Daguerre
Chicago.

THE
FINAL CONFESSION
OF
MABEL STARK

A NOVEL BY

ROBERT HOUGH

Atlantic Monthly Press
New York

First published in 2001 by Random House Canada, a division of
Random House Canada Limited

Photographs of Mabel Stark appear on pages i, ii, viii, 204, and 392
courtesy of Circus World Museum, Baraboo, Wisconsin.

Printed in the United States of America

FIRST AMERICAN EDITION

Library of Congress Cataloging-in-Publication Data

Hough, Robert, 1963–
    The final confession of Mabel Stark : a novel / by Robert Hough.
        p. cm.
    ISBN 0-87113-870-0
    1. Stark, Mabel—Fiction. 2. Women animal trainers—Fiction. 3. Women
circus performers—Fiction. 4. Circus—Fiction. I. Title.

PR9199.4.H66 F5 2003
813'.6—dc21   2002038415

Atlantic Monthly Press
841 Broadway
New York, NY 10003

03 04 05 06 07   10 9 8 7 6 5 4 3 2 1

To Soozie, Sally, Ella

CONTENTS

THE BARNES SHOW

THE RINGLING SHOW

JOHN ROBINSON / BARNES

PART ONE

THE BARNES SHOW

CHAPTER 1

THE ATHENIAN TAILOR

☞ HE IS: TALL, KNOBBY-KNEED, THIN AS A QUARTER POLE, IN HIS shop on Seventh Street, craned over his tailoring bench, applying white piping to a vest, when the pain in his lower right abdomen becomes a searing white-hot agony. He moans and keels over his work table, clutching at himself. This causes Mr. Billetti, the produce vendor in the market stall next door, to come running. After a moment of panic (arms flapping, hopping on one spot, saying, "Holy-a cow, holy-a moly"), Mr. Billetti throws his groaning friend onto an empty wooden cart, laying him on the flatbed ordinarily reserved for rutabagas and eggplants. He rickshaws Dimitri all the way to St. Mary's, bursts through the doors, and cries "Help! I needa help!" before collapsing at the toes of the Virgin Mary.

Ten minutes later, they scalpaled Dimitri open and removed what was left of his appendix, which by that point wasn't much, a squishy burst purple thing the size of a prune split lengthwise. Then they wheeled him into Ward 4 and parked him halfway down the right aisle, asleep and wearing a white flannel hospital gown. After about a half-hour or so, I wandered over and took my first long gander. He was lean and sharply boned and what the other trainee nurses called handsome, with his fine nose and wavy hair and olive-toned skin. Even unconscious he wore a smirk; later I figured out he wore it so much during the day his face had learned to fall that way natural when he was asleep.

As the poison spread through his body, he plumped up and turned the colour of a carrot. His hands looked like they'd burst if you pricked them. He slept around the clock, the only painkillers in 1907 being the kind that put you out like a light. On day three, I happened to hear two doctors discussing what all that stuff circulating through his body was likely going to do to him. "Either it'll kill him," the older one said, "or it won't. I suppose we'll have to wait around and see."

After three or four days, it became obvious Dimitri was choosing the second option, for his bloating eased, his skin returned to a colour more salad oil than carrot and he didn't look so mortuary-still when asleep. While emptying a chamber pot near his bed one morning, I took a moment to look him over, fascinated by the way his chest hair curled like baby fingers over the collar of his gown. Suddenly he opened his eyes and without bothering to focus said, "What is it your name, beautiful girl?"

Now this had a discombobulating effect on me, for not only was he the first person since my father had died to pay me a compliment, but he'd come out of what was practically a stone-cold coma to do it. I looked at him, perplexed at how he'd managed this, seeing as most people come awake so groggy and confused it takes them an hour to remember which way is up. I finally put it down to instinct, like the way you blink when onion vapour gets in your eye. When I turned and left I could feel his eyes struggling to get a bead on my crinolined backside.

"Maybe next time you stay longer," he croaked, "maybe next time, beautiful girl...."

That afternoon he asked for scissors, a bowl of hot water, a razor, a towel and a mirror, all of which I delivered when I was good and ready. Over the next half-hour he hacked at, and then trimmed, and then razored, the beard he'd grown over the past six days. When he was finished he looked at himself, closely, angling the mirror a hundred different ways so he could examine every nook and cranny, including the one burrowing deep and gopher-hole-like into the middle of his chin. "Aaaaaah," he exclaimed, "now I am feeling like new man!" Only his moustache remained, pencil thin and dark as squid ink.

Soon he was getting up and roaming around and starting conversations with other patients. Didn't matter those on the receiving end were weak and pallid and in no shape at all to hold up their end; Dimitri would sit and share his opinions on his country, or the tailoring business, or the hospital food, all of which he thought could be better. (He was the sort of man who smiled when complaining.) When he wasn't chatting, he was flirting with the nurses, both trainee and regular. Once, I was having a drink at the water fountain near the end of the ward when I felt a hand alight on my right hip and give it a little polish. Course, it was Dimitri. I spun around and slapped him and told him he'd better holster those mitts of his if he wanted to keep them. From then on, every time he passed me he'd look like we shared a secret—a secret he'd let me in on when and if it pleased him.

All this fraternization infuriated our head nurse, the jowly and old-before-her-time Miss Weatherspoon, no doubt because she was the only one he didn't turn beet-red with attention. She'd order him back to bed, only to have him grin, shrug his narrow shoulders and pretend he couldn't speak English. It was a show of insolence that perked my ears, for I'd had my problems right off with Miss Weatherspoon, my not being the world's greatest fan of people in love with their own authority. One day when Dimitri was up and roaming and responding to her bossiness in Greek, she grew flustered and decided to complain to one of the doctors. I happened to be walking by and saw her, salmon coloured, motioning with a crooked finger, face muscles tight as fencing wire. "But you said bedrest *only*" was the bit I heard. This caused the doctor, an older man named Jeffries, to roll his eyes and say, "Oh, all *right*, Beatrice, periodic bedrest if it'll make you happy." This put Miss Weatherspoon in an even worse mood than usual, which is saying something.

Suddenly everything needed doing all at once. Worked off our feet, we were. I got sore joints from scrubbing body parts. Two of the other nurses—lucky ones, I mean, with options—up and quit that afternoon. Right near the end of shift, Miss Weatherspoon decided Dimitri needed a sponge bath, so she ordered another trainee nurse named Victoria Richmond to do the job. Now, at that time it was popular for girls from good families to have a stint at nursing too, mostly because it gave them something to do while waiting to bag a husband. Victoria was such a girl: sixteen years old, skin like alabaster, blond ringlets, father a tobacco baron from the right side of Louisville, had a home to go to at night instead of the dorm for live-aways. In other words, she was the kind of girl I had trouble seeing eye to eye with, for every time Miss Weatherspoon told her to do something she'd lower her eyes, curtsey and say, "Of course, ma'am. Right away."

She did so this time as well, after which she turned on her heel, practically a pirouette it was, and went off to fetch a bowl and her favourite pink bathing sponge. When she reached Dimitri's bed she pulled the curtain and stepped inside, at which point I got bored and started doing something else. About a minute went by before me and everyone else on the ward, patient or staff, got interested again. And I mean *real* interested, for there was a screech, sounded like metal being sawed, and then Miss Richmond sprinted all girly toward the doors, elbows tight against the body, knees pressed together, lower legs wind-milling sideways. Her sponge was still gripped in one hand, and as she ran it left a series of watery drips on the floor. When she was gone it looked like an oversized slug had passed by.

When the commotion was over, Miss Weatherspoon marched to Dimitri's bed and turtled her head through the split in the curtain. We all watched. She extracted herself and stood, her face featureless as a plank. A thought crossed her mind—you could practically see it passing, as her eyes slendered and her features sharpened and the edges of her mouth crept ever so slightly in the direction of the ceiling.

"Miss Haynie!" she bellowed.

I moved fast enough so's not to be insubordinate but definitely not running like Victoria Richmond would have.

"Yes, Miss Weatherspoon?"

"It seems Miss Richmond has had to take her leave. I'd like you to complete the patient's sponge bath."

"Yes, Miss Weatherspoon."

"Oh ... and Mary?" She hesitated, savouring the moment. "If you enjoy your employment here, I suggest you be as thorough as possible. For unless I miss my guess, this patient is not the ... how shall I put this? This patient is not the cleanest of individuals, particulary in regard to his daily ablutions. His *private* daily ablutions. Do I make myself clear? I'll inspect him when you're finished."

"Yes, *Miss* Weatherspoon," I said again, this time stressing the part of her name that announced to the world she was unmarried and thick at the ankles and not about to get younger anytime soon. Truth was, I was annoyed and mightily so, for I barely had an inkling of what she was driving at, Miss Weatherspoon being the sort of woman who never said what she meant for fear of breaking some social convention invented so recently she hadn't yet heard about it. Instead, she went at things in circles, erasing her tracks with words that did little more than eat up time. Fortunately, with people like that body language generally makes up for any vaguenesses; the gloating leer plastered across her face informed me this task was lewd and distasteful and intended solely to show who was boss. My only defence was to pretend it didn't faze me in the least, so with as much calm as was musterable I turned and went looking for my sponge.

Upon reaching the patient's bed, I stepped inside the curtain.

Victoria's bowl of warm water still sat on the metal bedside table riveted to the wall. Dimitri, meanwhile, looked like a child who'd been caught lying. "I'm sorry," he said, "I could not help..."

I nodded as though I understood, even though I didn't, the upshot being his apology didn't relax me in the least, if in fact that's what it'd been meant to do. "Good morning, Mr. Aganosticus," I said all professional. Then I pulled back the bedsheet and took my first look at the body of my future first husband. Or at least I would've, had he not been furry from neck to spindly ankles and all points in between. On top of it all floated his crucifix, chain lost in the underbrush. Rooted and awestruck, I marvelled at how the hair swirled over his body, like a curlicued forest, growing lighter in some spots and heavier in others, the centre of the jungle falling in the exact vicinity of his privates. If he had a penis and testicles, they were lost under the jungle canopy, a fact that caused me to breathe a sigh of relief. My plan was: when I got to the critical part of the bath, I'd reach beneath the upper branches, give him a quick once-over and call him abluted.

I started on his neck, where gaminess can occur in the folds of skin. Dimitri closed his eyes. When I wiped his chest he sighed, which I took as a sign of encouragement. I moved my sponge over the area directly below the rib cage, where you can feel breath being drawn. Dimitri sighed again, and I felt encouraged again, and I proceeded to steer my hand a little lower, dampening the area where, on a less furry speciman, the stomach would've ended and the hair would've begun. I heard a gasp. I looked up and saw he had the same sheepish expression he'd been wearing when the sponge bath had begun. A second later, I saw what he had to be sheepish *about*, for there it was, his manly levitation, slow but unstoppable, rising through the jungle folds, like a totem pole being hefted by natives. I could practically hear the drumming. Though my heart was pounding and my insides felt airy, I couldn't bring myself to look away: long and log-like it was, with a gnarling of grey-green veins that seemed to funnel skyward and provide sustenance to a bulbous, maroon headpiece.

I swallowed hard, and found there was nowhere to look; every time my eyes settled on a spot it happened to be *that* spot, a phenomenon making it hard to think or get things done. Finally I whispered, "Now you look here, Mr. Aganosticus. My instructions are to give you as good a washing as I'm able, and while I'm not particularly pleased about it I don't have much choice in the matter. At the same time, I'm keen those on the other side of this curtain don't know what's going on in here. So if you make one peep, if you make one unnatural noise, party's over. You understand?"

He nodded, and I proceeded, lathering my hands until they were barely recognizable *as* hands. *Breathe*, I told myself, *breathe regular*, for I was starting to feel a little faint, society having a way of preserving eighteen-year-old girls in a sort of virginal aspic back then. After a bit, I reached out and made contact in the way you make contact when contact's a thing you're not sure you really want. Suppose *gingerly*'s the word. Or *tentative*. Problem was, I was so young I didn't even know when it comes to certain parts of the body a lightness of touch is the very thing that causes the most sensation. So I went ahead, not enjoying myself exactly but not hating it either: I remember feeling worldly for getting to know the contours involved and that particular way thickness can feel. After a moment, I looked up at Dimitri's face and saw he'd clamped one hand over his mouth and that tears had welled up like jelly in the corners of each eye—trembling he was, and red as a fire engine. His facial contortions so fascinated me, in fact, I neglected to put an end to what I was doing to cause them in the first place, the upshot being that seconds later I discovered what a grown man will do when treated to an excess of soapy rubbing.

I stood there, shocked. I was seriously considering giving the patient a whack across his sheepish-looking face, and surely would've were it not for the fact it was my whacking hand that'd gotten soiled. Then, I heard it. Shoes, comfortable ones, coming to a squeaky stop outside the curtain. I froze, which was a mistake, for the sudden lack or movement tipped her off. She whipped open the curtain and caught me, still as a figurine, right hand held out and messy with seed.

For the longest time she just stood there, not talking, arms folded across her stomach, one hip jutted, smiling like a crocodile.

Home for the next week was the hostel for Christian women on Portland Street. That weekend Dimitri and I married at the Greek Orthodox church on the corner of Seventh and Main, Dimitri insisting we had to, my honour now being his to protect and my being his sweet angel of mercy besides. It was a warm day, flowers blooming, air perfumed with honeysuckle, everything perfect.

After my folks died, I'd spent five years with my aunt in her terrier-filled apartment in downtown Louisville, an experience bad enough I'm in no particular rush to recount it. Still, blood's blood, and she did keep me from starving, so I swallowed my pride and sent her an invitation. She didn't answer, and later I heard I'd been disowned for marrying down, which sounded like something that auntie of mine would do. Dimitri was without family too, they being all in Greece, though the occasion was far from lonely. Seemed all of Seventh Street turned out: the fishmonger, the butcher, the neighbourhood cantor, both bakers, a half-dozen washerwomen, a letter writer, the gypsy tarot card reader, a tanner, a milliner, a sausage maker, that damn Arab (who had a shop where he sold carpets and, if you knew to ask, risqué Parisian photos), a hat blocker, a cobbler, a confectioner, the man who ran the numbers game, the ice man and Mr. Wong the Chinese herbalist, who at one point got me alone and, grinning and bowing, passed me a potion marked "For Marital Impediments." Rounding out the guest list was little Mr. Billetti, who looked dapper and taller than usual in a donkey jacket and high-hemmed pants (Dimitri having made the suit as a way of saying thank-you). They all brought their families, and after the vows every man, woman and caterwauling child crammed into the three-room apartment Dimitri kept over his shop. There were mountains of food and chatter in a half-dozen languages and as much dancing as was possible in the space provided.

The last guest left around three in the morning. The apartment fell quiet, like a person grown tired of talking. Dimitri approached me, looking solemn as a priest. With a grunt he picked me up and carried me over the threshold into our boudoir, his spindly arm muscles tightening like rope against my backside. I could tell some of the wives had been there, for candles had been lit and windows opened and flowers placed. After letting me take it in for a second, he lowered me to the bed as gently as he was able and whispered, "You can get ready now...."

He turned and walked out while I, eighteen-year-old Mary Haynie of Princeton, Kentucky, lay on the bed struggling not to cry. Lord, how I was mad at my mother, it being her job to take me aside and tell me how moments like this worked. (Course, it was an anger tinged with sadness, for even if she *had* been alive I probably couldn't've counted on her for this sort of information seeing as heart-to-heart talks weren't exactly something she enjoyed putting up with.) My throat swelled, I felt so sorrowfully ignorant, and what followed was my getting furious at myself for turning what was supposed to be the most glorious moment of my life into one of the saddest. I suppose I wasn't yet old enough to know this is a trick human beings are famous for playing on themselves.

Just then, it occurred to me that maybe taking off my wedding getup was what he meant by readying myself, so I wriggled out of my gown and pulled back the sheet, finding a dark towel where my pelvis would go; at least I knew what this was for, my being an ex-nurse and therefore knowledgeable of things physical. Outside the room, I heard the sound of a buckle undoing and pants being dropped.

Dimitri hummed softly as he opened the door. The light from the living room showed me the natives had already hefted his totem pole into place. I pulled the sheets up to my chin while trying to make my eyes look at least somewhat bedroomish.

Now, I don't have to tell you some things fit inside other things and some things just plain don't. If they're too big they're too big and that's all there is to it. By the same token, there's a fever comes over a man on his wedding night that robs him of the sense necessary to understand this simplest of mechanics. Dimitri sauntered over and slipped into bed. He kissed me on the lips and chin before moving onto places normally covered by clothing, though this didn't last particularly long as my new husband seemed unduly eager to get to the rubbing and coaxing and prodding part of the program.

Was no use. I suppose if I'd been at all interested it would've helped, the simple fact being I'd married Dimitri because it'd seemed to solve so many problems in one fell swoop. Unfortunately, I'd picked my wedding night to figure this out, instead of a day earlier, which would've been in time to do something about it. I could feel my cheeks burn I felt so stupid, my only hope being that Dimitri would mistake my flushing for wifely desire. To add to the awkwardness, I kept saying things like "Yes, darling, a little bit more, a little bit more," which ignored the fact those little-bit-mores were *so* little we could've been there all night and still had a ways to go come dawn.

Finally, he sat up and tried to look understanding. He stroked his chin and said, "Hmmmmmmmm." Yet his body language was all poutiness, every vestige of hope gone out of him. I was about to go sleep on the sofa when his face lightened.

"Wait!" he said. "Mr. Wong—he has give you something for this sort of problem?"

"Yes," I said, "he *did*."

The possibility there might be a way out of this logjam enthused me considerably, so I leapt from bed and fetched the little brown glass bottle I'd left on the windowsill in the living room. After unplugging the stopper I upended the contents into my mouth. It tasted bitter but not awful.

As I hadn't eaten much during the party (nerves) the potion took effect quickly, turning my lower body numb and my head giddy in a matter of minutes. When Dimitri plopped me back on the bed, in the middle of the towel, I had to fight the temptation to giggle like a schoolgirl, for it suddenly seemed so ridiculous what we women put up with. Plus I was hallucinating. This was new for me, and what helped take my mind off Dimitri being on top of me, eyes shut and mouth gone loose and rubbery like a cow's, was our bedroom ceiling coming alive with marching red-and-black toy soldiers. Gleeful and shimmering with light they were, and not prone to exhaustion: they marched and marched while my new husband finally managed to gain entry, all of which seemed like a tremendous amount of effort for the four or five seconds of pistoning that followed.

Next thing I knew, I was opening my eyes and could tell by the quality of daylight sneaking through the break in the curtains I'd slept somewhere close to noon. After waking totally, which took some time, I pulled back the cover; someone had removed the towel and put me in a white flannel nightie. I lifted the hem and inspected myself, half surprised and half not that everything looked like it had the day before. When I took my first step I most keenly recalled last night's deflowering, on account of I was tender as a hammered thumb. I stumbled toward the bedroom door. On the way I discovered no amount of favouring one side over the other helps when the soreness is coming from smack-dab in the middle.

To be truthful, all I wanted was a cup of hot tea and maybe a good cry, none of which happened because a woman I recognized in only the faintest sort of way was sitting on the living room sofa, knitting. I thought I recognized her from the night before, but with my head so fogged up I couldn't be sure.

"Oh!" she cried, "she is awake! You look so beautiful last night! You look so beautiful it make me want to cry!" As she said this, she put aside the knitting and ran toward me so she could hug me and kiss me and express all the emotion apparently caused by my radiance of the night previous. When finished, she took me by the hand and led me toward the sofa. She sat me down. Wiping away her tears, she said, "Oh, my child. Dimitri told me you are orphan? That your mother and father they die when you are just young girl?"

I nodded.

"Oh ... such tragedy. Such sadness we have. But you don't to worry. Dimitri he ask me to show you how to look after a home. Is all right I help you?"

I nodded again, which triggered another attack of tears and hugs and kisses on the part of this strangly comported woman. "Oh, is such a happy time. Soon you will have little ones, and I know it not sound possible but you will be even the *more* happier."

It wasn't till later, when we were in the market, and she was showing me how to thump an eggplant, that Mr. Billetti called good-morning to her and I realized how I knew her; she was married to Mr. Nickolokaukus, the baker from down the street, which explained why she smelled so warm and yeasty. Five minutes later and two stalls over, with her showing me the difference between good spinach and spinach readying to wilt, I asked, "Do you use the stems in cooking, Mrs. Nickolokaukus?" just so I could show I knew who in the hell she was.

"Oh please," she answered, "why so the Mrs. Nickolokaukus? *Georgina*. Please. My name is Georgina."

Over the next few days, Georgina decided I was pretty strong in the cleaning department, having done more than I ever cared to do at St. Mary's, and next to hopeless in things kitchen related, my having only the dimmest memory of watching my father prepare tortière and nettleberry torte. (Have I mentioned he was Canadian French? That my mother was English? That they were an odd mixture, she being stony and capable of the darkest moods, he being passionate and on the speak-your-mind end of things? That basically I'm a mixture of the two of them, personality-wise?) That week, Georgina showed me how to braise fiddleheads, how to roast potatoes in garlic and drippings, how to take home a baby lamb bound at the hooves and hold it down, panicked and bleating, before slicing its throat in a way the flow doesn't get on your clothing. ("You see, Mary? You must hold knife dis way....") She watched as I struggled through my first moussaka, as I charred my first piklikia, as I over-garlicked my first bowl of tsatsiki, as I put way too much onion in my first batch of spanakopita, and throughout she showed a patience that wasn't merited as I was still suffering from the gloominess that'd gotten a firm grip on my wedding night.

For instance—there I was, trying to bake some sticky monstrosity called a baclava, when it caught fire and I started shrieking and Georgina had to jam wooden spoons into the handles and rush to the window and shout "Gardyloo" before hurling it to the street. She leaned out, haunches wide as a baker's oven, a smouldering spoon in each hand, worried the flames might spread to the wooden stalls of Seventh Street, before finally saying, "Oh, the pot, it didn't break, maybe dent a little, nothing to worry about, fire is out...." When she turned I was slumped in a kitchen chair, face in my hands, aching all over, ashamed. She came over and put her arm around my shoulder, a kindness that loosened my guard and made me feel a hundred times worse.

"Oh do not have worry!" she said. "Please do not have ... is very difficult making baclava. Do not cry, it will be better next time...."

So I sat there, hiding my face, letting her think what was bothering me was the fear of disappointing my husband, when what I was really thinking was, *Why didn't anyone tell me marriage was just another form of busy-making? Why didn't anyone tell me a name change doesn't change things that've already happened?*

Those were my days. Every night at six Dimitri came up the stairs whistling. I'd put his hands in warm water and massage them, so as to get the crimps out. When finished, I'd present him with whatever creation Georgina had helped me with that afternoon. Like all lanky men, he ate enough to feed a platoon, and no matter how singed or dry or oversalty the food he'd polish it off while making delighted little snorting noises. Was a little like listening to a Pomeranian trying to breathe.

"Is good," he'd say, "is *so* good," the problem being he'd say this no matter how bad the food was (and many a night it was pretty bad) so that after a while he started sounding more like a father being patient with a child than a man discussing things with his wife. Generally, I ate little.

Next was the evening's recreation, Dimitri being fond of reading newspapers, listening to *oud* music recorded onto cylinders or having people over for games of cards. All this I would've enjoyed, as I do like music and've never had a quarrel with a spirited hand of whist, the problem being it was during this portion of the evening I'd start to worry about our nightly congress, which still wasn't proceeding in a way I figured was even close to natural. Mind you, I wasn't positive, my not having enough nerve to raise the subject with Georgina: could've been all women had to be elixired to the gills before dealing with husbandly randiness. I had no way of knowing, my own mother not being alive to ask, and I guess that's why I put up with it as long as I did; for all I knew *I* was being unreasonable.

Dimitri wanted children, you see. Wanted them the way a man lost in the Kalahari wants water. He craved them. Yearned for them. He'd wasted so much time setting up in America he worried he'd never have them, which to a Greek is as embarrassing as a forehead boil. What I'm saying is, he wanted to do it every night. And while we didn't do it every night—he was gentlemanly if I pleaded a headache or a case of the monthlies—we came pretty close. A routine developed. I'd tense up, his long loggedness wouldn't go where God had meant it to go, there'd be an excess of prodding, until finally he'd suggest I take a Chinaman bottle. After a couple of months we learned to skip the first two steps and springboard straight to the third, so that within fifteen minutes I'd be flat on my back, giggling and watching those damn tin soldiers on manouevres across our shimmering bedroom ceiling. I'd wake up sometime in the middle of the next day, feeling foggy and headachy and a little more like my grip on things was loosening.

Understand there *were* things I liked about Dimitri. He brought me flowers, often, one arm crooked behind his back as he came whistling up the stairs. He wasn't the type of man you had to follow around and clean up after, his having been a bachelor for so long, and he didn't drink, other than the odd glass of retsina. Plus, he'd given me a place to go, and at eighteen years of age it isn't hard to mistake gratitude for affection. It was just I was starting to mistrust his motives a little.

One night he suggested that different ways of coupling might make baby-making easier for us. "Do not have worry," he said. "I read in a book."

What followed was him suggesting *I* climb on top, a proposition akin to my trying to engulf a bedpost. Not wanting to disappoint, I agreed to give it a whirl. This turned out to be a mistake, as it gave Dimitri a green light to suggest other means of copulation, some of them more befitting barnyard animals than human beings. Over the next few weeks I watched those damn tin soldiers march not only across the ceiling but across the headboard, the wall opposite the foot of the bed, the pillow supporting my chin and, one night, when I somehow ended more out of bed than in, the chipped pine floorboards. What made it worse was Georgina had stopped coming, and though I'd always found her sugariness annoying I missed her fiercely nonetheless. Alone, I did a lot of sniffling and wondering how on earth everything was going to work itself out.

My answer came one day in the new year. We'd just moved to the bedroom, and I was about to unstopper a little brown bottle when Dimitri put a hand on my forearm and said, "Wait, I have other idea to make things easier."

With this, he took the bottle from my hands and went over to the bureau. He stooped and opened the drawer reserved for socks and handkerchiefs. He then pulled out a large packet, which surprised me for as late as that morning his sock-and-handkerchief drawer had contained nothing but socks and handkerchiefs (my having put them there, folded and de-lintified, myself). He sat beside me and unwound the string wrapping the packet. "This will help," he kept muttering, "I am sure," though he had difficulty unsealing the paper as his hands had gone shaky and unco-operative. Finally, he pulled out what looked like a breadboard-sized photograph, though I couldn't tell for sure seeing as he kept the face of it angled away from me.

Silence passed between us. Dimitri was reconsidering, I could tell, and he might've put the thing away had I not been so infernally curious. "Show me," I said, tugging his arm. "Give me a look." Finally he took a deep breath and rotated the sepia so I could see what'd been photographed. Which was: a woman, perhaps beautiful, perhaps not, wearing French stockings and a string of pearls, bare backed, kneeling before a nude man.

I couldn't move, couldn't say a thing, forgot to breathe, even; I could only look at that browny-bronze image and wonder what on earth possessed that woman to do what she was doing. Extreme thirst, was the only thing came to mind. In fact, I was so stunned it took a few seconds for it to sink in why Dimitri might've been showing it to me. Now this was a terrible moment, for all along I'd thought I'd been putting up with his nightly rutting so we could have a baby. And while I couldn't so much as summon a name for what that woman was doing, I knew for damn sure a baby wasn't going to come of it.

I suppose it was hurt and frustration that came geysering up, for the next thing I knew I was hitting him and slapping him and calling him a horny old goat born in hell, Dimitri having to throw me on my back and pin my hands over my head to defend himself. He was trying to calm me by apologizing and saying he loved me and promising to get rid of the photograph forthwith and heretofore. Had someone been listening in the next apartment (which someone probably was, the walls being thin as onion peels) they would've heard words like "Oh my precious petal" being yelled over words like "Let go my hands, you sweaty Greek son of a bitch!" Finally, he had no choice but to leap off the bed and race across the room to grab the Chinaman bottle. By the time he got back, the fight had pretty much gone out of me, and he didn't so much have to force the oozing brown contents down my throat as tip the bottle for me while I drank.

The next day, when it was clear I wasn't planning on getting out of bed anytime soon, Georgina came. She eased the door open and crept toward my bed, where I lay feeling low as an earthworm. Meanwhile she was crying and crossing herself and saying, "Oh my baby, this happen, this happen, is so difficult to adjust to early days of marriage. Is *so* difficult." Then she propped me up and wrapped her warm, yeast-scented arms around me, squeezing me and saying over and over how everything was going to be okay, just to wait and see, just to wait and see.

Georgina tended me over the next few days, bringing me cups of sasparilla and hot ox-tail broth, placing cool compresses on my forehead and cheering me up by telling me how normal this all was, despite it clearly being anything but. Still, if I hadn't felt so putrid I might've actually enjoyed my convalescence, for it was the first time since my parents died I didn't feel like I had to be somewhere, making up for who I was. I'd collapsed, and that was the person I was: someone who'd hit the floor and wasn't about to do anything but stay there. As for Dimitri, I had no idea where he'd gone to and was too tired to ask. All I knew was we were no longer sharing our marital bed, something that should've been a relief but, given my state, wasn't.

On day four Dr. Michaels came. He took my temperature, felt for my pulse, placed the back of his hand on my forehead and then turned me over and unbuttoned my nightie and thumped my back like it was one of Georgina's eggplants.

"Hmmmmmm," he said to Georgina, "looks to me like this is nothing too serious. An enervated system, due to mild nervous distress.

I understand she's an orphan? That she's just married? Not surprising, then. Not surprising at all. I think we can treat this here."

He gave her a jar of Carter's Little Nerve Pills and told her to see to it I took one every twelve hours on the hour. He then said he had other patients to see, though before he left he also handed her a black box about the size of a squared-off bread loaf, with a winding handle on the front and two long black thin cords leading from the sides. These wires connected to a pair of dangling black pads, each one shaped like a shoe sole. Georgina held it a little nervously, tipping it from left to right as if to examine it.

Seeing this, the doctor said, "I take it you haven't seen one before?"

Georgina put a hand to her mouth and turned the thing right the way upside down, inspecting its underside. Her eyes were big as spring potatoes.

"It's called a Faradizer. Sit the patient on the side of the bed, put her feet on the pads and give the handle a half-dozen good turns. Simple as that. I'd say one half-hour, three times a day, until she's feeling better. Understand?"

Georgina said yes, though as she did her lips trembled slightly.

"Good. I'll take my leave, then. Good day."

As soon as Dr. Michaels left, Georgina said, "All right, Mary, you hear the doctor." With that, she yanked on my hands till I was in a sitting position. Then she swung my legs around, heels landing on the floor. A few seconds later, the black pads were in place and buzzing away, jiggling the soles of my feet. This was relaxing, and I admit I didn't mind my Faradization sessions in the least, except afterwards my legs from the knee on down were tingly and unco-operative.

The nerve pills were another matter as I swore not to take them, having decided I'd had it with any sort of bottled remedy. Whenever Georgina gave me one—eight in the morning and eight at night, like clockwork, even if it meant waking me—I'd hide it in the back of my mouth, between teeth and cheek. When she left, I'd spit it out and push it into the soil of one of the pepper plants growing on our bedroom windowsill. Course, this could've been the reason all that bedrest and Faradization wasn't taking, for I was still interested in doing nothing but sleeping and having the occasional bawl; all I knew was I hadn't rested up when I should've five years earlier and that the tiredness had piled up inside me, forming layer upon layer, until I had no choice but to snooze my way through them, all of which would've been fine except this was 1906 and a dangerous time to take a long nap if you were a woman. Half-asleep, I'd hear them, gathered outside my room, discussing my condition. They'd keep their voices down, certain words jumping out in the low carrying rumble of voices gone deep with concern. *Hysteria. Neurasthenia. Daementia Praecox. Paraphrenia Hebetica. Undifferentiated Psychosis.* Always they were spoken as though followed by question marks. Meanwhile, Georgina would be crying away in the background.

How long was I laid up? Hard to say, though given the injustices being thought up in the other room I'd say it had to be a while, for you don't cook up that kind of spitefulness overnight. Call it two weeks. Maybe a little more. One day the door opened and in came Dr. Michaels, though this time he was followed by Dimitri, who couldn't look at me. Given the grave executioner's look on both their faces, I knew my goose was good as cooked. The only question in my head was how.

Dr. Michaels pulled up a chair and sat beside the bed. Dimitri hung back, staying near the door. As the good doctor went through the usual battery of tests—pulse, temperature, back thumping, saying *aaaaaaaaaah*—he directed a steady train of questions at Dimitri.

"She's been neurasthenic this whole time?"

"Yes, Doctor."

"And the treatment hasn't helped?"

"No, Doctor, I am afraid no."

"And you say she attacked you? She struck you with her hands and feet."

"It was terrible, Doctor."

"Hmmmmmmm."

(A long pause, Dr. Michaels sitting and thinking, Dimitri taking little shuffling steps near the doorway, me lying there trying to convince myself this was just one of the dreams I'd been having lately.)

"And," the doctor finally said, "you say she's hasn't been able to conceive?"

"No, Doctor."

"Hmmmmmmmm. Well, there's only one way to know for sure...."

With that, Dr. Michaels pulled down the covers and in a second smooth motion yanked up my nightie. Dimitri, who'd never actually looked at what was on display, turned away as though it was something meant to terrify. The doctor then directed my knees up and apart while he took a tube of goo from his black bag and smeared it all over the first and second fingers of his right hand. "Now take a deep breath," he said, and a second later he was inside me, rooting around like a man looking for lost change in a sofa. While it didn't hurt that much, it was cold and humiliating and I wanted to grab his hand and tell him to put it where it belonged. Throughout, he stared up and away, puzzling. After a half-minute or so, he pulled out his hand and stood. He was silent for a moment. Then he backed away and nodded solemnly at Dimitri, who'd sort of half turned, only his shoulder in clear view. The doctor's voice was low and sombre, and for a moment I thought he was going to tell Dimitri I had something that might kill me.

Instead, he murmured, "I'm sorry Dimitri ... it's just what I was afraid of.... There's definitely some displacement there. It's no wonder she's been acting the way she's been."

He left, taking his turn-handled Faradizer with him, which worried me for it suggested I was beyond the help a Faradizer could offer.

Dimitri then did something I've thought about for the rest of my life. He came over, fell on his knees and buried his face in my neck. "I never let you go, my little girl, never, never, never."

This reassured me, though later that day he must've changed his mind, for he went ahead and signed the committal papers anyway.

Next morning my few things were packed and Dimitri took me all the way to the hospital in a wagon borrowed from one of the grocers. The trip took four hours, and by the time we got there I was hot and smelling of horse and dust. After a long, tearful embrace (the tears were his, as I was stunned and stiff and feeling unaffectionate), he got in the wagon and drove off. I looked around. The lawns were thick and green and the flowerbeds blooming and the fruit trees commencing to bud. Strange, how beautiful everything was—seemed purposeful, as though designed to make you lower your guard. I mounted a flight of marble steps and passed between columns until I arrived at a high wooden door. There I used a lion's-head knocker as heavy as a bag filled with kittens to announce my arrival. When the door swung open, I found myself looking into the eyes of a nurse dressed exactly as I'd dressed at St. Mary's: nun-like, with a black skirt reaching all the way to the floor and a collar so high it chafed the underside of her chin.

"Yes?" she said, though she must've known why I was there as I had my little suitcase in front of me, hands clasped so tight on the handle my knuckles had gone white.

"Name's Aganosticus," I peeped. "Mary Aganosticus."

"Well, come in," she said with an enormous smile. "Please come in—you must be exhausted."

She took my suitcase from me and placed it next to the receptionist's desk. Then she had me sit in a waiting room, where she brought me a cup of tea with lemon. I was alone and frightened, though not as frightened as I'd been earlier, for I'd expected straitjackets and big men in white suits and the sounds of people screaming, and there was none of that. After a few minutes, I looked over and noticed my suitcase had disappeared. This triggered a disquiet inside me, the kind that won't stop until you do something about it, so I went and told the receptionist my bag had up and walked away. She looked up and offered me the same smile she'd used five minutes earlier. Then she told me everything was perfectly fine and I should wait and relax and she'd get me another cup of tea. This she did, and as I sipped the weak-tasting liquid I kept my worries focused and therefore small by concentrating on the square of floor space where my bag had been, telling myself so long as I got it back, then, yes, everything would be just like she said.

Everything would be just fine.

CHAPTER 2

THE YOUNG PSYCHIATRIST

AFTER FIFTEEN MINUTES OF NOT BEING ABLE TO CONJURE MY bag out of thin air another nurse came up and smiled and shook my hand and said, "Hello, Mrs. Aganosticus—I hear you've joined us for a little rest?"

I said I had, if that's what you wanted to call it, though mostly I put a lid on my natural tendency toward mouthiness. She told me her name was Miss Galt and asked me to follow her. I did, the whole time generating as much dignity as is possible when you're not exactly sure if you'll see the light of day ever again. (Was I terrified? Was my stomach doing somersaults? Was I hoping to God all this was some sort of dream I'd wake from sweating and whimpering and gripping at bedsheets? Course. If I stop to describe exactly how scared I was every time something scary happens, we'll be here for the next ten years. So do me a favour. At parts like this imagine how you'd've felt, and we'll both do fine.)

We walked through a set of doors and entered one of the hallways radiating from the front foyer. It was completely empty and for this reason foreboding: the only thing I could hear was Miss Galt's feet and my feet, our heels clacking against the floor. To keep from shaking with fear I invented a game, which was to make my feet go in step with her feet. Our clacking joined up. Was one sound where two belonged. After a bit she noticed, turned and smiled, though it was the smile you give a child who's just learned to use a spoon.

As we neared the end of this long, long hallway, I started to hear a low murmur, like voices well off in the distance. It grew louder—not loud, exactly, but louder—sounding more and more like the hubbub of voices you get in a theatre before the play starts. We reached another set of swinging doors, which were exactly like the first set we went through, only they were thicker and rimmed with rubber strips. Miss Galt stopped and placed a hand against one of the doors. "This is the ward for incurables. Now it's a little unruly in there. But don't worry. You won't be staying there. Is it all right if I call you Mary?"

I nodded, she pushed, and, oh, the noise.

It wasn't talking I'd heard coming through that soundproof door but wailing and shrieking and haggard bent-over women braying like donkeys and calling the words "Oh God oh God oh God." Every last one was dressed in a long grey gown, their hair gone straggly and wild, with scratches on their faces and forearms from where they'd dragged their fingernails. Those not up and walking and babbling incoherently were either strapped to their beds or unconscious. A few were banging their foreheads against cement walls or bed railings. There were no windows and the smells were awful and bugs were crawling up and down the walls. Rats, too—you could see them scurrying along the outer walls, awful rat jowls filled with heisted rat food. As I followed after Miss Galt, taking quick little steps, I kept seeing things that'd form foul little snapshots in my mind's eye and then refuse to go away: a woman, spaces between her teeth, spotting me and lifting her gown, showing me her privates. Another woman, young like me, but with blood pumping from a nostril and when she spotted me she smiled broadly, her smile against all that blood making bumps come up on my forearms. Or: an old woman, frail and the colour of fireplace ash, crouched between two beds, concentrating hard on pulling shit out of herself and using it to write a message on the wall, but because her shit was so crumbly the word wouldn't come out so she tried harder and harder and finally started shrieking in frustration, her hands crooked and covered with it. I took in all this in the time it took to snap my head away. Amazing, the way fear bends time around to squeeze things in.

We headed straight through, Miss Galt yelling over her shoulder that only God's mercy would help those poor souls. We passed through another short hallway, and through another ward like the first though muted somewhat, and without the scenes of absolute lunacy. Finally, we entered a ward far quieter than the first two, the occupants mostly sleeping or reading or lying on beds staring at the ceiling or chatting in small groups. There were fourteen beds, seven on either side of the aisle. None of the beds had restraints, which relieved me to no end, though I noticed there were locks on the doors at both ends of the ward. Basically, my eyes were moving like a ferret's, inspecting everything, too scared to settle on one spot. Miss Galt led me to the last bed on the left side of the room. A grey robe sat folded on the blanket. She asked me to put it on, and as she did she gave a funny little gesture with her right hand, as though her forefinger was stirring milk into tea. I hesitated, wondering if she really meant I should strip right there in front of everyone, though it soon became obvious that was exactly what she had in mind. After a few seconds' delay, her smile weakened, the corners of her mouth trembling and then turning downward slightly.

I turned my back and undressed and slipped into the robe.

"Good," she said, holding out her arms to take my clothes.

I was left sitting on the bed, all by my lonesome. I took a deep breath and tested the mattress by placing my palms flat against it and pushing. For some reason, I looked under my pillow, feeling disappointed that nothing was there but bedding. Mostly I was sitting there and fretting and wondering what it was exactly I was supposed to do when two women came over. One was about forty-five, the other maybe thirty, and we only had to lock eyes for me to know their stories weren't far off mine.

I pushed myself to the top of the bed to make room. They sat on either side near the bottom. We didn't bother with niceties or introductions, though later I learned the older one was Joan and the younger one Linda.

"How," I said in a loud whisper, "do I get outta here?"

Linda answered, also in a loud whisper: "First thing you have to understand is you *can* get out of here. You can. Simple as that. So many husbands are booking in their wives these days they have to let some of us out some time or another. Inspectors come around and make the decision. It might take a month, but you will get out."

"Yes," Joan echoed, "you will get out."

"So believe me, the trouble isn't getting out. It's getting out without being operated on."

"Yes," said Joan, "the operation."

"So just do what they tell you. Act pleasant. Make your purses. Don't go scrambling on walk days. Don't talk back or be ornery. And whatever you do, don't hit anyone or you'll go to the violent ward where they chain people to walls. There are padded cells down there too and orderlies with the self-control of goats. So toe the line is my advice, and you'll get out in one piece."

We talked for maybe an hour. After chatting about our husbands (bastards, all three) they filled me in on ways to get by: which nurses not to mess with and which inmates were dangerous and how to stay on the good side of the cafeteria servers, who'd starve you if they decided they didn't like the look of you.

"One other thing," Linda said. "There's a doctor here who's better than the others. Younger, with newer ideas. His name's Levine. Dr. Levine. Get close to him if you can."

I repeated the name five times quickly to myself so I wouldn't forget. See, my mind was spinning, as a mind'll do when desperate to land on anything it might mould a plan out of. That was how I first saw him—by taking a look at the picture in my head. What I saw was young. New ideas. Soft-spoken. Perhaps handsome, perhaps not. Probably a do-gooder, out to change the world, desperate for someone to prove his way of thinking.

With any luck, likes blond curls.

For the next two weeks, I took my walks and sewed my purses and ate my rubbery overcooked pancakes (no butter or syrup, only blocks of salt you chipped off with a thumbnail) and generally fought the urge to sock Dimitri in the mouth when he came around looking for his weekly forgivenesses. Wasn't easy, I tell you.

On the morning of day fifteen, Miss Galt fetched me. She led me to an examination room down the hall from the top end of our ward. Then she gave the little finger waggle that meant I was supposed to take off my clothes, something I'd by now gotten used to doing in front of others.

I sat naked on a table, covered with a white sheet. It was a little cold in the room, though not quite enough to raise goosebumps. I chewed my bottom lip and wrapped my arms around myself. After a few minutes a man wearing a white doctor's coat came in. He was middle-aged and homely, with plump twisted lips that looked a little like Jewish bread.

"Hello," he said, not looking at me, "My name is Dr. Sights."

"I'm Mary Aganosticus."

He nodded, again without looking at me, though he did raise his eyes to the level of my teeth and say, "Open." He peered down my throat, checked under my tongue, thumped my back, shone a light in my eyes and tested my reflexes. Throughout, he looked grim. Then he listened to my chest, flattening a thick grey ear against my left breast and then my right breast and then my left breast once more for good measure, which I knew from my nursing days was not in any way, shape or form how to check a heartbeat. Finally, he pulled away and wrote something on a clipboard and handed that something to Miss Galt.

"She'll be fine" was all he said.

That afternoon, Miss Galt came yet again and found me in the day room, where I was reading a four-week-old *Louisville Examiner*. All smiles, she was, though in a place like Hopkinsville it's amazing how things like smiles start to take on meanings different from those in the outside world. I stood, and she took me through the medium-crazy ward and the full-blown ward and into the front foyer where the receptionist had taken my bag fifteen days earlier. Here we took a left and walked down a hallway heading in a direction opposite from the women's wing; it was long and brightly lit and with doors every few feet. After we'd passed about a half-dozen, Miss Galt stopped and unlocked one, using a key from the hoop-shaped ring she always carried in her right hand. Inside was dark, though when she opened the door a bolt of light fanned over a goodly part of the room, enough I could see the walls were grey and the floors concrete and in the middle was a large, elevated tub. Miss Galt closed the door and opened the gaslight. She approached the tub, beckoning me to do so as well. She finger-stirred, and after I stripped, she folded my robe and put it on the floor next to the bath.

There was a leather sheet covering the tub, and running down the middle of the sheet was a heavy, metal zipper that looked like a bottle opener. She pulled down the zipper, steam puffing into the air. Then she took my hand, not so much for support but to direct me up the three steps leading to a small platform near the tub rim. From here I did what I imagined I was supposed to do, which was to put one leg, and then the other, through the slit in the leather. Soon I was sitting in a bath of hot water and salt. Miss Galt cradled my head until it rested on the back of the tub. Then she pulled the zipper to the top, where it formed a low tight collar around my neck.

Around this time it dawned on me the zipper handle was on the outside of the leather sheet, while my arms, and more particularly my hands, were *under* the leather sheet, meaning if the zipper was going to be pulled down it wasn't going to be pulled down by me. To make matters worse, it was equipped with a little latch fitting into eyelets on either side of the part, so I couldn't even thrash around with the hope the damn thing might lower on its own.

Now trapped is trapped, no matter how comfortable you are, plus the tub was coffin shaped and that can start a mind to racing. My heart picked up the pace, and I looked up at Miss Galt with what could only've been horror on my face. This made her smile even more broadly and say, "*There*. A nice hot bath. I wish I had time for one. I'll be back to get you in four hours."

With that, she patted the leather cover, turned and abandoned me; the last thing she did was close the light and cast the room into darkness. Course, the minute the door shut I began twisting and kicking and flailing and generally doing everything I could to get myself free short of hollering for help, which would've branded me as ornery and therefore suffering from hysteria. After a few seconds of this uselessness, I took a rest. Then I thrashed some more, took another rest and whaled my arms and legs one last time, though in a much less enthused manner: I was starting to figure the leather sheet was there to stay, and no amount of wriggling or commotion was about to change that.

This triggered a worse sort of panic. I could hear my blood pressure surfing in my ears and I could see angry jags of colour knifing through the darkness and I had to fight the inclination to vomit. And my heart—oh, how I called for Jesus's help. Whereas before it'd been speeding, now it was speeding *and* pounding, something a heart can't sustain, so every few seconds it'd up and miss a beat. Every time this happened I thought I was dying from fear, though at the same time staying alive to dwell on the process. A cruel set of dance partners this was, for the moment I started accepting my death as a mercy there'd be a collision in my chest, so hard it'd rattle my ribs and quake my stomach, and my heart would start charging along again until it missed the next beat, the whole thing repeating itself over and over and over.

It's hard to say how long this torture went on. Inside a completely dark place, time has a habit of looping around and doubling in on itself and playing tricks. So I can't say. Maybe it was ten minutes, maybe it was longer. Felt like longer. Felt like forever, if you must know, and that's a traumatic thing: finding out what an eternity feels like. What happens is the body exhausts itself, and you go completely still, and you feel cold and your fingers tingle and your bladder drains and your mind goes blank. Lying there, I reckoned this was the calming effect Miss Galt had promised, though it was the sort of calm you get nightmares about later on.

So I lay there, vegetabilized and chilled, maybe dead, maybe not, having completely stopped considering the possibility I might ever get out of that tub. The door to the room opened. Miss Galt opened the gaslight. I clamped my eyes against the glare.

"How are we feeling?"

I, defenceless as an old woman, weakly muttered, "Good." She let me out and I tried to dress, though I was so shaky she had to help me. We went back down the hydrotherapy wing, her walking and me shuffling, past the front desk and through the wards strung along women's wing A. She led me to my bed, and it seemed to me the ward was quieter than usual. Perhaps some of the women were having their tubbings, I don't know. Linda and Joan were there, and they hustled over and sat beside me, though neither one of them touched me.

Linda said, "Don't worry, Mary—first time's the worst."

Joan added in a softer voice, "Yes ... first time ... the worst," and all I could do was sit, nerves firing, glad they were there with me.

I had tubbings the following day, three days after that, and then the day after that, the scheduling of our hydrotherapy being something understood by the staff and the staff only .

The day after that I met my psychiatrist.

He came by late on a walk morning, just after we'd been led back in. I was in the day room attached to the ward, wishing I could knit something, feeling low and a little jumpy.

"Good morning," he said, "I'm Dr. Levine."

I smiled shyly, sizing him up.

"I thought maybe we should meet. Is that all right, Mrs. Aganosticus?"

He was a short, doughy young man, just shy of thirty, with thin dark hair pushed to one side of his forehead. As for his face, the nose was the primary liability, for it was oddly bulbous in shape and it flared at the sides, like a radish cut open to garnish a salad. As he was not the most attractive of men, he made up for it by projecting warmth and sympathy and a general all-round niceness. Immediately I figured him for being lonely, niceness being something women don't generally care for in men, and the thought in my head was, *Good*.

"Yes," I told him, "that'd be fine."

He sat looking at me. I wasn't sure whether this meeting would take place in the future, or whether we were having it now. As Dr. Levine was just sitting there, I figured the latter was the case, and that I better say something interesting to get it going. Problem was, I'd trained myself to be so cautious I couldn't think of anything to say. The pause lasted long enough I worried he might get bored and leave, so finally I figured I might as well up and out with it.

"I don't like being tubbed."

He smiled slightly, and I worried I'd made a mistake by complaining. My concern disappeared when he said, "Is it the darkness? The feeling of being trapped? The boredom? Yours is a common complaint, Mrs. Aganosticus. Sometimes I question the value of hydrotherapy myself. Particularly in light of some of the more progressive treatments coming out of Europe. Perhaps I can ask around, and see what I can do. Would that be all right?"

I was stunned.

"Yes," I peeped, "that'd be fine."

We talked a little bit more that day, mostly about the hospital and how I was getting along with the other patients. He left shortly after, though not before promising to see what could be done about my problem. I tried not to get my hopes up.

I had my fifth tubbing that afternoon; like Linda and Joan had promised, it was getting easier, though it was still miles from being easy. I now spent the four hours in a state of quivery boredom, not panicking exactly but feeling as though any moment I might. Linda had suggested I make up mental games to help pass the time; apparently, she'd pretend the tub was a magic carpet and she was soaring through space, visiting places she'd been and could conjure up in her head, like New York City or the ocean or the body of the man she should've married. I tried it too but didn't have much luck, imagination never having been my strong suit. Instead, I exercised my arms and legs, swishing them about in the water, flexing my wrists and ankles, for I didn't want my muscles going soft in case I was to need them.

After I'd spent a half-hour or so of arm and leg swishing, the door to the tubbing room opened and I got scared, for the orderlies had a reputation for sneaking in during a tubbing and unzipping the leather covers and taking their pleasures. Squinting against the light flooding the room, I was relieved to see it was Levine. He said hello and opened the gaslight enough to cast a dim, soft light over the room.

"Is that better?"

I told him it was. He asked if I'd like it lighter, saying he could do that too, and I told him it was a fine restful light if restful's a thing that's possible in a tubbing room. This made him smile, thank God. He took a stool and placed it behind the tub. In his other hand he held a note-book and pen.

"I'm afraid there is nothing I can do about the restraints," he said. "Hospital policy. However, I was thinking you might not be so bored if you had someone to talk to. Do you think that would help?"

I said I thought it would. He sat on the stool and, after a few seconds of rustling, said, all of sudden, straight out of the blue and without a moment's notice, "How did your parents die, Mrs. Aganosticus?"

Now, this question caught me off guard, my first reaction being, *That's personal, Mister.* But seeing as how he'd helped me a little already and it was something I did want off my chest I figured I might as well play along. So I told him how the TB scare of 1902 had gotten my father—how over a four-month period the air had seeped out of him, his face thinner and paler each day, the area beneath his eyes grow-ing darker and more sack-like as the ailment progressed. How when he coughed you could hear it coming from deep down inside him, rum-bling like the slow, distant thunder you get when the weather turns hot. How he died on a Sunday morning, a fitting day since he was a man who believed in God; I remember listening at the door of his room and hearing the doctor say to my mother, "He picked a good day to go, Lela. Heaven's got him now." How after the doctor left I cried and my mother just sat there, quiet as a log, which is the English way of han-dling strong emotion.

Throughout my little story, Levine sat on his stool, scribbling and saying, "Yes, yes, go on, go on," so I told him how a wagon pulled up and two men dressed in dungarees and work shirts came in and car-ried my father out in a burlap bag. Afterwards my mother thanked them and paid them, both of which seemed like crazy things to do con-sidering what they were taking away. The news must've spread, for the house soon filled with neighbours bearing food, some of them coming from so far away they didn't pay taxes in the same county. Course, many of them offered up their teenage sons to help out with the fieldwork, offers my mother turned down as she didn't like being reliant on the kindnesses of non-relatives. As a consequence, she had to spend more and more time out in the fields, tilling for next year's tobacco, it becoming my job to entertain the visitors. A big job it was, too; they kept coming and coming, loaded down with baskets and jugs and jars, all determined to help out the family of the man who, upon coming south from Quebec, had changed his last name to one that was old-fashioned and American sounding and, believe it or not, inspired by the sight of threshed hay. This went on for months, such that my biggest recollection of mourning, aside from the pure dog misery of it, was long awkward conversations had over cups of tea with people I barely knew. (That, and having people treat me like a thirteen-year-old one day and a full-grown woman the next.) When we weren't eating jams, pickles and mincemeat pies the neighbours had brought over, we ate root vegetables and cuts of meat preserved in clay urns filled with duck fat.

"And your mother?" Levine asked. "What happened to her?"

Well.

Here I told how she grew addled with pent-up sorrow, how she'd leave the house with only one shoe on or sometimes turn to me and you could tell she was seeing someone other than yours truly before shaking her head and coming to her senses. How one day, when the two of us had been alone for five months, she decided to buy an old dray cheap from a guy who'd spent time ranching in the Appalachians. The horse's name was Tom and he'd taken poorly to the wide-open spaces of west Kentucky: always snorting and stamping the ground and trying to manoeuvre his haunches so he could launch a hoof at your forehead, which was presumably the reason he'd been sold at the price he'd been sold at in the first place. A week after that, my mother decided she'd use Tom to harrow the northwest field, figuring the horse's spunk might come in handy at the end of a long day. Her second mistake came when she stood between horse and harrow while linking the trace.

Something spooked Tom, probably nothing more serious than a breeze or a moth fluttering by, and he bolted, dragging the harrow over his grief-witted owner. Course I was the one found the results. The sun was lowering and the cooking was done and she hadn't yet come in from the fields so I went out looking. Walked to the northwest field and from a distance saw the horse buckled to the harrow, just standing there chewing and thinking about whatever it is horses think about. Twenty feet away was a dark heap I couldn't make out. As I got closer it became pretty obvious what it was, though the mind's an optimistic thing, and needs to be shown the worst has happened or it'll go on believing the opposite. I got up close and took it all in. She looked like she'd been torn apart by wild animals.

Levine was still scribbling away, trying to get everything I'd said on paper, as though I'd recited the cure for smallpox instead of details I regarded as dreary and all my own. After a few seconds, the sound of his pencil scratching at paper stopped and he moved the chair around so he could look me in the face.

"Mrs. Aganosticus, I'd like to try something I have been reading about. I was wondering if you'd like to talk some more tomorrow."

"You mean like we did today?"

"Yes, exactly."

"Would it be during my tubbing?"

"If you'd like."

"Then sure, Doctor. Course."

That's how I started the first talking cure ever performed in the state of Kentucky. I didn't know it was controversial, and I had no idea it was contrary to hospital procedure. I didn't even know it was *treatment*, for as far as I was concerned cures involved something you could lay your hands on, like pills or bathtubs or turn-handled Faradizers. I just figured Levine liked to talk, and ask questions starting with "Tell me about..."

So I'd tell him. Not everything. But most things. Made up stuff too, just to keep the spice level high. To tell the truth, it did me good to get some of my mental goings-on into word form, particularly as regard to how much I missed having a mother. One day, after I'd been saying how cheesed off I was at her for about half an hour, Levine interrupted. "Why is it," he said, "you so rarely talk about your father, Mary? Obviously you were close to him too. Do you think that's significant, Mary?"

"Define significant."

"Important. Key. Germane."

"Out with it, Doctor."

"Could it be there was something about the nature of your relationship with your father that you're ashamed of? Something that makes you feel guilty and less inclined to discuss how painful his passing was? Something about the nature of your affection toward him?"

"Like what?"

Here he told me what he was thinking, which I won't repeat owing to the purity of its ridiculousness; in fact, I'm only mentioning it to illustrate what a feeble notion psychiatry is. It should also give you an idea how desperate *I* was, for instead of telling him he was talking nonsense I shook my head and said, "Hmmm, maybe, you've got a point there, Doctor."

This made Levine get all excited and animated, so he said, "Tell me more, Mary, tell me more."

In other words, he was taking a shine to me. He just was. As I rambled on my lips would get dry, so he'd hold up cups of cold water for me to drink. Or he'd cool my forehead if the steam rising from the bath made me too warm. Sometimes he'd get real worked up and say, "Yes, yes, yes?" using his voice like a cattle prod, though other times I'd say something that clearly didn't interest him and he'd steer the subject back to stuff he did want to hear about. After a while, I began to discern what he did and did not want to hear about. Jokes, offhand remarks, sarcastic complaining—none of that interested him. His pencil would stop scratching away and instead of saying, "Yes, yes, yes?" he'd say, "I see," in a tone more professional and sober. Then he'd try to egg me on in directions more sombre and revealing.

As the days went on, I gave him more "Yes, yes, yes?" material, and by this I mean comments along the lines of *when such-and-such happened I felt like such-and-such.* In my head I called them felt-like comments. Dr. Levine ate them up. Had they been food he would've gotten fat on them. Sometime my tears would come, mostly when I related what a donkey's ass Dimitri turned out to be, and though at first I thought this might annoy him the opposite turned out to be true, for after such visits he'd always say, "I think we made progress today, Mrs. Aganosticus. I think we made progress."

Had we *ever.*

Imagine. The tub water is hot, and the steam rising in my face causes one of my curls to become slicked to my forehead, where its tip annoys my eyelid. I blow on it, trying to free it up, but it won't work because my face is dripping and the spindle of hair's wet and sticking like a leaf blown against a windowpane. Levine reaches out and pushes it out of my eye. Now there're two ways you can do this. One, you're doing the person a favour, and another you're telling the person something you can't trust to words. Slowness, has a lot to do with it. And the way he uses three slightly curved fingers when one pointed index would've done just fine.

There ought to be a word for the feeling that sets in when you're ninety per cent of the way toward something and you know it'll all be for nothing if the last ten per cent doesn't get done. Jittery, with bursts of terror and euphoria. Sleep didn't come easily that night. To give myself something to do after lights-out I kept picturing Levine, pen in hand, signing my release, apologizing on behalf of the state of Kentucky for the shabby way I'd been treated. Naturally, I dressed the fantasy up with details. The skies would be bright blue. There'd be birds, warbling. I'd go to the best restaurant in Hopkinsville and order steak.

Stupid.

The very next day, Levine came and joined me at his usual time. I could tell right off he wasn't himself, for his "Good afternoon, Mrs. Aganosticus" lacked vim, and he was moving like the wind had been knocked out of him. He sat behind me, and when I started talking I didn't hear the usual sound of his pencil madly scratching. I was in the middle of describing something that'd happened to me when I was young (what, I don't remember—some girlish hurt imagined or real, I suppose) when the sound of chair legs dragging across the floor interrupted me. He'd moved so he could look into my face. Or not look, as the case may be, for mostly he stared into the side of the tub, taking only momentary glances in my direction. His body language scared me. Bowled over, is the description comes to mind.

In a defeated voice, he explained.

After that, everything changed. Staff who didn't pay attention to me before now paid an enormous amount of attention, and staff who did take an interest before now avoided me like I was marked by the plague. I suppose in a way I was. Suddenly I was the property of a nurse named Rowlands and the orderlies at her disposal. (The scariest thing she ever said to me? "You'll be going home soon, Mrs. Aganosticus.") She was older and far sterner than Miss Galt, and always in a rush. My treatment changed. My tubbing was cut down to two hours daily, though my mornings were now filled with other forms of hydrotherapy: cold packs, hot packs, foot baths, cold-bath plunges, wet-mitten friction, salt-glow rubs, jet sprays, needle showers, tonic baths—you name it. I was plunged and wrapped and sprayed and hosed down so often I got to feeling like a piece of meat that'd been dropped on the way to the barbecue. I was doused with water so hot it almost burned and water so cold it set the teeth to chattering. One of Rowlands's favourite tricks was to put me in a steam bath until I was so hot my temples were pounding, and then her orderlies—big men, with strong arms and shaved heads—would lift me out, always taking the opportunity to run their hands over my privates, before plopping me into towels so cold my body would start shivering uncontrollably. Believe it or not, it was these shiverings that were supposed to make me better.

And: douches. Fan douches, Scotch douches, spray douches, wet-pack douches, sitz douches, alternating hot-cold sponge douches. That part of me was washed out so many times I started thinking of it as a bodily affliction, good only for collecting disease. To this day, I don't understand the fascination they all had with that particular part of my anatomy. I only know they had it, and after a while I felt worthy of punishment just for daring to be female. That may've even been the point. After nine days of continual hydrotherapy—Nurse Rowlands referred to it as my "preparation"—I was examined again by Dr. Sights, who I sensed was behind all this, Levine having once mentioned that Sights made all the executive decisions in Hopkinsville.

In a brightly lit room, just the two of us, Nurse Rowlands ordered out, he gave me the same two-finger-with-goo treatment that Dr. Michaels had given me in Louisville. The only difference was Sights was rougher and seemed in no rush to get through it. Of course, this made me blazing mad, and I would've kicked him in the neck had two things not stopped me. First, I had nothing up my sleeve, no ace in the hole—all the losing poker expressions applied—so I clung to Joan and Linda's advice if I just played along and was polite everything would be fine. (This was suckers' logic, and one I haven't used since.) Second, my feet were in stirrups.

When he was finally finished, he stepped out in the hall. When he came back in Nurse Rowlands was with him. They both looked at me for a few seconds.

"She'll be fine" was what he said.

Later, I took a breather in the day room. Every part of my body was tingling from all the baths, which sounds nice but wasn't: it was extreme tingling, just this side of spasming. No matter how many deep breaths I took with my eyes closed I couldn't stop the nerves in my arms, legs, body, feet, hands and especially my womanhood from firing. Only my face wasn't trembling.

After a time, I sensed I wasn't alone and opened my eyes. Dr. Levine sat on the sofa beside me. For the longest time he didn't say anything. I was silent as well, for I was mad at him, giving false hope being one of the worst things you can to do a person.

Finally: "Is there anything I can do, Mary?"

I took a long time with my answer, for I wanted to wound as deeply as possible. What I came up with was something along the lines of "Sure you can. You can help me kill myself. You can give me a whole bunch of them barbiturates you hand out all day and I'll take 'em after lights out and all anyone'll think is I stole them somehow. I'm serious. I'm an orphan and all I need in this world is to get myself another family because a person's not a person without family, not really, not if you think about it, and if they take that possibility away from me I can't imagine a reason to stick around. You follow?"

He sat there, eyes on the floor, looking miserable. Couldn't even look at me.

"Yes," he said weakly.

I was kept away from dinner that night, which was fine by me. After supper, I mostly stayed in bed, Joan and Linda keeping me company not by saying anything but just by being close. After lights-out, I couldn't sleep for the longest time, though I eventually drifted into a light slumber—light enough that when someone crept up to my bed I heard the footsteps. I opened my eyes. Levine motioned for me to get up.

We crept, together and silent, through the ward for temporaries. He opened the door and pointed at an orderly sleeping on the sofa. I indicated I understood, and we tiptoed past him, through the door and into the hall separating the wards. Just before the medium-crazy ward was a door marked "Janitor"; here Levine stopped and turned the handle. We entered a dark room. Levine closed the door behind us and partially opened the gaslight, mops and brooms and buckets turning pale orange.

I felt a breeze, and it was this rustle of air that caused my eyes to fall on the reason Levine had brought me here. On the far wall was a window. He'd already unscrewed the wire-mesh plate and removed it and leaned it up against a drum of floor cleaner. He'd also opened the window enough a small body could squeeze through. At five foot one, I qualified.

Again, Levine put his finger to his lips, as if I was stupid enough to squeal with joy. Again, I nodded I understood. He gestured with his head toward a neatly folded pile of clothing sitting on one of the racks. Then he turned his back to me so I could change.

I put on a plain pale blue dress and bloomers and grey boots that buttoned up the side. I tapped his shoulder to tell him I was ready. When he turned and looked at me dressed like a normal woman, his eyes turned glassy. He wanted to kiss me, I could tell, and if he had I would've kissed him back just to show him how thankful I was and maybe let him have a little rub-up besides.

Instead, he blinked away his true wants and turned businesslike, whispering, "Tennessee is ten miles south."

With his help—his hand was soft and fleshy and damp—I put first my right leg and my left through the window so that I was sitting on the sill. I turned over so I was on my front, and pushed myself through. The fall was a few feet, the force enough that I carried on till my backside hit earth. I stood, brushing away turf, not knowing what to do, so I looked back up at Levine, who was leaning out the window with a small tin case.

I took it from him and opened it and looked at the contents: sandwiches, $20 and a compass. When I looked back up to thank him, he was pointing in the direction I had to go, which was across the hospital lawn into a forest. Truth was, I was scared stiff—scared of the forest and getting caught and the sheer production involved with escaping. See, it's a big moment, the day circumstances force you to become a doer. It changes your perspective and your sense of possibility and is not in any way gentle.

I couldn't stop looking up at Levine. Fact was, I wished he'd come down and carry me all the way to Tennessee. Instead, he did all he could, which was to point a second time in the direction of the forest.

That, and loudly whisper one word.

"*Go.*"

It felt good using my arms and legs and heart, oxygen pumping to all the nooks and crannies that aren't serviced in a hospital for the mentally ill. I reached the waist-high fence surrounding the property, hopped over it and ran like hell, though to be accurate *running* doesn't do much to describe what a fugitive does in forests: she more dodges and scampers and ducks branches and hurdles creeks and takes little tiny steps followed by full-out long jumps. Something about this zigzag stop-start sort of progress made me feel like I was in even more of a panic than I actually was, the upshot being I got hot and sweaty and kept imagining the sound of dogs barking hoarsely in the distance. Was a sound that'd make me stop in my tracks and turn suddenly cold. I'd listen hard, hearing cicadas and rustling trees and the surf-on-a-beach noises made by worried ears. Then I'd start off again, though within a few steps that infernal imaginary barking would start up again.

At the first clearing, I stopped to catch my breath and check my compass. Was then I discovered something. While a compass'll tell you where north is, from which you can figure out where south is, it won't make sure once you head off in that direction you stick to it. Owing to all that dodging and jumping and veering toward places where the undergrowth was the lightest, I kept getting off track. I'd stop and check the compass and find I'd been trudging more west than south, and on the one occasion I went a long time without checking, I got myself heading straight back from where I came. Plus I couldn't use the sky as any kind of guide, for it was the middle of the night, the moon in the same place the sun is at high noon, so no matter where I went it stayed in exactly the same spot: straight up and shining like a lantern. Every few minutes I had to realign myself and start off again, knowing I'd soon be charging in the wrong direction again. After a while I felt as trapped in that damn forest as I'd felt in that damn lunatic asylum.

Finally, I reached the edge of the woods. I took a step into a field gone fallow. It smelled dusty and earthless and like it needed rest. My progress quickened. A bit later I reached a lighter forest, more of a glade it was, and while crossing it I discovered a rushing creek. Here I wolfed down one of the cheese sandwiches Levine had given me and risked fever by taking a few swallows of water. Then I was on the move again, over a flatland of farms separated by strips of light brush, reaching a road around two or three in the morning.

I took a breath and was about to cross the road and keep on going when I heard hooves clomping against packed road earth. Was a farmer, someone's grandpa, delivering a load of wheat-brown caskets no doubt filled with sourmash. He looked at me, curious, and said, "You need some help, missy?"

"I'm going to Clarkesville."

"You *walkin'* there? In the middle the night?"

I nodded as persuasively as possible, which wasn't very, seeing as how my dress was wrinkled and my face marred with branch scrapes and my hair full of leaves. I watched him figure it all out, his face roiling, and I cursed both the full moon and myself for not running the instant I saw him. It was a strange moment, the two of us standing there trying to figure what to make of the other, my only hope being he didn't have a licence to transport whisky and so wasn't in any position to judge.

Finally, he said, "Well, you need a lift or not?"

I went with him the rest of the way to Tennessee. I didn't know the laws, so I didn't know for sure if I was safer there, but I can tell you

I sure *felt* safer once I saw the "Welcome To" sign. As for the bootlegger, he didn't make a word of conversation the whole way, and I followed his lead. By the time we got there, it was a cool morning bound to turn hotter. You could tell because the sun looked bleary and white, and because you could see bugs whirring atop grass stalks.

Wait a minute—I'm mistaken. Before dropping me off in the town square, smack-dab in front of the court house, he did say one thing.

Said: "Carnival's in town."

CHAPTER 3

JUNGLELAND

THEN, SUDDENLY, YOU'RE OLD. YOU JUST ARE. THERE'S NO getting round it. One day you're young and fresh and your skin's smooth as teak, and the next day you're lanolining your scars so they don't gnarl during the night. Believe me. If you think lost love'll spark a case of the maudlins, just wait till you can't tie your own shoes without a symphony of grunts and groans and hoarse respirations. Still, I'm not a complainer, never have been never will be, so I'll skip the drawbacks and jump to the thing I do like about aging. The mind gets supple. Believe it or not, it does. You start seeing around corners. You start picturing what's behind you without having to crane your neck (which you can't do anyway, seeing as it's getting stiffer by the day). It's the one recompense of being aged and wrinkly and sore: you learn the trick of being in two places at once. For instance, I can be in the grocery store, buying a six-pack of Hamm's, and my body'll be in this day and age, 1968 to be exact, while the rest of me will be in another place, like the Al G. Barnes 4-Ring Circus of 1915. It's quite a feat.

You get up there in years and if you let it, your imagination can get about as real as anything else. Maybe more so.

Basically, what it boils down to is time. The way it works changes. Used to be, I imagined time the way young people do, as something with an order and a flow, like sand through an egg timer. Then, around the day I started wearing orthopedic splints, I began to view time as something different, as more an accumulation than a march forward. If I had to describe how I see time today, I'd have to say it's like gumballs in a penny machine, all mixed together, jumbled up, rubbing the colour off one another. For example. That thing I did in 1927. Jesus. Was the worst thing one person can do to another person, and the hell of it is I did it without even trying. For years afterwards I divided my life into two. There was the *before*, when I'd hoped to the heavens I was a good person, and the *after*, when I knew for damn sure I wasn't and just had to keep going despite it all. (Try greeting each day with something like that weighing on you. *Tiring*, is the word comes to mind.) Then one day I woke up and I was old and my worst sin had come unhobbled in time. Started wandering, it had. Suddenly it was something I'd always done, something I'd always been capable of doing.

Suddenly, it was a part of me.

Another example. My men. Whew. Had a slew of them. The exact numbers I'll let you worry about but I know for a fact there were more than you can count on the fingers of one hand. Used to be when I looked back I saw them as a procession. I saw them as a parade. Now I imagine them like you would people in an elevator, clumped together and facing the door. Fact is I can picture every last one of them, as though they were sitting in front of me, my being in two places at once even now. The tallest? That's Dimitri, who's a good foot taller than Louis, who's the shortest. The richest? That's James, which is why he's dressed so fine and looking so damnably stern. The homeliest? That's Dr. Levine, who also happens to be the smartest. The oldest?

That's Art, the one I loved, while the youngest is Albert, the one made me fall out of favour with the Ringlings. The handsomest? Rajah, of course, though Rajah was a tiger and only thought he was a man, so I suppose he doesn't count. Otherwise, the handsomest by a country mile is Al G.; just look at those eyes, so piercing, so blue, don't even get me started on his jawline, Jesus he had a way with the ladies. The one with the chin cleft? Dimitri. With the ten-gallon? James. With the shoulders thrown way back and the backbone ramrod stiff? Louis. The one with the worried look on his face? Albert. The one with a general smugness about him? Al G. The one with the look of under-standing? Of sympathy? Of willingness to lend a hand?

Art.

All of which is a long-winded way of saying my preference would be to make my admissions the old person's way, gumball-style, the bits and pieces all mixed up and swirled together, conjuring why what happened happened throughout the whole story, instead of just at the end. It'd be a hell of a lot more accurate that way, and truer to the way I've been feeling of late. Still, stories aren't told that way, the danger being you'll write me off as an old woman given to rambling and I ... well. Let's just say I can't have that. See, there's a lot riding on you having a pure and clear-eyed understanding of the situation, so I'm going to have to tell it the standard way, the way I would've before age settled in and put its feet up and lit itself a slow-burning cigar. By the same token, there'll be times I take liberties with this thing called order, with this thing we pre-tend is time, if only because at my age it's hard as the dickens not to.

Like right now, for instance.

Problem is, I didn't sleep well last night, and by that I mean I slept even worse than old people normally sleep, which believe me is plenty bad enough. Was up fuming, worried, frantic. Tossed and turned for hours before finally nodding off, only to wake up in the middle of the night, 2:37 it was, eyes popping open like they were on springs. I was thinking so hard I could've sworn there was someone or something in the room with me, whirring. You ever get that? Where the mind's worked itself into such a lather your thoughts pick up where quiet leaves off, till it gets so you can't think for all the noise? Might as well've been sleeping by the side of a freeway. At least then I could've shut out the racket with earplugs.

Naturally, I could barely drag myself out of bed when the alarm went off at 4:45. Felt logy all day. Even Goldie noticed it—when I was finishing boning out her cage she gave me a good long look and an eye roll followed by a lazy high-pitched arf, which is tiger for *I know, I know*. The rest had fallen asleep by then, and were all wearing those restful housecat grins tigers get when full-bellied. You know a tiger licks his lips when he sleeps? Little dreamy tongue slaps that dampen his teeth and gums so they won't dry out? You know some tigers snore? And talk in their sleep? Sweep their tails when they dream?

Scares me, goddammit, the idea of doing without them. For the past thirty-six years they're what's kept my mind off the things I'm about to tell you. *They're* what's given my whirring mind something to focus on.

Please, make yourself at home.

Nice little place, isn't it? Cozy, paved driveway, bit of a garden out back, close to shopping. I'm the type of person who doesn't need much but likes to form attachments to the things she does have. A favourite coffee mug, comfortable shoes, a pearl-handled revolver bought years ago in Wichita, a gold-rimmed poster from the Barnes show, a bone rake I've had for so long there's a smoothness where my fingers, and no one else's, go. After almost eighty years on planet Earth, those're the things left to me.

In the early thirties I quit circus life—suppose I'd just plain had enough—and took a training job out at JungleLand. I've been there ever since, making me JungleLand's longest-running employee and the world's oldest tiger trainer. Not that that counts for anything. Uh-uh.

No siree. There are some pretty foul winds blowing out there, and I don't want anyone eavesdropping on our frank conversations. Plus we'll be more comfortable here, in my house, than in those little huts made to look grass walled but in fact are polystyrene. While the past couple of afternoons haven't been too bad, you get a hot one and the damn things'll heat up like a woodstove. Louis, the old owner, tried installing air conditioners about a year ago, but that caused havoc with the fuses. Was a lot of sparking and power outages and one day the dromedary pen caught fire so he took the units out and sold them for a quarter of what he'd paid for 'em. Course, that was always Louis's way of doing business: buying high and selling low and finding the whole thing damn funny. No wonder I liked him so much.

About six months ago, he found me at the snack bar. Was lunchtime, and I was tucking into the same thing I eat every day: a hamburger Annie had leaned on between paper towels to get the fat out, washed down with my second Hamm's of the day.

"Can I sit, Mabel?"

"Course, Louis."

He gave a little tug on his checkered slacks and sat. He was such a tall man he had to turn sideways so his legs would have somewhere to go. He twisted his body around so he faced me, and when he spoke it was in a lowered voice. His forehead was long as an egg flipper.

"Mabel, you've been here for how many years?"

"Thirty-six, or leastways close to it, Louis. Came when the Barnes show closed for good—you know that."

"Well, that means you've been here longer than anyone. So I want you to know first. I'm selling. I'm retiring. I'm going to spend my days watching rodeo in Santa Rosa. I'll make the announcement tomorrow. There just isn't any money in this business, Mabel."

"That's never bothered you before, Louis."

"That was then and this is now. Even Feld's Ringling show is going bust—who would've thought that could happen? I'm getting on, and problems start to wear when you're not so young anymore. It's high time I took a breather."

"You're kidding."

"Nope."

"Louis Goebbel leaving the animal business?"

"Running is more like it."

I was beginning to think he was serious.

"Who's buying?"

Here he started laughing. "A couple of candy butchers, if you can believe that. They go by the names of Jeb and Ida Ritter. Plus another partner named Ray Labatt. Seems he's got a rich wife who needs to lose some money for tax reasons. Mostly it'll be Jeb and Ida running the show."

"They know anything about running an animal park?"

"Enough, I suppose."

"They good people, Louis?"

Here he paused, long enough his answer didn't exactly fill me with confidence.

"Good enough, Mabel."

Three weeks passed, maybe a little more, till the day came when Louis was leaving for good and of course he threw himself a going-away picnic. Clowns on stilts wondered about, and there were kegs of free beer along with a banquet table covered with food. Word got out, JungleLand filling that day with old troupers, wranglers and carnies, half wanting to wish Louis their best and the other half attracted by the notion of free food. Must've been three, four hundred people easy. Midway through the afternoon I was standing at the banquet table, in front of the cheese-and-pickle roll-ups, waiting to get at the tray of devilled eggs, when I smelled something: menthol and perfume, with some spearmint gum thrown in for good measure. I turned and saw a woman in tight pink pants with a flowery shirt tied at the waist. She was bare ankled, and her hair had been lacquered into a beehive; a tornado wouldn't've ruffled it. With her do and her heels she must've stood six and a half feet tall. Her bracelets and big hoopy earrings jangled. When she bent over to reach a buttered bun at the back of the table, her navel almost grazed the roll-ups.

Now none of this bothered me unduly, though it's true I dislike it when women dress in a manner designed to redirect the eyeballs of men. What did bother me was her reaching hand held a burning Pall Mall, pinioned between the second and third fingers. The ash had gotten to be about half an inch long, and if it fell the breeze would've scattered it over the buttered buns, the cheese-and-pickle roll-ups, the pigs in a poke, the tuna-filled cherry tomatoes and most important the devilled eggs, which in my books are the only excuse for having a picnic in the first place.

She noticed me eyeing her.

"Oh hello," she said, while straightening. I had to lift my chin to look her in the eye.

"Hello," I replied, and I wish I could say there wasn't a hint of frostiness in my voice. If she noticed she didn't act like she did. Instead, she shuffled around her plate and her cigarette and her glass of rosé wine so it was all teetering in her left hand, thus freeing up her shaking hand. She held it out and said, "I'm Ida Ritter. How do you do?"

My whole body sank.

"Mabel Stark. I'm fine."

This answer caused her to chew more vigorously while looking up and away. "Wait a minute," she finally said. "Aren't you that tiger lady?"

Here I looked at her, trying to keep the daggers out but by God it wasn't easy. As you know I was centre-ring with the Ringling show of the twenties, and saying to me, 'Aren't you that tiger lady?' would be akin to going up to a Cadona and saying, 'Aren't you from that flying family?' or asking a Wallenda if he'd once walked a highwire. It was disrespect, pure and simple, not to me particularly but to the whole history of the circus. Had it been anybody else, I would've told them so and stormed off, devilled eggs or no devilled eggs.

Instead, I said, "Yes, that's right," and was pleased when someone recognized her and came over and told her how great she looked.

Well. With that introduction problems were bound to happen and sure enough they did. I was with my tigers one morning, about to lay down sawdust, when who should come up but Ida, this time wearing tight leopard pants, an insult to the leopard world if you ask me, along with cat's-eye sunglasses and a pink blouse tied just above her navel. She had a cup of coffee in one hand and a menthol in the other.

"Beautiful," she said, gesturing at my babies, "beautiful animals."

I stopped working and paid attention for I was still acting like there was respect between us.

"You got that right, Ida. There's nothing more beautiful."

"But chubby. I see some sway on a few of 'em. For instance, that one. What's his name?"

"Her name."

"Sorry. What's her name?"

"Goldie."

"Well, what do you think, Mabel, is it just me or is Goldie looking a little padded around the haunches? I was just wondering if maybe these cats could do with a half pound less of chuck a day."

Here I looked at her, doing my best imitation of calm, though inside I was seeing red, for tigers need at least fifteen pounds of meat daily or their coats pucker. Was nothing but cheapness, Ida's suggestion, and designed to aggravate; everyone knows if it were up to me I'd feed them their favourite hippo steaks each and every morning.

"Well now that's an idea Ida," I said. "I'll talk it over with Uncle Ben and see what he thinks."

"Good," she said and walked away, those teetery pink slippers making her ass wiggle.

A few days later, the same thing happened. I'd just thrown the cats their meat and was taking a breather when I heard those slippers slapping the ground. I turned, fearing the worst, and there she was, smiling and chewing gum, gesturing with a lit cigarette.

"Well, good morning, Mabel. My oh my those tigers are looking gorgeous as ever."

"Suppose they can't help it."

"Yep. They sure do look fantastic. You're doing one bang-up job around here, Mabel."

I took a deep breath and waited for it.

"But I couldn't help notice one or two of them have coats that could use a little shine. Like *that* one. What's his name?"

"Her name," I said, "is Mommy."

"Beautiful tiger. Beautiful bones. Ever thought of rubbing a little vegetable oil into her coat?"

Here I could've killed her, the benefit of vegetable oil being a wives' tale that got out on circus lots about fifty years ago, probably started by a vegetable oil salesman for it does nothing but make their fur look soggy plus it'll gum up pores and make them groggy. Was an insult, pure and simple, my having to take instruction from a woman who didn't even know *that*. Instead of losing control, I stared straight ahead, communicating my displeasure through wordlessness and an expression gone stern. After a while Ida took the hint and added, "Well, of course it's completely up to you. Bye now."

By that point I was fuming, so I went off to find Uncle Ben and told him he better talk to Jeb and get him to rein in his wife if he didn't want fireworks. Ben said he'd do what he could, which turned out to be not much, for the very next morning Ida was back again, smoking and drinking coffee and telling me how beautiful my tigers were, before suggesting I give them a little milk of magnesia.

"It's good for their bones," she added in that syrupy voice of hers, and it was the intent her chirpy tone was disguising that finally made me snap and call her the worst thing you can call a circus person.

"Listen to me, Ida," I said. "Listen to me good. You're a carny. You're a *concessionaire*. You really expect me to care what you think about tigers?"

Her face turned white and she stormed off, that silly back end of hers wiggling like electrical current was running through it. Since then we haven't talked. If we pass each other on the connection we both go stony and don't say hello. Thank God, Jeb and I get on, or I'd be out already. Still, you overhear things. Rumours, whisperings, snackbar chatter. Like Ida's pressuring Jeb something hard. Like she figures she's got more pull on account of she has a flat stomach and boobs propped high as mountain peaks. Like she figures she can get what she wants because a certain type of man goes for her.

Like the great Mabel Stark might retire soon.

Then.

A few weeks later. Young squirt, Irish mug, wavy red hair, tiny round eyes, keen as a wood plane, twenty-five at the most. I first laid eyes on him at the beginning of the day, while in the process of wheeling my big old Buick convertible off the Ventura freeway and into the JungleLand parking lot, where I was about to take my favourite spot by the fence under the giant oak. Was exactly 6:20 in the morning. Same time as I always got there. Only that day was different, for *as* I was wheeling my big old Buick convertible into the parking lot I noticed there was another car in the lot, and in that car was a guy behind the wheel, coffee cup in hand, staring at the front entrance of JungleLand so hard you'd swear he'd fallen in love with it.

So I got out. He got out. Instantly I knew he was a new cat guy and my day was ruined. First of all, he had marks on his forearms I could see all the way from the other side of the lot. Second of all he knew who I was—that much was obvious. He came toward me, beaming, and I looked at him, not smiling, until we got close enough I could see he was fixing on introducing himself. Just walked on by, I did, acting like he'd never entered my line of vision.

Shortly after nine, with the cats fed and dozing, I found Uncle Ben and asked him who in the hell the new guy was.

"The cage boy? Haynes is his name. Roger Haynes. From Oklahoma, I believe."

"Where they find him?"

"Working the Beatty show. Trained with Beatty himself before the cancer kicked in."

"Beatty!"

"That's what I heard."

"Oh Jesus Christ Ben, there you go! They have to spell it out in neon lights! No guy who's trained with Beatty *and* who's got his marks is going to take a job as a cage boy unless he figures he's not going to be a cage boy long! Oh Christ Ben you might as well start saying your goodbyes now cause if anyone ever tries to take my cats away from me I've got a neat little .38 in my bedside table. Oh Jesus Christ this is awful...."

On and on I went, practically hysterical—that's the way I get sometimes—until Uncle Ben started telling me I was wrong, no one's trying to take my job, that Haynes was taken on for the lionesses and no one's going to have to shoot herself anytime soon. On and on he went, painting a rosy picture, and because he has a voice that naturally calms people I started to feel a little better even though there wasn't a thing in the world to feel better about. In the end I promised I wouldn't march up to Ida's office and clobber her personally, Uncle Ben saying he was mighty relieved to hear that.

That was a Wednesday. Come Saturday, I was getting ready to do the biggest show of the week when who should turn up and start moving my pyramids around but Roger Haynes. You could tell he really wanted to prop the act, and for a second it occurred to me he didn't even realize he was there expressly to oust yours truly, a thought I immediately chased away because in the long run it really didn't matter.

This, more or less, was what I said: "You little son of a bitch. Don't you ever come around my goddamn tigers and don't you ever show up round this cage line and don't you ever walk up and down my cages." Then, because of the way I've been feeling of late, by which I mean broody and tallying the things I've done, I tossed in a piece of information even he didn't deserve. "I killed a man once," I told him, "and I'd gladly do it again now *get.*"

The boy went white, turned and walked off. As for me, I felt bad about doing it, and would've gladly felt bad doing it a second time. Suppose I'm fear-aggressive, a term normally reserved for wild animals but suits some people too.

Six months go by. I don't say boo to him. Pretend like he's not even there. Problem is the little bugger's so eager and driven he reminds me of me, and when that happens it's a struggle keeping your hostility at a pitch where it'll do any good. Plus it's obvious he has the tiger bug in him and he has it in him bad, and there's so few of us around who do it's hard not being gracious when you meet one. Plus he's always the first one to work in the morning, which is saying something seeing as how I'm there by 6:15, and I'm told he's often still there eight at night, offering to help where help's needed, a time I'm already asleep. And goddamnit if those lionesses don't look better than ever.

What I'm saying is, a little battle kicked up inside old Mabel. On one hand, he was obviously in the business of snaring my livelihood, whether he'd figured it out or not, so it was natural my giving him the cold shoulder and nothing but. On the other hand, he was working so damn hard he really did deserve an act of his own, especially considering he'd done it all before with that philistine Clyde Beatty.

Come July, and Uncle Ben took his annual two-week vacation betting on horses in Santa Anita. A few days before he left, he came up to me and said, "Well, Mabel. You're gonna need help in the morning."

"I know."

"I've asked Roger."

"Roger? You say *Roger*? Uh-uh. No way. Ain't no way that little Okie pissant's gonna gum up my cage bars with those ham-shaped hands of his. I won't stand for it, Ben, and you know it."

"Now, Mabel," he said in his smoothest simmer-down voice, "you and I both know Roger's the only cage boy with tiger experience, and you and I both know he's the most qualified." To this I sputtered something in protest, something with a few swear words thrown in, though we both knew he was right. In response he said, "Ah now, Mabel, don't you worry, I had a talk with Roger myself and I said point-blank, 'Listen here, kid. You tryin' to take Mabel's job?' You should've seen the look on his face. Horror, is what. Started stammering and saying, 'Shit no Mr. Bennett I'm not here to take her job. I'm here to learn from her and her only. Why you think I took a job as her cage boy? Oh Mr. Bennett don't think *that*.' So I said, 'You sure 'bout that, Roger?' And he said, 'Sure I'm sure. Beatty's up and gone and that makes Mabel Stark the greatest living trainer on the planet. Hell, she might've been that when Beatty was alive. I've learned the Beatty way and now I want to learn the Mabel Stark way.' He said that, Mabel. Said every word. You know what else he said? He said, 'Mabel Stark's a hero of mine, Mr. Bennett, and there's no way I'd ever do something like that to one of my heroes.' You gotta meet this kid, Mabel. Not an insincere bone in his body."

Course, all this was horseshit, though I have to say it was flattering horseshit, and if you're going to horseshit someone, dressing it up with flattery's a pretty good way to go about doing it. One more time I told Ben there was no way I was letting that little son of a bitch get within a country mile of my babies, though I said it with a faintness that hinted I was reconsidering, such that by the time he walked off it was general knowledge I had myself a new cage boy.

The next morning I showed Roger what he needed to know, figuring if they're fixing to give him my kitties he might as well care for them proper. How at 6:30 I got out my tools and lined them up in the same order against the same spot on the wall, and how you could tell they were in the right order by matching them to the places where the paint was scraped away. Then we put Goldie in the exercise pen and Toby and Tiba in the ring so we'd have three free cages and could move the cats around in order to clean all the cages. By seven I showed him how to sweep the cages, something he'd been shown a hundred times but never the Stark way, stressing you had to get every last flake of sawdust for if it gets on their meat it'll stick inside them and gum them up something bad. (Course, straw's different. That gets inside them and it'll act like a scour and clean them out. Problem is, straw's more expensive, so guess which one gets used?) After the cages were cleaned and the cats back in, we loaded up the wheelbarrow and I showed him how some of the cats are finickier than others, Goldie liking a shoulder blade and Mommy refusing everything but shanks. I also showed him how Prince and Khan can be dangerous, they way they lunge at the footboards, tearing meat from the fork tines.

At 7:45, with all the cats gnawing contentedly, I put on thick yellow gloves and showed Roger how you have to hose the blood out of the cage gutters, and then use a wire-bristled brush to scrape off bits of fat or tallow, for if they stay around they'll fester and cause disease. Then we had coffee—he took his black, which was encouraging—and by 8:45 we started boning out the cages and after that we put sawdust down, making sure each big shovelful hit the footboard direct so's the tigers could get at it and spread it around nice themselves. Then we filled the water pans, which is important because after a feeding cats get real eager to wash the blood from their mouths and throats. By nine o'clock we were finished, the cats sleeping and Roger rushing off to his lionesses.

Now. Did I look for the signs of laziness? Of him not wanting to get his hands good and filthy? Of him maybe thinking he was too important to scrub gutters because he had his marks *and* he'd worked with Beatty? Did I hope every day he'd come a minute late, or put my rake in the wrong spot, or get the least bit snippy?

Sure. Problem was, the kid was like a machine of hard work and politeness, and after a while you can't help admiring a man who's playing his cards right, even if he's using those cards to take your money. One day, after the watering pans had been filled and I was on my way to Annie's to have my first Hamm's of the day I said, "Roger, you want a drink?" Practically swallowed his tongue, he was so surprised.

For a good long time we just sat there, sipping beer, me brooding and him afraid to speak, when I thought, *Ah hell, this is ridiculous.*

"Roger. You tell me. You think the Professor's a fag?"

"Excuse me?"

"The Professor. I mean, he's got that Ginger all over him, day and night, randy as a jackrabbit, hooters the size of acorn squash, and still he puts her off. Sure she's about as subtle as a cannon act but Christ almighty, he's on an island of seven people—he can't be that choosy. Even if he *is* a fag they should get together. He'd be a good influence on her. Maybe tame her some. Give her a baby. I've known a ton of queers in my life and I can't say I've ever found them objectionable. Hell, I even prefer their company—they don't seem to have that fear of dying without leaving their mark on the world that makes regular men act so rash and self-centred all the time."

Roger looked at me, confused as I'd ever seen a person. It practically hurt to watch, he was so dying to add to the conversation or even understand one iota of it.

"Roger," I said. "You don't watch *Gilligan's Island?*"

"Uh, no, ma'am."

"Didn't you know Bob Denver lives right here in Thousand Oaks? Why I see him every time I go to the Oakdale market. And the Skipper's living just up the road in Ventura county. Christ Roger where you been? See you start tuning in. I like to jaw about it sometimes. There're reruns every night at seven. You'll like it."

Next day he came in and when we sat down for my first Hamm's I said, "Well, Roger, you tell me," and you what the son of a gun said?

"He's married to his work, is all."

Heh heh heh. Makes me laugh. Roger would say that. Married to his work. Could be he's talking about himself, you think? Working fourteen hour days, with a wife and baby at home, no less?

About a week ago, during break, I finally up and outed with it.

"Roger," I said, "you take good care of my babies."

"What do you mean?" he said, all innocent, maybe acting maybe not. Knowing Roger, probably not.

"Roger, you're going to have yourself a tiger act and you're going to have one soon."

"No way," he said, once my meaning had sunk in. "I don't want your job. There's no way I'm gonna be the guy who takes a job away from the great Mabel Stark. There's just no way."

"Listen to me, Roger. Big cat training's a dying industry. It's like scuttling coal, or sweeping chimneys. Not what you'd call a growth sector. Goddamn animal groups running around everywhere, people with TVs, theme parks the size of Rhode Island, even the Felds about to go bust, how *could* animal shows survive? If you're sure it's what makes you happy, you might have to do things you aren't proud of to get it. You follow?"

He blinked and said yes, though I really don't think he was getting it.

Nope, now that I think of it, he wasn't getting it at all.

Just so you know: I never saw Dimitri Aganosticus or Dr. Levine again. Dimitri's for sure passed on by now, and if I found out today he died slow and before his time I can't say as I'd be any the worse for it. As for Levine, it's my considered opinion he was one of two men who really cared for me, the other being my one true love Art Rooney, the man who sat me down sideways and taught me how things work.

Jesus. *Art.* These days you'd almost think I'm addicted to the hurt I get when I think of him, which I suppose in a way I am: when presented with a choice between achy remembrances and nothing, it's my experience people choose achy remembrances every time. I suppose it makes them feel like they've had their lives for a reason.

See, what you have to understand is this: I used to go up to him and bury my nose in that hollow between the jaw and neckline, and I'd have myself great big huge inhalations that'd make him go all high-pitched and girly (which, granted, for Art wasn't much of a stretch). I could barely help myself. I'd do it again and again, for the thing he smelled of was: familiarity. Places you liked as a kid. Food you had on picnics. Kites. Coffee. Neither one of us knew our parents past a certain age and if you think *that* doesn't scent a person, think again.

(Some free advice? You want to get yourself a good match in life, you take a cue from animals. You walk on up, you lean close, and you take a great big snootful.)

Goddammit, there I go. Telling the story like time was gumballs instead of flowing sand. Probably I'm confusing you already, not that you're the type to confuse easily—don't think I meant that.... Where was I? Oh yes. Levine. Dr. Levine. What always puzzled me was the fact he never laid a hand on me, never even *tried* to lay a hand on me, though most of the time he had me alone and helpless and up to my armpits in hot water. This is a curious fact, and one that contradicts my general opinion of the way men act when opportunity knocks. Basically, my hope is he's someplace nice and has himself a distinguished grey beard and a wife still comely and a whole lick of grandchildren. I also hope he's still sitting behind people while listening to them spill their guts and periodically saying, "I see. I see. But how did you feel?" Hearing that'd indicate there's a fairness to this world, and that's a concept I wouldn't mind coming nose to nose with these days.

My next husband?

That was the Texan.

CHAPTER 4

THE SOUTHERN COTTON MOGUL

I FIRST LAID EYES ON HIM FROM A BALLY PLATFORM IN BEAUMONT, just over the Louisiana border. I remember because he was the sort of man you couldn't help *but* notice, there being something in the shoulders and the slow sure manner of his walk that drew the eye. Plus he wore a big brushed-suede ten-gallon, and because he and his hat were so noticeable I watched as he took his seat, alone, in the back of the Superba tent, which I thought was strange as it was an afternoon show and the crowd was small and usually the men get as close as possible to the action. Maybe he didn't want to block anyone else's view, for he was real partial to that hat and showed little inclination to take it off. That or he didn't want to be seen, which didn't work because, like I say, he had a silent iceberg presence good for nothing but drawing attention to itself.

The show started, and because we were curious (we being me and the four other Dancing Girls of Baghdad) we kept peeking through the backdrop at him during the first half of the program. He sat there unblinking through the sword fighters, the knife throwers, the

Moroccan tumblers, the Whirling Dervishes of Constantinople, the midget who could stand on his head while circling the ring on camel-back and finally the old white-bearded swami who lured a cobra out of a basket while playing something tinny and horrid on a frigolet. The educator, a man named Ned Stoughton, then came on and announced a brief intermission to be followed by the beautiful and enticing Dancing Girls of Baghdad. "And in the meantime, gentlemen, if you'd care and if you'd dare, the Parker Amusement Company is pleased to offer you various diversionary pastimes...."

Grifters, in other words. Three of them, setting up on little folding tables called tripes, one with the shell game, one with a numbers board and one with three-card monte ("Keep your eyes on the lady, gentlemen, it's as simple as that—just keep your eyes on that pretty pretty lady"). By the time the plants made a big show of winning the rubes were lined up five deep, except for my future husband, the man in the big hat, who seemed content to sit perfectly still at the back of the Superba tent, hands folded and thinking about who knows what. The price of cotton maybe, or where he'd tell his wife he was at all day. The grifters went on for about twenty minutes, stopping just before the mood started to turn ugly. Then Stoughton sprang back on stage and said, "Showtime, gentlemen, showtime."

Meaning us. We went out, and while Sanjay and a bongo drummer played something whiny and Oriental we stomach danced, it being considered a talent back then to wiggle your belly while keeping your chest and hips as still as possible. This was followed by an excess of jeering and catcalls and men basically behaving like howler monkeys, the one exception being my Texan, who watched quietly from his stringer at the back of the Superba tent, legs crossed and applauding politely after each number, so well behaved it was hard not to have the suspicion he was up to something. At the end, he got up and walked out, straight-shouldered and looking far too composed for a man who'd just been to a girlie show.

Came every night, he did, and after a while it was obvious I was the one he was coming to see. Course, it wasn't me who figured this out, for he'd show interest in something else whenever I glanced in his general vicinity. Was the other Dancing Girls of Baghdad who filled me in, as they started noticing that anytime they looked *his* way he was in the middle of taking a good hard look *my* way. Was a theory they came up with the third night, and was a theory supported over the fourth, fifth and sixth nights, before being upgraded to simple fact our last night in town, when on his way out he momentarily looked up at me and tugged the brim of his hat, which I'd later learn is Texan for "I am not in any way displeased by your presence, ma'am."

We made the jump to Galveston, a short distance off from Beaumont, and he started showing up there too.

Now. Being singled out like that can make a girl conscious of what she's doing and more particularly what she's wearing, which in my case was: lamé slippers, the toes narrowing to the width of a lamp wick and then curling up into a backward somersault; billowing harem pants, the material not sheer enough to see through but coming close; a fake ruby stuck in my bare navel and kept in place with stickum; a sequined halter top that gripped my rib cage and upper arms so tightly it left red lines afterwards. Above my veil, which was lassooed to the ears with elastic, my eyes were enlarged with a thickness of makeup you didn't see anywhere else in those days (or leastwise not anywhere respectable). Finally, I had to bunch my hair on top of my head and tie it with a long yellow ribbon, not unlike the kind a flower girl might wear for a wedding. This was the most important part of the costume, Stoughton explained, as it lent an innocent touch that made the rest of the getup look extra slutty by comparison.

Every night and practically every matinee, my admirer was there, in the audience, at the back, a man in a fine suit and snakeskin boots and a hat made of fine brushed suede leather and sometimes you'd see him checking the time on a pocket watch that must've cost him a fair penny.

All of this added up to an aura of mystery, a hard fact being that the thing women like most about men is generally the thing they can't put their finger on. When he looked at me, unblinking, from back there in the Superba tent, I could never quite tell whether he was someone who'd do a good job protecting me or whether he was someone I needed protecting *from*, and it was this mixture that grabbed my attention.

We finally met the last night in Galveston. I was rounding the Superba tent corner, fixing on a cup of coffee at the pie car, when I ran headlong into him. He was so broad his shadow was twice the width of mine and for a second it felt like I'd wandered into the darkness cast by an eclipse.

He slowly removed his hat, and I had my first close look. His face was rectangular, the jaw and forehead taking up a goodly portion of surface area, and his hair was cut short enough it stuck straight up, looking sandy and stiff as brush thistles. Though he wasn't handsome, he was close to it, with the rugged look that comes from having the sun grow creases around the eyes. Plus he was older, probably Dimitri's age. (Advice to women: if you want to attract older men, just have your father die on you when you're thirteen. They can practically smell it on you.)

He just stood there, slowly rotating that big brushed-suede hat in his hands, until finally I had to say, "Is there something I can help you with, mister?"

"No ma'am," he said in a voice quarry deep, "I just wanted to tell you how much I enjoyed your dancing."

"Thank you."

"I think you're the best one up there."

"Well. Thank you again."

"No, really, ma'am. I mean it."

There were a few moments of silence. I suppose he was hoping I'd continue the conversation, a chore Texan men usually leave to the women. Finally, all he could do was say, "Name's Williams. James Williams. From Beaumont, Texas. Pleased to meet you."

"My name's Mary Aganosticus."

"Funny name."

"Funny world."

He smiled, and a whole whack of wrinkles I hadn't seen before came trampolining to life. Then he put his hat back on his head, tapped the brim and strode off. Late that night we made the jump to Pasadena, just outside of Houston, and he went back to whatever it was that kept him busy when he wasn't taking up space on the last stringer at a Superba show.

When we finally emerged from Texas (you can get lost in there for months, the damn place is so big), we spent the winter in Arizona, New Mexico, Nevada and Southern California, the first two not even states of the Union yet so it was like visiting different countries, with different money and cooking and types of houses. We headed north once the weather turned spring-like, which in a city like San Diego happens sometime around mid-February. Mostly I was learning how to fit in on a show, which wasn't hard, a carnival not being all that much different from a madhouse. For one thing, whenever people talked about themselves you heard pretty much the same stories as the ones I heard in the madhouse. Stories of woe, mostly, with heavy doses of bad planning tossed in. I was already used to sleeping in a room full of others, so occupying a stateroom with the other Dancing Girls of Baghdad wasn't a hardship. The food was a crime, powdered this and dehydrated that, without fruit or anything milk or meat related, but I was used to that too.

Also: in the hospital I had a place to go to when I needed to be alone. On walk mornings, when the lunatics began to wander in different directions, I'd drift off to a big old live-oak with a U-shaped limb that grazed the lawn before ricocheting back skyward. That's where I'd take up. If I was facing away from the hospital, I'd study the gaps in the forests or the knots in the fence or the types of birds scooping up worms after a nighttime rain. If I was facing toward the hospital, I'd watch those big-armed orderlies, ex-farm boys mostly, corral the lunatics. This was a difficulty in and of itself, for when a patient was led back to the middle of the lawn she'd often as not wander off as soon as the orderly went to grab another, so that after a while the orderlies got impatient and resorted to foul language and throwing the lunatics over their shoulders, like bags of sorghum, just to keep them in one place for a minute.

(More advice? In life you take your laughs where you can get them.)

Same thing on a show, and by this I mean people finding a quiet place to go off to. Otherwise the constant din and people were liable to drive you nuts, the consequences of which I've already related. It's called "finding a corner" and eventually others get to know where yours is and they respect it.

Mine was off the midway, in the Wild Animal exhibit, next to the cage filled with a big old Siberian tiger named Royal. Was the first tiger I'd ever seen in my life, which doesn't explain the attraction because I also'd never seen elephants, lions, zebras, camels, leopards, Friesian horses, Sicilian burros, brown bears, anacondas, tapirs, mandrills, cockatoos, bald eagles, dalmations, yaks, gila monsters or pygmy hippos. And if it sounds strange that a person could reach twenty-two years of age without laying eyes on a wild animal, remember there were hardly any zoos back then. Only travelling menageries, and if any had come to Princeton when I was little, my parents were too busy catching TB or getting torn to bits in farming accidents to take me.

Now, you take a Siberian with good bones and round paws, like a Bengal, and you've got the most magnificent creature you've ever seen, as they can weigh as much as eight hundred pounds with fur as orange as New Mexican soil. But most aren't like that. Most are leaning toward the scrawny end of the spectrum, with a tall arching backbone that adds a sway to the stomach when they walk. Long-limbed and a little dim, describes most Siberians, which is why they usually warm seats during cat acts. Royal was no exception, a moving bag of bones he was, though with eyes the green of jewellery and the dignified nature all tigers have. I'd come at day's end, when the crowds were gone, and keep him company, reading a book or doing my knitting or having a sandwich from the cookhouse while that lonely old tiger gnawed on a horse hock. Or sometimes I'd deliberately not bring anything, so as to force myself to do some thinking, my not yet understanding that the best pondering tends to get done when your mind's occupied with small, repetitive tasks.

After a while I'd get frustrated and say out loud, "What do you think's gonna happen to me, Royal? Something good, maybe? Something worth sticking around for? Just how is it a person's supposed to know?" To this he'd arf, or do nothing, or chew louder, or give me a low rasping *grrrrrrrrrrr* which in feline talk always means the same thing.

I'm a tiger. Don't take me lightly.

All of which I'm telling you because my fondness for Royal was the reason I got to know the guy who ran the Wild Animal Show. I'd seen him working before we met, a well-proportioned man in a donkey jacket and strawboater, ordering the groomers to clean out this tent or that, or give extra feed to such-and-such an animal, or scrub the mange off of this-or-that elephant. For the longest time we never talked, he being a boss and me a dancing girl and the line not being mine to cross. Yet one day, after I'd been with the show maybe a month, he seemed keenly interested on doing just that, for he came up and smiled and plunked himself beside me. With him was an older Negro, who sort of hung back to one side, looking fidgety.

"Now, you tell me. When you were a child and you went to the circus what was it you remembered afterwards? The clowns? The acrobats? The sideshow? Maybe. Maybe not. I'll tell you the thing *I* remembered the most. I remembered the animals. The elephants, the roar of the lions, the dog and pony, the dancing bears. Am I right?"

Was such a bald introduction I could do nothing but answer the question seriously.

"Can't say for sure," I told him. "I never went to the circus as a kid."

"Jesus," he said, laughing. "That twang. You really are from Kentucky, aren't you?"

"I am."

"I'll try not to hold that against you."

"I'd appreciate that."

"My name is Al G. Barnes. People call me Lucky Barnes. This is my educated valet, Dan."

I was feeling chagrined, for I've never taken well to teasing, which I realize is a fault but one I suffer from nonetheless. So I just said, "I know who you are."

Al G. was still grinning and looking into a place neither near nor distant. Seemed to me he enjoyed my being a little difficult, which is a trait common to men born for success: they look at problems as games instead of hindrances, as though they were nothing more than crosswords in a newspaper. After a time, he wiggled himself a little closer to me and resumed talking in a voice that'd lowered itself considerably. This hushing of tone signalled something to Dan, exactly what I wasn't sure, though within a few seconds Al G.'s educated valet was backing away and backing away until he just plain wasn't there anymore. Even Royal turned and lay down and farted.

"In that case," Al G. Barnes said, "I won't beat around the bush. I saw the Superba show again last night. Exquisite. There's something about you, Kentucky. Something I can't quite put my finger on, and that's what this show needs. Performers with mystique. Intrigue. Appeal with a capital A. Plus that stomach of yours—flatter than Iowa, especially considering what's above it and what's below it. I think I'll have a little meeting with Con T. about you. Maybe get you on to something better. Something that'll earn you a little more."

"You'd do that?"

"Sure I'd do that. I *will* do that. I'll do it tomorrow. So. How's about puckering up?"

Now there are two types of philanderers. There're those who do it because they never got past the age of sixteen and those who do it to scare. Al G. was the least objectionable of the two, so I let him kiss me a minute, mostly because I'd been feeling lonely and didn't mind the attention. His lips were warm and gentle, and like all handsome men he concentrated on his kissing technique rather than the person he was kissing. Still, I didn't mind, human closeness being human closeness, until I felt his right hand slip inside my blouse and squeeze my nipple between his second and third fingers. This I let continue for two or three seconds only, just long enough for it to feel silly, as I knew for a fact Al G. Barnes had at least one wife everyone knew about and another they pretended not to know about. So I pushed his hand away, saying, "There's a bit of my first husband in you" by means of explanation.

"Is that bad?" he asked.

"About as bad as bad gets," I answered, pretending to be more amused than I really was.

Without missing a beat he peered into the middle distance and said, "If all goes well I'll be out on my own again next year. A three-ring with *nothing* but animal acts. I've had a few setbacks but you just watch. What do you think of this: 'The Show That's Different'? It's got a ring to it, don't you think?"

I told him I thought it was fine, despite the real thought in my head: heavens to Betsy it's like his lips weren't just pressed against mine and his hands all over my chest. It's as though nothing like that even happened. At that moment I knew Al G. was going to do anything he set his mind to, the ability to recast history being rare and wondrous and one central to the art of crowd pleasing.

Naturally, I never really expected him to talk to Con T., the *I'm gonna tell the boss about you* being a tried-and-true way of getting young impressionables to open their hearts and, more to the point, their knees. Miracle of miracles, the next day I spotted Con T. Kennedy, manager of the Great Parker Carnival number-two unit and brother-in-law of C. W. Parker himself, sitting smack in the middle of the first stringer. He was eating midway peanuts and keeping a keen eye on what my belly was doing. Later that day he sent someone to fetch me. I went to his tent. He was smoking a cigar the size of a cucumber while eating a similiarly sized frank and bun; back then circus and carny managers did everything they could to be like John Ringling, and that included growing fat and impulsive.

"Mary," he said, "take a seat."

I did.

"Gonna make this quick"—here he took his cigar out of his mouth and pointed the soggy end in my direction—"I saw the show today and Al G.'s right. You got yourself an attitude that's interesting to the opposite sex. There's a bitterness in you and I'd bet my bottom dollar it's been hard won. Am I right? Don't bother answering, I don't need to know. I only know it's there and it makes the rubes think there'd be trouble were they to mess with you so naturally that's the one idea get's planted in their head and won't go away. Messing with you. Not the other girls. *You.*"

I sat there, blinking.

"We need someone to do a Serpentine at the end of the evening show. Something to give it a real kick. As of now, you'll be getting $6 a week."

He looked down, puffed on his cigar and started scribbling in a ledger. I waited for his not-talking to extend past a few seconds and signal the meeting was over. Finally, I figured we were through, so I got myself up and I walked myself out.

That night. Little Miss Mary Haynie of Princeton slash Mary Aganosticus of Louisville, hair dyed black and eyes festooned with fake lashes long as matchsticks, walks onto a stage gone completely dark. In front of me's a screen made of a fibre fine enough you could half way see through it when a light was shone. I drop my robe and, hidden from view by the screen, I'm naked as the day I was born, my body enfolded by hot beery tent air. I can practically *feel* it against my unclothed skin, and it's a feeling makes me scared and tingly at the same time. Behind me, Ned Stoughton lights a candle and magnifies it through glass so my silhouette is cast on the screen in front of me, and when he does I close my eyes and picture the languid way Royal moves when he has a bead on something, practically flow it is, more music than movement, and I impersonate that motion, writhing and moving in such a stimulating manner a roomful of men turn into a roomful of silent boys. They don't make a peep—in fact, they do nothing but sit and gape, like they were in church instead of a tent rank with cigar smoke and paraffin fumes and the perspiration produced by men who've just finished losing a week's feed money. I keep my eyes closed the whole time, feeling heady and warm and in control, which is a weird way to feel when naked in front of a tentful of men, a goodly percentage of whom have put their hats on their laps for fear of embarrassment. After exactly seven minutes, Stoughton snuffs the candle and I put my robe on and sneak out before the kerosene lanterns are lit and the rubes look at themselves, red-eyed and disbelieving and wishing they had different wives to go home to.

Soon I became one of the better known Little Egypts in a circuit full of Little Egypts, the Great Parker Carnival posters all stating I was 110 per cent authentic and that you shouldn't be fooled by imitators. My first taste of stardom, it was, and not in any way disagreeable. I started getting compliments, fan mail, boxes of chocolates, invitations to dinner and articles written about me in the local papers, some saying I was an artistic addition to the burlesque tradition and some saying I was the square root of all things evil and some even tracing my act back to the divan shows of the ancient Silk Road. And, oh, the flowers.

Rhododendrons in St. Louis. Daffodils in Fort Smith, Arkansas. Gladioli in Albuquerque. Roses in Bismarck (though how they got them up there I'll never know). Lilies of the valley, bunches and bunches of them, from an industrialist in Jefferson City, Missouri. And those're just the ones I remember. I'd finish a show and if it was an evening performance and we were in a town where times were good they'd be there, bouquets as big as yours truly, usually with a love note from some rich guy smitten not with me but the idea of me.

They'd ask to meet me. Stoughton, in that rich larnyx-bobbing voice of his, would tell them to beat it. I wasn't supposed to talk to anyone as Little Egypt, or admit to strangers I was none other, or otherwise display any intimate awarenesses of the Serpentine dance, the reason being it wouldn't take much more than my opening my mouth for people to figure out the famous Little Egypt was a pint-sized hick from the flat end of Kentucky. Your job, Stoughton would say, is guarding the mystique. My job is helping you do that.

Unless of course money was involved.

Here's how it worked. The interested gentlemen would pay Stoughton whatever Stoughton thought he could get from him, which would be anywhere from six bits in a state like Mississipi to upwards of $6 in a high-rolling state like California. Later on we'd split it. Was our extra little bonus, what troupers call cherry pie. For the first time, I started saving money.

Once the introductory fee was paid, Stoughton would lead the man into a feed tent we'd emptied of sacks and festooned with divans and veils and huge silken pillows and other store-bought items made up to look Arab. I'd be lying on a bunch of cushions, in harem pants and a veil, eating grapes straight from the bunch, and the man would stammer something like "Why yes Miss Egypt I just wanted to say how much I enjoyed your performance and how much I enjoyed your dancing and if you were free for dinner this evening I was just wondering...." Meanwhile I'd be doing nothing but pouting, head supported by my right hand, left hip jutting suggestively in the air, and it was the sight of this hip up close that usually caused the rube to get so short of breath he could barely get through what it was he wanted to get through. (Amazing, how easy it was to rile a man back in 1911.) After a minute I'd ease one of my eyebrows upward, as if to say, Me? With *you?*

This was Stoughton's idea and the result of Stoughton's understanding of John Q. Public: not once did a man react poorly to my rudeness, or do anything but bow his head and thank me for my time and back out muttering apologies. Stoughton explained this was because the rubes actually wanted me to do this, for it was in keeping with the general aura of Little Egypt. If I'd accepted an invitation, they'd know the great siren of Cairo didn't really exist, so in fact I was doing them a favour treating them like yesterday's breakfast.

After slipping into the state of Texas via Louisiana and doing our first show in Port Arthur, I heard from Stoughton a man wanted to meet me. We quickly threw together the Egypt tent. A few minutes later the flap lifted and in came none other than the Texan. We stood looking at each other. (Well, he stood and I lay, but given the air of superiority I generated while dressed as Little Egypt it felt like the other way around.) He had flowers with him, a dozen roses, and all he did was put them down and nod and leave. Didn't say a word. I guess he thought it was more dignified that way.

He came back the next day, his act more or less the same: he put the flowers down and took a good long look at me, only this time before tipping his hat and leaving he said, "I sure do enjoy the way you move up there, Miss Egypt," to which I fluttered my eyelashes and sent him on his way. The next time he came it was exactly the same routine, only he said, "I sure do enjoy watching you dance, Miss Egypt," and the time after that it was, "I sure do wish I could get to know you a bit better, Miss Egypt," (though with that one he dropped his dimpled chin, like a man guilty of strong emotion). I looked at him haughtily, raising my eyebrows and saying with my whole expression, Well, no *kidding.*

He left, only to show up the next night, wearing one of his expensive suits and a bolo tie and handing over another bouquet of flowers. We moved on to Baytown, and he kept coming, the jump to Houston doing little to dissuade him either, which is saying something seeing as travel between cities wasn't nearly what it is today.

His first proposition was something along the lines of "I was wondering, Miss Egypt, if you and I could get together, outside the circus I mean," a suggestion that was moulded the next night into "I was thinking, Miss Egypt, if you'd like to visit me in Beaumont, I own a real nice home and I know lots of nice people...." And then, near the middle of our Houston stand, he hit me with it in that slow solid Texan way of his.

"Might as well out with it, Miss Egypt. I'm here to declare my intentions."

Now I could only game-play for so long, especially once I started considering how much money that poor man was spending for the privilege of watching me eat grapes for a minute at a time. Fact is, he was wearing me down (or setting me up, he being a man) and on the night he actually got down on one knee and proposed, what could I do but break out laughing and say, "Lookit, mister. First off my name's not Miss Egypt. It's Haynie, Mary Haynie, from the ugly end of Kentucky no less. This is all just getup, a costume. There *is* no Little Egypt—she doesn't exist. I'm something they dreamed up. Oh, and by the way, we met last year but you just can't tell on account of this veil."

Well. You know what that big dummy did? He looked at me with those somber Texan eyes—like grey skies, they were—and he rotated his hat in those big leathery hands and he said, "I understand that, ma'am."

I won't claim this didn't have an effect on me, for it did, the ability to surprise being something women have trouble ignoring. At the same time I had no intention of running off and marrying, no matter how rich the suitor, given my general lack of interest in men and the bad taste I had in my mouth concerning the holy state of matrimony.

So instead I thought, *What the hell,* and walked over and got up on my tiptoes. This got me high enough to give his cheek a quick, dry kiss, like one a sister might dole out at a wedding.

"Don't come back, all right? I mean it. This is silly."

He looked at me sadly, for about as long as it takes to blink slowly three times. Then he promised he wouldn't, if that's what I wanted, but before he left he handed me a card and told me if I ever changed my mind I could cable him, day or night, let him know I was coming and no matter what he'd be waiting when I got there. Then he gave me a pitiful little nod of the head and left me eyeballing a gold-embossed business card. It read

James Williams III
Investments and Annuities

and it was one of those moments a thought you're not proud of pops into your head and you examine it with surprise and more than a little self-contempt before chasing it away.

Keep the card, Mary.

It was so hot and dusty that year by the time we made it to our last stops in the panhandle it'd started to feel like we'd been condemned to wander Texas for the rest of our natural-born lives. Everyone was bored and mad and restless, which is what happens to troupers when you force them to stay in the same state for an extended stretch—it feels like confinement and it cheeses them off. The animals were nervous and losing hair, and a lot of the workingmen were drinking and the ones who weren't had taken off, Con T. having to recruit more stake drivers and roustabouts from local men's hostels so of course they were drinking nonstop as was their nature.

Now. You take a group of sober men and place them next to a bunch of drunk men and the sober ones'll feel deprived, and believe me the thing men hate worse than anything on earth is feeling deprived. It's their greatest weakness. Go all crybaby, they do, probably from being spoiled by their mothers. So of course the drunkenness spread to the wranglers and the sideshow freaks and a goodly number of performers, the upshot being by the time we pulled into Lubbock we were all feeling crusty and in no mood, and in addition most of the men were suffering from headaches and the shakes.

Lubbock. Christ. Was practically biblical in its awfulness, and I'm a woman who's read the Bible more than once so I know what I'm talking about. When the China call went up and we all looked out the train window ... well, a sigh went round. The town was low and it was ugly, sitting in a dust cloud the colour of dried blood. When we detrained it got even worse, for Lubbock appeared on the schedule the same time of year the panhandle got eaten up by locusts, and as we moved our bags to the wagons those big old bugs set to work, flapping in our hair, running over our clothes, getting inside our shirts, their fat little frog-sized hindlegs rubbing together to produce an evil, gloating hum. Every towner who could be indoors was, meaning we pretty much had the place to ourselves. It was like a ghost town. Main Street was perfectly still, or would've been were it not for a hot wind blowing in from the plains, stirring up paper and scrub and brown-red dust. It got in your mouth and hair, choked the back of your throat and sent even the tee-totallers on the show running for the nearest beer.

So I went with them. The place was called the Town Inn, a big old saloon with only a few locals inside drinking when the entire cast of the Parker Carnival funnelled in. Whatever conversations had been going on stopped, townfolk generally regarding carnies as unwashed gypsies who dress themselves by stealing shirts off townie clotheslines, an idea incorrect only in the gypsy part: in all my years of trouping I never once met an actual gypsy though it's true we lived like them. No matter. When the barkeep saw we had money the draft beer started flowing and soon the room filled with chatter. I sat with the other

Dancing Girls, even though their chumminess had worn off considerably since I'd been named Little Egypt. Still, was a day we girls needed to stick together, for of all the people drinking beer in that bar to forget their glumness we dancing girls were by far the glummest, Lubbock being known as a town where the dancers more often than not got called on to help square the grift. Even as we sat there gulping, we knew Con T. was meeting with the chief of police to work out the details, the police in Lubbock being so mean and drunk and full of themselves they refused to barter with the advance agent, insisting on speaking with the boss man himself.

An hour later the call went out: Con T. needed to talk to me. As I walked over to Con T.'s tent it felt a little like the time I walked toward a bloody heap on an untilled tobacco field and nothing would make me believe it was my mother until I saw it all up close. *I* was going to have to fuck some fat greasy southern cop. That much was obvious. Yet as I went over there my mind took a little breather. If you'd asked me my name I probably would've looked at you blankly and said nothing more edifying than "Huh?"

It was when I walked through those tent flaps and saw Con T. sitting there, smoking a cigar and looking guilty, that reality came storming back. Started to tremble, I did.

He motioned for me to sit. I kickstarted the tête-à-tête.

"What's it gonna be, boss?"

"Usual stuff. Money. Whisky. Free tickets. A girl. I'm sorry, Mary. Seems Little Egypt's reputation has spread far and wide."

"His name?"

"Owen Lakes."

"What's he like?"

"Can't say he's a charmer."

"What do I have to do?"

"Go to his house. Be there at five. Have dinner. Dance with him if he asks. Wear your costume, of course."

I stared back, blinking, all the while searching my brain for a tactful way of handling this. One didn't come. In Hopkinsville, I'd sworn I'd never deal with someone trying to take advantage by acting nice and cute and hoping they'd take pity. But seeing as I was sitting in the office of Con T. Kennedy himself, brother-in-law of the great C. W. Parker and therefore a man with clout, I tried chasing it away and landing on a strategy a little more compromising.

Sure enough it didn't come, leaving me no choice but to do what I did. Got tired of waiting, I suppose.

"Nope," I said.

His face fell. His mouth looked like a pair of dropped pants.

"Whaddaya mean, no?"

"I mean what I say, Mr. Kennedy. This being the panhandle and the rough bit besides, I can picture Owen Lakes and what I'm picturing is fat and rude and sweating buckets, and I bet he's unkind to children and animals to boot. Under no circumstances will I go to his house, eat his food, listen to his music or in any way help him feel like a man. The answer is no. En Oh. You like Lakes so much you give him foxtrot lessons."

It was obvious no one had ever talked to Con T. Kennedy this way, much less a lowly dancing girl. He got up and circled round his desk and came toward me. I stood to meet him, and we both made our eyes go snake-like.

"Now you listen to me you little piece of West Kentucky trash. If it weren't for me you'd still be making wallets in the nuthouse so I'll say this one time and one time only. Tonight you will be entertaining the chief of police of the town of Lubbock, Texas, and you will be charming and you will be polite and when he asks you to dance you will say, 'Oh, wonderful I saw your cylinder player I thought you was never going to ask.' Am I making myself clear, Miss Mary whatever-you're-calling-yourself these days?"

"Sure are. And I hope I'm making myself clear too. I wouldn't go near that sewer rat if William H. Taft asked me and I certainly won't go near him for the likes of you."

"You will!"

"I won't!"

"Goddammit, you will!"

"Goddammit, I will not!"

Con T. Kennedy, brother-in-law of C. W. Parker and in charge for that reason only, chose *that* moment to put his cigar back in his mouth. This freed up his dominant hand so he could use the back of it to slap me across the face. Was something men did to women all the time back then; still do, I imagine, though it's mostly moved behind closed doors for the laws against it seem to get used more.

He'd swung from the elbow, meaning he hadn't hit me hard, though was hard enough my right cheek stung and my vision went jiggly and wet. At this point I knew I was supposed to give in, to suddenly pretend I'd come to my senses. Con T. had already put his cigar back in his mouth and gained that smug expression men get when they think they've dealt with a situation. It was this smugness I couldn't stand, more so than being smacked, so when I hit him back *I* threw from the shoulder, clipping him sufficiently hard the cigar flew out of his mouth and he bent over, holding his nose.

Now, when it comes to men, all you have to do is make the word *vulnerable* pop into their heads and they slink off like wounded boys, completely amazed someone's challenged their kingly status. (Lions are the same way, which I suppose is a reason I've always favoured tigers—punch a tiger in the face and he'll practically weep with gratitude you at least tried to make things interesting.)

Con T. straightened up. He was sputtering and pale and his eyes were messed with respect and he fought to get his breath. When he did, his yelling sounded high-pitched and girly, the content being more or less "You get the hell outta here, you're through you're fired I'll see to it your name's ruined you'll never work in this business again" to which I said, "Yeah well fuck you and your shitty little two-bit grifter show," which was quite an insult seeing as the Parker show unit two was probably the biggest carnival in the country.

By the time I hit the midway all eyes were turned and peering through dust. I couldn't calm my breathing, and the bones in my hand were aching fiercely. To simmer down I decided to go visit Al G., he being the only real friend I had on the show. Thankfully, his tent was up and he was in it, dressed impeccably as always, from his spats to his double-buttoned vest to his clean white straw boater, none of which had been dirtied by the air's brown dust. He was drinking a pale green liquid with Dan. When I entered they both looked up, Al G. giving me his charmer's grin. He pulled a chair for me and invited me to join them and I wanted to kiss him I was so thankful. Dan, meanwhile, looked rubbery with concern.

"So," Al G. said through a grin, "unless I miss my guess the Great Parker Carnival will be leaving Lubbock prematurely?"

"Looks that way," I said, though by then I was starting to come apart a little. Was all that adrenalin backing up and getting stuck now the fight was over; if you've never had it happen, believe me it hurts a fair bit more than the fist-swinging part. Trembly, I was, with a stomach ache thrown in. Plus I didn't have anywhere to go, *again*, something I'd learned to fear more than anything. I started blubbering, so Al G. gave me a finger of the apple brandy he bought in Amarillo and advised me to drink it down. This settled me enough to tell him I was thinking of marrying a Texan I'd met out Beaumont way.

"You love him?"

"Nope. You think that's wrong?"

"Kentucky," he answered, "*please*. There are so few things in this world that are just plain wrong. Murder, maybe, though even that can be a matter of necessity. Am I right, Dan?"

"You right, governor," Dan said, smiling now himself. "You just plain right."

I finished my drink so Al G. gave me another. As I wasn't a drinker, it hit me like a ton of hens, which was good because I needed a whole lot of courage to do what needed doing. Which was: stagger back to the Dancing Girls tent, announce the Little Egypt position was vacant, thank them sarcastically for their affection and support and loyalty, and tote out my unpacked bag.

Then I walked through dust and bugs and heat to the railway station, arriving bitten and hot and bedraggled. Bought myself water and coffee and a sandwich and got them all into me before taking the same train out of town that'd taken me into town.

I sat beside a housewife from Dallas and across from a Bible salesman from Utah. Basically I forced myself to chin-up, and by the time we hit our first stop, some rinky-dink place I can't remember the name of, I was starting to think what'd happened was not entirely bad.

In Dallas I sent a cable to the Texan. He came promptly.

I told him it had to be a city hall wedding, that I wasn't one for pomp and circumstance and *was* one for small numbers, such as, oh, I dunno, let's say for the sake of argument, two and two only? Course, my already having a husband back in Louisville along with a committal warrant bearing my name was the real reason any kind of production was low on my list of priorities. He agreed right off, which surprised me, for I'd heard Texans liked to do everything big, and I figured he'd want a giant banquet with an orchestra and shrimp cocktails and Chinese fireworks and sides of beef roasting over mesquite plus the entire population of Beaumont thrown in for good measure. Maybe it was him living so close to Louisiana, Cajuns generally being happier with simple things than Texans.

So I got married as Mary Haynie of Princeton, Kentucky, and became Mary Williams of Beaumont, Texas. I liked it that way, for it was as though Mary Aganosticus of Louisville had never even existed. Afterwards, we took the train all the way to San Francisco, which was

fine by me, California being far away from Kentucky, a place I wanted to forget forever and most particularly on my honeymoon. We ate
in the Continental and afterwards took a calèche to the Regency. Our
suite contained a French sofa and teak sitting furniture and a pond-
sized four-poster. The bathroom was the size of the car where I'd
slept with the Dancing Girls of Baghdad. We drank champagne on
our balcony, overlooking a bay gone beautiful with mist and boat
lanterns. From below we could hear the clip-clop of hooves and
the foghorns of freighters on the water. When it got chilly James
suggested we go inside, which was fine by me. I wasn't nervous, or at
least not unduly, for I was eager to figure out if my body could do
what a woman's body ought to be able to do, or whether my not being
able to have a baby was just hokum dreamed up to get me out of
Dimitri Aganosticus's hair.

I told James I needed to get myself prepared, at which point little Mrs. James Williams of Beaumont, Texas, retired to the Pullman-
car-sized bathroom, where an assortment of powders and lotions and
mists were applied to various and sundry bodily portions. A silky little nothing of a negligee, the product of two weeks' worth of cherry
pie, was pulled on. I looked magnificent. I just *did*. I opened the door
to the rest of the suite. James was waiting in bed, wearing pyjamas,
and before crawling in beside him I noticed his initials were on the
breast pocket. He leaned over. Gave me a quick kiss on the mouth. I
settled back for more, confident that under such circumstances I'd
soon be overcome and with the moist openness they talk about nowadays in romance novels.

Well. Did that happen? Did that happen to the misted and powdered and negligee-wearing Little Egypt of the Great Parker Carnival
company, unit two? To the greatest sexpot this side of the Mississippi?
Not on your auntie. James said good-night, rolled over and began snoring like a fat man.

All of this was severely curious business, for back when he used to watch me from the last row of the Superba his eyes practically flamed, even though the rest of him stayed still and respectful. I put it down to his age and the long day we'd had. Maybe he'd been tuckered by all the excitement. I, on the other hand, couldn't sleep, a problem that's bothered me my whole life, so I lay awake thinking about everything under the sun, the trouble with sleeplessness being that things you'd thought you'd put behind you have a way of popping up and staring you in the face and demanding attention.

Next day we started home, three full days through desert, looking at sand and cactus and rickety wood-plank towns that looked like their whole purpose was to give fire something to do. We ate in the first-class dining car and spent our nights in a first-class coach, him sleeping and me staring up at the ceiling while thinking, *Huh?*

Finally we reached Beaumont. From the town square James hired a Negro wagon driver to squire us along country roads and lanes; while I'd been told the house was out of town, I'd never imagining it'd be *this* out of town. Having passed miles and miles of cotton fields, swampy forest and squatters' shacks, James finally said, "Here we are," as we turned onto a narrow two-track lane.

We came over the rise, and there it was, his house, the sight of which made me say "Oh, my lord" under my breath. It was big all right, and getting bigger as we approached up a long driveway lined with live-oaks. I suppose most women would've been pleased, for you don't really understand how rich a man is until you see his house, and I admit a part of me was tickled pink: I may not look like much but I'm smart enough to know this bit about money not buying happiness is pure malarkey, the simple truth being rich people are happier than poor people on account of the things poor people have to do whenever the slightest bit of trouble flares up. So part of me was ecstatic. At the same time I was nervous, for in true antebellum style the house had marble steps and Greek columns and a high arching door; when put together under a coat of creamy white paint it looked a whole lot like the loony bin in Hopkinsville. I felt my shoulders levitate to my ears and my mouth parch. In fact I wanted to say, Let's live somewhere else, James, except he would've responded, Why, darling? and the fact of the matter was, at age twenty-three, I had secrets.

We went inside.

"Do you like it?" he asked, and of course I told him I did. As I took a look around—well, more turned on my heels with my mouth gaping—he rang a bell and before I knew it a pair of Negro women, each built like an elk, was standing in front of me.

"This is Melba, the cook, and this is Willa, our maid."

"Pleased to meet you."

"Our pleasure," they said, the flatness in their voices suggesting it was anything but. Worse, they finished up by muttering the word *ma'am*, which I found embarrassing seeing as I was half their ages and had figured my addressing them as ma'am might be more in keeping.

James took me on a tour. Quite proud of his house, he was; like all homes of that size it'd been in the family for generations. He took me from room to room to room. There were nineteen of them, not counting the cellar. In them were crystal chandeliers and Persian carpets and mahogony furniture and fine bone china and oil paintings in gilt frames. Beyond that, I won't go into any detail, for counting another person's riches is boring. I'm only mentioning the man's wealth so if later I tell you material things don't impress me you'll know it's a statement coming from a woman who, for a brief period of time, was about as rich as rich gets.

Plus James had a car. Every morning, after a breakfast of oatcakes and black coffee, he'd put on a pair of goggles and a funny leather driving hat that clung to his skull like a bathing cap, and he'd head out to his Model T. Some mornings I'd watch him getting his exercise with all the crank turning and lever pulling necessary to get the thing going, and then when it was finally moving it travelled no faster than a cart pulled by pair of workhorses. Furthermore, the thing usually stoppped before making it out of the driveway (which admittedly was a half mile long) and I'd watch him, off in the distance, jump out and start lever pulling and crank turning to get the damn thing mobile again. Then, to demonstrate his appreciation for all things automotive, he'd give three long blasts on the klaxon before turning onto the road.

He was in love with the motor car and often said it was going to transform the way America did business, that it was a genuine gift from the future and that he'd already invested money with Mr. Ford. As for me, I thought it a little suspicious he'd put so much stock in a sputtering heap of nuts and bolts when his very own Little Egypt was going untouched and unloved each and every night.

My days? Whew. Slow as tar, they were. Some days slower. You'd think after all I'd been through in the last decade or so I'd be eager for a little peace and quiet. Truth is, I'd thought that's what I'd wanted, only to discover that movement has a way of getting into your bones and making you feel disjointed when it's not there any more. It's like wearing a hat. At first you put it on and it feels scratchy and warm and tight. You wear it for a while, and you stop noticing it's there. Then you take it off and your head feels scratchy and warm and tight all over again, even though there's nothing to cause the sensation. The same with the business of shifting your body from one piece of ground to another. After a while it starts to feel like the earth beneath your feet is stable and still and reliable only when it's rushing.

To kill time I'd ask Melba to pack me a lunch ("Yes, ma'am," she'd say, her expression as flat as a board). Then I'd take long walks along country roads, making myself guess what was behind each bend, each gnarled and twisted live-oak tree, each rise in the camel-coloured earth. More often than not it was more of the same. I soon grew bored of this and started taking a blanket and setting myself in spots well away from anywhere in particular. I'd take a book and stretch out for hours. Sometimes I'd even unbutton my blouse and warm my flesh in the sun, all the while concentrating on the way air smells come autumn. For a time, I even managed to persuade myself I was happy, or at least that safe was a worthwhile substitute.

After I'd been Mrs. James Williams for almost three weeks I decided I was going to make myself a sweater. Winter was coming, and I'd wear it in the evenings, when even a bayou can get chilly. James picked up the wool I needed from town, and I drew myself a pattern on crepe paper. Was nice-looking, I thought, with piping and a high collar to come later. The buttons would be silver.

The next day I took my knitting stuff on one of my walks and started the sweater on the soft bank of a levee. I could feel the ground squish under the blanket when I sat. I did that for the next few days, until I got so intent on finishing I stopped bothering with the walks and started knitting on the front porch swing seat, letting Melba and Willa stay out of my way for a change. It took me a week to finish. I worked like my time on this planet was coming to an end. When the last pearl two was done I held the thing up to the light. Looked beautiful, it did, though at the same time something was wrong with it. Something peculiar.

Then I realized the damn thing was too small.

And not just small, but *small*, nowhere near big enough for an adult woman, even one of my slight proportions. I was astonished, for I'd followed the pattern to a T, and it'd come out looking exactly like it should except shrunk down. An eight-year-old would've had to exhale to get the buttons done up. I considered this fact for more than a minute, thinking maybe I really was crazy, when I recalled something Dr. Levine told me during one of our bathtub sessions. Seems we don't have one mind but two, one we know about and one we don't, and the one we know about isn't necessarily the one in charge. I kept holding up the sweater and scrutinizing it and thinking, *What could this possibly mean?* when suddenly my breathing went shallow and rabbit paced. Seems I didn't want to be knitting for an adult at all. I wanted to be knitting for a baby. I guess my two minds'd been duking it out the whole time and the sweater had landed somewhere in the middle.

I just sat there, looking at the garment, wheels turning, when finally a plan of action entered through my ears and pretty much hollered.

All right mister, said the voice. Enough pussyfootin' around.

That night I told Willa and Melba to vamoose to the servants' quarters once James had come home. I didn't even try to be polite; the other conclusion I'd come to was Melba and Willa would be a whole lot happier if I was rude to them, they being the type of people to get chagrined when their expectations are violated. I ordered them to put out the silver and to get two bottles of French wine from the cellar and to make sure there were flowers in the centre of the table. With a game hen roasting away in the oven, I shooed them away till morning.

Served dinner myself that night. I wore something loose so that every time I bent over to offer James more bird or cranberries or collard greens he could take a peek at the shapes that'd made me famous all over west and northwest America. My eyes looked dreamy and my lips moist throughout. Through opportunistic pouring, I made sure he drank more than his fair share of wine, thinking maybe reserve was the problem.

Afterwards I told him I had something I needed to show him upstairs. He took the bait and we retired to the master's chamber. There, I put my arms around him and told him I'd been lonely. He apologized, his voice even deeper and quieter than ordinary, saying there'd been craziness in the cotton markets lately and he'd been overworked and distracted by all the other things on his mind. This put me at ease, for I'd started to worry he was bent in some serious manner. We kissed. Kissed a second time. Everything seemed to going according to plan when he pulled away. He was wearing that expression men get under such circumstances, by which I mean half master of the universe and half needy child.

Was then he said, "Dance for me, Miss Egypt."

At first I recoiled, for I'd figured one of the upsides of marrying James was my days as a dancing girl were through. A second later I talked myself into it, thinking we all have our secret likes and dislikes, and there're sure a lot of things worse in this world than watching a young woman wriggle. Meanwhile James'd got up and was putting a cylinder on the player. He cranked the handle. Naturally it was frigolet music.

To make a long story short I figured if I was going to do this I was going to do this right, so I started dancing. And not just dancing but *dancing*, every limb in a slow tiger flow, eyes closed, whole body floating to music, soft sounds of delight coming from my painted lips, and to make sure my husband got more than any rube in a Superba tent I let the tension mount and then I ... well ... what it was was I started touching myself through my clothes, rubbing myself with the heel of my right hand, hard enough the veins on the back of my hand popped up, readying parts that ordinarily stay hid, and enjoying myself, too, for my dress felt soft and a breeze was blowing in the bedroom window and then, still dancing, I filled both hands with hair and slowly pushed blond curls off my forehead while at the same time running a tongue over pouty crimson lips.

Then I heard a groan. Well not a groan exactly. Midway between a groan and a grunt, like the sound a walrus makes when ready for dinner. I opened my eyes. My second husband, James Williams III, Investment Banker, Far East Texas, had himself out and was doing the job meant for me.

Was doing it frantically, if you must know.

I had to fight the inclination to leave the very next day, and would've gone ahead and done it had it not been a time when the mark of a good woman was the ability to endure. Truth was, I'd taken vows, and I'm a person who takes obligation seriously. I stuck it out for another two or three months, though during that time I promised myself I sure wasn't going to embarrass myself with another attempt at seducing my very own husband. If he wanted some loving, fine. This time he was the one who was going to have to come ask for it.

What followed was basically a repeat of the first month. James was in town most of the time, though when he *was* at home he was quiet and generally in his own little world. Melba and Willa padded around like they owned the place, and I worked hard at avoiding them, figuring at the very least keeping out of their line of sight gave me something to do. No one talked unless they had to, and even then it was in hushed tones. It wasn't long before I noticed how the house allowed for this crazy system: because it was so big, everyone could live and work and go about their business without ever crossing paths. Its very grandeur seemed to enforce a sort of institutional glumness and pretty soon I started to hate it, too.

One night, sitting in my chambers, twiddling my thumbs, thinking did I or did I not want to read a book, I finally decided I had to have some kind of talk with James. I descended the curving marble staircase and stood in the middle of the foyer. Though James was home, I didn't know exactly where he was and was readying to call his name. I'd taken a deep breath and was about to call out when I stopped myself. There was something about that house—its size, its stillness, its stuffy authority—that communicated what I was thinking of doing was a breach of decorum and therefore out of the question.

Instead, I went looking. I checked the parlour, the dining room, the kitchen (where sometimes James would have a slice of rhubarb pie while standing at the chef's table). They were all empty. I went back upstairs, found all the rooms darkened and then came back downstairs, heading through rooms I'd already checked till I reached the back of the house where the billiard room was. It, too, was empty, though I did notice the door on the far side of the room was open. This connected with a hallway running along the rear of the house toward the solariums. As it was almost twenty feet wide and therefore as much a room as it was a corridor, James had lined the hallway with his paintings. For this reason, he called this part of the house the "gallery"; everytime he said it he smiled, thinking how clever it was the word described both the room's functions in one fell swoop.

I moved toward the open door. James couldn't hear me, for the billiard room was covered with Persian carpets, so he didn't look over. He was contemplating a painting of a ballet dancer he'd bought in France. Even if he *had* heard me, I don't think he would've looked away, as his eyes were so busy following the soft, girlish lines of the dancer's body. All admiration, he was, like a dowager who'd finally found a vase that suited her sideboard. It was the same expression he always got when admiring the contours of his motor car, and for a second I felt proud that if nothing else, at least my husband was a man of discerning taste. The second after *that*, however, my heart skipped a beat, and I suddenly felt a little ill. The expression he had on his face— lips pursed, forehead creased, any pleasure residing in the eyes and the eyes only—was the exact same one he used to wear whenever he watched me dance in a Superba.

Next afternoon, I walked into town with nothing more than clothes, knick-knacks and some cherry pie dollars I'd saved. James had offered to give me some money, but I'd turned it down, saying I didn't need his help or anybody else's, my being too young to understand the difference between what was pride and what was just plain stupid. I caught the dusk train west.

True to Con T. Kennedy's word, he'd soured my name everywhere. Didn't even matter what that name was. Haynie, Aganosticus, Williams, I even tried Levine a few times before finally settling on a handle that just popped out of my mouth in front of a carnival owner in a place called Yuba City, California. I just liked the way it sounded, I suppose, and I've kept it till this day.

It didn't help. It's not uncommon for carnies to have five, six, even seven aliases, depending on how many states they're wanted in. In that world, you tended to go by faces and physical descriptions and reputations more than names, and everyone I talked to looked at me like they knew me. Finally I resorted to a job with the Cosmopolitan Amusement Company, that "Mastadonic Majestic Mighty Master of the Carnival World," on a flat-out cooch: after the entertainment and the grift we girls would come out and stomach dance and maybe do a balloon dance for good measure. After ten minutes or so, the educator would run on stage and stop the show so he could do what they called "the ding pitch," which meant any rube with another ten cents to spare got to see us take our tops off. Those who didn't got shown the door. Because the educator was the sort of man who could promise heaven as though it was his to deliver, most of the rubes would ante up no matter how much they'd already lost at three-card monte, and a minute later I'd be standing there, the blonde on the far right, half naked and newly named Mabel Stark, thinking how I'd once imagined a future for myself that was much, much different. It wasn't even the humiliation that got me down. Was the sheer lack of imagination involved. Believe me, it's pretty hard telling yourself you're doing something requiring talent when the whole point of your job is to stand in one place with your chest exposed. It hardly even mattered what expression you had on your face, for the rubes weren't looking there. The other four Harem Girls of Siam mostly opted for bored.

This went on for about a month. I got so low I thought about having myself a little neurasthenic holiday and probably would've if I hadn't been living so hand to mouth. Truth was, I didn't have time for a nervous breakdown, which in some ways was a blessing and in some ways a curse. In early February of 1912 the Cosmopolitan pulled into Venice, California, which back then was still considered a railroad town and not a part of Los Angeles. On our third date, I was standing up there, ding pitch over, reaching behind to unhitch my halter, when I got a cramp in my right thumb. This slowed me down considerably, and by the time the other four Harem Girls were topless I was still wrestling with my snap. Was then I heard laughter from the middle of the tent, the sort of laughter that doesn't so much rise as spurt to life, as though the person laughing had been holding it in for longer than was comfortable. The Harem Girls of Siam all looked at one another, puzzled, before peering into the glare. Owing to the magnified candle shining in our faces, it was difficult to see who was doing the laughing, or just what it was was so funny. Course, I was the one who figured it out first, ahead of the other girls and the educator and the frigolet player and the grifters who'd stayed for the show and even the rubes themselves, for when he finally quit guffawing Al G. called out, "For Pete's sake, Kentucky! How long is this likely to take?"

CHAPTER 5

THE HUNGARIAN MILITARY OFFICER

THREE WEEKS LATER, I PERFORMED A SLIDE FOR LIFE ON opening day of the all new Al G. Barnes Wild Animal Circus, a show Al G. really was calling "The Show That's Different." Was one o'clock in the afternoon and the parade was just returning to the lot. A goodly number of people had followed, the idea being the free act would keep them there and make them want to buy tickets for the matinee, which was always a harder sell than the evening performance. I started climbing a ladder anchored by guy wires. There were exactly two hundred steps of "Height-Defying Hysteria" and back then just seeing a thing stretch that high into the air was something. Meanwhile, the whole contraption was wavering and teetering and circling in the breeze, and with each step my legs grew weaker and my stomach more air filled and I promised myself if I survived I'd attend church and give money to the poor. All of this ran through my head as I climbed farther and farther into the heavens, seemed I'd never get there, though finally I reached a rickety little wooden platform at the top. Here I focused on Al G.'s suggestion that you didn't look down, even for a second, no matter how curious you got, though when you're that frightened advice tends to turn into a senseless string of words that function more to keep your mind occupied while you're standing knock-kneed and trembling and dizzy as a weathervane.

Around the time I began to wonder if a person can die from over-stimulation I reached out and squeezed my little hands around a padded triangle. It was attached to a metal pulley, and this pulley sat on a long, twisted metal cable that travelled from the platform to the ground at an angle not quite forty-five degrees but pretty damn close. Eyes clenched shut, I stepped off the platform, let rip a blood-curdler, and hurtled toward earth, my body twisting and kicking and jerking and flailing. I truly thought I was going to die for it didn't seem possible a mere pulley could hold a body gathering that much momentum, and because I figured I was a dead woman, time slowed and my head cleared and I had myself a moment to wish mine hadn't been a life in which survival had always seemed such an imposition. This got me sad as hell, so sad I almost forget why it was I was having such thoughts, it all coming back pretty quick when the cable took a dip at the bottom and headed back up skyward and then stopped. The triangle was wrenched from my hands, practically tearing my arms out of the sockets, and I went soaring, limbs akimbo, eyes clamped so hard they hurt. After soaring for about half the length of a baseball outfield, I felt netting strands go taut on my backside, dip me down low and hurl me straight back into the air, though with far less velocity. As I kicked and flailed, I started suspecting maybe I really would survive, a wonderful sensation when seconds earlier you were thinking for sure it's curtains. I crawled from the net, beaming, eyes teary, nose snotty, shaky from adrenalin and yearning to puke. People were cheering and laughing and pointing and saying, "Jesus Christ, you see that?" and was then I saw Mr. Barnes and his Negro valet, Dan, emerge smiling from the sideline.

"What did you think?" Al G. asked his assistant.

"It was somethin', governor. Somethin' fo' sure."

"He's right, Kentucky. You're a natural-born performer."

"Natural-born, Miss Stark."

Here I looked at the both of them, and when I'd finally caught enough breath to form a sentence it came out as "Al G., we have to talk."

Once I'd done a few more Slides for Life it began to sink in that just so long as I held on I'd survive, a rule I'd always subscribed to in life anyway. After a week or so I learned to style the act, bowing and curtseying on the platform, smiling through the plunge, pointing my arms over my head as I jetted airborne and then waving and smiling after I crawled from the net. Truth be known, it got to be sort of fun, like flying, which allowed me to concentrate on disliking my goat act and my riding act all the more intently. Meanwhile, the circus headed south.

So. Lithe little blond thing. Twenty-three years old and nary a scar, bone break or concussion under her belt (though the same couldn't be said about a sordid past). In the menage tent, near the cat cages, in the off-hours before the matinee, a time of day the monkeys stop chattering and the mules stop braying and the elephants stop trumpeting and the hyenas stop cackling. Even the horses and elephants close their eyes, not so much sleeping but enjoying the lack of commotion that part of the afternoon brings. My head on a rolled-up coat and that rolled-up coat on a pallet. I'm dreaming, almost certainly, for I've suffered from doozers all my life, so I don't even hear him march up and position those tall black leather boots beside my little blond head.

He waited a few seconds before impatiently rapping the heels of said boots against the floorboards. This caused me to open my right eye, blinking against the light filtering into the menage, before realizing I was staring at a man's shin. I rotated that same eye upward, and took my first look at Louis Roth, who'd been on loan to Hagenbeck-Wallace for the past half year.

This initial impression moulded my opinion of Louis's size, for from where I lay he looked to be about eight feet tall, with a huge ladle-shaped jaw and hair as thick and well groomed as Al G.'s. He was dressed in jodhpurs, black waistcoat and epaulettes, riding whip in one hand. As I lay there, coming awake, a thought passed through my head: *Whoever he is, he ought to wear a monocle.*

I got to my feet and discovered he was actually quite small, not much taller than five foot six, which is average on a woman but veering toward puny on a man.

"You are Mabel Stark?" he asked.

I said I was. At the same time I was noticing the smell of liquor. And I'm not talking about the smell of a man who'd had a quick mid-day bracer, something common on circus midways and in corporate boardrooms alike, but the smell of an odour on low ebb, dull but settled in, like grain and sweat on easy ferment. As he talked, the muscles in his face darted. It reminded me of the movements of a fly.

"You are ze vooman interested in tigers? In vorking viss them?"

"Yes, sir."

"I see."

Pause.

"Ver are you from?"

"Kentucky."

"How old are you?"

"Twenty-three."

Another pause, though longer this time and reading higher on the intimidation meter.

"I vill say this once. Forget about tigers. Go back to your horses or your goats or whatever it is you do. Go back to your free act. I vill never haff a vooman trainer again."

He stood there for another few seconds, letting me digest the news. Then he spun on his heel and marched off, his footfalls so heavy they kicked up tanbark and caused a general stir among the animals.

Seeing red, I marched out of the menage to the connection and strode toward Al G.'s tent. I was no more than ten feet away when Dan somehow stepped between me and the flap of Al G.'s office, all of which was an amazing trick for it seemed as though he'd stepped out of thin air to do so.

"Well hello, Miss Stark."

"Hello, Dan."

"Some weather we're having."

"Nice."

"What do you figure it looks like tonight?"

"Full house, I'd say."

"Full house fo' sure."

"Uh, Dan ..."

"And it's a good town, too. You been in? Pretty square. Two barbershops."

"No, Dan I was wondering ..."

"Plus a place to go for collard greens. Can you imagine, this far west? My, I do love collard greens. My momma made them all the time when I was little, fried 'em in pork fat for flavour, which of course made 'em salty but if you take your greens that way why it's sheer heaven...."

The whole time Dan was keeping his body between me and Al G.'s tent. Course, I knew what this was a sign for. Everybody did. It meant Al G. was inside, womanizing. I didn't know exactly with who, as I wasn't the sort who kept up with rumours, though I *did* know since Dollie Barnes had up and left him a few weeks prior he'd been busier than ever in the goat-like-behaviour department, which is saying something as he'd been pretty busy in that department even when she was around.

I thanked Dan for the pleasant conversation. Was a ladling of sarcasm in my voice, which seemed to hurt him and which I regretted immediately after, the upshot being I walked off with a soreness in my throat. See, cat training was supposed to be the thing that was going to give me purpose and options, two things you need plenty of at any age but most particularly when you're young. After a few minutes of walking around aimlessly, I figured I might as well head back to the menage, if only to give myself something to do before the evening show.

To make a long story short I kept on helping the menage boys with the tigers, no cherry pie asked for and none received, though it's true I'd lost a little of my vim now I was doing it just to kill time during lulls. Whenever I saw Louis I'd say good-morning or good-afternoon and then get out of his way pronto (though surely he must've noticed how the tigers purred every time I got near the cage? How they'd come over to me and rub their sides against the bars? How they hardly ever tried to hook their claws in my arm and pull?) The most I ever got out of Louis was a terse nod, and then the sound made by those knee-high leather boots stomping away from me.

When I next spoke with Al G., he told me to pay Louis no mind, that he had a sharpness about him and there was nothing I or anyone else could do to change that. Only time would bring him around.

This went on for weeks: my doing my goat act and my high-school riding act and my Slide for Life and in my off-hours hanging around the cats (while generally feeling logy and on the neurasthenic end of things). It might've even been months. Then one day I was in my corner, opposite King and Queen and Toby, reading a book though finding it hard to concentrate for I was thinking maybe I'd quit and try to worm my way onto another menage show. Louis came tramping down the aisle between the cages. The ground was damp that day, and his heels hit the earth so hard he kicked up divets.

He stopped in front of me and held out a twisted willow whip.
"Here."

Was the first whip I'd ever held, a long piece of leather smooth and comfortable and with a smell halfway between worn wood and

Louis Roth. He led me outside, through the backyard, and into an empty stretch of dirt beyond the lot. It was a hot day, sun blazing. Louis was wearing his meat belt, and he reached in and grabbed a hunk of horse and dropped it on the ground. Then he walked me a dozen feet back and said, "Wait for ze flies to come and when zay do start flicking zem off. When you can flick off one fly so zat another is not disturbed, vee can haff a talk. Are you understanding me?"

I nodded yes and he walked off. I stood there, alone, with a whip and a piece of meat fixing to turn rank, which in the noon sun wasn't going to be a long process. After a bit I started contemplating the thing in my hand, impressed mostly by how it managed to be so smooth and rigid at the same time. I shifted hands and noticed how my sweat had seeped colour out of the handle, leaving a copper smear running diagonal over my palm. I put it back in my right hand and squeezed, and by God its firmness reminded me of Dimitri the day I sponge bathed him, by which I mean dead stiff though with a hint of sponginess.

By this point, the meat was starting to turn a dull grey green and a trio of flies were doing a zigzag dance in the air above it; it looked like they were deciding which one got the honour of being the first to make a landing. I waited, it being a measure of my desire to follow Louis's directions to a T. I didn't even think of practising until those flies were on the meat. One landed, and another. I raised my right hand, circled the whip dramatically over my head and let loose, snapping my wrist at what I figured was the perfect moment for wrist snapping, the idea being the force of that snap would travel down the length of the braid and translate so hard into the popper it'd make a snap could be heard on the far side of the lot. Instead, that long, long whip unrolled like a carpet on a hill. By the time my wrist snap wound its way to the tip it'd pretty much worn itself out, the popper flopping silent into the dust, a full ten feet from the target. It didn't disturb the flies' business one iota.

I cursed that nervous little Hungarian, for it occurred to me he'd given me the biggest whip in the business and the last thing someone would ever learn on. Basically he was putting me off, thinking I'd get discouraged and forget the tigers. Had this not occurred to me it might've even worked, but the plain fact was I was mad, and anger's always motivated me about as well as anything else. I spent all afternoon trying to make that damn thing snap, quitting only when I had to go eat and then get ready for the evening show.

That night we jumped over the Colorado border to New Mexico. When everyone was bunking down for a midday nap, I found Louis polishing his boots in the menage tent. A pint of Tennessee sipping whisky was beside him.

"Can I get another piece of horsemeat?"

Naturally I could've gotten my own piece of horsemeat—could've borrowed a slab from a cage boy or bugged the cookhouse staff or visited the butcher in town, for that matter. The point was, I wanted him to know I hadn't given up yet. He looked at me, surprised I was going to miss my sleep a second day in a row, and sighed.

"All right," he finally said. "Tell Red I said it vass okay."

Around the end of *that* day's whipping session, the meat gamey and green and so ridden with flies it hummed, I started to get that popper to snap. Not powerfully, mind you, not the way Louis could, but a snap nonetheless. I'd been thinking a lack of strength in my arms was the problem when in fact it was my technique: the arm-circling has to be tight and purposeful, the wrist snap coming at the exact moment the power generated by all that arm circling is at its maximum (and not a tenth of a second earlier or a tenth of a second later, a mistake not difficult to make). The first time the popper actually popped I practically jumped out of my boots—I thought some rubes with pistols had wandered on the lot looking for trouble (which was something that happened all the time back then, especially if the workingmen had been out stealing shirts off clotheslines the night before). When I realized what had really happened, I grinned.

I made the whip crack a few more times before having to quit. Next day, I was at it again, forgoing my sleep, giving Louis the may-I-have-another-piece-of-horsemeat? act, spending a hot two hours twirling a whip over my head and yelling, "Yah!" That day I figured out a good way to get the popper to go off more ferociously was to jerk the whip back just as it was about to snap. While this certainly did add a zing, it was also a little dangerous; midway through the session I mis-fired and the whip end rebounded and caught me on the cheek, leaving a red welt that burned for days. Was lucky I didn't put my eye out.

My main problem now was accuracy: I couldn't get close enough to those flies so they'd so much as get nervous, never mind leave their supper. Season ended and we came back to Venice and I got myself a room at the St. Mark's, and like many of the women who didn't get jobs over the winter I danced a little burlesque in town to keep myself fed. But only a little. During the day I devoted myself to whip training and staying near the three tigers I hoped to work. Day after day after day, I practised. If Al G. was interested in what I was doing, he didn't show it—in fact, he never once came round to check my progress or offer encouragement or tell me what I was doing wrong, something I attributed to his being so busy with skirt-chasing and running a circus.

Instead he sent Dan. One day, with no warning or footfalls approaching, he was there, watching me, mouth parted, till finally I lost my composure and said, "You got something to say, Dan, then say it."

His hands got lost quick in his pockets and his shoulders shrugged up and he watched his own foot make a pattern in the dirt, until finally he upped and outed with "I knows what you doin' wrong, Miss Stark."

"Well then Dan why don't you tell me what that is?"

"Gots to aim two feet behind the piece of meat. Gots to pretend like its in the *way*. Gots to whip through the target, ma'am. Not at it."

"Is that a fact?"

"Natural-born fact. I seen Al G. do it. Back on the dog-and-pony. He may not look it now, but that man he's got the gift too."

We looked at each other.

"Was that all, Dan?"

"Yes ma'am," he said before walking off.

Standing alone with my whip and my stinking meat I saw a little red, for Dan's advice sounded so ridiculous I wondered if it was something Al G. had told him to say so as to put me even further off track. Still, I wasn't having much luck my own way, which was to stare at that putrid meat for a good five seconds before letting fly. So I gave it a whirl Dan's way. Didn't even really try, seeing as I had no confidence in his suggestion, just delivered the whip in that general direction, wrist snapping at some imaginery spot of dirt maybe two feet behind.

The meat bounced skyward and set the flies to buzzing.

After that, it was a matter of me wanting to hit that piece of meat every time and therefore not being able to do so, no way nohow, and wasting three more days before realizing the secret of doing anything artful is to try as hard as you can while at the same time not trying at all. With this bit of swami knowledge under my belt, I soon got so eight times out of ten I could send those flies into a commotion, though I'd long figured out that no one, and that included Louis Roth, could ever hit one specific fly while leaving another be.

So I went and got Louis. Rapped on the door of his parked Pullman car and told him I had something he needed to see. Immediately I knew he'd been drinking, for his accent was thicker than usual, almost to the point I couldn't understand him: "Vell vell vell, ze girl she hass somesing to show ze boss, mmmmmmm?" We headed through the backyard, Louis walking stiff and rapid-fire as always though with the occasional off-course sidestep. Every few feet, I had to skip a little just to keep up. We reached my training space, out in an empty yard behind the menage tent. There he watched as I picked up the whip and aimed and not-aimed at the same time. After a quick arm twirl, I let loose a wrist snap that was a millisecond tardy. A dozen feet away, a pair of flies were sniffing and dancing over the target. One was way over on the left, one was way over on the right, and the fact my slightly off-course lashing got close enough to scare the right-side fly only I put down to sheer fluke.

Louis's mouth went to hang open, though he stopped himself just as his lower lip cleared his teeth. I watched his jaw muscles grind beneath tight skin as he looked at that day's meat being bothered by a single silent fly. Just kept looking at it, he did, until finally he turned to me and barked, "Come."

So what did I, twenty-four-year-old Mary Haynie of West Kentucky slash Mary Aganosticus of Louisville slash Mary Williams from East Texas slash Mabel Stark of the St. Mark's Hotel *do?* Followed him, best as I was able, for Louis practically bolted through the back-yard, across the midway and into the training barn. Without benefit of a cage boy, he started shifting cages so his two best lions, Humpy and Bill, connected to the tunnel leading into the steel arena. This exertion made him sweat, and this caused him to give off the scent of alcohol gone sweet with exertion: was like camphor lozenges, though stronger. He yanked the tunnel door rope and the lions filed into the tunnel. He opened the second tunnel door and they entered the ring. Then he brushed by me—not so much as an *excuse me*—and stepped inside. Humpy roared and Bill flopped on his side and Louis barked, "Children! Seats!"

Humpy took the pedestal to the left and Bill the pedestal to the right. Louis stood between them, dropping his whip on the floor. Then he reached out and pressed a hand against each lion's throat, both arms disappearing to their elbows in tawny mane. With this, the lions lifted their heads and placed their chins on Louis's shoulders. Louis turned to his right and pressed his lips up against Bill's mouth and he kissed the lion for five or ten seconds. Then he turned to Humpy and kissed him even harder than he'd kissed Bill, his hand furrowing through Humpy's mane to the back of Humpy's head before grabbing up a handful of cat hair and pulling, so that Humpy's gums and lips and tongue were forced over the lower half of Louis Roth's face, smearing it with saliva and hay bits and fragments of horse. Then, as man and animal kissed, Louis slipped his hands into the sides of the animal's mouth and, with a steady pressure, craned it wide open. Head then followed hands, Louis now inside a lion from the neck up, the tips of Humpy's incisors making pointy-shaped impressions in the skin of Louis's neck.

In a second Louis was out, not a hair mussed though his face was dampened and speckled with mouth debris. He walked out of the ring and stood beside me, smelling of cat and whisky. We were both silent. His jaw muscles worked and he folded his arms tight over his stomach. The *things* that man could say without speaking.

I opened the cage door and stepped inside and walked to the point between the pedestals. I was shaking inside, half from fear and half from wanting to do this so bad. Humpy grinned and Bill growled, a deep distant-thunder rumble that got inside and roped up and down my spine and got turned into my own voice once it reached the inside of my head. *Go back*, was what it said.

Instead I craned my neck and kissed the lion as he was still growling and maybe thinking of having himself a kill, though he calmed with my lips against his and my hand tickling his neck. When his growling stopped I turned and put my lips to Humpy and kissed him too, the big cat lolling his tongue out of his mouth so it lathered my tongue and teeth and gums before parting his jaws a little to signal he expected hands to slip inside. Taking this cue I pulled his jaws apart and put my head in the animal's mouth, and it was while inside Humpy's head I felt myself go dead calm, for at that moment there was no question what was going to get me—was going to be the jaws of a lion, reeking of tartar and animal flesh going to rot between molars, and in this certainty there was a warmth difficult to describe. Fact was, I didn't even want to pull my head back out.

After a bit Humpy widened his jaws. When I felt the point of his teeth leave my neck I pulled out. I left the cage and stood beside Louis, and for the next thirty or forty seconds we had ourselves a conversation without one word being passed. Humpy and Bill had both flopped and were flicking at flies with their tails. When Louis finally spoke, was for the record only.

"All right," he said. "Tomorrow vee start."

That night I went back to my room and did a curious thing. I'd kept some mementoes from my pre-Stark life, cards and letters and even a menu from the Continental in San Francisco. I was sitting on my cot, looking at them, when a hopeful feeling came over me and the next thing you know I had out scissors and was cutting and cutting and cutting.

Next morning, I met Louis bright and early. He had huge grey wells under his eyes and wrinkles in his face that weren't ordinarily there, but otherwise he looked impeccable: hair combed and boots polished and training suit pressed. The cage boy, Red, met us too, the three of us shifting tiger cages until they connected with the steel arena. Red went inside and shifted three pedestals so they were in a row, calling "Props ready!" when finished.

Louis darted off, back bobbing ramrod stiff. I looked to Red for an explanation, and he shrugged. A minute later, Louis returned with a pair of overalls on his arm. "Here," he said, "put ziss on. If zey catch a nail in your skirt zey will keep on tearing. Zey luff the sound of things tearing."

I ducked behind a tool shed to change, and while I was doing so Red and Louis released the tunnel doors. The tigers slunk into the ring, looking shaggy and consternated. Toby roared, and I trembled, for it wasn't the roar of a lion showing off but of a tiger indicating displeasure, and there's a world of seriousness separating the two. This roar bothered King, who took a swipe at Toby, and in a second the two tigers were at each other, on their hind legs and exchanging a flurry of quick clawless blows before crankily taking steps backward. Queen peered at Louis and me, her gaze slowly taking it all in.

I slipped into the ring with a buggy whip and stayed close to the bars. The tigers had seen me outside the ring for the past six months, and I had to give them a chance to get used to the idea of bars no longer separating us. Queen stayed still, watching me, while the other two paced around the far side of the ring. After a minute, King flopped on his belly and Queen rolled on him and it was only Toby who was still fixed on figuring out what I was doing in there. So he came close. Came within four feet and then stopped and peered at me through green slits. He was panting loudly enough the liquid gurgling in the back of his throat sounded like its own deep voice. He could've been thinking about killing me or he could've been thinking about that day's weather, for all he showed.

It was then I focused my gaze on his eyes and time froze and I knew. I knew exactly what that animal was thinking, would've mistaken it for my own thoughts had I not seen it written across his kelp-green pupils.

I'll test her, that tiger was thinking. *I'll just see.*

So he came forward another foot. The crowd gathered outside the steel arena hushed. I cracked my whip and my voice rang clear in the silence of the menage—"Seat!"

Toby stood his ground and I cracked the whip again and issued the command again, until finally he slunk back toward the pedestal but to show he couldn't be cowed he lay beside the pedestal instead of taking his seat, all of which is tiger for *Fuck you*. Still, I was encouraged he hadn't taken a swipe and that he was even halfway near where he should be. I called Queen's name, followed by the seat command, and was surprised when she actually did it, looking happy with the activity. I did the same with King, only he got serious-looking and he came toward me. Again, I looked into a tiger's mind like it was a shelf in a grocery store, and again I knew exactly what it was he was planning. Which was, *Think I'll act as if nothing's concerning me and then rip her stomach clear out, just to see the look of surprise on her face.*

In other words, I jumped before that forepaw shot out, sprang clear out of its path and watched it sail by. I could see muscles reticulating beneath the surface, like a fit man's, only it was covered in orange-and-black fur and ended in a fluffy white dangerousness. Then it was my turn for surprises, so I brought the whip down hard on his nose. This froze him—not the pain of the whip but the shock caused by my being able to read his thoughts, which is the only real way to get the word *vulnerable* rumbling through the head of a tiger. I hit him again, this time harder because he was still and I had more opportunity to wind up. He hissed and swiped the air one more time and with a rumble of disgust slunk to his pedestal and took his seat.

By this point, I had two cats seated and one sprawled on the arena floor, which is more than anyone expected I'd get done, seeing as how the cats had gone half rogue since killing their trainer a year and a half previous. As for me, I was bathed in sweat and trembling from having tensed my muscles too hard, so I nodded to Red and he roped open the tunnel door. Each cat rushed toward the exit, and after some nasty pawing at the gummed-up opening they left in the following order: King, Toby, Queen.

On the outside I towelled off. Truth was, I felt like I'd taken a Chinaman bottle, meaning numb and euphoric and seeing stars. Louis could do nothing but shake his head, not believing. Around us people were chattering, workingmen mostly, and though their words bedspreaded all over one another I knew they were talking about what they'd just seen.

That night, Louis Roth invited me to dinner.

I'd never seen a man eat so precisely. He cut each piece of roast with a sawing rhythm that lasted exactly eight saws, even if it took only six to get through, the last two squeaking against china. He'd then lay his knife at a forty-five-degree angle across the top of his plate—carefully, so as not to make a clatter—before returning his fork to his right hand and then putting the morsel of food into his mouth. Then he'd chew exactly eighteen times. Count, I did, for he wasn't a man who needed to hear the sound of his own voice, or the voice of anybody else for that matter, meaning there were pauses in the conversation. Every third bite he'd take a swallow of red wine, which he drank too much of, more than a bottle and a half, though you'd never know he was drunk except his accent thickened and his movements got a little less darting.

Otherwise, the meal was businesslike as businesslike gets, Louis willing to discuss only tigers and what my plans with them were. So I informed him I wanted to go straight to the top, and he told me the top was a good place to be if you could wrap your head around the fact there was only one place to go afterwards. I had soup, salad, fish and potatoes, and a slice of chocolate cake. Later that evening he dropped me off at the St. Mark's before heading back to his own car on the lot. He didn't try to kiss me, there being nothing during dinner to predict it, our first touch being a handshake on the street outside the lobby, my fingers disappearing in a big sinewy hand that looked out of place on such a wiry little frame.

"Good evening" were his last words before heading down the darkened street. I was left puzzling, though over the next few days I figured out that dinner had been his way of saying he was going to take me on without actually out-and-out saying he was going to take me on. Once it sank in that Louis Roth was going to mentor me, and maybe I was finding myself out of the mess my life had been for ten years ... well. The sheer *relief* of it. Was a feeling infected everything I did over the next couple of days. Sometimes I'd look at myself in the mirror and see how happy I was and I'd actually say, "Can't you wipe that grin off your face, Mabel? Can't you? Go ahead, *try*," and there I'd be, wrestling with my mouth muscles, the lunacy of which would make me break out laughing, and I'd be giggling at nothing but my own reflection and it'd occur to me, *Jesus Mabel, you really are crackers* and it'd be this thought that'd sober me up quick. (The worst part of being sent to a nuthouse? For the rest of your days, every time you have a purity of emotion, you worry, *Uh-oh here I go again.*)

My education started the very next day, around eleven. And what an education it was. Remember, back then Pavlov hadn't yet been invented, so no one was really sure what it was made an animal do anything. Most trainers got their way by battering the animal until it did what it was supposed to, the reward being if the cat stepped on the pedestal he'd stop getting his hind end flogged with a cane whip. Problem was, the animal didn't learn much more than how to get out of the way, the tricks full of miscues and inaccuracies and those errors in movement trainers call splash. Plus over time the animal usually developed a keen interest in killing his trainer, which is a foolhardy relationship to have with any animal that kills by seizing your shoulders and pulling you on top, at which point anything not protected by rib cage gets torn out by a single swipe of hind-leg claws. You die watching the tiger feed on your mess. It isn't even particularly quick.

It was Louis who figured instead you should give the cat something good when he did something right. He called his method "gentling" and it was "gentling" he taught me throughout January and February. Whenever King or Toby or Queen did what I wanted, or anything close to it, I'd hum, "Good little kittie," or scratch their throats or drop a piece of horseflesh at their feet or purr in their ears until they started purring right along, a sound like a motor idling. I worked this way with the tigers for five weeks, rewarding every time they came close (and then closer) to doing what I wanted, giving them a wake-up smack if they got ornery, jumping out of the way whenever my sixth sense flared. If I made a mistake Louis let me know about it pretty quick. He was good at that, though after a while it also got so if I did something good his jaws would flex and he'd say, "Yess yess, that iss it."

By the end of that time Toby could do a sit-up and a rollover, and the three cats could lie side by side without slashing at each other. For a finale, they'd move into a pyramid in the middle of the ring, Toby on the high pedestal, wearing an expression that looked like pride but was actually a cat waiting for a hunk of meat and knowing he was going to get it. Seeing this, Louis not only said "Yess yess, that iss it," but grinned while he said it, for putting three tigers in a pyramid was what passed for something in 1913.

One night about two weeks prior to the start of the season, Toby started convulsing. For the next half-hour, I held his head in my lap while I spoke softly and stroked the spot low on a tiger's belly where they feel a keenness of pleasure. He was so sick he didn't even try to bite or claw, normally the first thing an ailing tiger will do. Finally he arfed weakly and his body shook and a film of white spread over his eyes. I bawled like a little girl, Louis and Al G. and Dan standing off to one side with their hands in their pockets, feeling bad and wondering what they were going to do vis-a-vis the photo of newcomer Mabel Stark and her "Pyramid of Fearsome Feline Ferocity!!!," which was now on Barnes circus paper all up and down the West Coast. This'd been Al G.'s idea, his opinion being nothing but nothing styled a tiger act like a blonde, especially considering how everyone knew the last woman trainer on the Barnes show had been pulled down forward and fed on. Only problem was, all the styling in the world wouldn't make a pyramid out of just two cats.

Was it my bawling? Was it the gravity of the situation? Or was it that Louis Roth took this moment to notice his protégée was young and lithe and looked at him with crossed eyes through curly blond bangs? All I know is when Louis Roth, a man not know for kindnesses or human considerations, offered up his two best lions for a mixed act, I could only blink a few times and think to myself, *Hmmmmmmmmmm.*

We started by putting King and Queen in a cage next to Humpy and Bill so they could get used to the sight and the smell of each other. This phase lasted a week, though longer would've been better. Then we put them all together in the cage, the lion pedestals and the tiger pedestals as far away as the cage diameter allowed. Over the next week, we kept moving their seats closer and closer, rewarding every time they took them, until the day came when we flanked the lions with King and Queen. No one liked this but Louis and me; the lions roared and pawed and growled and put on all the fake bluster lions are famous for putting on. The tigers went silent, which was worse, for if you looked carefully you could see their muscles were tensed and their ears were shifted backward ever so slightly.

I needed the twisted willow that day, along with a lot of imitation purring and "Good kitties" and lower-belly scratching. I threw down a lot of horsemeat, too. This went on for several more days before I tried kissing the lions with the two tigers looking on, a move truly nervous-making for I had to drop my whip to do it and I wondered if the tigers would interpret this as a signal feeding time had commenced. Louis advised if a tiger stalked I kick it hard in the whiskers with a boot heel and then pull back quick so a claw didn't take hold.

We opened March 8 in Santa Monica. Three rings, with thirteen displays, all of them animal acts. I rode high school in the fourth display, and put on my mixed act in the tenth, a centre-ring attraction flanked by dog acts in rings one and three and a performing bear doing a hind leg around the hippodrome. Was a good little act for its time: after marching the cats around the cage perimeter I got them on their seats and had King, my performing tiger, run through his sit-up and rollover. Then I kissed Humpy and Bill and for a finale moved the two tigers down and close, forming a four-cat pyramid.

The applause? Was like music. Was like the crescendo of an orchestra. You hear applause like that and for as long as it lasts everything you ever thought about yourself thins and gets blanketed with *Hey, you're a person people clap at.* Only problem is, it can and will turn you foolish: the moment the applause started to dim I was dizzied with a need to stretch it out, so right off I lost my head and turned my back on those cats and took a bow, something no one had ever done before in the circus and a piece of foolhardiness that got written up next day in the papers. Louis was furious, Al G. delighted. A week later, Al G. issued new paper, his posters announcing "Mabel Stark Subjugates to Her Will the Most Dangerous Killers Ever Recruited from Mountain Fastness and Jungle Lair." Was a claim followed by five exclamation points.

Following Santa Monica, we played six days at a Shriners' convention in Los Angeles, a rarity for we mostly jumped every night. From there we moved into the Mojave and then crossed the Tehachapi Mountains to get to Bakersfield, Porterville, Reedly, Selma, Tulare and Coalinga before drifting Oregon way. Houses were good, it being the tail end of what they call the Golden Age of the Circus, before roads and cars offered people in small towns choices. When we came to town, banks closed, as did all schools and businesses. Attendence was routinely more than 80 per cent of the people in any given town. There were two shows daily, plus a Tom Mix–style Wild West in place of a concert after the show. In addition to my horse and cat acts, I rode in the lion cage during parade, behind bars with four of Louis's gentlest. Al G. got a new goat trainer and Slide for Lifer, his feeling being that either act would've destroyed my mystique. Soon I got used to signing autographs and dealing with reporters, most of the questions having to do with, *Is it true women are more able to soothe the savage beast?* or *Do you really hypnotize your animals?* or *How's it feel filling the shoes of Marguerite Haupt, seeing as how she got killed wearing them herself?* Imagine what this was like for a little orphan from the homely end of Kentucky: encircled by men in trench coats, press cards tucked in Fedora bands, scribbling every word you care to utter, then fighting to get the next question in.

Well.

Was lovely and exciting and nerve-wracking all rolled into one, my being a woman who's always found pure happiness a commodity difficult to deal with. Course, I suppose that's why I was drawn to the tigers in the first place. No matter how well things're going, you always know it's only a matter of time before a claw catches, or a tooth snags, or a forepaw lashes, and your contentment feels bearable again.

Here. Let me show you something. This photo was taken November 5, the final show of 1913. Sacramento, California. The man with his arms up is Louis. Now, you can look at this photo in two different ways. You can look at it like a rube would've, and if you do you'll see a little man making seven adult lions, two of them black-maned Nubians, perform a simultaneous sit-up. You look at it and think, *Jesus Murphy, I'm hugely and mightily astounded.*

Or you could look at this photo the way I do. Then, what you'd see is the second lion on the left slouching, and the far-right lion yawning and about to lose his sit-up before the trainer wants him to. You look at this photo the way I do and you'd see splash. You'd also see a man facing a wall of adult lions, and instead of having one leg slightly ahead of the other, knees bent and ready for action, he was standing straight-legged, weight on his heels, the front of his body as open as a can of worms. You look at this photo the way I do, and you'd get a little nervous. Your palms would sweat a little, and your breathing would go shallow. You look at this photo the way I do, and you'd see disaster looming.

We wintered that year up in Portland, Oregon, instead of Venice, California, the rumour being that Dollie Barnes was divorcing Al G. and his assets were in danger of getting seized if he set foot inside California state lines. I stayed at a hotel where they rented rooms by the week, though Al G. gave me a job at winter quarters, meaning I didn't have to dance burlesque to make ends meet. One day, shortly after we'd set up in Portland, Al G. and Dan came up to me when I was boning out my cages. As usual, Al G. was smiling, so I looked at Dan, whose expression was generally a more accurate indication of what was going on. He looked bothered, like he had an abscessed tooth.

Al G. hooked his thumbs in his vest and rocked back and forth on his heels. Then he took a deep breath, like a man who'd just climbed a mountain and wanted to sample the altitude.

"Ahhhhhhhh. Don't you just love the air up here in Oregon?"

I told him I did, though wearily. Like most people on the show I was tired of hearing Al G. insist an ugly divorce was not in any way, shape or form the reason we'd hightailed it out of California. Yet now that Al G. was on a roll, he wouldn't be dissuaded by body language or a disbelieving tone of voice.

"Ah yes, Kentucky. I do believe Portland's going to do the Al G. Barnes Circus just fine. Did I tell you feed up here only costs six cents a pound? Down in Venice I was paying eleven. Now that's a considerable savings...."

On and on he went, detailing how even the constant drizzle suited him just fine, until Dan noticed my eyes were glazing over and I was itching to get back to my cages. Was then he did something he hardly ever did, by which I mean he interrupted his boss.

"Tell her, governor."

Al G. stopped talking and for a second looked chastened. Then he obliged, his demeanour going solemn.

"Kentucky," he said, "it's about Louis."

I looked around, checking we were alone. I didn't want anyone else to hear what we were about to talk about, even though Louis's problem was known to everyone from the dwarf tumblers on down to the dog-eating sideshow freaks.

"What about him?"

"Now you know and I know Louis is the greatest trainer ever to appear in the American circus. Or any circus, for that matter. Better than Bostok. Better than Van Amberg. I've never seen a man read an animal's mind the way he can. But he drinks. And he's drinking more than ever. It's only a matter of time before he hurts himself and there's no way I'll be able to replace a man like Louis Roth."

I looked at him, blinking and maybe saying something naive, for

Al G.'s eyes widened and he said, "Kentucky, you *do* know why he's hitting the bottle, don't you?"

"I figured it was just his way."

He shook his head.

"Well, it is and it isn't. It's you, Kentucky."

"Me?"

"You."

"I don't think so."

"Kentucky, please. Let's have a look at this as though you weren't one of the people we're talking about. He let you put his two best lions in with those ill-mannered tigers of yours. Do you have any idea what those lions are worth? Thousands and thousands, Kentucky. Maybe more. Plus he's shown you about all he could show you in the time you've been here. *Plus* he invited you to dinner. What's the man have to do? Put an announcement in *White Tops*? Kentucky, the man has gone moony over someone and that someone is you."

This was a lot to digest, there being a big difference between suspecting something and having it confirmed. Mostly I was waiting for Al G.'s plan, Al G. being a guy who always had one. His expression perked up, as though an idea had just occurred to him.

"Tell you what. You want yourself an all-tiger act, right? Well then sidle up to Louis. Make him forget the bottle and I'll owe you a favour."

"Can't," I said. "I never see him anymore."

"Oh no?"

At this Al G. gave his all-purpose smile, the one he used whenever he had an idea or was about to slip his hand under a woman's skirt or was just plain disguising the way things really were. What irked me was I looked over at Dan and saw he was smiling too. Obviously, they'd cooked up something and they'd cooked up something that was going to have a less-than-subtle effect on the life of yours truly. By the time I put this all together, Al G. was on another damn tangent, something about how much he liked Portland's mountain backdrop, and through-out he kept looking at Dan and saying, "Am I right?" to which Dan would reply, "Surely are, governor. You surely are."

The very next morning I spotted Louis coming toward me, a forefinger bent and gesturing for me to come. I put down my tools and followed him out of the menage tent and across winter quarters. At the door of the training barn I kicked mud and tanbark off my boots while Louis sat and scraped the undersides of his with a stick until they were as black and new-looking as the tops. He stood and said, "Come viss me," and I followed him into the middle of the barn, where Red was stand-ing next to a big male lion. We pulled a little closer, and I saw the lion was Samson, a cat too old and docile to do tricks. Louis mostly used him to warm seats in his finale.

Louis stopped about a half-dozen feet from the cat, and I pulled up as well. We both stood there looking, Louis silent, letting me figure it out. The lion was sitting on a platform cornered by ropes, and all four of those ropes were looped over a single pulley rigged to the top of the barn and then connected to a winch on the barn floor. Turning the winch would've lifted the platform straight into the air, and it hardly took take a genuis to figure why a winch, a lion, a platform and a young blonde might all be in the same barn at the same time.

I walked over to the lion and stood beside him and patted his mane and said, "Good boy." Instead of throwing my leg on over, I went all girly and extended my hand for support; when Louis took it, I gave his hand a little squeeze that wasn't exactly necessary. I threw my leg over sidesaddle, hoping this would be another reminder I was a girl and an unwed one at that. I stood for a second, weight on my feet, before lowering myself. Meanwhile, old Samson panted and looked around and belched raw horse. When I put my full weight on his back he became a lion again, for he turned his head right around and looked at me. At the same time, he made the rumbling full-throated growl only

an animal with a larnyx the size of a ham can make. I could see teeth
and the pink cavern of his mouth.

Louis purred at the cat, saying, "Good boy, good boy. Zat is it,
good boy." This calmed him, and I lowered my weight again, the lion
growling and generally getting ornery until Louis hugged him around
the forequarters and kissed him on his nose. I settled my weight again
and this time the lion was a little better, for instead of growling he
stayed still, hissing. Louis said, "Good baby," and gave him a generous
lump of horsemeat. Red walked over to the winch and started turning
so that little old Mary Haynie from the tobacco fields of Kentucky was
lifted into the air while seated on a six-hundred-pound lion. The whole
time Samson trembled so bad he wasn't a danger to anyone or anything
with the possible exception of his own heart. At about ten feet, Red
stopped winching. After letting us sit in mid-air for a half-minute, he
lowered the lion and me back to earth, and again I held out my hand so
Louis could come and take it and sample its warmth.

"Vass good," he said, though to toast that morning's work he
pulled a flask out of his jacket pocket and had himself a sip of
Tennessee's finest.

The next day, we practised the balloon act again. (Even though
the winch was in plain sight, the audience was supposed to think
Samson and I were being lofted into the air with balloons, a denial of
reality that only seems to work when people are in a tent and have paid
to see a circus.) We went up twenty feet that day, Samson trembling
every second. Somehow I'd forgotten to do up the top button on my
blouse, so when Louis took my hand and I leaned over to get off the
lion, he saw a mixture of shadow and flesh. Next day, we went up thirty
feet. This time, when I stepped off the lion, hand extended and blouse
drooping like a hobo's pants, Louis said, "I sink ze lion he likes you."

Figuring this was as close to a joke as Louis Roth was ever going to
make, I laughed and with my free hand touched his elbow and said, "Oh
go on with you," which any man with half a brain would've translated as

I am a woman and I am touching you in not one but two places and you're now formally invited to figure out what this might mean.

Was then it hit him—what all my handholding and shadow-exposing and weak-joke laughing of the past few days might actually have meant. His eyes went wide. His face drained of colour. He licked his lips. Before recovering, he said, "Tomorrow vee vill continue." Then he bustled off.

This went on and on—my giving him little glimpses of flesh and having him touch me at the slightest call and laughing at jokes that were barely even jokes. Nothing happened. No dinner invitations, no professions of love, no inappropriate fondlings. Nothing. Around the time we perfected the balloon act I decided the whole thing was hopeless, that Louis Roth was the type of man who preferred a state of misery to one of happiness. (A lot of men are like that, for it gives them an excuse to act mopey and boy-like. Plus it makes drunkenness feel noble, and over the years a lot of men with the weakness have told me noble drunkenness is the best kind of drunkenness there is.)

I went to practise the next day and got on the lion the way I would a horse. This time my blouse stayed fastened to the top and I barely spoke a civil word to Louis. I generally acted like we were having a lovers' spat without ever having been lovers, which I realized was a case of putting the cart before the horse but having run fresh out of ideas I figured at the very least it'd make me feel better. That day, old Samson and I got hauled to the top of the tent and I set off the battery charge with my foot. Fireworks went off all around us, blue screamers and red shooters and frog-green twirlers and orange nightriders, all exploding against the top of the tent (which for some reason never struck us as a stupid idea seeing as the tarpaulins were waterproofed with paraffin and couldn't've been more eager to catch fire).

Those fireworks kept screeching and screaming, Samson kept trembling and hissing, and throughout I felt like a pillow that'd been torn on a bedpost. I came down with an emptiness inside. I stepped off the lion. As I passed Louis he said, "Vood it hurt you to smile?" to which I said, "I dunno, Louis, would it hurt *you* to kiss my ass?"

I spent the rest of that day sulking and keeping to myself. The day after that, we opened in a place called Roseburg, Oregon; was April 9, almost a full month after the Barnes show normally opened, everything having been delayed by Al G.'s legal troubles down in California. Was a straw house, meaning we had to put down bundles of straw for the overflow crowd to sit on. That morning Louis had given Samson a bath and a blow-dry, which was accomplished back then by washing and towelling the animal and then waving a piece of cardboard until the cat fluffed up like a show animal. Some animals don't like it, though if Samson was one of them he didn't show it; he even purred a little as I led him into the lights and the noise. I put him on the platform, and as we lifted into the air he commenced with tremoring, which didn't bother me as this was just his way of saying he didn't particularly like the act but would do it for the horse hock he got after.

We reached the top and I kickstarted the fireworks. A second later I heard it: rasping, like a needle scraping the end of a cylinder, a much higher-pitched sound than a lion'll usually make and scarier because of it. Immediately, I realized the rubes were making him nervous, and I cursed myself for not practising the act with some groomers watching and making as much noise as possible. My heart started to pound, seeing as I was stuck forty-five feet up with a panicking cat, a flaw in the design of the act I was amazed I hadn't considered previously.

As those damn fireworks kept firing and those damn rubes kept applauding, I called up every gentling technique in the book along with some that hadn't yet been invented; luckily, Samson was glued to the spot, so I had the opportunity to apply them. I told him he was a good kitty, and I purred in his ear, and I scratched low down on his belly, and I promised him all the meat in the world if he didn't make me die face to face with the top of a centre pole, with people watching and music thundering and fireworks going off to make the event more memorable still. He seemed to listen. The fireworks stopped and we started to come down and the only thing left was some weak applause and the odd powder burst. His rasping faded, and when we reached tanbark his shivering lessened as well, both of which I was mighty thankful for. I swung my leg over and a razorback came running up with Samson's leash, which I snapped onto the collar he wore around his neck. (This was for the benefit of the audience only, there being little a hundred-pound woman can do should an adult lion decide to make a run for it.)

I took a step. I waited for Samson to walk off the platform. I took another step and felt the leash go tight. I turned, looked at Samson and it happened: a paw snapped out and took hold of my arm. The whole thing happened so fast I never even saw it coming.

The pain was sudden and spectacular though tempered by the fact that things were about to get much worse. The rubes, meanwhile, were howling, thinking this was the funniest thing they'd ever seen, a lion resting a paw on his trainer's forearm as if he didn't want to leave the ring. Course, what the rubes didn't realize was Samson had latched his hooks good and deep into my arm, the blood flowing free and warm down my sleeve and pooling where the sleeve bends at the elbow. We just stood there, Samson and I, looking at each other, though I knew very well what was about to happen: he was going to yank my arm so sudden and hard he'd pull the ball out of joint until nothing but skin stretched thin as paper was holding it in place. Then, because it's fun, he'd swipe it off with his other paw, in effect showing me what would happen if I or anyone else tried making him go up on that damn platform again. Wasn't a doubt in my mind this was going to transpire; I even started wondering if I could learn to handle a whip with my wrong hand. The only thing I resented was it taking so long, and that four thousand rubes were being entertained by it. Meanwhile, Samson kept peering into my eyes and panting lazily, obviously enjoying himself, stretching both my arm and the moment, the weight of his paw making a statement on my sorely stretched shoulder joint, when a thing can't happen, happened.

Samson pulled three of his claws from my arm. Now this is a move requiring a dexterity lions don't have, but one I can prove *did* happen by the oddity of those particular scars on my forearm. My arm was now hooked by only a pinky; his paw looked like a society lady's hand holding a cup of tea. I glanced back up into those gleaming golden eyes. While tigers can't smile, a lion can, and he gave me a big one, something made the audience start laughing harder still. He dug the single claw in deeper, through the cutaneous and subcutaneous layers, reaching where the body gets pulpy and blue. Then he ripped. Pulled open my arm as slowly as you or I'd open a letter, neatly dividing cloth, skin, muscle and sinew, leaving a clean straight tunnel. Just before the wrist, he calmly stopped, extracted his pinky nail and smiled, and as he smiled it occurred to me he clearly thought he deserved a reward for not tearing my arm off. He was actually just sitting there grinning, waiting for me to pat him on the head and say, *Good kitty.*

Funny thing was, I obliged. Scratched him behind the ears and said, "All right Samson, you made your point." Then he got up and led me to the blue curtain, as well behaved as a Dalmation, the audience clapping and howling and wiping away tears. Outside the big top, people saw my costume had turned red from the elbow down. There were screams, though not loud ones. I was starting to stagger from faintness, and blood was beginning to make its way over my fingers, the colour red mixing with field earth. My good hand, gone ash white, was still holding the leash of that panting contented lion, seeing as Louis was in the menage and was no way anybody else was going to lead Samson off. I stood there for minutes and minutes, feeling silly and weak, the trickle of blood from my sleeve turning to actual flow. After a bit, the ground started to teeter like a see-saw, the voices around me turning slow and unnaturally deep.

I woke up in darkness, circus-lot sounds nearby. My eyes adjusted to the dimness well enough I knew I was in a rail car, though I didn't know whose until Louis came in with a lit kerosene lamp in one hand, a bowl in the other, and a cloth over his shoulder. He must've just finished the evening show, for he was in his performing getup. Steam from the bowl rose into his face. I looked around the car. It was full of old furniture, lots of dark wood and red velvet, the walls covered with framed photographs of Louis: with his platoon back in Hungary, performing in the George R. Rawlings show, putting his head in a lion's mouth, guiding a trio of lions through a rollover. In another he was posing with Al G., Al G. beaming and draping his arm over Louis's shoulder, Louis looking stonefaced and uncomfortable. Was also a framed *New York Times* article from 1905, reporting that Louis was the first to ever put his head in the mouth of a lion, which was pure horseshit seeing as Van Amberg was doing it back in the 1800s.

A sheet separated myself and the bedspread, and my arm was resting on a mat of towels. The wound was stinging, no doubt from carbolic acid. Because it was animal inflicted, they'd left it open so it could froth up and drain. Louis sat down. Instead of looking in my eyes, he looked at the wound, gently turning my arm so as to inspect it from different angles.

"So," he finally said, "vee haff had a little accident."

"Looks that way."

"Hmmmmmm. I haff seen much vorse."

"It'll scar?"

"Oh yess."

"Good."

He took the cloth and dipped it in the hot water and began to wipe the wound. The cut looked long and pristine, like a canoe, though built with layers of pink softwood. Louis kept looking at it, couldn't take his eyes off it, and might've stared at it for a whole lot longer had the rail cars not started shunting. He left, saying he'd be back, and an hour later, when the train was built and we were about to make the next jump, he returned carrying another bowl of hot water and another clean cloth. He washed the surface of the wound till it was pretty and pink and glistening in the soft light cast by burning kerosene.

"Zer," he said, though he didn't stop, for he then poked an index finger into the cloth and dipped the point of the cloth into the warm solution. The train started to pull out of the station, Louis waiting for the jiggling to settle into regular motion before he did what he was intending.

Which was: press that carbolic-acid-and-warm-water-soaked cloth, made pointy with an index finger, into one end of my wound.

"We must make ziss thoroughly clean," Louis explained. He put a bit of pressure on the tip of his finger so that it separated the folds of the wound and dipped inside, producing a stinging that didn't, in any way, stay confined to the length and breadth of the wound. I wriggled a bit and tried to stay ladylike, though it was hard seeing as Louis's finger was moving toward the centre of the wound, splitting deeper layers of skin, the sensation mounting in a way that was practically vengeful. Air hissed through my teeth, and I arched my back, though I didn't yell out—I wanted to show him pain was something I had a higher than average tolerance for.

"Zer," Louis kept saying, "zer zer zer. Iss better now, I sink. No chance for infection. Vee don't want you getting meningitis."

I lay there a bit longer, may've even fallen asleep, while Louis took a chair in the corner, polishing his boots and the buttons on his tunic. When he felt the wound had stopped seeping for good, he pulled out a roll of sterilized gauze and wound it snug around the arm, wrapping the bandages to just beneath the elbow.

"I sink is better now you get some sleep," he said. "In ze next town maybe we let it drain some more and get some stitches, no?" I was just about to oblige when a thought occurred to me.

"Louis," I said, "where're you gonna sleep?"

"Me?"

"Yes you."

"Ziss is not a problem. I vill sleep in ze chair. I haff done so many many times. Ziss is a talent I haff developed...."

"Now Louis don't you be ridiculous. This is your car, and if anyone's going to sleep in the chair it's going to be me."

"This is not possible. You must keep your arm supported or ze ache will be horrible. I vill not allow it."

"Then you're just going to have to climb in. I'll skitter over and make room. Thankfully, there's not a lot of me so I don't take up much space."

"I don't ..."

"Louis. There's polite and there's just plain stupid, and you bunking in that chair overnight is nothing but stupid. You're a cat man. If anybody needs to be fresh come morning it's you...." With this his face soured—he was seeing things the sensible way, even though the sensible way also happened to be my way and he obviously didn't like being wrong. He got up and blew out the lamp, and I heard clothes being pulled off and on in the dark. I wriggled to the side of the car, and he got in bed wearing a long white flannel nightie.

Course, the tension made sleep impossible, and for the longest time we just lay side by side, not touching, staring up at the car ceiling, listening to each other breathe lightly and rapidly. Was after who knows how long I finally heard Louis whisper, "Mabel?"

"Yes?" I whispered back.

"I vass hard on you in ze beginning. I am sorry."

"That's all right, Louis."

"Many sink they can be cat trainers. Zey know vee are paid well, and zey sink it is glamorous. If I don't chase zem avay, zey can get hurt badly. It's for zer own good."

"I know that, Louis."

"I didn't understand you had ze gift."

"Water under the bridge, Louis."

There was a long pause, Louis and I lying there listening to rail sounds and rumblings. Finally he said, "Al G., he tells me you are an orphan?"

Another long pause. I could feel Louis's eyes on the side of my face. Meanwhile, I was considering whether I really wanted to get into the whole orphan thing or not.

"Nope. Don't know where he would've heard that. Funny how rumours get started."

"So you're parents, zey are alife?"

"Yep. Back in Kentucky. Working tobacco."

"Hmmmmmm," Louis said while doing something I'd stopped expecting: one of his big sinewy hands crossed the great divide and took hold of the two smallest fingers on my good hand. The word *finally* popped into my head, and though I was tired enough to beat the band I wiggled toward the centre of the bed and I sidled up. A second later I felt Louis's lips on mine—his breath was warm and tasted of sourmash—and I felt one of his hands slide inside my blouse.

After a bit of kissing and massage, I encouraged his hand to travel southward; though he did nothing more than rest his fingers on the spot where I'd placed them, his hands and fingers were trembling so badly there was a natural vibration that was not in any way unpleasant. Meanwhile, I reciprocated, pulling up his nightie and giving him a caress; he was tiny, that man, perhaps the size of a thumb, something that gladdened me for it wouldn't take much eagerness on my part to accommodate him. After a lot of kissing and touching, I rolled over and reached between my legs and guided him inside.

After a few slow-moving strokes—men do that to show they're gracious, though you can always tell they consider it an annoyance—he began to move like greased lightning, one hand on my shoulder and one on my left breast, the bed now jiggling faster than the rail car holding it, and throughout Louis was completely silent except for a *ffffffffft* sound coming right at the end. Was like a punctured tire, though I took it as a signal he'd had his share and was ready for sleep.

He got out of bed and, without looking at me, washed his face and hands and privates as thoroughly as he'd cleaned my wound. Then he got back into bed, tried to say he loved me, couldn't, and fell asleep. I stayed awake, counting rail lights, heart beating like a rabbit's, a single thought doing circles and loop-de-loops and Slides for Life in that curly blond-haired head of mine.

Al G. would hear about this.

He'd hear about this come morning.

True to his word, Al G. bought me a wild Bengal from an Indian captain who had his freighter parked in San Francisco Bay. I named her Duchess. She was so wild for a while it looked like I was going to have to use a collar and chains to break her, which is a terrible way to train, carrying grudges pretty much being a hobby with tigers. Finally I gentled her onto her pedestal, though it took more than a month, and the first time I mixed her with King and Queen she opened a gash on Queen's nose, and to keep order I had to buggywhip Duchess harder than I'd ever hit an animal. She turned on me and lashed at my hand and would've done worse had Louis not been beside me to bring a whip down hard on her nose and eyes, which backed her out of the strike range but only just. She sat growling and looking scary. Meanwhile, Queen arfed at the tunnel door and King stayed on his seat, though his eyes were slit-like and fixed on Duchess's every quiver.

While Red got the cats back into their cages, Louis held my injured hand in his own. The injury wouldn't've been so bad except a nail had caught the ring Louis had given me a few weeks previous, and it was the ring that'd torn through skin and muscles and fractured the joint, the finger now flopped over and hanging on by nothing more than skin and tissue on the far side. It took more stitches than you'd think a finger could take and never worked right after that. The one consolation was Louis nursed me again, and that nursing resulted in more nighttime affection, which pleased Al G. for the more Louis and I were together the less Louis seemed to drink. Even I was happy, for I wanted a baby and figured Louis would be as good a man as any to have one with.

I had more wound cleaning later that season, up in Washington State, after Al G. gave me a new stallion to work during the riding act. First day in practise it bucked me, my head hitting frozen ground, opening a gash over my eye and breaking three ribs and putting me in a coma for a week. When I finally came to, I suffered from bad neck pain and partial blindness and a dizziness that was better some days than others but was never totally gone. Louis put cold compresses on me, and if I was up to it he'd clean the twisting gash above my eye with the mildest of ammonia solutions. To restore the vision in my left eye, he'd have me sleep with a witch-hazel pack, a remedy he swore by but did nothing but fill the car with the smell of fermented bark. For a full year my eyesight bothered me, until the next tiger Al G. bought me, Pasha was her name, took a swipe at me during a matinee in Leavenworth, Kansas. She opened a gash wasn't that serious but that bled like only a headwound'll bleed—women were fainting and children screaming. Oddly enough, my vision started coming back in my left eye, and the double vision that'd bothered me every time I turned my head went away too. The doctor said the cat must have ripped away a blood clot caused by the horse fall. Who knows? While I lay in hospital Louis went out and bought a half-dozen hats for me to look at, as I needed something to wear while the shaved patch grew back. I told him I couldn't decide, seeing as they were all so pretty. Louis clicked his heels, went back out again and paid for them all.

Or: in 1916, Al G. sent me and Louis to San Bernadino to put on a lion act for some Orangemen. Midway through the act, an attendant decided he'd help out by reaching through the bars and slapping a stubborn cat on the rear. The lion screamed—not roared but screamed—

and after that all hell broke loose, cats attacking everything in sight including the pedestals and the bars and the other cats and of course me, my only distinct recollection being I was dragged around the cage by the arm until Louis ran in and tried to save me, getting himself chewed something furious on the right leg. Was a blur of panicking lions and screaming people and men rushing in with guns loaded with blanks and the air filling with flying hair and gob. When the cats were finally cleared out, Louis and I were left lying in bloody heaps. We looked over at each other and, I swear, smiled.

Louis and I recuperated together, my cleaning him as best as I was able considering my arm was wired in two places, Louis cleaning me as best as *he* was able given the slightest movement caused him pain that sliced up and down his body like a knife. I was proud of him. The jostling of the rail car at night caused him such pain he couldn't sleep, and even then he stayed clear of the bottle. We were both a mess of bite and claw marks, Louis joking I'd brought him good luck, for until then a lot of people described him as the best unmarked trainer in the circus whereas now he was the best, period.

Basically, we had ourselves a system. We'd take cloths and dip them in a boric solution before rinsing them thoroughly and hanging them on a line stretched across our rail car. Those we used for wound cleaning. We also mixed up several different batches of iodine solutions, each one slightly less strong than the one before. We kept them in Mason jars, lined along one wall on the floor, and as we recuperated we used weaker and weaker solutions, until the seeping got mild enough we could get stitches and wear bandages and move around. Once we started with bandages we changed them every day, Louis insisting we wash our hands in an ammonia solution. If the rips got sore, say if we hadn't stayed still enough during the day, we'd numb them with ice or creams cooling to the touch, for I didn't trust painkillers and Louis worried he might develop a taste for them. Or we'd talk our way through, diverting the mind being a lot more powerful weapon than people generally realize. It worked like a charm, every bit of it. We both got through without so much as a hint of infection, and that's saying something when you're dealing with cat marks.

In three weeks time, we were both more or less healed and raring to get back to work. I decided to visit Al G., and as I walked across the lot the pain I felt with each step was so light I could almost pretend it wasn't there. After chatting my way past Dan, I found Al G. relaxing in his rail car, a smile framing the spot where his cigar stuck from between his teeth. Was a third of the way through the 1916 season, and he had a lot to smile about. He'd more or less won his divorce case, having settled for a lot less than Dollie had originally asked for, and his circus had grown to four rings with well over a thousand animals. Even the matinee houses were full, Barnes's theory being that a lot of young men were taken with the idea of seeing one more circus before America started sending soldiers to France. He'd bought a private rail car with a bathroom and electric lights, his other theory being that show owners ought to make the papers once in a while with what he called "demonstrations of flamboyance." It'd belonged to the millionaire William Holt, so we all called it the Holt car. Al G., feeling this undignified, named it Francesca.

"I'm through with the lions" was what I told him. "Just don't have the knack. Louis does, but I don't. And I know that's hard to believe, what with every trainer on earth saying it's the lions that're easier to read. Hell, Louis is one of them—he can't believe I prefer the tigers, but I can only tell you my experience has been the exact opposite. Those lions are like a mystery to me. Maybe it's because they're pack animals. All I know is I get their signs mixed up every time. Tigers are what I want. If you got me one or two more, I could put on an act every bit as famous as Louis's finale. So what do you say?"

Al G. pretended to think it over, his fingertips pressed together so they formed a church steeple. After a bit, an eyebrow lifted and he smirked.

"Was there anything else, Kentucky?"

"Well, just so happens there is, Al G. There is at that."

A week later I headed into Boise city hall as Mabel Stark, born Venice, California, my proof a fake birth certificate one of the grifters got for me from who knows where. I came out as Mabel Roth, wife of the greatest big cat trainer of all time. The ceremony was in the Idaho capital, thanks to a blowdown cancelling a show and freeing up a night; we had the reception right on the lot, Al G. paying for everything, something he offered to do when Louis asked him to be best man. Was a couple of roast pigs and bathtubs full of beer and ice. Everyone came, from the performers to the workingmen to the Wild West performers to the sideshow freaks, which is why if you look at the pictures of my third wedding you'll see a girl with arms skinny and hairy like a spider's; a pair of Siamese twins from Patagonia named Eco and Ico; a man from Russian Alaska whose body was covered in fish scales; our famous dog-eating Ingorrotes of the Philippines; a half-and-half named Geraldine who wore a beard covering the right side of the face only; and Bosco the glomming geek, who bit the head off a live squirrel and then swallowed it as part of a toast to the bride.

The minstrel band set up and played until dawn, and we all danced as the wind whipped our hair and clothing. In the distance was the town, giving off a soft glow, and seeing as we were all dancing and feasting and generally having ourselves a good old-fashioned bacchanal it was hard not to feel like a band of drunken gypsies, parked on the outskirts of town. Everything went right that night. Though the workingmen got so drunk most of them could barely stand, they were kind enough to keep the fighting and town looting to a minimum. As for Louis, he stayed sober, though not so sober he didn't crack a smile and dance a little himself come midnight.

And Al G.

Good old Al G. Laughing and beaming and telling stories but

mostly just presiding and strolling the circumference and admiring the little city he'd built. Sometime around one or two in the morning I noticed he'd disappeared, though a bit later he came back and was wearing a trench coat, which I figured he'd put on because of the wind. I was dancing with one of the Wild West boys when he came up and apologized to my partner and asked if I could come with him. I excused myself and followed Al G. to the sidelines, away from the merriment. There, he looked at me. He was so quiet and serious I thought maybe I'd done something wrong. After a half-minute he couldn't contain himself any longer and he broke into a big smile.

"Thought I'd let you have your wedding present now." Then he opened his trench coat and showed me the real reason he'd changed; two Bengal punks were hanging on, their claws dug into Al G.'s vest. They were fluffy and mewing and red as pottery. I'd never seen anything more beautiful in all my life. Tears came to my eyes and I put a hand to my mouth and I drew breath through fingers and no matter how I tried I couldn't find the wherewithal to get out the thanks lodged in my throat.

Instead, I named them on the spot. The one on the left I called Sultan. Was the other I named Rajah.

CHAPTER 6

THE BENGAL PUNK

THE NEXT DAY, SULTAN LOOKED SNOTTY AND SHAKY AND when I checked the wicker basket the morning after that one of the punks was moving and one of them wasn't. Sultan just lay there, nose caked, spirit gone out of him. Funny how you can tell when someone or something's up and died: they take on a stillness that has the look of forever.

Louis and I didn't tell a soul, at most maybe one or two cathouse groomers who saw my agitation. Somehow the news spread anyway, and it took less than twenty minutes for the sideshow manager to come looking for us, offering to buy Sultan for a pittance so he could put him in a jar and add him to his pickled punk display. Even though he was a good half foot taller than Louis and stockier, he backed off quick when Louis waved his riding stalk under his nose and accused him of being a goon.

That afternoon, Rajah and Sultan and I went for a walk in a forest near the lot, Rajah in the crook of my right arm and Sultan in a wicker basket I'd slung around my neck like a fruit picker's trough.

Once we got there, I took it off so I could start digging. The ground was tough, but not too hard to get the shovel tip through. Though Rajah was old enough he could walk in a stagger, he mostly stayed close to me, fidgeting and rolling in leaves and chewing my pant cuffs and generally not paying the attention the circumstances were due. Meanwhile, I dug a little hole and kept Rajah amused by talking to him.

"Now I know what you're thinking, little tiger, that your brother dying means you're all alone and believe me I know that can be a frightful prospect. But you don't have to think that way, on account of you've got yours truly to keep an eye out for you, which believe me is a better deal than I ever had. And I know I'm not a tiger but for some reason I can think like one, in fact there are times I think maybe I was one in a former life. God knows stranger things have happened, so I'd say I'm pretty much the next best thing, wouldn't you?"

On and on I went, blabbing about tigers and loneliness and how the two somehow go together, until I'd made a nice little hole and placed the shoe box containing poor old Sultan inside. I shovelled over the hole and tamped it down nicely and when I was finished I marked it with wildflowers.

"There. Should be an okay place. Won't get too hot in the summer, nice view through the leaves, I like the way the sun dapples...." We stood there for a few minutes more, letting Rajah pay his final respects, though to be truthful he was more interested in gnawing nervously on his own tail than in feeling mournful. After letting a wave of sadness come and go, I bent over and put the basket back round my neck, though this time with Rajah in it. We tramped out of the forest and back to the circus. On the lot I looked for Louis, as he'd promised to get me a live nanny goat seeing as how Rajah was having trouble wrapping his head around the idea of a baby bottle and hadn't eaten much for two days.

As it turned out, the goat trainer had flatly refused to volunteer one of his, saying Rajah would tear the goat's stomach out the day he turned tiger. Hearing this, Louis turned and walked away, his feeling being that trying to persuade anyone of anything was a chore undignified and therefore beneath him. Instead, he'd gone into town and bought a farm goat, who was waiting for us when we got back, tied to a side-wall peg and chewing something not ordinarily considered food.

Was a tough sell, acquainting Rajah with the nanny goat, both of them bleating mightily when we put them together. It occurred to me I could lure Rajah by putting some sweetened milk on my palm and leading him to the nanny's teat, which I'd also lathered up with sweet stuff. After a few tries, Rajah got to suckling, though the goat whinnied at having something other than a kid's mouth come in contact with her. Still, she was swollen to discomfort, and once Rajah started to relieve that discomfort she stopped complaining and returned to gnawing on a boot sole.

Later, I put Rajah in his basket with a jackrabbit and a mongrel pup so as to stay warm, my fear being he had his brother's weakness for pneumonia. That night I tossed and turned with worry, and when we finally reached town I darted to the menage car to make sure Rajah was okay. Though I found him playing with his two bunk mates, rolling over and under them and taking friendly little nips, I considered this as evidence I'd just been lucky. Practically shaking with worry, I asked Louis if he minded my taking the three animals and putting their basket in our stateroom. He agreed, mostly because he'd been kept up by my tossing and turning and sighing.

Days, I'd do my acts and tend my cats, and when I wasn't doing that I was with Rajah, playing with him and tussling with him and taking him on strolls. On occasion I took him to town with me, carrying him if the streets were wet so his paws would stay dry and he wouldn't get chilled. These shopping expeditions always attracted stares and attention, so it was fine with Al G., though they stopped the day I got on a streetcar and the conductor told me I couldn't board carrying a live tiger. I asked why not, and he told me cats and dogs can't by law ride public transportation in the city of New Orleans. Naturally I said Rajah was a tiger, which is neither cat nor dog and therefore had nothing whatsoever to do with the city's ordinances.

I was wrong, of course, a state of affairs that generally makes people argue all the more vigorously for their way of thinking. So I told the conductor, who was Louisiana-fat and perspiring badly because of it, that only a damn fool would ever confuse a Bengal tiger cub with a common tabby, to which he said he couldn't give a shit if it was a purple Chinese puma, a tiger's a feline and that's all there is to it. Next thing you knew, we were in a yelling match I wasn't about to lose, the only problem being a reporter was on the streetcar and the whole thing got written up in the next morning's paper.

("Mabel," said Al G., raising an eyebrow, "this kind of publicity I don't need. You know how much these Dixie cops are taking *as it is?*")

With all this fresh air and attention, Rajah grew as fast as he would've in the wild, though he still had a tendency to jump if he heard loud noises, such as car horns or a pistol shot. His tigerly instincts settled in with his muscles: one morning when he was about two months old, I came awake to find Louis standing over the basket, his face curdled. "For Christ's sake, Mabel," he said, "look at vat your tiger has done!"

I zipped out of bed and took a gander. Sometime during the night, Rajah had gutted the rabbit and then worked on the neck of the puppy. The fact he'd done it without waking us showed he'd killed them fast as a lightning bolt. This pleased me, for it indicated he was growing into a tiger and not some strange barnyard hybrid, though I lost my smile the moment I noticed one of Louis's favourite performing jackets, a heavily brocaded riding coat with epaulettes and gold buttons, hanging on a hook just above the basket. Somehow, during the melee, bunny entrails had splashed upward and ruined the sleeves and waistband, a fact now causing Louis to be in a mood and a half.

"Jesus I'm sorry, Louis."

He finally picked up the coat and waved it in my face, saying, "I do not know if ze stains will come out!" There wasn't anything I could particularly say to defend myself or make him feel better, so I said nothing, and after waggling the garment for long enough to make his point, he stormed out, leaving me to feel guilty and clean the mess as best as I was able. Meanwhile, Rajah mewed proudly.

The season ended two days later. We returned to Venice, Al G. going around and telling everyone the price of feed had gone up in Portland and that's why he'd moved winter quarters back down to Venice. Louis and I took a room at the St. Mark's, and because I couldn't bear the thought of putting Rajah in a cage, he came with us. Louis insisted Rajah had to sleep between me and the side of the bed, instead of in the middle. That way, Louis wouldn't have to put up with getting pawed and scratched whenever the animal dreamed, something that was a nuisance but that I didn't mind so long as I knew my little baby was safe and happy.

This living arrangement lasted until the manager complained his chambermaids were afraid to go near our room, so we rented a furnished apartment on Pacific Avenue overlooking the ocean. From the rental office you could hear waves and gulls, sounds I'd learned to associate with California and being between seasons and having time to collect myself. The manager's name was Randall, and after asking our names he gave us an application form. In the space where it asked about pets, Louis looked at me with a smirk and, in a rare display of wit, wrote: *one*.

We moved in that day, me with a lone circus trunk, Louis with boxes and boxes of clothes, equipment, medals and memorabilia. His collection of whips and crops alone took the better part of a steamer trunk. That night, he went back to the lot and returned with Rajah mewing pitiably in a leather duffel bag. We opened the bag. Rajah poked his head out. To show his displeasure at being transported thusly, he stepped onto the carpet and micturated like a Roman fountain.

Using this same bag, I'd smuggle Rajah out of the building and down to winter quarters, where I'd play with him for hours, rolling him on the turf and scratching his ears and teaching those little teeth how to chomp down without breaking skin. When we tussled, I'd squeal like a child, something that made people stop and watch for I wasn't the sort of woman known for making sounds of delight. If Rajah forgot about his claws, I'd purr to him, or I'd rub him low on the belly and say, "Now, Rajah ..." until he learned to be gentle as possible with me. Around this time, I rewarded the nanny goat for loyal service by weaning Rajah, figuring it was only a matter of time before he disembowelled her as well.

That day was the first day I gave Rajah a shank King had completely cleared of meat. Rajah sniffed the bone a few times before putting a paw beneath it and a paw above it and chewing on the joint, tilting skyward. He licked his lips and started to purr afterwards. The next day I gave him another bare shank, and this time he learned the trick of snapping the bone in two and getting out the marrow by turning his tongue into a dipping spoon. When his teeth and stomach had strengthened, I started giving him bones with a little horse left on, which is exactly how a mother tiger weans a kitten, though in the middle of the night I still had to give him a bottle brimming with heated goat's milk or he'd cry something horrid. Problem was, this necessitated fumbling with a hot plate and metal spoons, and no matter how quiet I was the clinking would wake Louis. He'd sit, remove his eyeguard and hiss "For Christ's sake, Mabel! Can't ze fucking tiger sleep elssver?"

Then.

Was just after the New Year, 1917, a time when it seemed everything was changing. The country was gearing up for war and Dixieland music had come north and for the first time baseball games were played on Sunday. Mary Pickford was big, as was Charlie Chaplin, who made a million dollars a year, unheard of then—even John Ringling didn't make that much. Communists were fixing on taking over Russia, and the Charleston was all the rage. I knew all this because Louis loved the papers, loved riffling through them while shaking his head and saying *ffffffft* whenever he saw something that riled him. Oddly enough, it was the same sound he made at the height of his physical affections; were I to make a list of the things I remember most about Louis Roth, that sound would be on it, along with his drinking, his fussiness, his accent and his wee privates.

Which brings me to the night I'm recalling. After midnight, we were all in bed, by which I mean Louis and me and Rajah, who by this point was the size of a golden retriever, though much stronger and with a beauty no dog's ever going to possess. Louis came awake with one thing on his mind and started to nibble my ear, a sensation like being bothered by a horsefly, but one I pretended to enjoy for Louis was a man and like all men insecure in the lady-pleasing department. This progressed to kisses on the neck and one of his big hands sneaking over my body and taking hold of a breast and squeezing it like he was testing an avocado for ripeness. After a bit more fondling, that hand travelled downward and took hold of the hem of my nightie. He pulled it up, with me adjusting myself so he could get the hem over my hips, until it was rolled up around my armpits like a life preserver.

This gave Louis free roam, and because I was his wife and had duties I whispered encouragement, nothing too specific but words promotional in tone. I felt him rooting and rubbing and generally causing friction in places men think women enjoy their friction. Throughout, I had my back to him, the front of my body facing Rajah, who was sleeping and licking his lips and making little high-pitched tiger snoring sounds.

Louis's hand landed on the inside of my left leg. He applied a little pressure, indicating he wanted that leg bent and lifted. I complied, and a minute later felt him ease his thumb-sized manhood on inside.

Now, there're adjectives that can always be applied to a man's lovemaking style, and the ones describing Louis Roth's were frantic, silent and tireless. Went at it like a muffled piston motor, he did, not a sound escaping his lips, working himself to such a frenzy the bed started to squeak and buck something rabid. Meanwhile, all of Louis's plunging pushed me forward, so the front of me started rubbing up against Rajah, and when I say front of me understand it was the front of me that *counts*, the sensation made all the more notable by the fact a tiger's coat is covered in oil, and that oil was rubbing off and turning me slick and warm as an oyster fried in butter. Soon as this happened, I found I couldn't catch my breath, my discovering for the first time how safe and wonderful not catching your breath can feel: I was practically dripping in tiger oil, and other effluents besides. Meanwhile, Louis was pistoning and Rajah was snoring through his nose and I was between the two of them, though at the same time I didn't particularly care who or where I was, for until that point I'd always considered my body a necessity, a thing that carries you around and nothing more. That night I discovered it was also something that can give you a ride, like the ceramic horse on a Carry-Us-All, and that when this happens if you close your eyes your body will let you go and you can soar. The sensation built and built, to the point I was starting to wonder if I was about to explode—not a bad way to go, if you ask me—and as this question got posed louder and louder inside my head I clenched my eyes and saw an image of a bed containing a man and a woman and a tiger, a frenzy of motion beneath the blanket, the women opening her mouth and groaning in a way that would've made a longshoreman blush.

Which woke Rajah.

He sprung ceilingward. In mid-air his entire body revolved, so that he landed claws down, hissing and growling and taking swipes at Louis, though he really couldn't do much given I was between them, and it would've defeated Rajah's purpose of defending me if he'd scratched me to ribbons in the process. Course, Rajah's fury was nothing compared to Louis's, as his pistoning had been disturbed and if there's anything that'll turn a man nasty it's disturbing *that*. So he hisses, "Oh for Christ's sake I haff had it," and he gets out of bed and seizes Rajah by the tail and pulls hard enough I thought the tail might come away in Louis's hands.

Rajah's belly hit the floor with a splat, and the sound of his nails being dragged toward the door set me to screaming, "No no no, please Louis you're hurting him," to which my husband replied, "Ziss cat is out of control." Then he opened the apartment door and, swinging Rajah by the tail, pitched him into the hallway. I lay there for less than a second, listening to my baby yelp and yowl and generally sound ter-rified, before I jumped out of bed and ran into the hallway, gravity pulling my nightie back down into place.

Rajah was cowering in a corner and peeing. I went to him. Reached between his hind legs and tickled his pleasure spot.

"You just never mind about him. He was in the army so he has ideas about orderliness that don't include sleeping with his wife and a tiger. What I'm saying is, it's his fault, little tiger, not yours...." Hearing this, Rajah snuggled into my arms like he used to do as a punk. Shaking like a leaf, he was. I lifted him and stood, a movement requir-ing all my leg power and then some, as he was up to maybe 150 pounds. At this point, I heard voices and footsteps, and I could tell by their urgency that the people making those noises were not in any way relaxed. So I did the only thing occurring to me, which was to step inside the communal washroom and sit in a darkened cubicle and cra-dle Rajah, the whole while saying, "That's all right, baby. Don't you worry—nothing's going to bother you, not while I'm here, baby...."

Well. You wouldn't believe how many people come running when you throw a live screeching tiger out of your furnished room in the middle of the night. Police. Firemen. Randall, his hair standing on end and a pair of pants pulled on over his pyjamas. Neighbours, all looking sorely aggrieved, as if we'd started a grease fire in danger of spreading. Emergency-type people with thick denim gloves and axes in hand. Reporters with little flip pads and hats marked Press. A dog catcher holding an oversized butterfly net, who took one look at Rajah when I emerged from the bathroom and said, "Holy shit," before turning tail. Even the odd drunk and insomniac wandered in off the street to see what all the noise was about. Was a scene and three-quarters, and the best thing I could think to do was carry Rajah back to the room and hold him and whisper into his ear. Meanwhile, Louis stood outside, a foreigner with a thumb-shaped impression in the front of his long underwear, trying to provide some sort of reason why we shouldn't be arrested for disturbing the peace and endangering the public and generally living like wild gypsy animal hostellers.

After a bit of sputtering he came up with "Vee are viss the circus. Vee are viss the Barnes show. Vee are circus *people*."

Funny thing was, it was an excuse people seemed to buy.

We were evicted again, this time forced to live in our parked Pullman, which bothered Louis for he'd gotten used to electricity and a flush toilet in the off season. Rajah was relegated to his own cage in the menage, which made him about as happy as Louis was: soon as I closed him in he took to pacing in front of the bars and crying. When I went to check on him the next day, I noticed a few spots on his body that weren't quite bald but were coming close: up high on his right shoulder, in the middle of his forehead, two-thirds of the way down his tail. Next day, more hair fell and the next day more still; within a week his thin spots had graduated to full-fledged bald spots, poor Rajah now more skin than coat. Two days after that, when he'd lost pretty much all the fur God had given him, I leashed him and walked him across the lot to the Holt car. I knocked, and Dan let me in.

Al G. was inside, smoking a cigar and looking pleased as punch about his latest acquisition, a mountainous blond vaudevillian named Leonora Speeks. Tall as a giraffe, she was, for she wore heels and bundled her hair atop her head in a wilting celery arrangement she referred

to as a "waterfall." To achieve this effect, her hair was pulled so tightly away from her forehead it tugged on the corners of her eyes, giving
her a look that was vaguely Shanghai. I suppose *exotic* was the word for
Miss Speeks. When she walked, her whole body looked like jelly set in
motion during a faultline tremor.

She was the first to speak when we entered Al G.'s car, and by this
I mean she took one look at Rajah and jumped to her feet and squealed,
her palms thrust upward like a holdup victim's. It was mostly effect,
this, Miss Speeks taking any opportunity to jump up and down in those
high teetering shoes, a movement that set her bosom to bobbing in a
way was practically dangerous.

"What on earth is that?" she cried while throwing herself into Al
G.'s lap and wrapping her arms tightly around his head, all of which
had the net effect of pressing Al G.'s face in the cavern formed by Miss
Speeks's chest, a bit of theatre causing Dan and me to look at each other
and roll our eyes. Al G. said something, though I couldn't make out
what it was, given the muffling job still being performed by the endow-
ments of his latest wife.

Now, you'd think any man would be embarrassed at having such
a nitwit for a companion, but of course here I'm thinking like a woman;
when Miss Speeks finally rose from Al G.'s lap and straightened her
dress, he looked like he'd conquered an ocean, by which I mean red-
faced and beaming. Course, this expression didn't last long, for he was
finally able to take a good long gander at Rajah. His blue eyes widened.

"Jesus, Kentucky. That poor animal." He rose from behind his
desk and walked up to Rajah and crouched and let Rajah sniff his hand,
and because Al G. had the gift you could practically see Rajah relax. Al
G. sat there a minute, thinking, until finally he said, "Attention,
Kentucky. Some TLC. It's about all I can think of."

That afternoon I took Rajah for a walk along Pacific Avenue. Every
five minutes or so kids would come running up to see what unusual

breed of hairless dog I had, stop within ten feet and get scared and run off, a rejection poor Rajah sensed. He'd start arfing, and I'd get on one knee and hug him and say, "You pay those kids no never mind. You'll get your hair back, trust me, and heads'll start turning." To this, he'd start panting and his ears would come forward, a signal he could live with that promise for the time being.

Every morning I'd give him an egg bath, something he didn't enjoy but seemed to tolerate, for I told him over and over how it'd help grow his fur back. I gave him sulphur for his blood, lime water for his stomach and cod liver oil so if his coat did come in again it'd come in thick and glossy and worthy of stares. On Sundays he got milk instead of meat, which is good for a cat as it gives the digestive tract a rest. I washed his eyes out with sugar of lead whenever I could get him to hold still, a treatment that makes the whites of their eyes as white as clouds, and whenever I put Rajah back in his cage I gave him a little treat, like pig knuckles or the soft end of a rib, so he'd start associating his bars with things pleasant, something we all have to do when you stop to think about it. With these ministrations Rajah's coat started coming back, oddly enough, in places where humans have hair: the top of his head, under his arms, in a soft tuft covering his loins. For a while he looked like a cross between a tiger and a clipped French poodle.

Here. Let me show you some photos. I took them on Al G.'s old tripod, which tended to let light in and turn things a wash of grainy grey; for this reason they look a lot more melancholy than the moments they were meant to capture. Truth was, they were some of the happiest moments I've known, though I don't think I realized it at the time because I was pent up with aspirations and kept thinking life would *really* be good once Rajah made me famous. (The problem with ambition? If you let it it'll act like the blinkers on a horse.)

Notice how in all of them it's twilight, the sun either on its way up or on its way down, for with Rajah getting to be the size he was, I took him to the beach only at times when there weren't many townies around. This one I like. Rajah, just coming out of the ocean, shaking water off his new fur. The way the sun's catching all those droplets and the way those lit-up droplets are framing my tiger, Rajah looking like there's no such thing as problems or worries. Eyes sparkling, and though you can't see it here, they're the green of emeralds. His incisors white as ivory. And his whiskers ... you know if you look close at the black of a tiger's whisker, it turns out it isn't black at all, but a swirl of violet and deep blue and kelp green.

Or this one: if the beach was deserted, which it often was given the time of the year and the time of the day, I'd let Rajah off his leash and let him charge at the seagulls. Lord, how he loved that, leaping and jumping and pawing at those birds, which is why he's airborne here, back paws all the way off the sand, body twisted and a paw reaching as high as a tiger paw can go. Or this one: looks like he's fixing on doing a back flip, for he'd jumped just as the bird passed overhead and kept on tracking it till his back was arched as a hairband. To me, it's a photo of determination, something me and tigers have in common.

Or this one. Just an empty beach scene, right? Look harder. Much harder. See that dot, disappearing into the sun's belly? Isn't a dot. It's Rajah, and what happened was I'd taken him off his leash and we were both standing on the beach when he did what tigers do in place of smiling. By this I mean he got himself a look of clear understanding: the ears perk and the eyes pierce and they radiate a purity only tigers have. Then he took off. Just started running at hunting speed, not at all bothered I was yelling at him to stop. This left me thinking, *Oh great, there goes fame and fortune, worse he'll probably head into town and kill a child and they'll blame me and throw me in a place where the criminal minded never see the light of day.* Was such a dour moment I could do nothing but sigh and duck inside the camera bellows, if only to record the moment for posterity. Rajah kept on running. It felt to me like he wanted to find out the meaning of forever, a question bothers animals as well as humans. Finally, and I mean finally, the speck stopped and stayed the same size for the longest time, an orange blip in a blurry gold distance. Then it looked like it was a little bigger, and then for sure it was getting bigger, and then Rajah came back panting and happy and wanting to roll around in the sand.

I figured I'd better start training him.

Now. The way you pick animals for tricks is you look for natural behaviours. You get a tiger with good balance, you make him your ball roller. You get a tiger likes waving his paws up in your face, you put him in your sit-up chorus. You get a cat that's heavy and graceless, last thing you do is send him jumping through a burning hoop. With Rajah, the natural inclination was toward bodily contact, for he liked nothing more than jumping on me and lying on me and letting me lie on him, all the while batting at me with leathery paw undersides. So I started encouraging this. Then I started teaching him to do it on signal, something no more difficult than giving him meat every time he began frisking me *if* I'd whistled first.

So. February 15, 1917, and the Santa Monica opener is three weeks away. America's official entry into the great war is six weeks away. A smiling and proud Mabel Stark finds a groomer and asks him to tell Al G. to meet her by the training arena in the cathouse. With Red's help, I shifted cages and let Rajah into the arena. After Rajah'd been up on his pedestal for a few minutes I heard feet against floorboards. I looked up, and there was Al G., looking handsome and slightly portly, as he'd been eating a lot of steaks and potatoes fried in butter and ice cream sundaes of late, it being his belief a man larger than life had to literally *be* larger than life. (Course, it was a belief he'd gleaned from guess which famous circus owner?) Naturally, he was with Dan, who'd recently started wearing three-piece suits himself, though of a slightly inferior quality to the ones worn by Al G. Miss Speeks wore a bright red dress, loose at the bosom and tight at the caboose, all in all a dress engineered to be fetching to men and an embarrassment to women. Seems we were all in costume that day, for around this time I'd started wearing a tight black leather bodysuit. And despite what you might see in old circus paper, in which a hundred different adjectives were used to suggest I had a way of riling men—*enchanting* was a favourite, as were *tempting* and *seductive*—my suits weren't in any way an attempt to outdo Miss Speeks in the sexpot department. For me, it was simply a matter of safety, the leather offering protection against claws and the tightness offering nothing to take hold of. My shoulders were padded, shoulders being a favourite grabbing spot for tigers, and I wore a thick black leather hat I'd patterned after the one my second husband wore whenever he drove that Model T of his.

(And what of Louis Roth? What of the ex-Hungarian military officer turned head catman of the twelve-hundred-animal Al G. Barnes circus? A man who knew how hard I'd been working and who hadn't helped me one iota despite it being his job to govern all cat acts? A man I'd married in the capital of the potato state and who'd been annoying me with his thumbness ever since? Where was *he* on the day I first showed people the most famous cat act in the history of the American circus? Well, he wasn't there, is all I can tell you.)

I got myself into the cage. Walked to the middle of it. Stood looking at Al G. and his entourage, all three of them slack-jawed with curiosity. I whistled. Rajah lunged off his pedestal, charged me, and without my so much as turning to defend myself I let him leap up and get me by the shoulders and push me down and start rooting in the space separating a woman's shoulder and jaw. Already he weighed almost three hundred pounds, for despite his runty start Rajah was going to be big for a Bengal, maybe even over five hundred, and with his size he easily rolled me around on the floor with those big paws. Meanwhile, Miss Speeks shrieked and Dan started yelling, "Oh my God, governor, he's killing her!"

To show them he wasn't I got an arm up and around Rajah's throat and I held him and rolled him over and got on top, and was then I felt those hind legs slip up to my belly. The disembowelling reaction was what it was, so I got my mouth right close to his ear and said, "No no no, Rajah," in that soothing tone he loved so much. When his hind legs drifted back down I replaced them with my left hand and started scratching his pleasure spot, such that he started arfing and hugging and licking my face with his barbed wet tongue.

At this point I heard Al G. laugh, for it was then he realized the whole thing was an act and I'd never really been in danger, or leastways not in any danger I couldn't control. Hearing this, I wrestled a few seconds more before pushing myself away and hollering, "SEAT!" Rajah went to his pedestal, looking dejected, and while I exited the arena Red got him out with pieces of horse.

I looked over at Al G. He and Dan were smiling more broadly than I'd ever seen. Miss Speeks looked at me like what I'd just done was slatternly and disgraceful, which I suppose was appropriate seeing as that was pretty much what *I* thought about everything *she* did. I was covered with a layer of sweat, and my face was sticky with cat gob.

"Will you mix him with the others?" Al G. asked in a voice more a laugh than a question.

"Oh yeah," I answered, "get him sitting up there, King and Queen and Pasha and Duchess doing all the tricks, until the audience figures Rajah's there to warm the seat and nothing but. Then I'll turn my back and whistle."

"You know what this means?"

"Not sure I do, Al G."

"It means you've broken the first wrestling tiger act in history," to which I said, "Oh, right, *that*," which was a joke Al G. thought so funny he came over and kissed me and hugged me, something I enjoyed mostly because it made Leonora Speeks's face fold in on itself like an origami horse. Pulling away, Barnes stopped at my ear and whispered, "A wrestling act, Kentucky. I'll be very pleased...."

Which was code for: do this, and you'll get more kitties.

Next day, I decided to acquaint Rajah with the other cats. After shifting cages I took the pedestals out of the steel arena, leaving it completely empty, something I figured would encourage mingling. As soon as King stepped inside, I knew I'd made a mistake, for I could see Rajah start to quake and pant while King did slow, quarrying circles around the younger tiger. I was already calling for King to tunnel when he stepped up and growled and hit Rajah on the shoulder, a blow not intended to injure but to leave no question who was boss. Still, it was hard enough poor Rajah got knocked to the cage floor, and when he tried to get back up he was so panicked his hind legs couldn't get a grip on the tanbark, so they kept spinning and slipping as he tried to make it to the side of the cage. There he whimpered and peed and looked for me through the bars. King was already through the tunnel door.

I stepped inside the ring and went over and soothed Rajah by explaining this was just the way King was, that he'd warm up to him and before he knew it Rajah would be enjoying the company of his own kind. Rajah kept shivering, though this subsided when I put my arm around his neck and hugged him and rubbed his belly spot. After I did this for more than ten minutes Rajah seemed to calm down, a calm I made the mistake of trusting.

I stood and had Red hand me a pedestal, which I lugged to the centre of the ring. Rajah immediately went over to it and climbed aboard and started grooming. After a minute or so, I decided he was tractable enough to practise a little wrestling, just so the day wouldn't be a total waste. I turned my back and whistled and a second later felt those paws hit my padded shoulders hard and knock me over. Now there's playful knocking a person down and there's let's-make-something-clear knocking a person down and this was clearly the worse of the two. My knees and palms stung and I had trouble gaining my breath. I had the full weight of a tiger on top of me, and while I normally liked this sensation, Rajah chose not to support any of his weight on his legs and forepaws, giving me his full tiger bulk to deal with. It felt like I was drowning in fur and muscle. He bellowed in my ear, and then I felt his jaws take hold of my right shoulder. And while he didn't bite down nearly as hard as he was able—he could've taken my shoulder clear out if he'd wanted—it was enough I knew I was being held down, something makes the question *for what purpose?* grow large and loud in the mind.

Now, I want to make something perfectly clear. Rajah could've killed me if he'd had half a mind to, was nothing Red or I could've done, and though what he did was bad remember in a tiger's mind he was being gentle as he possibly could while still getting his grievance across. What he did was: take a big rubbery paw and stick it in my face. It felt leathery, like the padding on a boxing glove, though coarse with pebbles. The worst of it was I couldn't breathe, for he was holding me hard enough his paw had closed around my nose and mouth, so I panicked. I flailed my arms and legs, none of which made much impression against the weight and strength of a tiger.

Figuring he'd made his point, Rajah pulled his paw away, and to this day the fact his thumbnail got caught in my left eyelid I put down to accident. Course, I wasn't thinking that then. I was thinking more about the sensation of that big hardened orange nail dragging along the surface of my eye, something that hurts more than you can imagine, the eye being about as sensitive a part of the body as there is. I thought Rajah had torn it plumb out, something a tiger'll sometimes do to disable its quarry. Worse, it was an impression confirmed by all that adrenalin pumping through my body, adrenalin being a substance that makes the mind race and bend and play tricks on itself. In other words: I swore I felt my eyeball pop loose and roll down my cheek and settle in tanbark, and it was this belief that made everything spin and a second later go dark.

I woke up in our rail car. Louis was above me, and when I peered at him through my right eye he smiled weakly, though his face looked wavy and dreamlike. There were silver clamps closing the tear in my left eyelid, and I knew they must've coated the wound with an anaesthetic, for I couldn't feel any pain (and believe me, it hurt like a raging son of a bitch later on). It wasn't bandaged, the worry being infection, so I just lay there seeping over my cheekbones, feeling foggy headed and strange, Louis periodically wiping one of his disinfected cloths over my slitted eye.

"Mabel," he finally said, "I sink you must give up on zis wrestling tiger business. It is foolhardy."

Here I shook my head, causing Louis to withdraw his hand for a second.

"I shouldn't've put Rajah and King together without pedestals. I was hurrying things, and not thinking of the cats. Was my fault, not Rajah's."

Louis laughed, and I caught a whiff of Tennessee's finest, though with my head acting up the way it was, I wasn't sure whether I was imagining it.

"Is funny. All trainers say zat. You know, I vas there when Marguerite Haupt vas killed. A mean old cat did it. Far vorse than King. Put him down afterwards. Vas no one's fault but his. Anyway, Marguerite is lying zer and you can imagine vat iss coming out of her, and vis only a minute or so to live she says to me, "It vas my fault, Louis. I should not haff vorked ze tiger in ziss heat. Vas too hot for ze tiger, Louis."

"You trying to scare me?"

"Yes."

"Guess you know it won't work."

"Yes." He chuckled. "I am avare of ziss."

Louis didn't say anything more for a long time. Neither did I, choosing to concentrate on the nice feeling of warm water dripping off the cloth onto my face. After a few more minutes, he decided the worst of the seepage was gone, so he removed the silver clamps and let me sleep a good long time. I slept and awoke feeling fine. Louis had another look at the wound and was so satisfied he replaced the cotton and secured the new cotton with tape. When he was finished, I thanked him, though I suppose I did it a little too formally for he started thinking about the problems we'd been having of late.

"It has been a while since you and I ver as man and wife."

"Yes, I know. I'm sorry, Louis."

"I haf been missing you," he said, and because I'm a woman and that's a state of affairs that comes with duties, I suddenly felt sorry for him. I invited him into my arms and kissed him. After a minute or two of this, he moved down and unbuttoned my blouse and started giving me tender little kisses, though I wasn't enjoying the sensation at all for the ceiling was all colourful and bendy and I couldn't figure out what was wrong with me.

"What did you give me, Louis?"

He lifted his lips from my chest and said, "Give you?"

"For the pain. You gave me something for the pain."

"Oh, yes. Vas some morphine is all. For zee eye. You vill discover nothing hurts more than an eye scratch."

My heart started pounding. Luckily, Louis didn't notice my galloping pulse, as he'd moved farther south, and I didn't say anything if only because I didn't want to do any explaining. Instead I took a few breaths and told myself I was going to get through this, no matter what it took, for Louis had been deprived of late and he was a man and I was determined to make it up to him. When I heard him lower his jodhpurs and extract himself, a switch got thrown, and here I'm talking about the one that takes unpleasantness and instantly upgrades it to nightmare. One second you're hanging on, the next you're trying your damndest not to scream at the horror of it. See, I was seeing those damn tin soldiers, watery and grinning, red jacketed and on the prowl, taunting me, and the memories they brought back made me start to cry and shake and peep, "Please, Louis, please ..."

He rolled off and hitched his pants and stood above me while I lay on that bed weeping and nude and not caring. My hands were over my eyes, though I took a second to peek with my good eye through slit-ted fingers, just long enough to see the worry and confusion on his face.

"Oh" was the only thing he said, though it could've been air coming out instead of an actual word. Crawling in bed beside me he said, "Zer are sings I do not know about you, Mabel Roth. Maybe one day you vill tell me, hmmmmmm?" and was then he put the full weight of a jacketed arm over my chest, a bit of bodily contact I both needed and couldn't, in any way, stand.

The season opened in Santa Monica, California, the atmosphere so hot and heavy when the rain finally settled on hot concrete wispy clouds rose off. The show started with an opening spectacle called "The Conquest of Nyanza," Nyanza being a name made up to sound African, Al G. wanting to distinguish ours from all the Far Eastern specs logging miles around America. A chorus dressed in loincloths chased around a gold-painted chariot pulled by a team of bears dressed to look like Masai plainsmen, and if reporters with the *Santa Monica Reporter* knew there was no such thing as an African bear they were nice enough to keep it to themselves. Meanwhile, an orchestra blared, and there was an excess of drumming and chanting and spear waving and, for no reason I could ever figure, the sideshow Wild Man riding willy-nilly on a llama. In the middle of the melee was Leonora Speeks herself, barely dressed in a drooping cavewoman outfit and roped tight to a quarter pole, being carried through the air by savages, as though being led away for sacrifice. Course, she loved it, for it afforded her the opportunity to do a lot of shrieking and wriggling and calling attention to herself. Rumour had it the savages were under strict instructions to carry her straight out of the big top and over to

Al G.'s car, where she stayed tied up for another twenty minutes, if you understand my meaning.

After the spectacle—I played a camel-riding tribeswoman, which isn't as easy as it sounds seeing as camels are foul, nasty and lazy by nature, though at least my eye patch was newly off and though my eye still throbbed I could judge depth again—I didn't come on again till the twentieth display, when every able-bodied female performer had to mount a high-school horse and ride around smiling prettily. Five displays later, I put on my new seven-tiger act, Al G. having bought me another two Bengals named Kitty and Ruby. Was a decent little act, all seven tigers sitting up while in a pyramid, something no other trainer was doing with tigers back then. Plus I got five of the seven to do a rollover together, the two holdouts being Queen, who looked at me with blank blinking eyes every time I tried teaching her something new, and King, who had a tendency to start fights if he got touched by another animal's fur. He more than made up for it with his hurdle jumping and hind-leg walking, though.

Display thirty was the clowns, and after that the big top went dark; the Barnes show was the first circus in history to travel with generators and electrical lights, so just making a big place suddenly go dark was enough to impress. Was no introduction, no hyperbole, no swell of music, nothing. Just a light, suddenly shining on the steel arena, Rajah sitting on his pedestal. Then I came in myself, wearing tight black leather with a pair of black boots that tied up the inside and stretched to the knees. Felt like something, I did, for I was strong from all that cage work and limber from jumping out of the way of paw swipes, and if there's one thing the body's good for when young and fit it's parading itself.

I stood eyeing the congregation of rubes, as though I'd completely missed the fact a tiger grown to almost five hundred pounds was sitting behind me. Grinning, I was, in a way suggesting I was either naive or stupid, and in either case in a state of high vulnerability.

Meanwhile, Rajah was squirming and licking his lips and adjusting his paws and basically acting like a tiger yearning for action. The house fell silent. Completely silent. Was a silence I pretended confused me, my flummoxed expression stating, "Hey, we're in a circus—ain't no place for quiet. I even put my hands on my hips and scrunched my face to play up my perplexity. The calls started: "Look out behind you" and "Mind the tiger" and "For Pete's sake—over your shoulder lady!" In response, I bent at the waist and put a hand to my ear, as though I was hard of hearing. This made them call louder, and pretty soon each and every rube was screaming to beat the band, while I stood there cupping my ear, pretending I'd chosen that moment to turn stone deaf. I was also trying not to laugh, the ears being amazing things in that they somehow filter the din and let the funnier warnings sail through. For instance: the man in the front straw row, standing red-faced and frantic, shrieking, "Fer the love of Christ, lady, you're gonna get your ass et!"

Was then I whistled. None of the rubes knew I did it, for they were noisy and I'd lowered my head so no one would see me doing something different with my lips. The only thing *they* knew was their worst fears were coming true, something that excites people and makes them feel good: Rajah stormed off that pedestal and hit me three-quarter force and roaring, knocking me down and leaping on top in the process. The whole world went away, both my hearing and vision muffled by soft orange. Once I turned my head to get a breathing passage, I was completely safe, and would've even been comfortable were it not for the weight on me getting serious every time Rajah took a breath. Plus his belly fur tickled.

Later, the workingmen told me when Rajah hit and my neck whipped back, the whole audience thought he'd snapped the bone clear in two, a suspicion confirmed by the fact my hands and feet, the only parts of me poking out from underneath the tiger, weren't in any way moving. Apparently the screams and cries were deafening, ladies fainting and children screaming and some of the braver men rushing the steel arena to rescue me, though what they thought they were going to do once they got there is beyond me; it took a dozen clowns and elephant groomers to hold them back. Meanwhile, Rajah roared and growled and aired his back teeth, acting for all he was worth like a tiger guarding its kill. I lay under a mound of animal, thinking it probably all looked mighty funny from outside the cage. After a bit, I pulled my right arm underneath Rajah and scratched his pleasure spot, a signal to him that everything was fine and dandy and that despite the addition of hollering rubes the game was the same as ever. With that, he rolled off me onto his back, something a cat normally hates to do, and let me roll atop him, at which point he crossed his paws over my back and hugged me like we were slow dancing.

Well. Was a crest of applause—a crest one part relief and one part resentment at having been scared witless and one part disappointment they weren't there the night Rajah the wrestling tiger ripped apart his trainer. These three parts got all whipped up into a din had a life of its own. The din expanded to fill the big top, where it sat like rain clouds trapped in a valley, getting louder without even trying, when finally it began to transform into laughter, and here I'm talking about the laughter caused by people realizing they've been had and had bad. Even after Rajah and I had stopped rolling around and we'd taken our bows, they were still holding their stomachs and wiping tears, though as I walked Rajah out of the arena toward the blue curtain they started applauding as well. And whistling. *And* standing on their feet *and* cheering; was like I'd just showed them all the secret of immortality. Inside the curtain, I handed the cat off to Red and looked at Al G., who was beaming and not because he'd just feasted on the tied-up lusciousness of one Miss Leonora Speeks.

He had to yell to be heard over the applause: "Well, go out and give them what they want, Kentucky!"

So I did. I went back out there and bowed. Was just a quick dip at the waist, for despite Al G.'s generosity the one thing a trouper never does is interrupt the flow of a performance. Still, during those five or ten seconds everything that'd ever happened to me suddenly seemed sensible and worthwhile, if only because it'd led me to this. I ducked back behind the blue performers' curtain and floated on air through the dancing bears and the bucking mules and the elephants parading around the hippodrome while wearing giant tutus.

Then came the finale, Louis's lion act, the numbers having been cut from twenty to twelve for Al G. had recently developed worries about Louis handling a group that large. Though the act ran smoothly, Louis suffered from a slowness of step that would've been dangerous if his cats hadn't been so well trained. In fact he looked like he was wading through water; though the cats were doing their sit-ups and rollovers and pyramids, they weren't doing them with the crispness that separates a good cat act from one just getting by. Truth was, his cats were lollygagging, and normally in the world of Louis Roth there was no worse sin than that. I half watched the act, and half watched Al G. watch the act—his eyes were narrowed and his jaws muscles flexed under powdered skin, though his showmen's guise bounced back into place when Miss Speeks squealed, "Look at all the lions, sweetheart!" and started to hop on both feet. The act ended with a group sit-up that impressed the rubes but seemed to drain Louis: he had to struggle to keep them all paws up at the same time.

That year the after-show was a bunch of magic and song-and-dance acts we called a Vaudeville Presentation, Miss Speeks herself acting as the woman who gets herself sawed in half by a dastardly magician. Was put on in the sideshow tent so we could get to tearing down the big top right away. And when I say *we*, I'm being literal, for there was a war on, and most of the workingmen had taken farm jobs that'd opened up on account of young farmhands all across America feeling patriotic and signing up. A few of the workingmen had gone off to fight as well, though not many, the typical razorback being too afflicted with alcoholism, nervous problems or pederasty to get by a draft board. There were so few workingmen left, in fact, that Al G. had to inform the performers if they didn't chip in and be troupers that big top wasn't about to get up and down all on its own.

The main performance ran till ten in the evening. Normally, the workingmen would get the big top down and rolled and loaded by midnight. Took *us* till four in the a.m. that first night, tear-down being a complex job involving precision and timing and a whole team of elephants pulling up tent pegs with their trunks. The boss canvasman, a guy named Peterson, yelled till he was blue in the face, though all the yelling in the world couldn't change the fact we didn't know what we were doing. There were slowdowns and fuck-ups and rigging injuries galore. That night I mostly ended up bandaging people who'd been hit by sliding bail rings, and putting icepacks on noggins conked by toppling quarter poles (for as you know, I'd worked as a nurse and was therefore knowledgeable of things medical). The whole operation bogged down around half-past one in the morning, when the centre pole team somehow got way ahead of everybody else, meaning the whole tarp came wafting down with everybody still underneath it, and if you want to get an idea what disorientation's all about try having a canvas tarp bigger by half than a football field fall on your head. Suddenly the whole world was screaming and pitch-blackness. For the next twenty minutes we were all occupied by crawling our way out. More than once I bumped into someone confused and heading back toward the centre, and when we were all finally out from under we had to figure a way to go back in and retrieve all the fallen half poles and aerial riggings and electric light stands. Jesus, what a kerfuffle. Poor old Peterson got so agitated I made him sit still and breathe into a brown paper bag and think pleasant thoughts.

By the time we were finally done, I was tired and cold and my fingers ached. I went off to our stateroom, not having seen my husband all night and knowing full well for what reason. The stench was terrible, practically manufactured it was, Louis lying spread-eagled in the centre of the bed, his boots and uniform not in any way bothering him seeing as he was practically in a coma. Thankfully, it was one of those times when there's enough good going on in your life you sort of need a dose of bad, if only to balance things out and keep the gods happy. I closed his eyes, pushed him to one side and crawled under the covers. That night I dreamt of the way applause has a rise and a fall that's as close to music as something non-musical gets.

We all left as tired and sore as it's possible to be, and made it so late into San Diego we had to cancel the matinee, which left Al G. mighty sore. Thankfully, it was a two-night stand, and we caught up on some sleep before a night in Escondido and three full days in Los Angeles. Then there was the Mojave and over the Tehachapi Pass to Bakersfield, where we played all the usual towns in the San Joaquin Valley before heading up to northern California and San Francisco, a place that always made me feel a little agitated owing to my wedding with that rich voyeur James Williams. Still, things were good, Al G.'s theory about wartime attendance holding firm, for the houses just kept getting bigger and bigger. According to *Bandwagon*, Sells-Floto and John Robinson and Hagenbeck-Wallace were all doing sellout business too. The only difference from before was the faces belonged to kids and grandparents and women without men, all easily entertained because they needed it so badly.

Al G. bought me three more tigers, including a cantankerous Sumatran named Jewel who tried killing me on a number of occasions, Sumatrans being extra dangerous because they're so small and quick. The way I was feeling back then I could've dodged bullets, so I took her natural tendency toward springing and turned her into a hoop jumper par excellence. When *White Tops* reported I'd done the impossible by mixing a Sumatran in with nine Bengals, I scoffed out loud at the article. "No such thing," I said to myself, "*as* impossible."

Rajah knew it too. As he crept up to his first birthdate, he reached his adult weight of 550 pounds, which is huge for a Bengal; I've known

smallish female Siberians that weren't that big. He was the most beautiful tiger I've ever seen: face shaped like a heart, eyes the green of a
jewel, fur thick and gleaming, whiskers long and delicate and purple
black. Plus everything the right size for everything else, something you
don't find that often on a big cat. Plus he'd gotten an ovation every
night since Santa Monica and don't think that won't swell a tiger's head.
Soon he had himself a regalness the other tigers lacked (except for
maybe King), and by this I mean he moved slowly with his head up and
his shoulders back, not unlike a deb learning to walk. Dignified, he was,
his bearing reminding me a little of Louis when he wasn't on the drink.

Which brings me to the topic of Louis.

I'm in the Holt car, talking to Al G., Dan having gone to town
with Miss Speeks.

Al G.: "That husband of yours, Kentucky. What are we going
to do?"

Me: A shrug, as it seemed unfaithful for a wife to out-and-out
admit her husband was lost to the bottle.

Al G.: "Talk to him, Kentucky. Spell it out. Though do it in a way
he doesn't realize he's having it spelled out for him. You hear what I'm
saying? Use tact and niceness and your God-given wiles."

That night, Al G. lent me his rail car and I made Louis a dinner
of goulash and dumplings he was practically too drunk to eat. When I
suggested maybe his crapulence was getting on Al G.'s nerves and that
bosses' nerves were something you definitely didn't want to get on, he
became defensive and upset, and the next thing you know he spat out a
subject reserved for wounding and wounding only: children, or to be
more exact, the fact we didn't have any.

I saw red. The fight could be heard all over the lot. I even hurled
a dish or two, which irked Al G., for he'd had them shipped all the way
from Provence. I decided to spend the night in the menage car, bunked
beside Rajah, one of his paws on my chest. In the morning I awoke with
straw marks on my cheeks.

That day, we pulled into a little town in southeast Nebraska called Falls City. Though it was nothing but a tiny dot on the map, it was memorable to Barnes troupers in that it represented the farthest east the show had ever gone, the Barnes circus being a West Coast show and nothing but. It was late July and hot, the smell of fresh corn hanging over town like an overcoat. I had some time before parade so I went downtown as a little treat, wearing a hat pulled low. Was a nice place, Falls City. Course, most towns were before the interstates: the town square had a gazebo and carved wooden benches and a place where a band played on holidays. Plus a neat little courthouse and a drugstore that sold penny sodas. It was a Saturday, and because the stores had closed for the circus, there was a little open-air market in the square, bonnetted women selling preserves and baked goods.

Despite my fight with Louis, I was feeling good about the world. After parade, the usual gaggle of reporters asked for interviews, and believe me when I say it wasn't Louis they wanted to talk to. Nor was it Cheerful Gardiner the elephant man, or Captain Stonewall the seal man, or Al Crook the producing clown, or even the charismatic owner, a man known throughout the circus world as Lucky Barnes. Uh-uh, wasn't *any* of them.

That night during the wrestling display, I stood in the steel arena, Rajah seated behind me, peering into the audience, pretending to be deaf or stupid or both, while the audience hollered out variations on "My God, look over your shoulder!" I whistled, and Rajah came jetting off his pedestal and knocked me down, and as sometimes happened he jumped on me before I had time to roll over, such that my belly was down and the right side of my face pressed against tanbark. I entered my world of heavy furry silence, though this time something different happened: Rajah gave me a bit of air and he leaned his jowls beside my ear and he offered up a little rumble that sounded both affectionate and dangerous. He licked the side of my face, and was then I felt both big paws settle on my shoulders, his claws sinking deep into padding. He held me down. He opened his jaws and closed them over my neck, eye-teeth pressing against skin, me saying, "Rajah, no no no," which he ignored. For a second, I thought something was going totally wrong, and that maybe it was true you never could trust a tiger, even one you've raised from birth.

Rajah began rubbing his body against mine. To the rubes it must've looked like he was fixing on having me for breakfast, which in a way he was: I could feel his manhood, about the size of a whip handle and covered with a white wispy down, searching for an entrance in my leather. Finding none, it contented itself with rubbing against me, a motion that shook me like a Raggedy Ann. Rajah let go of my neck and roared the way a male tiger does when so occupied, the rubes screaming and yelling for help and the usual assortment of bravehearts rushing the cage and getting held back by groomers and cage boys and clowns, a sight that got the rubes whipped up all the more. Rajah picked up the pace and, with a roar that scared even me, finished and then rolled me over with a paw and buried his face in my neck and gurgled. I hugged him as the rubes' screams turned into screams of relief.

He rolled me around a little more before I finally pushed him off. I took only the quickest of bows. Truth was, I was embarrassed as hell, for his spunk had got all over my back, and when he'd rolled me over the tanbark shavings had stuck to it, my beautiful black leather uniform about as messed as it was possible to be: quite frankly, I looked like I'd been tarred and feathered, something I'd seen happen to more than one sideshow grifter. I left the arena red-faced, and as I did I passed two men who'd been standing just outside the door. The first was my tunnel man and cage boy, Red, who realized what'd happened, and who was laughing and pointing and enjoying the well-worn sight of me.

The second was Louis, who also knew what'd happened, and who didn't find it funny in the least.

CHAPTER 7

JUNGLELAND

JESUS CHRIST I'M GLAD YOU'RE HERE. IT'S ALL HAPPENING and if there was ever a time I needed a shoulder to lean on it's now. Was a few days ago. A pair of them, in black suits, like twin funeral directors, poking around like curious sons of bitches, inspecting cages, huts, wagons, I even saw one of them standing outside Annie's steam-belching snack hut and shaking his head like he couldn't believe what he was seeing. To add further emphasis in case anyone was watching he kicked it. Looked ridiculous, he did, like it was a used vehicle he was beginning not to think much of, pulling his foot back and inspecting *it* instead of the scuff he'd made on the side of the building.

They were with Jeb and Ida practically the whole day, and on the odd times they weren't you'd see them having their breaks together, sipping iced tea and scheming. When I asked Roger, "Who in the hell're those two?" he told me he didn't have a clue, so I asked the same question of Uncle Ben. He shrugged as well, saying, "The only thing I know is they're in from Omaha. I'd ask Jeb if I were you." This was easier said than done, for I couldn't confront Jeb when Ida was around, and I sure as hell couldn't pin him down when he was showing around the strangers, they being the ones I wanted to talk about in the first place. In other words, I had to steam about it pretty much all day, until finally, near the time I was about to go home, I saw Jeb heading across the connection. As usual, he was wearing a cowboy hat and the frown that comes from owning a money-losing business. I timed it so I turned a corner and we practically ran headlong into each other.

"Mabel!" he said after a quick sidestep.

"Jeb! Christ, you scared the bejesus out of me."

He laughed and made to move around me, causing me to shift into his line of vision, a signal I was in the mood for a chat.

"Quite a day," I said.

"Quite a day."

"Sunny. Not too hot."

"Wish it was always like this. Business would sure be better."

"What we used to call a real circus day."

"Oh, it's a circus day for sure."

"See you got some visitors."

"Visitors?"

"Those men in suits keep following you around."

"Oh. Them. They're hardly visitors, Mabel. To be visitors you have to be invited. They just phoned up and told us they was coming and I didn't have much choice in the matter."

"That a fact?"

"Well, Mabel I gotta ..."

"Who are they, Jeb?"

He peered at me for a second.

"Who's who, Mabel?"

"Oh for Christ's sake, Jeb, the guys in the pallbearer suits!"

Here he took a breath and looked at me squarely.

"Insurance folk, Mabel. The company that holds our policy got sold, and the new company says they have to poke around."

"Oh."

"Nothing to worry about."

"No, course not."

"One thing we never have to worry about is your tigers, Mabel, and neither will they. Not with the way you labour over them."

"No, I'm not worried, just curious was all."

This was followed by a few more seconds of awkwardness. We parted and walked in separate directions, me feeling jittery and air filled.

Problem was, he'd told me I had nothing to worry about *before* I told him I was worrying.

They were there again the next morning, poking about, generally trying to sink into the woodwork though achieving the exact opposite with their latest Nebraska fashions. Everyone was on tenterhooks and then some. Then, at midday, Jeb tracked me down in the cathouse and said, "Uhhhhh ... Mabel?"

"Yes, Jeb?"

"You're needed in the office."

"What for?"

"Those men. They need to talk to you."

Was my turn to be cagey.

"What men would that be, Jeb?" though I immediately regretted it for Jeb wasn't my enemy, no matter who his wife was, and he gave me a spent look reminding me of that fact. I followed him out of the training barn and then headed alone to his office, where the men had set up on a card table in front of mounds of paper. I entered and suspected right off this wasn't going to be pleasant.

The two men. One was taller than the other, and he wore his hair in a fashionable cut, by which I mean silly: Little Lord Fauntleroy bangs and wisps travelling down over his ears before doing a little flip up sideways. Why a man close to forty years of age would let himself get influenced by what those hippies are doing is beyond me, but there it was: he had himself a hairdo that made me yearn for the 1940s, a time men knew how to dress, as opposed to today, a time men just plain don't. The other man was older, maybe in his fifties, and slightly more dignified, his hair greyer and sparser so he was less tempted to follow the trends. Both were in cheap suits, poorly stitched and dumpy, the older of the two with a ketchup stain on his tie that sacrificed what little he had in the dignity department.

"John Fischer," said longhair.

"Mabel Stark," I said, taking his hand.

"Kevin Taylor," said ketchup stain, to which I said, "Mabel Stark" and gripped *his* hand. We all sat down around the card table and the two men started shuffling through papers and generally looking perturbed.

The younger one started the talking: "Now, Mrs. Stark ..."

"Miss Stark."

"I'm sorry. Miss Stark. We understand you're the head tiger trainer here at JungleLand."

"The *only* tiger trainer at JungleLand. Or leastways the only real one. Have been for thirty-six years."

"Really?" he said. "That's quite an achievement."

"Yes," said the older one, "we understand in the circus world you're something of a legend."

"Suppose you could say that."

"It's an honour to meet you."

"Yes. An honour."

"We just wanted to talk to you because—and I'm sure it's a clerical error, or something along those lines—but there doesn't seem to be any record of your employment here."

True enough. The fact of the matter was I'd always been paid under the table at JungleLand. I preferred it that way, for I'd signed a contract once before and it'd almost been the end of me. Course, Louis understood, a fear of restrictions and legal responsibility being a common trait among ex-troupers.

"We suspected something like that. We just wanted to clear it up with you. Nip it in the bud, so to speak. So you are an official employee here ..."

"Course. And I'll thank you to keep your insinuations to yourself. They may not have told you but I'm a lady who doesn't like to be riled."

Here they seemed to start up their own little two-sided conversation.

"Of course not."

"No, of course not."

"Who does like to be riled?"

"Nobody. No. Nobody."

"It's just that we have some questions pertaining to, well, our business here, and it's difficult to get some answers without the proper papers ..."

"We're not questioning your status here at JungleLand—that's not our intention at all—it's just that, well, we have to have some information in order to be able to do our jobs."

"Let me approach this from a different direction. Jeb tells me you're sixty-nine years of age. Is that, uh, accurate?"

I looked at them, blinking. While it was true sixty-nine was my official circus age, it was also true I always lopped about ten years off my real age so I'd never have to account for years I'd rather not account for. Truth was, my eightieth birthday was on the horizon, something I never thought would happen and something they sure as hell weren't going to find out from me.

"Yes," I said, "that's accurate," and the fact I said this through slitted eyes amply communicated I was getting tired of being questioned. They rustled in their chairs and shot glances at each other.

"Well then," said ketchup stain, "that's all we need to know. You'll get us something we can copy and show head office, a birth certificate, perhaps, and we won't have to bother you again."

With that, they were both on their feet, hands sticking out of those cheap dark sleeves, saying good-day and acting like they were doing me a favour. I shook both their hands, and left, thinking I had myself a choice to make. Though I didn't have a birth certificate, I did have a driver's license complete with fake name and fake age—believe me it's not hard to get—and I supposed coughing it up would be enough to keep them satisfied. On the other hand, I didn't like the way they made me feel—i.e. creaky and past my prime—so I wasn't exactly in a hurry to make their jobs any easier. I pondered this all day. Did my tiger act by rote. Percolated. Kept asking myself if this was a situation calling for my policy of never rolling over or whether this was a different situation altogether. Finally I decided it was something different altogether, so I caught up to the two insurance rubes at a time when Ida was with them, thinking at least I'd get the satisfaction of seeing her figure out her trap wasn't going to work.

"Gentlemen," I called out, jogging up in a way someone wearing splints ordinarily can't. "Been looking for you all day."

I handed my driver's license to the older one, who by then had changed his tie and was looking a little less ridiculous. He glanced at it and passed it on to the younger one, who hadn't done anything with his hair and still *did* look ridiculous. They both smiled and said, "Thank you, Miss Stark, we'll get this back to you later today," to which I said, "No hurry, gentlemen. You have a good day."

And Ida?

You could've broken an egg on her face, it got so tightened up.

Whether this'll work or not I don't know. Most likely not. Whatever Ida's cobbling together is going to get cobbled together no matter what I do about it and that's a truth I'm just going to have to learn to deal with. Frankly, at this point I'm a little beyond caring: if the end comes tomorrow at least I won't have to worry about regret, which I'm pretty sure is a feeling that haunts a lot of townies once old age hits.

Think of what I've done. *Think* of it. I've been to every town in America, small or large, most of them more than once. I've seen the mountains, the swamps of southern Florida, the buttes, both oceans. All of them were sights, every last one. I've heard every kind of accent, including the funny ones, and here I'm thinking of southern Louisiana. Or that valley in the middle of Connecticut where they speak like the Queen, only gone silly-sounding with hiccups. Or northern Minnesota, where we used to go when taking the long way into Canada; you'd swear they were all Swedish lumberjacks, which of course a lot of them were.

Tell me this. You ever seen a vanishing point over water? Course you have—Art used to say if a person didn't gaze out over water from time to time it could have grave implications for the health of that person's spirit, something I began to believe myself. Yet it doesn't compare to seeing space vanish over *land*, like you do on the plains of western Canada, not a tree or building or butte in sight. Was something I saw every year on the Barnes show, and I can tell you quite honestly there isn't anything like it.

Or: the sun setting fire-engine red in the desert, where it'll plant itself for hours, casting a violet hue over the cactus and sand and tumbleweed, before finally dipping over the edge. Beats Key West, where you're liable to miss the whole show if you blink at the wrong time. I know because I've seen 'em both more than once.

I've been to Cecil B. DeMille's house. I've ridden parade with Mae West. I've kissed Douglas Fairbanks (though not in any way meaningful). I've wrangled on a dozen movies, so many the idea of being a star no longer impresses me, probably because I used to be one myself. I'm a woman who's had John Ringling give her flowers. I've visited the Tower of London, I've tried Devonshire cream, I've seen the Changing of the Guards. I'm a woman who's had her beer at room temperature. I'm a gal who's eaten raw steak in fine restaurants, who's swum in a salt lake of all things. I'm a woman who's worn spangled costumes, who's ridden in limousines, who's breakfasted on mountains, who's been deafened by applause. I'm also a woman who, on a steamy day in Bangor, got what she deserved and was torn limb from limb by tigers, and if there's anything that'll zest up a life faster than that, well, you'll just have to tell me about it.

Sorry. It's a subject gets me worked up, my losing my babies. Haunts me, if you must know. Without them, I'll have hours and hours each day, and I know very well I won't be thinking about all the places I've been and all the things I've seen and all the worthwhile things I've done. Instead it'll be springtime, 1927, North Carolina, Mabel finally in love with a man she's married, a rainstorm brewing and the circus gets hooked up to the wrong water supply and people start getting sick and was it my fault I was a nurse? Was it my fault I could help out? Was it my fault I couldn't tolerate contentment pure and simple?

Well?

Jesus. There I go. Guilt. What a smiting *that* is. Worse than any tiger mauling, I'll tell you right now. You let it get to you and pretty soon you can't sleep and you can't eat with your normal gumption and you start to wondering why you even bother going on.

So I called Dr. Brisbane's office.

Because he'd been treating me for years and had a sympathetic secretary, I got an appointment the next day. On my lunch hour I piloted that big old Buick of mine to his office. I parked and took the elevator and entered a waiting room full of other old circus folk. I gave a series of half nods and sat. Across from me was Luigi Concello, last of the original Concellos, who, like all old flyers, suffered from terrible elbow and shoulder pain and was probably in having his weekly freezing needles. Next to me two chairs over was a midget I knew only by sight though I'd heard he'd been with Yankee Robinson back when that show was something. He now suffered from the back pain that sets in when a midget gets old; often I'd see him shopping at the Safeway, wincing with each step. To my left was a Cole Brothers veteran named Eddie the Cannonball Frecoldi. Supposedly what happened to him was he hit the net funny one matinee such that his head stayed in one place while his whole body carried over and made a loud popping noise from somewhere between the neck and shoulder. Apparently his suffering demanded an armload of pills, such that Eddie was always either a little bit out of it or a lot out of it, depending on a number of factors like the dampness of the weather or the strenuousness of the previous day or how brave he happened to be feeling. When I nodded at him, he nodded back with a fearfulness in his eyes; you could tell he was hoping he really did know this person and it wasn't someone just tricking him into looking stupid.

I sat there reading one of the *Billboard*s Dr. Brisbane was smart enough to put out. There was more news about the Ringlings' new owner and whether Mr. Feld could really make a go of it and save the circus in America. Given the dourness of my mood, I figured probably not. Funny. I'd joined the circus in its golden years and then stuck with it, directly or indirectly, for the rest of my life. Made me feel like its story was my story and vice versa and that I ought to be in a museum because of it. Course, the same could be said about pretty much everyone else in that orange-carpeted waiting room.

As I moved up the waiting list, a parade of old troupers came in and got half nods from yours truly; you've never seen a sadder gathering of limps and manglements and people just plain moving in a way not normal. Though I'd been to Dr. Brisbane's office dozens and dozens of times, for some reason his waiting-room pageant was bothering me more than usual, so I was relieved when his secretary finally looked up from her desk and called "Mabel Stark" in a loud croaky voice.

I went in. He had his desk and bookshelves set up in one corner, an examination table in the opposite one. As usual, he was sitting at his desk, so I took the seat across from him and waited another few seconds while he scribbled something with a pen so fat it looked uncomfortable to write with. He was wearing a white lab coat with a tie underneath and his black plastic Steve Allen glasses.

"Mabel!" he said. "How nice to see you. How *are* you?"

"Fine," I said. "Just fine."

"Tigers treating you okay? Had any scratches lately?"

"Not a one."

"Good. Good. One of these days I'm going to come out to JungleLand with my little grand-niece. Cute as a monkey's tail, she is. Two years old and lives right here in Thousand Oaks."

"Well if you do make sure you tell them you know me and you can come backstage and meet the cats in person."

"I'll do that, Mabel. I'll do that. Now what's the problem?"

Here I paused so as to make it clear I wanted the conversation to shift gears.

"Sleeping. Sleeping's the problem."

"Having a touch of the insomnia, are we?"

"Yes."

"The kind in which you can't get to sleep or the kind in which you wake up in the middle of the night and can't fall back to sleep?"

"The kind I wake up in the middle of the night and stay that way."

Already he was reaching for his fat pen and prescription pad.

"I wouldn't worry too much, Mabel. This happens a lot when people get a little on in years—"

"No," I interrupted. "This is ... well, this is different. I can't fall back asleep because I've got memories popping up and staring me in the face. I don't suppose you'd have something that medicates against memories, would you?"

He looked at me for a second, puzzled, before regaining an expression that beamed with confidence and comfort. Often I've told myself I'd go to see Dr. Brisbane even if that expression was the only thing he had in the way of medicine. Fortunately it wasn't, for he handed me a paper covered in chicken scratch and said, "One before bedtime. If that doesn't work, make it two."

I made it through the day, tired as usual, just wishing something would happen for anything'd be better than this infernal waiting game. On my way home, I stopped at the pharmacy and got myself a vial of red-and-white capsules. I washed two down with a Hamm's right after *Gilligan's Island* and put myself under the covers. Next thing I knew, morning had come, and though it took a cold shower and an extra cup of coffee before the cobwebs started to clear I had to admit I felt better, by which I mean rested and less raw, the only side effect a mild fuzziness on the tongue.

So now my pills sit on my bedside table. They're next to a silver hairbrush, a glass of water, a .38 calibre pistol bought years ago in Kansas and a silver frame holding a photo more than forty years old. Was taken on our wedding day, my *last* wedding day, thank you very much, which explains why Art's wearing a tuxedo and pink frills. The smile that man had—there are smiles born from manners and there are smiles born from an understanding of how bad things can get, and by now I hope I don't have to tell you which one I consider the most attractive. Hell, I'd show you what I mean except his picture's in my bedroom and no one other than myself has set foot in that room in the thirty-six years I've lived here. I'd probably die from the shock of it.

But if I *did* show you the photo, you'd see a man, handsome in a well-worn sort of way, smiling, eyes grey blue, skin reddish, moustache bushy but not ridiculously so, and I guarantee the first thing you'd say to yourself is, "Jesus Murphy. That mascara?"

CHAPTER 8

THE HANDSOME BIGAMIST

I DIDN'T SEE OR HEAR FROM LOUIS ROTH FOR THREE YEARS. Even then it was out of the blue, a letter arriving from the Great Wortham Carnival, a tiny grift show with a menage I'd thought had up and died years earlier. He wanted a divorce. With three husbands to my name I had no qualms thinning the crowd a little.

The letter went on to propose we sign the papers on May 20, 1920, in Portland, a date coinciding with the arrival of the Barnes show. We'd do it around eleven in the morning, between set-up and matinee, before the crowds.

I cabled him back, agreeing to everything.

That morning I awoke early (nerves) and gave Rajah a kiss on the head and squeezed the folds of his ears together, a gesture that tickled him and made him generally agreeable. When he came awake I scratched the downy fur of his underbelly and told him Mama was busy that day and he'd have to go to his *c-a-g-e*; was a word he understood even when spelled, so he arfed and made himself sad-eyed and limp in the tail.

"Shoo," I said, reinforcing the point, "you just shoo," and here he lifted his head off his forepaws and moved off the bed hind end first.

After leashing him I walked him all the way to the lot where he ran around while waiting for the workingmen to set up the menage. When he'd had enough, I treated him to some brisket and brushed him and gave him a big kiss on the snout before putting him in his cage. Around ten o'clock, Al G. told a gilly driver to take us into town. Ten minutes later, we stepped out in front of the address Louis had given me. It was on the wrong side of town, the buildings dirty and the sewers open and a pair of ragamuffins already tugging on Al G.'s arm and bugging him for pennies. He handed them quarters and said, "Well, Kentucky, good luck."

"You're not coming?"

His face widened into a grin.

"People to see, Kentucky. People to see...." which was a statement that shouldn't've surprised me for he was without Dan or Miss Speeks and Portland was a town he knew well (it being a source of cheap hay and all). He wandered off, whistling, a tall-backed man in a nice suit sauntering into a coal-black tenement and if you want an image summing up Al G. Barnes that's about as good as I can do.

I went inside. The steps were rickety and one of the vestibule lights was burnt out. I was afraid to touch anything, for dirt was everywhere and back then there were some pretty misguided rumours concerning the way you get diseases common among the poor. (Scabies, for one thing, and conditions that make going to the bathroom a horror.) After a bit of poking about I found the office I was hunting for, on the second floor just down from the stairwell. Here I opened a door and found a waiting room that was surprisingly clean and well lit.

I also found Louis Roth, flipping through a paper.

He gave me the thinnest of smiles. In three years his face had gotten wrinklier and slim to the point of gauntness, gauntness being

something that looked bad on a man like Louis: the skin on his face had
to stretch to accommodate his pail-shaped jaw, the effect being skull-
like and a little eerie. His thick dark hair had thinned a little and gone
grey at the temples, something that must've bothered him for he'd
always been so vain about it.

"Mabel," he said.

"Louis."

He stood, took my hand and shook it like we were about to sign
a land deal; he even brought his heels together in a click before retak-
ing his chair. Frankly, I wished he'd kissed me. It would've made the
whole thing less weird.

Instead, we sat, staring at the door to the lawyer's office, listening to the dull hum of a ceiling fan. If Louis was thinking what I was
thinking it had to do with the way one minute two people can be close
enough to clean the inside of each other's animal wounds and the next
minute be worse than strangers. It was a maudlin thought, so I passed
the time dwelling on it, for I've always considered maudlin to be one of
the truer ways of feeling.

After a few minutes the door opened and a rumpled little bowling
pin of a man with muttonchops invited us in and handed us the papers.
I'd seen a copy already, Louis having sent one with his letter, and I was
fine with the stipulation we both just walk away with whatever we'd
brought to the marriage, no money or property or ill will changing hands.

"Any questions?"

We both said no by moving our chins. Louis then asked, "Iss zer
anysing else?"

The lawyer shook his head. Louis put his fountain pen back in his
jacket pocket and stood and straightened his jacket and said, "Goodbye,
Mabel. It vas nice to see you again."

He marched out. The sentimental fool in me felt a twinge at the
sound of Louis's boots smacking the floorboards; I suppose I was
thinking if his boots still had the sound of authority there was a better

than even chance Louis still carried it around somewhere inside him as well.

After a few seconds, there was nothing left to do but shake the lawyer's hand and thank him for his time. I did so, and he informed me I owed half the fee, which seemed fair so I paid it and thanked him again and left. When I made it to the street, Louis was nowhere in sight.

The whole thing had taken about five minutes. Both Al G. and I had figured it would take a whole lot longer, so we'd told the gilly driver to come back in an hour and a half. With time to kill, I caught a taxi across the railway tracks and had myself a soda float in a nice department store. When I finished my soda I ordered another, my weight or lack thereof having always been a problem. After that I browsed through magazines and talked to people who recognized me from my picture on the posters the advance agents had put up all over town. Then I left the store and walked for a bit, feeling happy, for I was discovering that a feeling of freedom sets in after a divorce that's not in any way unpleasant. If only I'd had the same opportunity with hubbies one and two.

Was a nice warm day with a nice warm breeze. I took my kerchief off and let my blond hair ruffle up, and when I passed a store with a bright blue dress I liked in the window I went in and it fitted perfectly. Because the shop owner was a circus fan he insisted I take it free, so long as I'd let him put a picture of myself in the window along with a sign saying "Mabel Stark the Tiger Queen Shops Here."

In other words, I was feeling good, something that normally makes me nervous but for some reason didn't that day. I walked until the town started to turn seedy, at which point I hailed a cab and took it back to the meeting place, where Al G. and the gilly were both waiting. Al G. was in a good mood, and by this I mean a genuine good mood and not the good mood he conjured when trying to get what he wanted from others—he was whistling and smiling and talking sports with the driver and teasing me about being a free woman. He even told me I ought to smile more often, on account of how pretty I looked when I was happy. To emphasize this sentiment he put his hand on my knee and gave me a quick little fresh-bread squeeze, which was the first time he'd tried something forward with me in ages. I laughed it off and pushed it away and wasn't the least bothered.

"Mabel," he said, "why is it you and me have never *been* together? It's unnatural."

"It's not unnatural," I said. "It's just plain sanity."

This made him laugh hard enough his eyes went into slits, the wrinkles caused by countless hours of midway sun popping up like desert crevices. We were both feeling mirthful and younger than our actual ages—me about thirty, Al G. maybe forty-five—when we pulled into the lot and Dan came running.

He didn't say a thing. Just gave Al G. his something's-wrong face, a face Dan wore at the best of times but was particularly pro-nounced that day. Al G. jumped from the car and went off with him. Ten minutes later, Dan was marching up and down the midway with his hands cupped over his mouth calling "John Robinson, John Robinson" which is circus slang for blowdown weather's on the way so we better get the show over with quick.

Strangest thing, though. I looked up, and there wasn't a grey cloud in sight.

Still, orders are orders, the circus being more like an army than most troupers care to admit (albeit one that doesn't discriminate against felons, drug takers, dwarves, communists and arse lusters). "The Conquest of Nyanza" was cut to shorter than ten minutes, just a quick circle around the hippodrome and we were all back through the blue curtain. The clown segment was reduced to one pie in the face and one tiny car sprouting three dozen chubby arms and legs. We omitted the aerial monkeys and the rube parade and the fabulous bucking mules. Al G. also killed the spec in the middle of the show—an African hunt with Spanish stallions and Indian elephants and brown-skinned girls with jewels in their navels and red dots pasted to the middle of their foreheads. Lotus the hippo, the Blood-Sweating Behemoth of Holy Writ, rode a cart instead of doing his normal lumbering walk around the tent. No doubt there were other cuts too, though I forget what they were. I only know when it came to the show's finale I stayed under Rajah for just as long as it took him to do his business, my having substituted a white leather uniform for a black leather uniform so as to avoid the embarrassment I suffered the first night Rajah started using me as a rubbing post.

After a quick announcement, the after-show was cancelled and we were done. Two hours and twenty minutes packed into less than one and a half. By the time I got Rajah back to the train, the workingmen had taken down the cookhouse and pie car and had made good headway with the big top. Still there wasn't a cloud in the sky, and as the gillies started getting poled onto the train, we all stood around speculating that the real problem was probably some woman trouble Al G. had got himself into. Maybe a pregnancy or another wife we didn't know about, Al G.'s weakness being not so much his love of women as his love of marrying them as a means of being accommodating.

We left Portland before four in the afternoon, a day early, in a state of high confusion. To fill time before the Tacoma date we made an unscheduled stop in a place called Cape Disappointment, Washington, where we did an impromptu night in a field about eight miles from town—without sponsors or paper up or newspapermen lured with free barbecue there were no more than four or five hundred in the crowd. In fact, there were so few people the start was delayed twenty minutes, all the troupers walking around scratching their heads and saying, "What's it look like tonight?" when the answer was as plain as egg on toast. It looked *bad*.

Was lunacy, this, lunacy pure and bug-eyed and top-of-the-lungs raving. The only explanation was we were hiding out, an explanation supported by the fact no one had seen Al G. or Dan. Even the stars were disguised by a sky thick with grey, mashed-potato clouds, making everything look shadowy. After the performance we loaded the gillies like normal. In the middle of the night, with everyone asleep and my arm thrown over Rajah's shoulders and Rajah snoring weakly, the train sailed right through Tacoma, a town known for having good crowds and reasonable cops and nice restaurants besides. Imagine our consternation when we all opened our eyes and threw open our Pullman curtains and instead of seeing buildings and lights and the offerings of a city we looked into drizzle and low shit-brown mountains dotted with settlers' cabins. That was looking out the left side of the train. When we looked out of the right side we saw potatoes. Saw them for miles and miles and miles, which would've been fine except a potato field's about as interesting to look at as a potato itself.

The place was called Sandpoint, Idaho. Though I never saw the actual town, I heard it was one of those places that isn't a really a place, just a name given to a naked intersection so folks could get mail. We played to exactly 180 rubes that afternoon. Each and every one of them, children included, was chewing tobacco. Afterwards a team of working-men earned cherry pie by cleaning spittle off the stringers.

We were there two more days, a Sunday and a Monday besides, the words *unscheduled holiday* circulating through the cookhouse and pie car and blue car. Was around then a rumour started that Al G. had gone mad with either syphilis or stress or a combination of the two. It wasn't hard to believe, for Al G. was still holing up in his car, seeing nobody and keeping his mouth shut, behaviour that was normally against his nature. Dan, meanwhile, turned away any and all visitors. The closest I ever came to Al G. in those weird two days was seeing Miss Leonora Speeks strolling down the connection, hips swaying and cheeks ablaze with colour. She was smiling too, suggesting what she and Al G. were up to in that fancy rail car wasn't pinochle.

I said, "Let's go," to Rajah and tugged on his leash and we caught up to her. We all walked side by side for a few seconds, Leonora not looking at us, until finally I said, "Well what is it, Miss Speeks. Why are we parked in the middle of this drizzly nowhere?"

She stopped and peered at me through the white veil hanging from her chapeau. In the process I noticed her eyes for the first time: orange, like a marmalade cat's, with flecks of black to spice them up. Even I had to admit they were something.

"Quarantine, Mabel," she said, saying the word like I was slow. "Quar ... ann ... teen."

Then she gave me a smile suggesting she didn't care whether I believed her or not and jiggled herself off, humming.

There was a possibility she was telling the truth: during a two-month stretch in 1918 when influenza broke out in the northwest, the show rerouted itself so as to avoid places where it might be seized and shut down till the panic was over. Yet there was no good reason Al G. wouldn't have announced this, staying one step ahead of health inspectors being a time-honoured circus tradition. That night, with the train idling on the tracks, a few of the groomers hooked a radio to a generator and listened for news of influenza or red death or a water-borne menace. If there was one it wasn't mentioned that night, the only news being from Europe and how they were making progress clearing bombed-out buildings.

In the middle of the night we started moving again. Though this normally wouldn't have woken me, I must've been pretty anxious to feel some motion again, for my eyes opened and I felt as alert as a gal who'd slept well. Rajah's eyes opened too, and he murmured and turned to me and yawned, his meaty breath wafting into my face.

He rolled over and fell back asleep with his face against my neck. As the train rumbled east, I stayed awake, waiting for a change of direction, hoping against hope we'd head toward civilization instead of vast western Canada emptiness. No such luck. After fifteen or twenty minutes a whistle blew and I felt the train taking a slow turn, straightening out so we were heading more north than anywhere else.

We didn't travel long that night, maybe an hour, and when we stopped we were in some dinky station, a single light illuminating the words "Grand Forks." Beyond that was a blackness interrupted only by firefly light.

The sun came up on a misty cool day, like every day we'd seen over the past week. The transport wagons took us past little home- steader shacks to a field laid to fallow in the middle of nowhere. It had the feel of weirdness, this place, for it was completely deserted, no evi- dence whatsoever of stores or saloons or meeting halls, only a big clapboard church with Russian letters across the steeple base. We did- n't bother with a parade, so we didn't see the townsfolk until the hour before the matinee, when they began straggling toward the main entrance. They were like ghosts, appearing in the mist, wearing long white robes sashed at the waist, the men wearing beards that obvious- ly hadn't been trimmed for years, the women looking plain and tired and hooded.

After a lot of milling about and head scratching, the robe wearers began to filter in; within a few minutes it became clear that in addition to their strange sartorial sense, the other defining quality of Doukhobors was they were way on the frugal end of things. There was- n't one rigged game of skill played that day. Not one drop of tincture, elixir or nostrum was sold by the cure-all vendors. Not a single sideshow ticket was sold, despite the efforts of both the outside talker and the free act, a guy named Jorge who could swallow a fistful of swords and still sing the Honduran national anthem. I did see one little white-robed girl buy a live chameleon from one of the bug men, though when her father found out he opened the matchbox and overturned it. The squishy sound of him stomping it made the girl go teary.

Finally, it was showtime, "The Conquest of Nyanza" spilling onto the hippodrome in a trumpet of sound and colour, and I remember thinking this would break them out of their stupor. It didn't; we all stood outside the performers' tent, listening to the silence, one of the spec riders breaking the tension by saying, "Maybe they're sitting on their hands to keep them warm." Nor did things get any better, each act finishing to not so much as a cough (though the clowns did get the odd laugh from the children). During my twelve-tiger act, an act so exciting the audience was usually standing by the end, there wasn't so much as a peep; throughout, I couldn't stop myself from taking little sidelong glances, if only to try to figure out why they'd bothered coming in the first place. The cats were doing the same thing. With pupils shifted to the corners of their eyes, they did their sit-ups and ball rolls and hoop jumping nervously, as though worried that something was being thought up in all that quiet. When we got to our finale, poor Rajah was so upset he crawled off his pedestal, limped over and stood on his hind legs, more hugging me than pretending to attack. I had to ham it up, pulling him down on top of me and reaching behind me to scratch his pleasure spot in order to get his blood up. I even wiggled my exposed arms and legs to suggest I was in trouble.

It wouldn't work. Rajah just sort of lay on me, panting and shivering and looking around. When the orchestra struck up a minute later it sounded ten times louder than normal.

Finally, it was over, nothing left but the national anthem and the after-show. Since it was obvious these people weren't about to part with another penny that left the national anthem alone. The orchestra struck up "O Canada" and it happened: grumbling and yelling and every man, woman and child covering their ears and rushing for the exit. I even watched one woman with a baby trying to cover her ears and the baby's ears simultaneously, finally making do by pulling the sash off her white gown and wrapping it tight around the baby's head. Within two minutes every last one had vamoosed.

This behaviour inspired a chill in the membership of the Al G. Barnes 4-Ring Wild Animal Circus. We started packing up as quick as we could, the workingmen taking the big top down so fast they were in danger of tearing it in two. Within an hour and a half the last wagon was rolling toward the parked train. Meanwhile, the entire population of Grand Forks, British Columbia, had formed a standing patrol on the far side of the tent, arms folded over bellies and faces locked in scowls. It looked like they wanted to assure themselves we were leaving as fast as was possible, and as far as we were concerned we were going to oblige. The workingmen started poling the wagons onto the flatbeds and ratcheting them into place. Meanwhile, our watchers' expressions never changed, for better or worse, and for a second I wondered if somehow the whole town was taking the same personality-flattening drugs I'd been given in the nervous hospital.

As if that wasn't weird *enough*, after the whole train was packed up, not a twitch of hay or a crumb of animal feed left behind, we sat idling, as though we couldn't move without the protection offered by darkness. Rajah and I curled up on the bed and I calmed myself by pushing my face into his fur. We stayed this way for hours, Rajah drifting off and me too nervous to read or knit, so I lay there, smelling his fur and letting my hand comb the thick white hair between his front legs.

Come evening there was a knock at the door. Immediately I figured it was a posse of rubes, out to get me for the tightness of my uniform and the fact I wore my hair in curls men found pleasing. For a second I told myself I wasn't going to answer. The knocking came again, and because this time it woke Rajah I decided I'd answer after all, figuring five hundred pounds of tiger goes a long way in calming disgruntled townies. I pushed my car door open and saw a great big white-cloaked Doukhobor standing under a hood. He looked like a small upholstered hill.

A voice came from beneath the bedsheet that didn't at all sound like what I imagined a Doukhobor voice would sound like. Polite, it was, the diction precise and school taught.

"I was wondering," it said, "if I might have a word with you, madam."

I swallowed.

"About what?"

"It's a ... it's a delicate matter. Do you mind if I step inside."

"Yes, I do mind. You can state your business from right where you are. I've got an animal in here who doesn't particularly warm to strangers."

He tilted his face upward, something that suprised me for he was clean-shaven and meaty around the jowls.

"Please ..." he said, and it was his Barnes-like charm that made me involuntarily back away. He had to duck to get under the doorway, and when he was inside his cloaked head practically touched the ceiling. He had to have been six foot three, his body weight triple mine, with dark eyes and prominent lips and a fighter's jaw. He wasn't handsome, but at the same time had a way about him that just suggested importance. I studied his face, exploring the strange feeling I'd met him somewhere before. He pushed his cloak off his head, revealing thick black hair gone wavy with pomade.

"My goodness. I was beginning to think we would never have the chance to meet. That Al G. Barnes. You have to to hand it to him. One wily customer. Of course, he *is* a circus owner."

With that he bent over so he could take the hem of his robe in his hands, an effort that made him groan. He started pulling it over his head, revealing a crisp, beautifully tailored virgin wool suit underneath. It must've cost $500 if it cost a nickel.

"There," he said, "that's better. Now perhaps we can talk."

He dabbed his hair, even though it hadn't been mussed, and he evened his tie. When he reached inside his jacket pocket for a double corona I realized how I knew his face. My heart sped, and I felt a rush of heat to my cheeks and brow. In danger of fainting dead away, I took a series of deep, slow breaths to save myself the embarrassment.

Meanwhile, he held the flame from a solid gold lighter to the tip of his cigar, the flame dancing and bobbing as he sucked. Within a minute my rail car filled with tobacco smoke so fine you could smell apple and sandalwood.

John Ringling was pointing at Louis's old scroll desk and saying, "Tell me. Is that real Bohemian pine?"

One half-hour later I walked the length of the idling train. This being a moment of high emotion, both good and bad, just the way I like it, pretty much everything about that walk made an impression. My feet were making sucking noises in the mud. I could smell elephant dung, dark earth and rain. When I looked up through the drizzle, the fields had a cottony greyness about them. I passed groups of workingmen sitting around playing cards on overturned crates, laughing and passing bottles and not minding the weather for it was better than being in their cars, crammed three to a berth. The sky felt low and thick, like a cozy.

I made it to the front section of the train and stopped in front of the Holt car. There I waited for a few seconds to get my nerve up, Rajah yawning as if bored and wanting to get out of the mist. I knocked on the door, hoping Dan might peer out the window and see it was me and open up. It didn't happen, so I knocked again, louder this time, calling, "Jesus Christ, Al G., I know you're in there," and when this didn't work I went to the side of the car, underneath a window, and hissed, "Al G., you open the door. Goddammit I *know* what's going on...."

The stillness lasted a few seconds more. Then the car door opened, both Rajah and me snapping our heads to the right, where Dan was standing underneath the awning with his worry face. I passed him into the car. He didn't say, How is you this evening, Miss Stark? or even hello, for that matter.

Al G. was sitting at his desk, a mountain of train schedules and maps and circus paper in front of him; it surprised me to see him hunched over and fretting. He looked up and our eyes met. Leaning back in his chair, he linked his fingers over his stomach and, after looking sick for a few seconds, gave me a pained smile.

"Found you, didn't he?"

Rajah was pulling me toward a space of carpet next to the hearth so I let him go and he lay down beside a burning log.

"He did."

This made Al G. laugh in the way people laugh when something isn't at all funny. Dan was standing beside me, while Leonora Speeks was sitting on the antique sofa filing her nails. We all just looked at him, worried by the giddiness of his reaction.

"Let me guess," Al G. said between howls. "He ... he used a costume didn't he?"

I nodded.

"Ha! I knew it. You've got to respect a guy who'll go to those kind of lengths to get what he wants. He's been trailing us since Portland, you know."

"I sort of figured that."

"I'm sure you did, Kentucky. I'm sure you did. Of course, there was no way I was going to win. A whole circus cannot outrun one man with his own locomotive. With his own *railroad*, for Christ's sake. Am I right, Dan?"

"You right, governor."

"It's putting up the fight that's the fun of it. That's the *whole* point of it. Remember when he wanted those Peruvian flyers from Cole Brothers a few years ago? *The whole circus bribed their way into Mexico.* Thirty rail cars worth of circus, and they wandered around Chihuahua and Sonora for a month, four hundred people stuck with Montezuma's revenge and the workingmen all drunk on mescal. They didn't win either but I bet it was worth it. Or the Robbins Brothers. Have you heard this story, Kentucky? They paid a local sheriff to lock up their star wire walker, and then they spread a rumour he'd been kidnapped by Bolsheviks. The point is they did it, am I right, Dan?"

"You right, governor."

"Tell me, Dan. How long did I say it would take John Ringling to catch up with Kentucky?"

"You said three days."

"And how long have we been making ourselves scarce?"

"Five days."

"So we did all right, didn't we, Dan?"

"We did, governor."

"I think maybe Ringling's getting a little old and fat for this game. It's slowing him down. Let me guess, Kentucky. He offered you twenty tigers? Each one Bengal and cage bred and as handsome as Rajah? Plus twice what you're earning here? No. Let me guess. Three times? Plus your own tent on the lot. A tent with fresh flowers every day, like Lillian Leitzel has. Is that the deal, Kentucky? *Is* it?"

Was then I noticed something I wouldn't've thought was possible. Al G.'s blue eyes and high cheekbones and thin straight nose somehow weren't adding up to handsome, and it occurred to me he hadn't slept for some time. Frustration and fatigue had ganged up on his features and it'd made them plain. He must've realized it, though, for it didn't last long. Was like he willed it into oblivion, a half-second later becoming the same Al G. who in just over a decade turned a dog-and-pony into one of the biggest circuses in America—as big as Cole Brothers or John Robinson or Hagenbeck-Wallace, all of which had been around since the last century.

"Ah hell, Kentucky, I'm just a little sore. You can't blame me. I should be happy I'm producing acts John Ringling wants to pirate—it's a sign of progress. No. Really. I'm glad your time's come. No one deserves it more than you. Are you leaving immediately?"

"I'll join them at winter quarters."

"So you've got time with us yet."

"Yes."

"Well, then. Let's toast your success. We'll have some Calvados, imported from France. What do you say?"

"Sure Al G."

With that, Dan got up and retrieved a decanter of greenish liquid from the sideboard, along with four snifters. For the next while, we all sat sipping a warm alcoholic beverage that tasted like heaven, Al G. telling Dan and Leonora stories about how we met. Like a true gentlemen, he left out the embarrassing and compromising parts—like my being a mental institution runaway and a bigamist and a cooch dancer. Come to think of it, there was a whole lot he had to leave out, enough he had to pretty much start making it up: in his rendition I was a talented young dancer with clout instead of a girl earned her living by dropping her harem top in a Superba tent. Seems he'd wooed me with promises of riches and stardom and fancy dressing rooms before I'd even considered joining his woeful little operation.

When Dan offered me another snifter I accepted, and with each warm sip what'd just happened sank in a little further. Leonora and Dan each had a second helping as well, Leonora growing flirtatious and tipsy and even Dan beginning to smile a bit. Just when I thought Al G. might offer us another, he slapped his palms against the writing pad on his desk and used the momentum to carry him to his feet. He stood, hands on his hips, beaming.

"Well. No point staying here, wasting coal. If we turn around now we might even make those Chicago shows."

The next thing you know old Dan was walking up and down the car line ringing the big copper bell that was used to signal the cookhouse was open or it was fifteen minutes to showtime or the train was leaving the station and if you were fixing on coming along now was the time to get on.

What's more, there was a happiness in the way he was ringing it.

So we got out of Canada and we got out quick. Burnt an entire ton of lump fuel charging through the northern states. Al G. didn't explain his lunacy of the past five days to anyone else, but he did apologize by stopping the train in North Dakota and having a huge barbecue with steaks and beer. A band of Indians formed a curious lineup a little way off, some of whom were recruited to play whooping parts on the Wild West. While we were stopped Al G. sat next to me and kept my plate filled with potato salad. I reckoned it was to prove there were no hard feelings.

Of course, a bunch of the workingmen ran off, took up with squaws or got themselves killed in bar fights for all I know, so we had to stop in Bismarck so Dan could go recruiting in the hostels and clap wards. Stopped again in the middle of Minnesota to water the animals, and we all gillied into a local town where Swedish meatballs were on the menu. Then we chugged straight on through Wisconsin and made it to Oak Park, Illinois, for two days' worth of shows come the tail end of May.

After the first matinee I leashed up Rajah and tickled his ears and said, "You and me and Al G. have something important to talk about. Something regarding *you*, my baby. Let's go see if we can catch him in." We walked through the lot at the same time the rubes were coming out of the after-show, so Rajah and I attracted a crowd of people trying to get close enough to have a look but not so close they were in danger of getting bitten. Rajah just licked his lips, like he was looking at breakfast, something that made them all laugh. They followed us past the freak banners to Al G.'s tent by the main entrance.

Dan was there when Rajah and I came in, so as politely as possible I told him Al G. and I had some personal business to attend to. This news doured his expression—suddenly it looked like pea soup brought to a simmer—and he looked over at Al G.

Al G. nodded it was okay and Dan left.

"Well, Kentucky," he said. "Caught your finale today."

"You did?"

"I did, just for old times' sake. No wonder the Ringlings want you so bad. Scares *me* every time I see it and I've seen it a hundred times if I've seen it once. Don't you worry Rajah will go rogue one of these days?"

"Rajah? Doesn't know the meaning of rogue."

"Let's just hope he keeps it that way. I'd hate to see you torn up before you go off to fame and fortune."

"Actually, that's what I wanted to talk to you about. Mr. Ringling wants to buy Rajah. He says he'll give you more than he's worth."

This set Al G. to thinking, though whether it was real thinking or Al G. pretending his plan was spur of the moment I couldn't be sure. He was pursing his lips and making a church steeple out of his fingers and pointing the taller ones into his forehead. He looked up and said: "It's Sunday, Kentucky. No show tonight. Why don't you and I go for dinner? We've known each other for almost ten years now and we've never once had dinner together. We'll paint the town red. Spend some cash. What do you say?"

Here I looked down at Rajah; my intention had been to spend the evening with him, as he'd been a little unsettled by the hysteria of the past week and had taken to getting into my underwear drawer and ripping what he found to shreds. At the same time, I couldn't bring him into town and there was no way I was going to miss this meeting with Al G. After I'd accepted the offer, Rajah and I went back to the car. While I dolled myself up I explained to him I had to go out, but to make it up to him I'd have one of the butchers bring by a hip bone. Hearing this, Rajah arfed and turned less mopey.

A half-hour later I inspected myself in the mirror. This was something I rarely did, for looking at myself without getting a clenched feeling in the pit of the stomach was a talent I'd never really developed. Far as I could tell, I had everything right. A drop-waist dress, tight at the top and bottom, with a belt that made my waist look like it was the same thing as my hips. A Japanese parasol made from oiled paper, and why women needed this for evening jaunts I didn't question, my having long accepted fashion as something intended not to make sense.

Buckled evening slippers with what they called lavatory heels. (Again, you tell me.) Velvet evening gloves. A chapeau that fitted the head like an elasticized salad bowl, my only opportunity for showing off my best feature being to pomade two tight little curls so they stuck out from the hat edge and curled around my ears. To top it all off, a fox stole with a clamp sewed into its mouth, so that even in death it could prevent slippage by chomping on its own tail.

Still, there was no denying the bloom was off the rose. The first problem was my arms and legs, which weren't as bad as they are today but were still a mess of scars; though the trend was to wear sleeves rolled to the elbows, I had to keep mine tight to the wrists, something that made me look a little grannyish. Likewise with dress hems, which were drifting up toward the knees, though for obvious reasons not on yours truly. And though I had a few minor nicks and scars on my face that could be disguised with foundation, that damn rip to my eye had done something permanent to the muscles in the eyelid. Truth was, it hung a tiny bit lower than its partner, the upshot being if you thought about my face for more than a few seconds you realized it was a little bit cock-eyed. Seeing this, I squeezed my eyes shut and took deep inhalations; there'd been people in Hopkinsville who'd looked this way, and by this I mean just not quite right in the face. Least I had tigers to blame.

I walked away from the mirror and knelt in front of where Rajah was lying. I cupped that face in my hands, whiskers tickling what little of my wrists were exposed. Two emeralds looked up as I said, "Look what you're doing to me, you naughty tiger. You're going to put men off me...." He grinned and licked his nose and generally practised being an imp and a tiger simultaneous.

When I was finished teasing him I kissed him and stood and looked in the mirror once more and took a deep, nerve-steadying breath. I stepped outside and saw a car waiting. A chauffeur was holding the door open, though most of what I could see inside was shadows.

There was, however, a leg protruding from the gloom, covered in striped material and ending in a polished spat, and my assumption was it belonged to Al G.

I got in the car and was proven correct.

That evening Al G. took me to one of the best restaurants in Chicago, and though I forget the name I remember the menu was all in French French and not the uncommon French they speak in the Bayou. The table was decorated with candles and fresh flowers and real silver, and there were men in tuxedos who wandered around playing whatever you wanted on the violin so long as you gave them a dollar afterwards. Al G. joked we should ask for something minor key and frigolet-ish, a joke that made me chuckle, though in the end he paid for "I Dreamt I Dwelt In Marble Halls," a song popular back then and one I liked because it was something I'd dreamt as well.

Was the twenties, you see, and with all that money starting to float around people were looking for new ways to spend it. Everything we ate that night had names I'd never heard before: Waldorf Salad and Lobster Newburg and Oysters Rockefeller and Baked Alaska. Before dinner we started with a brand-new drink that came in a long-stemmed glass with a cone-shaped bowl. They called it a martini, and it tasted a little like the ethyl propolene we used to run the generators (though with a hint of taste given by the olive plopped in the middle of it). The sight of all these people in expensive suits and fox stoles sipping these drinks like they were the nectar of the gods was enough to make me believe old P.T. had been right when he'd said the public could be made to believe anything. Hell, I even tried one myself. After two I could've yodelled from a mountaintop.

Still.

I figured we were here to discuss business, and around the time the white wine came, along with the funny salad crammed with nuts and apples and slices of celery, I upped and outed with it: "Al G. We have to talk about Rajah. Mr. Ringling needs an idea what he's going to cost."

Al G. looked weakened. His mouth shrivelled and his eyes rounded and his eyebrows slanted up and toward the middle, so that they looked like the sides of a pup tent. He wiped his mouth on a linen napkin and said, "Kentucky. *Please* ..." and without giving me enough time to figure out what that *please* was supposed to mean he started telling me about the first sideshow act the Barnes dog-and-pony ever employed, a prestidigitator with a sickness that made him keen on burning things to the ground. One night, when they were playing in a room above an Odd Fellows Hall, this particular prestidigitator went back to the hall in the middle of the night and did just that, the building reduced to a mound of cinders in minutes. The whole town got in a ruckus and when Al G. heard about it he knew what'd happened. In a flash he packed up his dog, his ponies, his performing mule and his Edison Vitascope and he hightailed it out of town before the rubes figured out the travelling show was the culprit. As he fled he kept looking over his shoulder and seeing smoke funnel toward the skies, and as he did he wished he had a pair of horses instead of two short-legged ponies incapable of flat-out running.

Course, it was a story that made me laugh heartily, for being chased by rubes is a panic I'd known once or twice myself. As I laughed, it occurred to me this was the best sort of story there is: sad then, funny now, with miles and miles of honest picked up along the way.

The fish came and after that a huge slab of meat, château something or other, that Al G. and I were meant to share. I lost count of the glasses of wine the waiter brought, though I do remember they kept changing colours, from white to garnet to a light green one we had with our flaming ice cream. Throughout, Al G. kept telling one story after another, and as the wine made me number and number and his stories made me giddier and giddier, I began to feel like a spoilsport for wanting to discuss matters of commerce. Afterwards we took a walk down Michigan Avenue, the Windy City not living up to its name that night for the air was balmy and still and the sidewalks full of people strolling. It felt good to be with someone I'd known for nearly a decade and had never rubbed the wrong way. It was like it proved something good about myself.

When Al G. finally brought me back to the train it was after one in the morning and I was drunk as a skunk and, for the first time in my life, wishing I could slough the next day's matinee off on someone else. Maybe it was the high time Al G. and I had just had, or maybe it was the fact I was going to be leaving soon, both of which are states of affairs that make people do things they've always wanted to do but never realized they wanted to.

What I'm saying is: I came a hair's breadth from inviting Al G. in, though thank God before the words came out of my mouth I gave my head a rattle and contented myself with a quick sisterly peck on the cheek. "Good night, Al G." were the last words out of my mouth. I went inside my stateroom, at first being quiet so as not to rouse Rajah, but then thinking the comfort of a body warm and soft was just the thing I needed. I undressed and got under the covers and stroked Rajah's cat ears, and as he started to purr I helped myself to some rubbing that made the front of me slick with coat oil.

Next day, the jump was to a place called Clinton, Illinois, and after that the circus started making long jumps south, training straight through the west tip of Kentucky and down through Mississippi before entering the state of Florida during a tropical storm that turned the Barnes show into a regular old mud show—we put a full ton of tanbark down on the midway and when it sank into the quagmire we switched to straw and when this didn't work we finally resorted to hay, only to see it eaten up by the mud and rain as well. Didn't matter, though. Folks couldn't get enough of the circus, and not only did the houses get filled but they got filled by people wanting to lighten their pockets. That year everyone on the show made more money than they would've ever thought possible, from the candy butchers to the chameleon vendors to the sideshow freaks. There were grifters who made so much money they left the show mid-season to buy small farms or ranches, saying they were bound and determined to straighten up and fly right and maybe even have a kid or two. Most were back by the end of the year, having lost their deeds in high-stakes poker games and looking not at all regretful.

From Talahassee and Baton Rouge we were on to Natchez, Mississipi, followed by Port Gibson and Vicksburg and Greenville and Clarksdale before making a 123-mile Sunday jump to Wynne, Arkansas, where cold damp weather again had no effect on the size of the houses. This was followed by another hundred-plus mile jump, this time to a place called Yellville, Kansas; seems the Yellvillians had never seen a live hippo before, and they were so fascinated by Lotus we could barely get them out of the menage to start the main performance. Then it was on to Colorado, Utah and Nevada before winding our way back into the state of California via the north end.

Now, all this is a matter of public record. What *Billboard* and *White Tops* and the dailies didn't know is in the top end of Mississippi, in a town called Holly Springs, Miss Leonora Speeks left the Al G. Barnes 4-Ring Wild Animal Circus. No one knew why—was a rumour her mother had passed away, something no one believed for she looked more aggrieved than grieved. All we knew is one day she was Al G.'s big-hipped wife and the next she was standing outside Al G.'s rail car, surrounded by trunks and suitcases and dress bags and hat boxes, looking exceedingly wronged. When her car came she let the driver move every piece of luggage while she stood looking impatient. Then she got in, flashing a last bit of leg for the workingmen.

There was one other thing *Billboard* and *White Tops* didn't know. While the well-endowed Miss Speeks prepared a divorce suit back in Oregon, Al G. Barnes, a man whose fortunes were growing by leaps and bounds, was turning his attentions to a certain blond tiger trainer whose fetching days may or may not've been behind her.

If there was a particularly good performance, say I'd gotten another cat to ball roll or sit up, there'd be flowers and a congratulatory note. Sometimes he'd come in the cookhouse when I was eating and sit with me; this gave me the status of management and was therefore hard not to appreciate. During an evening show someplace in Colorado, one of the cats, Lady was her name, got a little pissed off about something and took a swipe at my arm. It wasn't serious, though her nails had taken a good rip out of my white leather bodysuit. Instead of having Mrs. Mac, the head of wardrobe, stitch it up, I came back to my car and found three brand-new leather suits with a note from Al G. saying he couldn't afford to have his star act looking dingy out there (even if it was only for the rest of the year).

Then. During a matinee in Carson City I finally got that evil little Sumatran to ball walk. It'd taken over two years of gentling and was something you do for personal satisfaction only—though *Billboard* made a brief mention of Jewel's new trick, the vast majority of rubes never realized it was a trick once considered impossible, given how mean and pouncy Sumatrans are. Al G. noticed, though. Two mornings later, I was sitting in my car, resting, when there was a knock on the door. Al G. was standing there, alone. He was carrying a round cardboard tube.

"Good morning, Kentucky."

"Morning."

"Do you mind if I come in?"

"No," I said, stepping aside. "Please do."

He walked in, all smiles, saying, "I thought you might like to see my newest paper."

I said I would, and he walked over to Louis's old desk and pulled the master copy of a poster from the tube and laid it on the desk, flattening it down by leaning on it with either hand. I walked over and so did Rajah, who sensed something interesting was about to happen. I stood to Al G.'s left, and Rajah planted his forepaws to Al G.'s right, something that made Al G. a little nervous for he always believed it was only a matter of time before Rajah started acting like a normal tiger.

I looked down. My eyes turned misty.

The line running across the bottom of the poster read, "The Queen of the Jungle Presents a Notable Congress of the Earth's Most Ferocious Performing Lions and Tigers." Above it was a picture of my face, filling the whole poster. Furthermore, it was my face before I'd had accidents, back when I was unscarred and perfect, skin like porcelain, eyes as blue as Kentucky skies. Was like my face when I was eighteen, and as I looked at it one word kept popping into my head.

Before. *Before before before.*

Plus the poster was gold. The border was gold and my hair was gold and my uniform was gold, thick and pure and solid. This was something that never happened back then, gold being a colour printers had a tough time with, and it must've cost Al G. a fortune. But there I was, smiling and beautiful and eighteen again, in the first gold poster ever in the history of the circus. Was sheer stupidity, Al G. only being able to use it for another two months, but it was a stupidity that made me feel warm and wanted, and that's a feeling few women can resist. Even Rajah started purring, though I had to keep him away from the poster so he wouldn't paw it to shreds.

Later that week, when we pulled into San Franciso, Al G. took me to dinner again. Was a lot like the first time, there being a violinist and French on the menu and each wine a different colour than the wine previous. By the time we hit the meat course there was no doubt what was going to transpire when we returned to the train, something that made the rest of the meal practically solemn. We skipped dessert and rode back to the train in silence. We stopped in front of the Holt car, and he held the door for me. I took a good look around while Al G. poured apple brandy: the ceiling was dark wood and there were brass fixtures and a huge polar bear rug covering a floor made from beech. There was a hearth and a dining table for eight. The bed he escorted me to was framed in mahogany.

We never even sipped our drinks, for what commenced was a flurry of kissing and clothing removal, and the next thing I knew I was on my back, naked except for my jewellery, thankful the lights were dim and Al G. couldn't see my scars. Took his time, he did. I could tell he considered himself a Casanova of the highest order, for there were flourishes and fine touches and figure eights that simply didn't need to be there. He even suckled a part of me I thought men simply wouldn't, the sensation being one of astonishment more than anything else. Suppose I shouldn't complain, for there was a sureness and a slowness I'd never noted in a man before. Plus he was so handsome he didn't even lose his looks when it came to *that* moment, a time when most men's faces tend to flap slightly and lose their definition. He was gentle about it, too, meaning it all took a while, such that when he finally sped up and yelled, "Oh my Sweet Dinah," I was starting to feel a mild cramping in my upturned legs. To make him feel better I called out myself, something to do with the heavens above, and dug my nails into his shoulders.

Was then he pulled off me and a strange thing happened. With no more lust or desire between us, the situation attained a clarity and announced itself as surely as a new day announces *it*self. At exactly the same moment, we both understood why we were together, in Al G. Barnes's sumptuous rail car, and with that came a weight. It settled over us like a bank of heat. Was a weight that talked, too, meaning we didn't have to say a thing, the weight having the conversation for us.

Him: You still joining the Ringling show?

Me: You still refusing to sell Rajah?

Him *and* me, chiming together like a choir: *Yes*.

I dressed in silence, feeling slutty and used and guilty Al G. probably felt the same way. At the door I took a quick glance over my shoulder and had a last look at that handsome, handsome man, lying naked under a sheet, looking up at the ceiling, barely able to believe he hadn't got what he'd wanted. It must've been a shock to his system. Was the only time I ever saw him looking sad (and it still strikes me as odd that Al G. looking sad is the Al G. I picture whenever he comes to mind).

And what of me? What of Mary Haynie slash Mary Williams slash Mabel Roth slash Mabel Stark, soon-to-be Ringling star? What did *I* do? Went back to my car and pushed my face into Rajah's fur and bawled at the prospect of leaving him. Rajah woke but he didn't get playful or mad. He just lay there, quiet and listening, maybe licking his lips a few times. Was this bit of comfort that made me decide I couldn't do without him. So I got up and dressed and threw a few clothes into a bag and got Rajah off the bed and put a leash on him. I opened the door to my car and looked both ways.

The problem was I'd never stolen anything in my life, and if you're going to steal something as big as a 550-pound tiger it's good to get some practise beforehand. After all these years of hard work and trying to stabilize my life, here I was, in the dark, readying to flee, relying on nothing but reflexes and pluck *again*. Was a misery there I had to ignore if I was going to get this done, so I bucked myself up and whispered, "Come on, Rajah, there's a good boy." Doggone it if Rajah didn't pick that moment to grow a sudden attachment to the Al G. Barnes Circus, for he looked over his shoulder and gawked at the train and his whiskers turned down like a person regretful. Or maybe he saw the foolishness of a woman and her tiger just wandering off planless into a dark field, animals sometimes showing an instinct for preservation that most humans lack. Whatever it was, he planted his royal orange-and-black haunches. Just sat them in the dirt and refused to budge.

"C'mon, Rajah," I hissed, pulling hard on his leash. "Come *on*."

Course, there's no way even a large man can move an animal the size of a full-grown Bengal, though in times of desperation simple facts tend to get lost in the kerfuffle. By the time another half-minute of tugging had gone by, I was at a forty-five-degree angle from the ground, pulling with all my might, feet digging into the dirt, pleading through tears, "C'mon baby please please *please* we have to go...."

And then Dan appeared out of nowhere.

"Mabel," came a voice.

I stopped heaving, looked up and saw him, his expression saying what I was doing was cheap and felonious and worthy of pity all at the same time. I couldn't believe it. I hadn't even gotten off the lot and the jig was up. Feeling as though a pinprick had let any and all energy out of me I dropped the leash and half fell and half sat in the dirt. I couldn't look at Dan or Rajah, could only sit with my elbows on my knees and my face in my hands, feeling like an old scarred woman, even though I'd barely cracked thirty. Didn't even cry, for I didn't have the gumption, and believe me that's about the worst way in the world a person can feel.

Time got lazy playing itself out. It felt like we stayed in those positions, frozen like chess pieces, for minutes and minutes, though it was probably just seconds. Throughout, Dan just stood there, monitoring, while Rajah panted and for some damn reason looked pleased. Finally, I just got up and walked back to the rail car and left the door open, and when Rajah followed me in I closed the door and told him in a sharp voice he was sleeping on the floor.

I slept heavily and dreamless that night, and then woke late, feeling achy and tired. By the time I got to the lot Red had done more than half the work, which was bad for he was already mad enough at me for getting friendly with Al G. and not him.

What happened then is still a mystery. Maybe Dan had had a word with Al G. Maybe Al G. had stopped to consider how I'd feel if Rajah was taken from me. Or maybe he woke up remembering a circus owner is a businessman, first and foremost, and that the moment I left for the Ringling show Rajah would pretty much be worthless. *Or* (and this was the one I found the likeliest), maybe he couldn't stand the prospect of leaving a bad taste in a woman's mouth, particularly one he'd been with the previous night. All I know is I found an envelope with my name on it stuck to the door of my Pullman room. I opened it. Was an offer to sell Rajah the Wrestling Tiger for $10,000, roughly twenty-five times what a healthy trained adult Bengal went for in 1920.

Still, it was an offer, and I had it delivered to John Ringling, who apparently wrote out a cheque without thinking. I never even had a chance to thank Al G., Dan telling me he'd gone off to Nevada to over-see the construction of some house he was having built in the middle of the desert. After that, I finished out the season as quietly as possible. Word got round I was giving up the Barnes show for the Ringling show, and though there were a lot of congratulations and back-slapping there was a feeling on the lot I wasn't "with it and for it," which meant a slight frostiness every time I came upon a group of people. Or maybe it really was jealousy, something that brings out the worst in people. Mostly I spent my time with the tigers I'd have to say goodbye to.

The final show was sometime in late November in Tempe, Arizona. I didn't even go to the farewell party, just locked my door and listened to the hooting and hollering rage on outside while Rajah and I had a quiet evening in. Next day, the circus packed up and moved to temporary winter quarters in Phoenix, Arizona, the rumour being that divorce lawyers hired by Leonora Speeks were already picking apart everything back in Venice *and* Portland.

I spent the next day and a half reading and knitting and taking Rajah on field walks. Was a happy time, being alone with a cat and a rosy-looking future. Midway through the following afternoon, the eastbound came. A Negro porter deboarded, having been instructed to be on the lookout for a white woman, a steamer trunk and a housecat the size of a sofa.

PART TWO

THE RINGLING SHOW

CHAPTER 9

THE RINGLING ACCOUNTANT

☞ IT TOOK THREE DAYS TO GET RAJAH ALL THE WAY TO Bridgeport. At every whistle stop I'd gentle him and coo at him through wire mesh, and if the baggage hands were susceptible to flirtation I'd leash him and take him out for little walks around the rail yard, Rajah arfing and moaning when I put him back. He lost weight and piddled like an old person.

By the time we reached Bridgeport, there were already spots where his hair was growing sparse. A different winter quarters with different people didn't help much either. Within a week and a half, he was bald as a pool cue, *again*, meaning I was subjected to the usual jokes about my prize tiger and how if old P.T. was still alive he'd advertise him as a rare hairless sabretooth from the northern plains of Manchuria. I was living in a hotel in downtown Bridgeport that didn't allow pets, much less wild ones, and though Rajah spent all day following me around I still had to put him in a menage pen at night. Slowly he adjusted to his new life, though I do mean slowly: we'd been there a month and only small, plum-sized patches of hair had grown back, his coat looking more checkerboard than regal. Two weeks into the new year, I started to worry my famous wrestling tiger might not be ready for the season opener in New York City. Nervousness or no nervousness, he had to start working again.

That afternoon, I leashed Rajah and let him into the practise arena. He went to his pedestal, in fact he looked sharp doing so, which is why I suppose my guard was down. I turned my back and gave the signal and a second later I had a tiger around my shoulders, nuzzling the spot of neck between ears and back. He leaned his weight against me, this being Rajah's way of pushing me down and smothering me with fur and body. Lying under him, I felt pleased, so I said, "Good Rajah, that's real good," and to show he understood he purred and began a series of wriggles and warm undulations.

At which point a tapir wandered by.

Now I don't know if you've ever seen a live tapir. In this day and age there're zoos in pretty much every decent-sized city and the average person knows a whole lot more about animals than the average person in 1921, so I assume you have. But just in case you haven't, believe me when I say a tapir could just be the ugliest animal ever put on this green earth, and that's saying something given we also have pugs, duck-billed platypuses and the naked mole rat. In other words: wrinkly black body, a little like a donkey and a little like a horse and a little like neither, along with a face that'd be nothing worse than mopey except for a long, dong-like thing dangling where a nose should rightfully be. What this tapir was doing wandering free is anybody's guess, though at times the menage hands did let the gentler animals out when they cleaned their cages. Though it was strictly against the rules, it meant they didn't have to find other cages to put them in.

Anyway, I was lying there, peering through the gap between tiger and floor, when the tapir stopped and looked and let his face-dong waggle with curiosity. I suppose he'd never seen a big naked cat lying atop a woman before, and I suppose this bizarre sight inspired him to let out the screechy barking noise tapirs make when they want to comment on something. Suddenly I could feel Rajah's muscles clench, and I knew something was wrong. He growled, stood and started toward the tapir, who was braying like a lanced mule and waggling his dong-thing so furiously it was practically a blur. The one thing the tapir *wasn't* doing was backing away from the cage bars, common sense never being a trait among animals who defend themselves by looking weird enough to frighten.

Meanwhile, Rajah was stalking his way toward the outer cage, his ears back and his body low. It was clear once he reached the bars he was going to reach through and take the tapir's dong-thing clean off and probably its head right along with it. And while the thought of a dead tapir didn't upset me greatly, it was equally true I didn't have much clout with the Ringlings, seeing as so far my world-famous act had amounted to nothing but a bald tiger whose sorrowful arfing kept the other animals up all night. Under no circumstances could Rajah kill that tapir. By the time I figured this out, however, he was exactly one tiger step away, meaning all I could do was lunge forward, yell, "Rajah no!" and take hold of his tail.

Was sheer stupidity, my forgetting Rajah was tiger, for he chose that moment to take out all his perturbation of the past six weeks. Meaning: he turned and swung a forepaw full force at my head. He kept his claws in, which proves he was only trying to issue a complaint (though even if he had killed me I wouldn't have blamed him for it was my fault trying to work him so soon). In the end, it didn't make much difference who was at fault and who wasn't at fault, for I was lying flat on my back out cold. At least I was doing better than the tapir.

I woke up in the Ringling infirmary with a jackhammer for a head. When they asked me if I was all right I assured them I was fine, though in truth I was soon pestered by headaches and dizziness and, most worrisome, periods in which my hearing would go on the fritz, everyone sounding as though they were standing a long way off and mumbling. Around this time, I stopped kidding myself that Rajah would be ready for the season opener in New York. If I wanted to keep my reputation I needed to find something interesting and cat-like to train, and I needed to find it quick.

So I went for a good long walk through the Ringling menage. I'd done it before but this time I had my eyes peeled and that's a different experience altogether. I saw black bears, brown bears, grey bears and polar bears taken from Eskimo villages in Greenland. I saw nilgai, black bucks, aoudads, gemsbok antelope and the tapir bought to replace the tapir Rajah had beheaded. I saw six giraffes from the plains of Ethiopia; because of their specially built car, the Ringling circus had to be routed so it didn't encounter any tight tunnels or low bridges, which was possible only because the Ringlings owned half the railroads in the country. I saw hippopotamuses from the Transvaal, orangutans from Borneo, howler monkeys from British Honduras and tiny rhesus monkeys from the jungles of India (who by the way are the only monkeys on earth with a natural friendliness about them, chimps being testy and gorillas being grumpy and the orangs being out-and-out vicious). I saw Peruvian llamas, Ecuadorean pumas, Mexican macaws, Nicaraguan toucans and oscillated turkeys lifted straight from the jungles of Guatemala. I saw sea lions, sea elephants and sea turtles. Saw rhinoceruses, elephants and Jumbo the hippopotamus (who like Barnes's hippo was fed only water dyed red, it being the fashion back then for circus hippos to sweat what was supposed to be blood so they looked like something from the Book of Revelation). I saw kangaroos, koalas and hairy-nosed wombats. I saw bats and snakes and spiders and serpents and salamanders, all sideshow-bound. I saw camels and horses and zebras (though back then troupers called zebras convicts, owing to their stripes). I saw yaks and bison and Vietnamese water buffaloes. I saw a white stallion with a papier-mâché horn that'd be billed as a unicorn if someone could figure out how to stop the horn from shaking free every time the horse hiccuped. I saw pigs and Sicilian burros and goats and deer. I even saw a wild boar or two, with their tiny, pig-like eyes and wine-cork-length horns.

Plus I saw Nigger.

Now I know that's a dirty word today, but back then people used it all the time and if you want me to apologize for the sins of an age well maybe I should. Still, there's no denying when I first laid eyes on him, I was struck by how dark he was, darker than the darkest of the Negro stake drivers. Even in sunlight there wasn't a suspicion of purple in his coat or the spots that lay underneath; right then and there I decided I had to work him, a pure blackness being something that's mighty rare and beautiful to look at.

I admit there was also a healthy dose of my own vanity at work here, for until then there hadn't been a trainer in the history of the circus who'd tried working a jaguar, probably because every other trainer in the history of the circus had had the horse sense not to, jaguars being evil, flat-foreheaded beasts who in addition to suffering from extreme hostility are fast as greased lightning. The only upside was if they attacked, they were small enough you'd most likely survive.

This one had been bought by a Ringling animal hunter in Barbados and had been shipped to Bridgeport in a wooden crate. Throughout the trip he kept trying to batter his way out, so the Creole deckhands had driven nails through the sideboards. The upshot was the cat had gotten scratched and punctured and perforated on the way over, something that didn't help his disposition one iota.

I started breaking him. Thankfully, the rest of the act was trained, for it took all winter, hours and hours a day, a whip in one hand and a sawed-off broom handle in the other. Was ages before I even got Nigger to entertain the notion of taking a pedestal, and even then I had to put a second pedestal between the two of us, seeing as he had a bad habit of acting quiet and kitten-like before launching a sudden spitting swipe at the eyes. The key, of course, was rewarding him every time I drew close and he *didn't* launch one of those big muscled forepaws at my eyes (jaguars having paws of a size that wouldn't look out of place on a Sumatran).

I told him he was a good baby a hundred times a day. I dropped him enough hunks of beef to feed an adult lion, his nervous energy burning it off as fast as he could lap it up. When he was on his hind legs, pawing the air, I'd tickle his pleasure spot with the broom end, a niceness that confused him and made him spit. Then one day it happened. *You're a good cat* crossed his mind. You could see it pass over him. Just sat there, he did, head cocked, mulling the whole prospect over. Was as though I'd convinced him tenderloin wasn't good eating.

After that, Nigger was still miles from being docile, but he did start considering the possibility of being agreeable on the occasions when there was something in it for him. I got him to sit up, something he'd been doing all along, only now he was doing it for meat and not because he wanted to wave his claws in my face. Then I started sending him through hoops, his size and agility allowing him to jump twice as far as a tiger. Plus I got him to do tricks with the Bengals in the steel arena, something that wasn't supposed to be possible with a jaguar, no how, no way.

Late one afternoon, about two weeks before the season opener, I was sending the last of the Bengals through the cage tunnel when I smelled cigar. I looked over and realized John Ringling had been watching the whole thing. Though it was winter and the cat barn was chilly, there was no cause to be wearing a full-length Italian virgin wool coat and kid gloves besides. He looked at me for a few seconds, sucking on his cigar. Then he pulled it from his mouth and walked away, looking not at all displeased.

So.

April 22, 1921, Madison Square Garden, Ringling Brothers Barnum & Bailey Circus, the Greatest Show on Earth. We opened with a spec the Ringlings had been putting on for years called "The Durbur of Delhi." As the name suggested, it was East Indian in flavour, and included four dozen elephants, each mounted with a howdah and a waving red-dotted girl inside, two dozen stallion-drawn Roman chariots and a float done up to look like the golden dragon Chu Chin Chow.

Then came the aerialists, a picture act pure and simple, intended to please the senses rather than thrill. The bandmaster, Merle Evans, would spur the orchestra into something lush and romantic. Then thirty-six girls, each one dressed like an Andalusian, with red skirts and black net stockings and a rose between her teeth, would invert themselves and hang from a rope crooked through the knee. Then they'd rotate slowly and in syncopation, bathed in red and green and gold, their arms extended and their smiles fluorescent. Was a thing of beauty, seeing all those young women rotate in tandem, particularly if you consider slow precision a form of beauty. Plus a lot of chest area was caught by swirling light, giving the dads in the audience something to remember now that the citizen groups had pretty much railroaded cooch into carnivals and burlesque halls and the lowlier wagon shows. After a few minutes, the music would wind down and the girls would get lowered to the big top floor and Fred Bradna—top hat and monocle in place —would announce, "Ladies and gentlemen, all eyes on the centre ring steel arena ..."

In other words, me. The Ringlings believed the cat trainer should go on soon as possible so they could get the steel arena out of the way early. With an orchestra blare I came in wearing my white leathers, waving and smiling and cracking my whip for effect. Then came the tigers: eight of them, beautiful Bengals all, beef fed and straw bedded and mighty pawed, their coats gleaming from egg baths and visits with a real veterinarian. Then it was Nigger's turn, lurching down the tunnel, looking left and right.

The audience hushed, for Nigger started pacing the arena like a caged animal, which I suppose was fair though it upset me anyway. I followed him at a respectful distance while shouting, "Seat, Nigger! *Seat!*" When this didn't work I kept trying to cut him off to get him to his pedestal, which is impossible to do in a circular arena, Nigger doubling back and crossing behind the line of Bengals. I finally got him on the pedestal around the seven-minute mark, the time at which the display would normally be over.

Truth is, I was starting to get nervous, for the Ringlings were sticklers for punctuality, believing flow was what made a circus and not the contribution of any single act or performer (the one possible exception being the elephants). So I flowed. Or leastways I tried to. Sent the Bengals through their sit-ups and rollovers and hoop jumps as fast as was possible, forgetting Nigger completely until it came time for the finale. This was the only trick I couldn't excuse him from, for he was the top, and without him I would've just had a bunch of tigers sitting in an odd-looking clump instead of the world's first tiger-topped-with-jaguar pyramid.

He wouldn't do it. Just plain refused. As the Bengals took their positions, he kept taking little runs at me from his seat, which I'd fend off by sticking my broomstick into his mouth. Or I'd pull out my gun and fire blanks in his face, cats not being fond of loud noises or the smell of gunpowder. He'd slink back to his pedestal and snarl and glare and generally do everything in his power to look menacing. It was around then the world went silent.

It didn't particularly bother me, my damn hearing picking that moment to up and go, for blocking out all the noise and clamour did help me focus on the problem at hand, something I sorely needed with a pissed-off jaguar lunging at me every few seconds. It was like we were alone together, everything quiet and thick as though underwater. Meanwhile, I had to keep an eye out for the Bengals, for even the best tiger on earth will turn ferocious if it detects a weakness in its trainer. In other words, I had a lot on my plate. By the ten-minute mark I was soaking wet. Around the twenty-minute mark, John Ringling himself left his box and came arena-side and started yelling, "Give it up, Mabel!" Truth was, I couldn't hear the man, didn't even know he was there, though later I was told he went pink in the face and the skin padding his chin started to wobble. Even if I *had* heard him I probably wouldn't've obeyed for if a cat wins a battle even once you can never work that animal again. At the thirty-minute mark I decided I was good and angry, and to hell with who was watching and any sensibilities might be involved. So I walked up to that snarling almond-eyed devil and I stared him straight in the eye and I unnerved him by smiling.

Was a move dangerous and foolhardy and one resorted to only in the spirit of absolute frustration, for I was offering up my body as a target: had he leaped, there would've been nothing but nothing I could've done. This was the point, for I'd found in the past if you show an animal you trust them completely it can have a calming effect. Course, I'd forged this theory with Rajah and trained Bengals and not on a bitter black jaguar who still yearned for palm trees and warm ocean trade winds. I tried it anyway. Instead of springing, he looked at me perplexed, as if to say, *Now what could she be up to?* Then he relaxed. You could practically see the tension flow out of his shoulders and jaw. Next thing I knew he was jumping off his pedestal and not just moving to the top of the pyramid but moving there sharply. The applause came in the form of a roar, which I heard because my hearing had come back, though to my left ear only, meaning for a second I thought one half of the tent had liked the trick and the other half for some reason hadn't. Sightlines, I figured.

As I exited through the blue curtain, the performers from the next display all patted me on the back and said, "Way to show 'em, Mabel! Way to hang tough!" Was a case of them being nice, I figured, so I headed straight to my car and collapsed beside Rajah and spent a long, miserable night holding my tiger. Here I'd been paid to provide flow and spectacle, and instead I'd taken thirty minutes to get an animal no bigger than a large dog to move from one seat to another. Mighty impressive. As I didn't sleep well, I slept late, wakening to the sound of knocking on my car door.

I answered with a robe wrapped around me. A Ringling porter told me he had a delivery from Mr. John Ringling, and when I moved out of the road a second porter who'd been standing to the side carried in the largest bouquet of red roses I'd ever seen in my life, each one long stemmed and prickly as yours truly. I could barely even see the second porter for the foliage, the bouquet looking as though it'd sprung a pair of legs and was using them to walk in on. I spent the next ten minutes counting them, giving up around the hundred mark, though I suspected I was looking at a gross of flowers, poking out in every angle conceivable from a brass vase the size of a saloon tub. It took up most of the back half of my stateroom.

"Look, Rajah," I squealed, and he jumped off the bed and came over and bit at one of the flowers, whimpering and jumping back when a thorn caught his lip. Seeing this, I laughed and suggested we get some air, though I was thinking more that I had to get outside and prove to myself this was really happening. I got dressed and leashed up Rajah and went to the corner newspaper box and there it was: a front-page article in the *New York World* saying how a girl weighing one hundred pounds wet had provided the greatest thrills during the opening show of the Ringling Brothers Circus, 1921 season. Note: it hadn't been Cadona or Con Colleano or Emil Pallenberg or May Wirth or Bird Millman or Luciano Christiani or Poodles Hannaford or that prima donna Lillian Leitzel. It'd been *me*.

Later that week, *Liberty* magazine caught up with the show and did an article on Mabel Stark. This got followed up by bits in *Collier's* and *Saturday Evening Post* and *Harper's* and local papers by the score. I did radio interviews too, dulling down my hick accent as much as was possible. In every one I promised I'd be working a wrestler by mid-season, which of course they believed as they'd all heard about Rajah from my Barnes days. One day, about a week after we left New York City, the train got adjusted and I found my suite had been moved, so I was up near the wire walker Bird Millman and the trick rider May Wirth, though way back from the entire cars occupied by John and Charles Ringling. Hacks started coming around, wanting to write my life story, promising best-sellers and maybe even a movie. Was fame, this, all because I'd sweet-talked a fierce-tempered jaguar into taking a pedestal. Once I got Rajah wrestling again I figured I'd get even more of it, a possibility that made me so excited I had to force myself to breathe deep every time I thought about it.

Now, the funny thing about fame is you start believing you're the cause of it and not the press agents. You read the articles and you believe every word, especially if it drowns out suspicions you've been trying to drown out as long as you care to remember. Believe me. The flip side of having your insides moulded by sadness is that with a minimum of encouragement you start considering yourself the second coming, someone they're probably going to invent an antidote to old age for. Here's an example of how skewed and wonky this celebrity business makes your thinking, particularly if it sneaks up and bushwhacks you the way it bushwhacked me: not once did it occur to me that having my face plastered in every newspaper in the country might not be such a good idea, seeing as I was a woman with a past and still considered a fugitive in certain parts *of* that country.

From New York City we started acting like a circus, packing up after every evening show and travelling through the night, cherry-picking our way through Pennsylvania and Maryland and the Virginias. We stayed in towns with fine lots and populations sufficient to pack a big top that held twelve thousand people, more with straw bundles down. We headed southwest, sleeping on good mattresses and eating good food off tables set with linen, china and fresh-cut flowers. (Course, in the workingmen's cookhouse things weren't quite so civilized.) By March we slipped into Kentucky, doing one show in Lexington before moving on to Louisville, and if that bony-arsed old aunt of mine was in the audience she sure wasn't carrying a sign to let me know about it. From there we jumped to Bowling Green, which is in the middle of the state though slightly off to the west side and near the Tennessee border. We played two straw houses there, people needing something to spend their money on now that liquor wasn't an option (or leastways a legal one). The draft, war, prohibition—back then it seemed like everything, bad or good or somewhere in between, worked out well for the circus.

After my evening performance I was feeling a little tired and a little worried about Rajah, who was still foraging through my underwear drawer when I wasn't with him, ripping and tearing and shredding whatever he got his paws on. I'd tried washing them in bleach, thinking maybe his nose picked up a scent not removed by normal laundering. When this hadn't worked I'd finally resorted to bagging them and slinging them between two hooks I'd screwed into the ceiling of the car. Often I'd come home and find Rajah on his hind legs, taking swipes while breathing hard.

With the idea of saving my undies I decided to leave shortly after the intermission, before Bird Millman's wire walk and May Wirth's backward somersault from one moving horse to the next and Lillian Leitzel's left-handed planges and Alfred Cadona's triple somersault. Because I left early, the midget brigade wasn't ready to escort single ladies back to the train so I set out alone. It was a short walk, through a neighbourhood of rickety low-standing wood buildings lit by naked light bulbs, in a part of town deserted and therefore quiet, which I suppose had a lot to do with it being circus night.

I could hear my heels clacking against the pavement, steam escaping from pavement grates and tabby cats mewing. After walking a couple of blocks, I reached the point where I could continue on the main street, taking a left after a couple of blocks and then doubling back so as to reach the rail yard using the major streets. This would take another twenty minutes. My other option was to sneak through an alleyway running into a long, thin, dark space separating a box factory and a tenement. This route would take two minutes, and we'd been warned by the lot manager not to use it. Everybody did anyway.

I entered the alley. To my left was the sound of people talking and arguing and laughing and being randy. To my right was clanking. I walked quickly, having great confidence in my own surefootedness, and as I walked I was conscious of the grime existing on the walls inches from my shoulders. The alleyway jogged slightly and I passed through a pitch-black courtyard, picking up the alley on the other side. In the distance I saw a rectangle of light and the rail cars beyond. I think I slowed my walking a titch, though I can't say for sure. What I do remember is the smell of the hand that darted from an alcove and smothered the lower half of my face, the crook between thumb and forefinger clamped beneath my nose. In moments like these the senses sharpen, and I could pick out sweat and leather and tobacco and dirt and the salt of male seed. The hand was big, too, meaty and plump and no stranger to rough work. The other hand grabbed my right wrist and bent it around back until the muscles in my upper arm screamed. Without a word, only rough breathing, he turned me around and frogmarched me in the direction I'd come. A tear dribbled out of my left eye and dampened his hand and I wondered if I could soften his resolve with the wetness of it.

He marched me toward the courtyard but instead of picking up the other half of the alleyway he turned me right into the gloom and after a few steps I made out a parked jalopy. He stepped me up to the hood of the car and moved his hand away from my mouth and put it on the back of my head and slammed the side of my face into the hood. I was silent despite the pain for I figured probably my life depended on it. Was never a word spoken, just him roughly grabbing the top of my skirt and panties and yanking them straight to my ankles, exposing my ass to the night air, me suddenly knowing what this was all about and wanting to die because of it.

Then the man lifted his right hand in the air and brought it down hard on my buttock, making a slap would've been heard a full block away were it not for the clanking sounds of the factory. I yelped, and was preparing for Sodom-like humiliations when he reached down and seized the waist of my skirt and panties and with a single violent jerk pulled them back into place. Then my arm was forced behind my back and the other arm was forced to meet it, and when my wrists were crossed I felt a rope binding them together in a tight, scratchy knot. He pulled out a long red bandana and twirled it in the air so it went into a tube. When this was done he pushed it against my mouth, the force of it parting my teeth and chafing against the corners of my mouth. My tongue was forced to the back of my mouth and I started gagging. Was this in combination with pure dog fear that made tears skitter down my cheeks and jawline and by the time they'd dribbled down my neck they'd gone cool. He pulled at my collar and spun me around. He was breathing heavily, and while he caught his breath I took my first look at his unshaven face through eyes gone so wide I couldn't've shut them if I'd tried. I could feel a welt coming up on the side of my face and a palm-shaped bruise on my buttock, and it was the understanding this violence was really happening that made my nose get so snotty I could barely breathe through it. His arm shot out, and I prepared to be hit, though instead what he did was seize the back of my collar and spin me around again and march me to the passenger side door.

He opened the door and pushed my head down and shoved me into the car and ordered me to stay there or next time I'd get myself a spanking that'd leave my ass as raw as the Dakotas in winter. One of my feet was still a little ways out of the car, the man kicking at it until I pulled it inside. He slammed the door behind me and locked it.

He got in himself and started the engine, and when it came to life it belched and farted and generally sounded like an old man sputtering at the end of a nap. He backed it up and took a lane bisecting the blackness in the other direction. I didn't know what my survival would or wouldn't depend on, so I blinked away tears and forced myself to look hard at everything. I figured I was being driven to another grey tenement, or maybe a farmhouse way in the country, where I'd be held, barely fed and subjected to round-the-clock buggery until the life was gone from me. In other words, I was on the lookout for avenues of escape. Being trussed up like hog bound for slaughter made it difficult to imagine one, so I was visited with a single overriding thought: *Why in Sam Hill didn't you bring Rajah?* I spent the rest of the car ride imagining what Rajah would've done to the driver and believe me it was as bloody as bloody gets.

We drove through streets with broken lights. I kept hoping we'd pull up beside a cop on the beat and he'd notice that the woman in the passenger side was gagged with a bandana turning wet with gob, snot and tears. Course, it didn't happen, there never being a cop around when you need one (and cops back then tending to work on a user-fee system anyway). I kept taking quick glances at the driver, who was dark and hairy at the neck. He wore an overcoat in need of repair, which I mention to show how crazy the brain goes in moments of extreme stress: I saw that frayed brown fabric and for a moment felt sorry for him and the circumstances that could make a boy grow up as foul and bad-smelling as he was. Meanwhile, I watched where we went, hunting for information that might be useful should escape present itself. Was impossible. The car kept taking turn after turn after turn, the steering wheel big and plastic and grooved and grey and tilted forward like a bus's.

When we stopped in front of a police station everything finally started making sense.

He shut off the motor and, as he walked around the back of the car, it clanked and sputtered and caused the car to shudder. After flinging open the side door he grabbed hold of my right upper arm and pulled hard, saying the second thing he'd ever say to me: "Out."

With that, I was on my feet and getting marched into the precinct. It seemed to me I wasn't the first person to ever get this brand of treatment, for when we came bursting through the doors not a single head turned. The man pushed me up to the desk sergeant, and once again I was flung forward, the front of me hitting the wooden desk.

"Here," he barked, and walked out.

They'd been expecting me. The desk sergeant, a jowly owl-shaped man with no hair and considerable midriff, nodded and came around and took my arm and double-timed me to the back of the station where the cells were. We passed the lock-up holding that evening's allotment of drunks and reprobates, and of course seeing a women with her hands bound sent them to hollering whatever lewdnesses came to mind. I glanced over and recognized a few of the workingmen in there and was glad they were paying me the honour of not yelling out vile, venal things like the others.

We finally stopped in front of a small cell holding one other woman. The sergeant told me to turn around, and when I did he untied the gag and the rope binding my wrists. My jaw ached and my wrists came away chafed and sore. The sergeant then opened the cell door and I considered it a small measure of kindness when he more guided me than shoved me inside. He locked the door with a clang and walked away, hollering, "Pack it in!" when the lock-ups started yelling how he was fat as a pig and smelled like one besides.

The jail fell silent. I sat on the bunk not occupied by the woman, who'd obviously been working the same streets we'd driven through to get there: the heaviness of her makeup spoke volumes. Now that the immediate danger was over, my heart leapt into overdrive, and the nerves in my head started firing so fast the cell filled with shards of colour. It took a minute of slow, even breathing to get me in a state one ratchet down from panic. I closed my eyes and tried to moisten my lips. I also thought about saying hello to the woman but could see she wasn't in the mood for chatter as she hadn't so much as glanced in my direction. Impatient, was the way she looked, for she was loudly chewing her gum and bouncing a foot in the air.

The long and short of it is I was there all night, not a phone call offered or a word spoken or bread and water brought. I was too revved up to sleep, the sense of boredom and containment soon getting harder to tolerate than what I was going to have to face come morning. Sometime in the middle of the night, with the men in lock-up snoring like wood splitters, two guards approached the cell. I kept still, hoping whatever they were there for had nothing to do with me. My cellmate took the gum out of her mouth, stuck it to the metal cot and approached the bars. There was whispering between the two guards before one sort of stood aside while the other crowded the bars.

Even though I was on the far side of thirty and spent my days working side by side with workingmen, there were still ways I was a little naive. As the woman sauntered toward the bars, I honestly thought her time was up and she was about to be released, the only thing striking me as odd was them doing it in the middle of the night.

Next thing I knew the woman had dropped to her knees and I could hear the sound of a zipper being pulled and I realized what was happening was the same thing I'd seen in that sepia photo of Dimitri's so long ago. The slurping sound lasted maybe a minute, the guard throwing his head back and emitting a noise like an after-meal burp. He zipped up, and a second later the other guard was pushed against the bars and helping himself to the sepia treatment as well; he finished pretty much like the first, after which the woman stood and wiped her mouth with the back of her hand. The first guard then detached a key ring about as big around as a dinner plate from his belt. He opened the cell and let the woman out. The three walked off, and that was the last company I had till daybreak, when another guard brought a red wooden tray holding a bowl of cold oatmeal and toast and chicory coffee as thick and tasty as gravel.

I sat glumly chewing. Once I finished eating what I wanted, which wasn't much, I put the tray on the other bed and sat with my hands folded in my lap, desperately missing trains, rubes, cats, Rajah, applause, the smell of elephants, anything circus. Meanwhile, the place was getting loud. People were screaming they had to get out and they needed to call their lawyer and they were innocent and they knew their rights. Some of the others were screaming for dope, which was worse, for they added a layer of racket that was high-pitched and frenzied and that worked at your nerves like a fork. Every ten minutes or so a guard would come walking down the hallway clacking his billy club against the cages and shouting, "Pack it in goddammit, pack it *in!*" and the noise would stop for two, maybe three, minutes. Then it'd start up again, a murmur at first then growing into a roar. Was like cycles, and I occupied those early hours listening to it flood and recede, flood and recede. Outside, the sun was barely above the horizon.

As the morning progressed it got hot and airless in the station, which added smell to the whole equation; after a time I got so bored and anxious I thought I might even do some yelling myself and probably would have had I not still been clinging to the whispery notion I was a circus queen and had to act as such. Was then a pair of guards came walking down the hallway accompanied by a man with mussed hair and the pissed-off expression of someone who'd been woken early. He wore a suit and carried driving gloves in his hand, which he waved around as though he was directing traffic.

All three stopped in front of my cage. I looked up and immediately felt like I recognized the man who wasn't a guard—was the thinning sand-coloured hair, the wire spectacles, the jowliness of the bottom half of the face. In fact, it looked like a face I'd spent a goodly amount of time trying to forget, and as soon as *this* thought passed through my head I knew who it was. I was looking up at Horace B. Sights, Superintendent, Western State Hospital for the Mentally Insane, Hopkinsville, Kentucky.

That son of a horse's ass just eyed me, stretching the moment out, for it was clear he'd been waiting for this a long time and was delighted it was finally happening. He even made a show of taking off his glasses and wiping them on a starched white handkerchief before perching them back on his nose; was as though he was saying *I would-n't want to make a mistake, Officers, no I wouldn't want that*.... Then his beady, raincloud-coloured eyes roved up and down my body, and it wouldn't've surprised me if I'd found out he was picturing me nude, specifically those parts of me he'd poked and prodded every time he'd inspected me for female irregularity. He even stroked his chin, as though he had a thoughtful side he wanted to put on display.

He turned to one of my jailers and nodded.

"You sure?"

"Oh yes," Sights answered.

The three stared for a while longer, and when the guard in charge turned and gestured that he could go Sights hesitated a little and said, "May I speak with her?"

The two guards looked at each other, for a long time actually, as if they were inspecting each other's mouth corners for yolk. Finally, the one in charge shrugged, pulled his keys, opened the cell door and said, "Five minutes."

Sights sat. He looked at me, stared at me, in fact, letting a wrinkly little worm-wriggle of a grin infect the right side of his lips. Was probably the happiest he'd been in years. Mostly I kept my eyes on the floor, though I kept taking fleeting glances at his smirk, true ugliness being something difficult to keep your eyes away from.

He spoke. "I just wanted you to know something, Mrs. Aganosticus."

Here he obviously wanted me to mutter, "Oh really, what's that?" so I didn't say boo, though I did shudder at hearing myself called by Dimitri's surname.

"It wasn't hard figuring out how you escaped, Mrs. Aganosticus. Your blessed Dr. Levine admitted it the moment we confronted him. In fact, he seemed quite proud of it. He accused me of practising barbaric treatment methods. Of course, it's against the law to aid the escape of a lunatic so I just wanted to know what you did to persuade him, hmm-mmmm? I imagine a woman such as yourself has ways of being persuasive, hmmmmmmm?"

Here he looked me up and down as lecherously as is humanly possible.

"Four months in jail. Too bad. He was an educated man. Kind, sensitive, gentle. A *Jew*, and you know how much they enjoy the pleasures of the mind. Cerebral pursuits were more his cup of tea. Ill-suited for prison life, I'm afraid."

He got up and crossed the cell and sat so close our legs touched. I wiggled away, and then noticed it out of the corner of my eye: a bulge in his pants the size of a banana. Sights started whispering inches from my left ear: "No one makes a fool of me. No one. Two days from now you will be back in my care. Two days, Mrs. Aganosticus. *My* care."

Hearing this, I stared ahead, thinking there was no way I was going to give him any satisfaction, so even though I was trembling inside I acted like a tiger would've, meaning my eyes narrowed and my jaw muscles flexed and in a voice gone as bitter as possible I said, "Yeah well go fuck yourself."

At this he attempted a laugh though it sounded false and in that there was the smallest of victories. Then he stood, walked to the bars and waited for the guards to spot him.

So. What did Mary Haynie slash Mary Aganosticus slash Mary Williams slash Mabel Roth slash Mabel Stark slash Mabel the Jailbird *do*? I did what people always do in times of deep and grievous stress: I waited until Sights had slunk off before flopping on my knees and clasping my hands and peering up like an altar girl. My eyes were wet from pure fear.

"Dear Lord," I started, "I know I've done some bad things in my life, but it seems to me I've been punished enough, especially considering I *try* to be a good person, I really do, you have to admit I do bring smiles to people's faces and I do make them forget about dry growing seasons and the price of feed and wars going on in Europe. Please, Lord, I wouldn't ask you except I've got no one else to turn to, I really don't, but if you could see me through this one little jam I promise I won't feel entitled to your kind deeds ever again and will work hard to make it up to you."

After that, I got good and tired. I'd had a long day and a longer night and an even longer morning, and suddenly I'd had it. I lay down on the tissue-thin mattress and guarded my chest with my knees like a baby and had myself a long happy dream about being a normal woman. One with kids and a husband and a house and a calmness of spirit. Later I awoke and got up and looked out the tiny window at the back of the cell and saw that the shadows cast by trees had grown long. A woman looking pretty much like the woman who'd been in the night before sat on the bunk opposite, no doubt waiting to sepia her way out.

I was still tired so I lay down again, though I was disturbed by a guard bringing me a supper of chipped beef and bone-dry potatoes. I tried to eat, couldn't, and lay down with my eyes open. About twenty minutes later a guard came by. He was more boy than man, still fighting acne and gawkiness. While unlocking the cell he looked at me and said, "Ma'am. This way please."

I stood, fighting sniffles. As far as I knew a bus was waiting to take me back to Hopkinsville and whatever horrors Sights was having fun thinking up for me. I kept my head down as I shuffled, trying to shut everything out and muster courage. The daylight, though it was waning, made me feel worse for I knew it'd be the last I'd see in a while. For a moment I thought about bolting, or hollering for mercy, or crying like a girl, none of which would've helped. The guard trailed behind me, steps matching mine. At the front of the station he pushed open the door and said, in a way practically made me swallow my tongue with surprise, "I'm a big fan, ma'am."

He pushed open the door, signalling I was going out while he was staying in. I suppose he saw the confusion scribbled all over my face, for he said, "You're free to go, ma'am" and nodded toward the street. There, parked at the curb, was a car. A nice car. Plus a man was holding the door open with his left hand. In his other was a bouquet of white tulips he handed over when I approached.

"Good evening, Miss Stark," the man said, smiling and holding out a gloved hand. "My name is Mr. Ewing. Albert Ewing. I'm the Ringling Brothers' accountant. John and Charles Ringling asked me to deal with this matter personally. I can assure you they were incensed. Enraged, actually. It's a pleasure to finally meet you."

I took his hand. Was the handshake of a man who'd never gripped anything tight in his life, and given the last hand I'd felt on my body it was a welcome change.

"On behalf of Mr. John and Mr. Charles and myself I'd like to apologize for any, er, discomfort you might have experienced while a ward of the city. I assure you we did everything in our power to secure your release as soon as was possible. Would you care to join me?"

He stood aside and I got in. After closing my door he walked around the car and climbed in and asked the driver to go. Then he turned to me and said, "I'm afraid the circus has left Bowling Green, so we'll have to catch up to them in Nashville."

I leaned back, enjoying the feel of soft leather. The whole car smelled unused.

"You know," he said, "if you don't mind my saying, you might want to secure yourself some management. Such a move might prevent these sorts of occurrences in the future."

"*Will* these sorts of occurrences occur again?"

"Probably not. There were some negotations. They went rather smoothly, all things considered."

"What about Sights?"

"I suspect he won't be bothering you again."

227

No doubt the Ringlings had bought his co-operation as well. Mind you, there was a possibility that Sights had refused, given his thirstiness for revenge, so I asked what happened. This caused the accountant to go a little quizzical about the mouth and eyes.

"Well, of course, I don't know. I wasn't there. Apparently there were discussions. At first Mr. Sights didn't understand that a Ringling star is, well, beyond reproach."

"What kind of discussions we talking about, Mr. Ewing?"

Here his face broadened into the grin.

"As far as I understand it they were, well, *discussions*."

Funny how sometimes a euphemism can be like music to the ears. A deep contentment took root, the kind that comes from feeling powerful. Was as though I was friends with gangsters or politicians or people with money, and that's a sensation everyone should have a least once a lifetime. I closed my eyes and thanked God for helping me out. I rode this way for quite a while, not sleeping but relaxing, and when I opened my eyes again I had a good long look at the side of Mr. Ewing. He was a medium-sized man, with freckled baby-soft skin, thin curly hair and some mild lumpiness around the jawline. On the plus side, he had dimples and high cheekbones and green eyes. Even though he was slightly younger than me, thirty at the most, he carried himself with the weight of a fifty-year-old, and if the truth be told weariness is something I've always thought looked good on a man. Plus what was left of his curls was a pleasing shade of marigold.

All of this I mention because when I opened my eyes he was in the process of taking a good long gander at the tightness of my leather costume, particularly as it pertained to the length of my left leg. (I always did have nice gams—comes from chasing after tigers all day.) Had he known I was watching he no doubt would've pretended he was fascinated with the floor of the car or the workmanship of my boots. But seeing as how he *didn't* know I was watching there was no denying a simple fact, one I could either do something with or leave completely alone.

All eyes, he was.

We got married halfway through the season, during a three-day stand in Portland, which I picked because my divorce happened there and I figured my divorce had worked out a damn sight better than any of my marriages. Both Ringling and Barnes troupers came, though more of the latter seeing as I'd been on the Ringling show for only six months and was having my usual trouble making friends. I wore white—cheeky, I know—but by then white was my signature colour so I figured I had an excuse bordering on legitimate. Rajah was my best man, he and I turning heads when he walked me to the altar. There I handed him off to my Barnes tunnel man, Red, who Rajah had always liked and respected and had never once tried to eviscerate. They both took seats in the front pew, Rajah for the most part behaving himself though afterwards Albert and I did get invoiced for one chewed-up Bible and one torn-to-shreds book of wedding Psalms.

There were streamers and daffodils and a soprano with piper, all of it tasteful and sophisticated and too good for the likes of a farm girl from the ugly end of Kentucky. My only disappointment was Al G. wasn't there, though he did send a telegram expressing his condolences; thankfully, he hinted his wranglings with Leonora Speeks were the culprit so I didn't blame the weight that settled over us the last time we'd seen each other. The only other invitees who couldn't make it were John and Charles Ringling, Mr. John having gone off to Italy on an art-buying trip and Mr. Charles looking at a four-hundred-year-old violin someone had turned up in an attic in Durban, South Africa. To apologize, Mr. John sent me another gross of roses. Mr. Charles must've heard this, for the day of the event he sent a bouquet containing two gross in an arrangement the size of a Ford.

When we got to the part where the minister asked the question answered by "I do," he had to ask it twice for my hearing picked that moment to go on the fritz. After an uncomfortable pause, I realized what everyone was waiting for, so I said, "I do," and Albert said, "I do," and we both signed the book and then we all went to the New Westminster Hotel where we had a sit-down dinner for forty, speech making and dancing and cavorting afterwards. Fred Bradna, the French-born ringmaster, was the emcee, and he made a toast wishing us a long and happy future after joking that he knew Albert would be as "tame and tractable as all the other wards of Mabel's stable." At this everyone but everyone laughed.

Course, *White Tops* and *Billboard* were there—*ravenous* is the word comes to mind when I think about reporters—so to give them something good I did a quick two-step with Rajah, who I could tell had had a few sips of the hooch being brought in through the service entrance. Practically placid he was, and more in step than usual. He didn't even blink when flash pods went off.

We danced till three in the morning, which was probably longer than Albert cared to, seeing as by one in the morning he seemed pretty eager to get up to the room. Naturally, this ran counter to my desire to stay out of the room as long as possible, seeing as I was a woman who'd never had much luck in the wedding-night department. Still, there came a time when he approached me with that look men get, half Valentino and half child wanting a cookie, and I realized I'd have to face the music sooner or later. We went upstairs. Of *course* there were flowers and of *course* there was champagne in a bucket. After a bit of preliminary kissing, I asked Albert to turn out the lights. We both undressed and climbed into bed and came together and it was:

Fine. No inabilities or weird noises. Nothing I felt too much or not at all. Nothing made me want to break out laughing. Nothing left chafe marks or bruising. Nothing produced rank odours or odours period. Was just a good old-fashioned man-on-top roll in the hay, and without a lot of fussing or frills, so it had the advantage of not taking all night. (Sorry, Al G., wherever you are.) Albert was even gentlemanly enough to stay awake until after I'd fallen asleep, something I'd never had happen before, there being something about losing their seed that makes men as drowsy as a snake in hot weather.

Throughout the rest of the 1921 season Albert and I settled into a life of quiet ordinariness, or at least as ordinary as a pair of circus people could ever hope for. My days I spent fussing with my Bengals and Rajah and Nigger. Albert spent his days in the red car, fidgeting with the books, as he'd been hired specifically to look for ways to trim the budget. This was no easy feat, given he worked for a circus that, each and every day, went through three hundred pounds of butter, three hundred gallons of milk, twenty-five hundred pounds of fresh meat, two thousand loaves of bread, fifteen hundred pounds of fresh vegetables and two hundred bushels each of oats, ice, coffee and loose tea. "And that," Albert moaned one night, "is just for the humans. Have you ever counted how many elephants are out in that menage? Four dozen. Four *dozen*. Of course, I suggested to Mr. John if he sold off a few it would help things considerably. 'Wonderful idea, Al,' he told me. 'Wonderful idea. I'll get on that immediately.' The next day he bought a half-dozen more from a circus that had gone out of business and was stranded in the middle of a farmer's lot in Oklahoma. He told me he couldn't afford *not* to buy them."

I'd listen attentively and then give Albert a shoulder rub, my latest husband being a man who took things too seriously for his own good. Meanwhile, Rajah would watch, his head cocked, from the shelter I'd had built into the end of our Pullman suite. Once Rajah had nodded off for the night I'd ask Albert if he felt like burning off any excess tension. If he didn't, his usual complaints being fatigue or stress headaches, I'd shut the lights and undress so as not to dim any future appetite with my scars. If he did, we'd jump in bed and proceed, keeping as quiet as a couple with a baby in the room. After a couple months of no results, I started doing handstands afterwards, though I told Albert it was a means of strengthening my shoulder muscles. Or I'd prop my waist on my hands and sit on my shoulders, legs poking straight into the air. On such occasions I'd tell him I was practising yoga tips I'd picked up from Colombo the Indian Rubber Man.

We finished that season on November 4 in Richmond, Virginia. Back in Bridgeport, Albert and I moved into a little bungalow in a neighbourhood filled with circus folk, meaning no one batted an eye at a couple with a Bengal tiger in place of a toddler. Soon after I checked myself into a hospital and they took pictures of the inside of my head with an X ray; afterwards, they told me an abscess of the tissue of the brain was likely the cause of my headaches and dizziness and periodic deafness. They also told me if I'd waited another three days to come in it likely would've killed me. Course, it was far from the first time I'd been told I had days to live, doctors having a habit of telling you that so you'll be happier paying for whatever costly procedure was being proposed. An hour later, they lanced the abscess with a long glass tube snaked up through my nose. When the ether hangover wore off a few days later I was fine.

Shortly into the new year the menage caught fire and killed a bunch of animals, a tragedy that added a huge figure on the debit side of the circus and therefore caused Albert neckaches and irritability and stress-related indigestion. One of the animals who died was Nigger; though he wasn't burnt he took in one too many lungfuls of smoke, and despite my best efforts to nurse him back to health he passed from pneumonia three days later. I spent most of that morning feeling sniffly and wet-eyed, though after a can or two of beer in the blue car I marched back to our bungalow and leashed up Rajah and informed him he'd had enough coddling. That afternoon we went to the training barn and I let Rajah into the steel arena and a minute later I was lying prone under five hundred pounds of humping hair and muscle. When Rajah streamed over my back I felt like things were getting back to normal.

I debuted him three months later in Madison Square Garden. You should've heard the screams, the applause, the cheering. After that, I couldn't hang a bra out to dry without some reporter popping out of the bushes and asking me whether lacy or non-lacy was better for training tigers.

What I'm trying to say is this: Albert and I managed to achieve an ebb and flow that would've looked a lot like married life if you took the circus out of the equation. Problems came along, but I would've been nervous if they hadn't. He had his work and I had my work, and at the end of the day we talked and had dinner together and on Sunday nights we went to the pictures. There were afternoons we took walks, sometimes with Rajah and sometimes without, and in the evenings we enjoyed games of cribbage and backgammon for Albert was fond of pastimes requiring an understanding of risk and numbers. He was always polite, never raising his voice or being critical, and if he showed a less than burning interest in my tigers it was because he had more than enough problems of his own. Throughout, I was still hopeful my handstands and yoga moves might one day take effect, and when you boil it right down, hope is what we talk about when we think we're talking about happiness.

A month later we reached Boston for the only other arena show of the season. After the evening show a bunch of the other performers were going out and invited Albert and me along. Though I didn't particularly want to go, I'd been thinking that part of my attempt at living regular should really include making some friends who weren't husbands or tigers. Plus Albert was going through a difficult time, Mr. Charles having bought himself a 200-foot yacht he named *Zalophus*. When Mr. John found out, he bought himself a 220-foot yacht called *Symphonia*. Both boats got listed as circus expenses, meaning Albert needed some relaxation and he needed it badly.

That night, after the show, I got dolled up in my evening finery, including my fox stole and my drop-waisted dress and my evening gloves stretched to the elbows. Albert put on a suit that positioned him near the handsome end of the spectrum. Then we all met out by the ticket wagons and tipped some workingmen to take us into town, we being Bird Millman, the wire-walking sensation, who never went any- where without her pet parrot on her shoulder; May Wirth, the Australian trick rider; the Spanish wire walker Con Colleano; the acro- batic clown Poodles Hannaford; the bear trainer Emil Pallenberg; and that bossy little plange-turner Lillian Leitzel, who of course brought along her insane husband, the trapeze artist Alfred Cadona.

We pulled up in front of the classiest of the nightspots that'd opened in Boston since prohibition. You had to be either famous or mob or a high-ranking police officer to get in, and since we classified under the first category the red velvet rope was withdrawn and we were welcomed inside. The doorman wore white gloves and a tuxedo, and seeing Leitzel his eyes lit up and he led us to a big round table right in front of the bandstand, where a group of black musicians was playing a new kind of music on piano, drums and an assortment of horns. To me, it sounded like bedsprings getting a workout.

This was my introduction to the Roaring Twenties. I can't say I liked it much, for it was loud and there was smoke everywhere and I was uncomfortable around people as haughty as Leitzel. Plus they were all chattering away in different languages, switching from French to German to Spanish to weird East European tongues with even a little of that Hungarian Esperanto tossed in for good measure. I, on the other hand, was that rarity of rarities among circus performers: American- born, and therefore burdened with a curse common to all Americans. No matter how many different languages I heard, the only one that ever made any sense to me was English. Leitzel, on the other hand, knew eight or nine. Mostly she used them to curse more dramatically when she wanted something.

So as I sat at that big table amid all that smoke and laughter and music, I mostly felt alone and yearned for our Pullman. Frankly, with all that noise and all those different languages it wasn't that different from being deaf, my only meaningful conversation coming when Leitzel leaned over and said, "You had better keep an eye on zat huss-band off yours. It seems he has vondered off. You know vat they say, Mabel dear. The quiet ones are the ones you have to watch out for."

She was trying to get a rise out of me, not because she had any-thing against me but because she was the type of person who just plain enjoyed doing it. It worked, too, but not because I had any concerns over Albert; was more my feeling that someone ought to cut Leitzel down to size. Luckily, I was smart enough not to act on that feeling, so in a voice rich with fake appreciation I said, "Yes, of course you're right, Lillian. Perhaps I'll go find out where he is."

So I excused myself. If the others noticed, they didn't care enough to stop yammering and smoking and laughing. I walked past tables peopled with chiefs of police and chiefs of the waterfront, jumping out of the way of cigarette girls wearing flapper dresses, dodging black musicians smoking a tobacco sweeter than any I'd smelled previously. Found Albert over by one of the wheels of for-tune. I stood beside him. At first he didn't notice me for he was con-centrating hard on that little white ball, his face having gone all pursed, the way it did whenever he was concentrating on his ledger books. After a bit, he leaned over and kissed my cheek, but he still didn't say anything.

Not particularly wanting to go back and join the others, I watched him watch the others place bets on that spinning little ball, wondering what on earth the interest could possibly be. Albert, mean-while, couldn't look away; riveted, he was, jaw muscles clenched and eyes burning holes.

Finally, and I do mean finally, for I'd been standing beside him for the better part of twenty minutes, he leaned over and whispered loud in my ear, "Do you see that, darling?"

"Do I see what?"

"The wheel. I've watched every hand for the past hour and I've noticed it has tendencies. It favours certain numbers. Look. It did it again. The wheel likes high, odd numbers. Colour red. I am sure of it."

"Really?"

"Yes ... look."

I looked and the ball hopped into a slot showing a low even black number, though when I pointed this out to Albert, he said, "Tendencies, Mabel. Observe." I did, and his theory failed again, though the third time it worked. He told me it'd worked seven out of the last twelve times, though before that it hadn't worked for ten times in a row, which was another part of his theory, for apparently there were stretches when the wheel tendency worked and stretches when it didn't.

"Is the tendency working now?" I asked him.

"Yes."

"Then why not put some money down?"

He looked at me, eyebrows arching. "Really?"

"You might get lucky." Course, I was joking, for like most people I didn't really believe luck was the reason things happen. What I figured was Albert would bet, the ball would spin, we'd get all excited, he'd lose some money and we'd rejoin the others. "Live a little," I even said, and it was this encouragement Albert had a tough time turning down, accountants being people who go through life having to prove they're neither boring nor cheap. So he turned and bought some betting markers from a flapper chewing gum so loudly you could hear it over the music.

Just before the "All bets in," Albert dropped the markers on a single number. The little white ball spun around and around before slowing and hitting the number-slot edges and bouncing and hopping and finally settling into the very number Albert had bet on. The ball spinner acknowledged the win with a nod, and he pushed a pile of markers in Albert's direction. Albert, looking flustered and pleased, picked them up and I followed him to one of the cashier windows. He pushed his dominos through the window. A stack of twenties was pushed back at him. Trying to look nonchalant, he took them and folded them in two the way gangsters did. A few seconds later, in a corner of the speakeasy, he counted it. Seven hundred dollars and change.

When I heard the amount I gave a little hop with an accompanying shriek that embarrassed Albert but at the same time made him beam with pleasure. His win seemed to give the evening a totally new complexion, for it suddenly felt to me like the people we'd come with were my best friends and needed to share in this windfall. So I rushed over and leaned my head into their circle, making sure I was right beside Leitzel.

"You wouldn't believe what just happened! Albert won $700 at the wheel game!"

At this a cheer went up, Colleano yelling "Ole!" and Millman's parrot squawking. Though Albert continued playing he held on to most of his winnings so at the end of the night we all went to another speakeasy Poodles Hannaford knew, one where they served champagne and salmon breakfasts on white linen, which of course Albert paid for. We both came home feeling flushed and happy, and before putting Rajah into his shelter I scrunched my cat's face up and kissed him and said, "He's a genius, that daddy of yours, a natural-born genius!"

It was eight o'clock in the morning. I took myself a nap that lasted a couple of hours before the parade bugle. Was no jump that night, so Albert and I took it easy and stayed in and played cribbage. Around ten o'clock I said good-night to Rajah and put him in his shelter, and when his sides were rising and falling in a way that was wave-like Albert and I had ourselves some time together, after which I turned myself upside down so the seed might go where it might do some good. By then he'd guessed why I'd become so interested in handstands and yoga, it being a relief he supported my plan. In fact, he held my hand during my inversions, after which he held *me*. We chatted some, mostly about places we'd like to visit and people we'd like to meet and things we'd like to accomplish. In other words: future stuff. Hopeful stuff. After a bit, my thoughts drifted into nonsense.

In the middle of the night I woke up with a thirst and reached for the glass of water I kept on my bedside table. I took a sip and looked over at Rajah. Moonlight was sneaking in through the Pullman windows, and some of it caught Rajah's coat and made it gleam a ghostly orange. Was then I felt it, in that way you feel the presence of something different: taking hold at the back of the neck, tickling hairs, a quiet *too* quiet.

I spun around. Albert's side of the bed was empty.

CHAPTER 10

THE EX-POLAR BEAR MAN

NOW. THE PROBLEM WITH TELLING THE STORY THIS WAY AND not an old person's way? With telling the story as if time was a straight line, with a beginning and a middle and an end? As if time has itself some sort of plan? As if it has a purpose?

I'll spell it out for you. You look at that line and you think, *Hmmmmm. Needs sprucing up. Hmmmmmmm. Needs decorating.* Next thing you know, you're drawing in peaks and valleys so as to give time a meaning it probably doesn't deserve. You're picking out moments on that line and assigning them importance, based solely on what came before or after. Worse yet, you start looking for significance, for an overall reason, and if anything will drive you crazy it's that. I'm not saying it's not there. I'm just saying it's not something you'll ever find.

Still, you keep looking. You just do. Fact is, you'll do anything to spot it. I look back on the moment I found Albert's side of the bed empty and I can't help but see a peak, everything sloping upward before it and downward from then on. One second prior, I had the best animal act in America. One second after, I was on my way to burning my bridges with the Ringlings and spending five years stuck in a contract saying I was to be "generally useful" and not much else. So you think to yourself, *How could so much have happened between those two seconds? How could so much misfortune squeeze itself* in? And then, because you're a human being, and you're cursed with a brain the size of a toaster, your mind gets around to the only question that's really worth asking.

Just whose decision *was* that?

Quite frankly, it's enough to make you dizzy. Besides that it's an invitation to gloominess, for the other tendency is to look at that line and see that high mark and paint everything that happened afterwards with the same dark brush. Course, this is inaccurate, for though my star did fall after that one crammed-full space between seconds, there were still plenty of good times after that. There were still plenty of starry nights and warm days and waterhole swims. There were still plenty of real circus days. Moment or no moment, I remained a trouper, and though the hours are long and the conditions miserable, the one thing you can say about circus work is it's long on giddy moments. Hell, *Art* came along after that moment, and he was the best thing ever happened to me.

Ooops. There I go again. Nothing like that man's name to get me off track. Fact is, we're still on the topic of Albert Ewing, Ringling accountant, a topic I usually work hard at forgetting. The sad truth is, it didn't take long before Albert burned through his money and my money and money that didn't belong to either one of us until one night in Bridgeport I'd had about enough.

"Uh-uh," I told him, "no more, the well's gone dry, the bank's closed, your loan officer's retired, you want to gamble till all hours, go ahead. You just aren't doing it with my money."

"Please, Mabel, be reasonable. The game's with rubes. I'll triple our stake in two *hours*. Believe me, Mabel, it's the end of our problems. Two hours and I'll get us back in the black, Mabel. My luck's changing I can feel it. Two hours, I *promise*."

"I've heard that one before."

"Mabel, I mean it."

"No."

"Mabel, it's for us."

For a second I looked at him, tempted, for there were nights he'd go out and do what he was promising, coming back flushed with triumph (the only problem being those nights were few and far between). Plus the phrase *it's for us* was put on earth to make women lose their sense; appeals to our yearning for safety, I suppose, something men learn right around the time their voices deepen.

"Albert," I finally said, "it's for you and you only."

With that, he stormed out, slamming the door to make his point. In the middle of the night he finally came back, creeping in, making as little noise as possible, getting in bed all considerate and sheepish. Had he won, he would've come bounding in, waking me and Rajah and recounting every hand and just generally basking in it.

He didn't ask me for money after that. God knows where he was getting it; I only knew he'd get it and then he'd go out and then he'd lose it. Made me mad as an orangutan, this did, and for a time this contributed to some mightily frenzied nighttime activity, the kind that can take the place of jogging or shadow-boxing. Course, it couldn't last. One night, with Albert slack-lipped and humping, he looked into my eyes and I looked into his eyes and what we saw was enough to make blood ice over. He pulled off and we went to either side of our big bed and that's pretty much where we stayed. I even got in the habit of taking Rajah out of his shelter and letting him lie between us, something Albert didn't object to so long as I washed the sheets.

Talking went too. I couldn't so much as look at the man without feeling spiteful so I figured it was foolish trying to communicate with him. It even got so I'd take my food out of the Hotel (which was what the Ringlings called their cookhouse) and eat it with Rajah in the Pullman so others wouldn't have their appetites ruined by our frostiness. And if you're wondering why we didn't break it off right then and there its because it was winter and troupers have a long tradition of going a little squirrelly between seasons. All that motionlessness makes us ornery. Though I can't speak for Albert, my game plan was to wait for the next season and see if things improved.

The arena shows in New York City came a little earlier that year, the beginning of April, if memory serves, most of the stars showing off acts they'd been working up over the winter. That first night, May Wirth did a *forward* somersault, pretty much a miracle on a cantering mare. Poodles Hannaford somehow got a saddle on the belly of a horse and, arms flailing like a drunkard, rode around at full gallop while clinging to the horse's underbelly (though how he did this without taking a hoof to the head is anybody's guess). Con Colleano did a one-armed stand on a slack wire, once again making the rubes question what is and what is not possible, something people trapped in townie lives need once in a while. Not to be outdone, Lillian Leitzel turned 160 left-arm planges, the rubes starting to count off each one by the time she'd reached 50. To top it all off Alfred Cadona debuted the first quadruple somersault in the history of the trapeze, a feat that wouldn't be copied for decades.

And what of me? What of Miss Haynie slash Mrs. Aganosticus slash Mrs. Williams slash Mrs. Roth slash Mrs. Ewing? The next night, lying beneath my roaring and rubbing Bengal, I realized the one drawback of working on the greatest circus show ever assembled was that acts went stale fast. When I finally rolled out from under Rajah, my leathers as sticky as midway floss, there was applause you could call mighty. But there weren't screams and there weren't ladies fainting and there weren't children crying.

A week later we pulled out of Grand Central station, the Ringling show so big it needed a total of four trains to pull all the cars. A giddiness took hold, for each year the routing changed, meaning different towns, different scenery, different people. Different surprises, too: that year a Jack Londoner demonstration was waiting for us in Philadelphia, a lot of angry men, women and children waving placards and shouting. It was something I didn't take too seriously, the idea that circus life is hard on an animal being nothing but dreamt-up bunk and the result of a certain overly privileged segment of society having too much time on its hands. We had a straw house anyway, and when we pulled out of Philadelphia it was like those placards had never been there.

But the best thing was Albert seemed to settle down and take his job more seriously. He started getting up on time, and he avoided the poker games that went on nonstop outside the workingmen's cars. Instead, he played solitaire, betting against imaginary banks with wooden matches as markers, which I figured wasn't the greatest state of affairs but a damn sight better than losing real money. As a show of thanks I veered closer to the civil end of the spectrum. We started eating together again, and since we were on opposite sides of the table I guess we both figured we might as well start communicating again.

At first the conversations were light. Weather, cat talk, gossip about who was screwing who. Then one morning, in Baltimore, my husband slash manager looked up over his coffee and broached the subject needed broaching the most.

"Mabel. I know things have been rotten but I think I've got this thing under control, I really do, and I know I deserve the way you've been treating me but now that I'm getting better I think we should work on liking each other again."

I looked at him, letting my eyes say I was unconvinced but willing to hear him out anyway. He spread some marmalade on toast and said, "I have a proposition. The Hagenbeck show is routed an hour away in Annapolis, and I thought we could go see that new mixed act everyone's raving about. Clyde Beatty, I believe, is his name. I thought maybe we could go tonight. Maybe we'd get some ideas for how to steer your act. What do you say?"

"That's all well and good, Albert, but you might remember I work nights."

He produced a slight grin. "I spoke with Curley and told him you needed the night off. Professional development. The Argentine will run your Bengals through their act. You've got those cats trained so well *I* could probably do it. So the only thing the crowd won't see is Rajah but I figure Rajah could use a rest once in a while as well."

I looked at him, wondering whether I'd be able to tolerate my husband's company for a stretch of several hours, at the same time weighing this against the fact I really *was* curious to see what kind of an act an ex–polar bear man could come up with and why everyone was yammering about it so. After the matinee, Albert and I got in one of the Ringling automobiles and so we'd be alone Albert did the driving instead of a workingman. We talked most of the way there, Albert saying he'd come to the conclusion his gambling had been caused by work stress and the fact it appealed to his mathematical side and the nervousness caused by us not being able to get in the family way. You have to imagine how Albert talked: laying everything out in such a precise, logical way that after a while you started to feel irrational for not agreeing with everything that came out his mouth. Three-quarters of the way there we stopped at a diner. Over a plate of smothered chicken and peas, I told him if he kept on the straight and narrow maybe we could start acting like husband and wife, the key word being *if.* Just saying that cheered him so much he whistled and tapped the steering wheel all the way to Annapolis.

Now. The Hagenbeck-Wallace circus was an old outfit started in America by a German animal breeder named Karl Hagenbeck. For years, the Hagenbeck circus had been a respected and honest menage show, which is of course why it went broke. In a public auction it was bought by a man named Ben Wallace, one of the sleaziest two-bit grift operators in a business crammed with sleazy two-bit grift operators.

For PR reasons, he kept the Hagenbeck name, a decision causing old Karl Hagenbeck so much grief he sued to get his name taken off, the judge deciding the name of his circus was part of the sale and that Ben Wallace could do with it what he liked. Hagenbeck moved back to Germany and shortly thereafter died of heart problems no doubt brought on by extreme humiliation.

By 1923 Wallace was dead, too, and his circus had become about as reputable as any of the second-tier circuses in America, by which I mean sort of. About the same size as Barnes and Sells-Floto and John Robinson and Cole Brothers, it had four rings and a decent menage and, with straw down, seating for maybe eight thousand. When Al and I got to the ticket wagon I was recognized and taken in as a special guest of the circus and placed in the front row of seats with stars painted on the backs.

A few seconds later the lights went down. An Oriental-style spec was followed by the aerial display, neither of which were as big as the Ringling counterparts but at the same time not in any way shameful. Then the tent went dark and the ringmaster bellowed, "All eyes on the center ring steel arena ..." for by then everyone was following the Ringling idea of putting the cat display third. With that, the centre ring lit up and three male lions were fed into the arena. Heaven knows I'm no fan of lions but these ones were so lopey and unbarbered even I felt embarrassed for them, a sensation heightened when two snarly, bedraggled tigers were fed in next. All five cats took their seats slowly, and even just sitting there they looked growly and uncomfortable, taking little air swipes at one another. Every few seconds a lion would roar, and I noticed both tigers had gone completely quiet and still, a sign they hadn't been mixed or seat-trained properly.

Truth be told, I was relieved, for I'd been hearing the Hagenbeck-Wallace show had itself a mixed act that had to be seen to be believed. But the moment I saw how irritable and poorly groomed the cats were, I knew the whole thing was a press agent concoction and something the crowd would see through in a second.

A spotlight followed Clyde Beatty across the big top. He was a handsome kid, maybe twenty-five years old, with a strong jaw and wavy dark hair though like all male big-cat trainers he was a short son of a gun. He wore a white shirt and jodhpurs and tall black leather boots, and he carried a whip in his right hand. In his left hand he somehow gripped both a pistol and a wooden kitchen chair, the peculiarity of which was yet another sure indication of how bad his act was going to be. Yet the thing that amazed me was just *how* bad it was; no sooner had he beckoned one of the lions from his seat than the lion was roaring and taking air swings and generally not doing anything close to what he was told. Beatty started yelling, and to get the cat moving he swung his whip over his head and cracked it somewhere around the cat's shoulder, which got him moving, all right—got him charging straight at Beatty. Would've eaten him, too, had Beatty not jammed one of the chair legs down the cat's throat, making the lion gurgle and choke in a way made me sick. The cat chewed on it for a second and when he was finished just sat looking cowed and bitter while the other cats growled and swiped and generally looked pissed off. Beatty indicated for a rollover and again the cat balked and again Beatty cracked the whip and jabbed at him with the chair leg until finally he did a single sloppy half-hearted rollover, from which he came up swinging and taking jabs and roaring. (By contrast, I could send eight tigers through the cleanest simultaneous rollover you ever saw in your life and I could do it with a single motion of my chin.)

After the rollover, Beatty tried to get another of the lions to come sit beside the sore-headed lion on the arena floor, which he did by yelling and snapping his whip on the cat until finally the cat had no choice but to come roaring off that pedestal and have a blank pistol cartridge fired in his face. In this way Beatty got two lions to not so much sit side by side as occupy the same general area of floor space though when it came time for them both to sit up he had to flick the whip in their eyes and kick at their paws and fight them off with his chair before they sort of teetered back and lifted their front paws for maybe a half second and not at all simultaneous. At this point all hell broke loose, for though tigers hate lions I suppose one of them figured out what she had in store, for she came flying off the pedestal with an intention to kill, getting so close to Beatty he had no choice but to stick the pistol in her face and fire and singe her with powder. She screamed, a sound makes the blood run cold, and then the tiger and the lion on the pedestals started fighting and the two lions left on arena floor started fighting though taking turns heading for Beatty, who kept yelling, "SEAT! SEAT! SEAT!" though it was difficult to say who exactly he was yelling this *at* for he'd completely lost control of his cats and was only staying alive by firing his pistol and flicking his whip and jamming his chair leg down the throat of any cat that came within striking distance. Beatty was sweating so much his skin showed wet and pink through his drenched shirt, a situation that wasn't improved when he tried to move down the final male lion, who to that point hadn't done anything worse than fight with the tiger seated beside him. His name was Bongo, and when Beatty yelled his name and whipped him and tried to bring him off his seat he just sat there, getting madder and madder, finally coming off his pedestal in a way indicating that nothing short of a bazooka was going to stop him. Was then Beatty ran. Just turned tail and raced across the ring and ducked into a little safety cage he'd attached to one side, the lion pinning him to the back of the safety cage by taking swipe after swipe through the bars, the whole time roaring at the top of his lungs, Beatty pressed against the bars and looking like he'd wet himself.

Ten minutes this anarchy had gone on, and in that time Beatty had managed one flopping rollover and a two-lion sit-up so poor it barely even counted. The cats heard the tunnel boy rattle the door and they all raced out, though not without stopping and fighting each other at the bottleneck, the cage boys prodding the cats out by poking sticks through the bars of the cage and jabbing at their haunches.

The lights went out, coming back as a spotlight on centre ring. Meanwhile, Beatty had let himself out of the safety cage. I turned to Albert and covered my mouth and tried not to laugh, even though I did feel sorry for Beatty, who hadn't had enough sense to stick with polar bears. I also felt sorry for Hagenbeck-Wallace; must've been mighty slim pickings for the press agents to splash Beatty's act all over new paper. Most of all, I felt sorry for the cats themselves, having to work with a man who felt no compunction about provoking them instead of training them properly. Was no wonder the Jack Londoners were getting themselves worked into a lather.

I intended to comment on Beatty's pitiful excuse for an act, and I suppose it was something in Albert's expression that caused me to notice something I for some reason hadn't noticed before. There was applause happening in that big top, applause that wasn't in any way subtle or soft or reserved. I turned from Albert's sallow expression toward centre ring. Beatty was standing in the middle of the steel arena, his costume turned pink by a blue flood. He took bow after bow after bow, waving and smiling and then crossing his arm over his waist like a Spaniard and doubling over. He had to. The cheering wouldn't stop. It just wouldn't. It simply refused. It would've gone on forever and ever had a midget-clown interlude not taken it and turned it into laughter and then general enthusiasm for the act next to come.

On the way home, Albert and I had an argument that'd been brewing for well over a year: was about gambling and babies and my supposedly unwholesome attachment to tigers and how I was stupid gentling them, though after a bit it wasn't so much about arguing as about spearing each other with words and seeing who could stick the spear in deepest. I can't even blame Albert totally, for it's a game I'll gladly play when riled. When our throats got sore we stopped haranguing each other and rode the rest of the way in silence. When we got to the Ringling lot we parked in front of the Pullman. First thing Albert did was come inside and change and then go out. Rajah was asleep on the bed, though the sound of the door slamming caused him to lift his head and cock his ears and gurgle. As Albert changed I sat not watching, though when he finally left I put on my night things and poured myself a drink of Tennessee's finest and, not feeling the least bit tired, crawled into bed and held Rajah close.

The next day, I got up early and went to the cookhouse and instead of eating breakfast I asked the Nicaraguan food doler to give me a leaned-on fried egg sandwich and a thermos of black coffee. Take-out in hand, I headed out to the training barn. There I met my cage boy, Bailey, who helped me shift cages so the Bengals were let into the practise arena. I didn't even feed them first, hoping this'd make 'em a little testy. Got my whip and training stick and strapped a pistol loaded with blanks onto my waist. Then I joined them.

Their names were Zoo, Queen, Princess, Dolly, Rowdy, Ruggles, Pasha the Himalayan, plus the twolings Boston and Beauty. You couldn't've named a more beautiful outfit of tigers in all of America, and until then this was a fact that'd always made me happy to wake each day with the dawn. That morning their beauty didn't impress me in the least, and in fact made me a little irked, each one zipping like a mechanical rabbit to his or her pedestal and sitting there looking ramrod straight and beautiful and awaiting instruction.

The biggest of the lot, and the only one with anything approaching a mean streak, was Zoo, for he'd reached that year before a tiger normally goes rogue and was starting to show signs of crankiness. He was about as big as a Bengal's going to get, as big even as Rajah, and owing to the size of his paws and the thickness of his shoulders he wasn't particularly good in the tricks department. Mostly what I used him for was topping the pyramid at the end of the display, though this alone earned him his keep for he was regal and beautiful and as big as a Siberian, though with the handsome form of a Bengal. He enjoyed it too, for like most males (tiger or human, if you ask me) he was vain and fond of being gawked at.

That morning, I decided he was my next ball roller.

"Zoo," I barked. "*Come.*"

He rumbled to the middle of the ring and sat, chin held high. I stepped outside the cage and fetched the big red Indian rubber ball and put it a foot away from him. He looked at the ball by shifting his pupils to the sides of his eyes. His brow furrowed.

"Zoo," I barked again, for no specific reason other than to display the sharpness in my voice and to indicate things were going to be different from then on. I slipped a piece of horsemeat onto the training stick and placed the point of the training stick on top the ball. All of this was sheer foolishness, the best way to ruin a well-trained tiger being to give him conflicting messages: he knew he was the pyramid topper and that Pasha was the ball roller, the weirdness of my request making him rumble deep in his chest.

"Zoo!" I shouted again and for added effect I snapped the whip about six inches behind him. Was a noise didn't frighten him in the least, Zoo being on the taciturn end of things and not quick to startle. After a minute of thinking he put both paws on the ball but before that he did something couldn't have pissed me off more and by this I mean he yawned. Just opened up that big tiger mouth of his and lolled his tongue and released a cloud of meat breath so as to indicate he was indulging me and that was all. Then he licked his chops and let his eyes go sleepy.

I didn't reward him, a betrayal that made his eyes go narrow with complaint. Then I gave a signal he'd seen a hundred times when I was training Pasha: I tapped his hind end with the training stick, a signal I wanted his hind paws to go where his front paws were. He looked at me, expressionless, before calmly raising the right half of his upper lip and showing me one of his eye teeth. This made me mad so I hollered, "Zoo!" and tapped his hind end. He showed me his eye tooth again, though this time he added a low rumbling growl.

Good, I thought, *now we're getting somewhere*. To show him I meant business I hollered "Zoo! Ball!" and tapped his hind end in a way was more a slap than a tap, all of which had the net effect of causing Zoo to pull his front paws off the ball and put them back down where he liked them. He turned and faced me and sat rumbling, cheesing me off for he should've been mad enough already to take a run at me.

Was then I did it. I twirled that whip and for the first time in my entire career touched an animal for no fair reason, the popper smacking Zoo right on his ass, my plan being to either stick the training stick down his throat or fire the pistol once he charged. But instead of meeting me with a full tiger rage he did something even crueller, something that let me know he was tiger and nothing but and in his own way would always be the one in charge.

He sat there. Didn't even sway his tail. The message in his eyes was, *I could tear you into little tiny bits in a second but I won't because I don't care to. You're too puny. You don't deserve the nobility of my tiger rage, not with the way you're acting today.*

You're the animal. Not me.

With that, Zoo turned, and to show he wasn't scared of any whip he walked as slowly as was possible to his pedestal and took it. Once he was on it he looked at me and sighed. I skittered out of the arena with my head down so Bailey couldn't see I was crying.

Next day I gentled Zoo like he'd never been gentled, buying him hippo chunks with my own money and telling him over and over he was the (second) most beautiful cat I'd ever seen. Then I more or less did the same with the others. If I had myself a picture act, so be it, I was bound and determined to make it the best one in the country, the thrills provided by my wrestler. I worked a precision and a grace into the act that'd never been seen. Plus I kept my front to the audience as much as possible, cueing the cats with hand movements done behind my back, seeing as from a distance I was still blond and I was still lithe and I was still more or less young. In other words, I figured I could still style an act in a way Beatty would never be able.

So, I worked. You feel things slipping and that's what you do: you put your head down and you get at it. I'd work through siesta, something that was unreasonable for my cage boy so I started tipping Bailey each time he helped out. Even with giving him a little bit extra he started showing up later and later and grumbling louder and louder, which I understood, for he was a workingman and with that came a lack of understanding of how a little extra money can help out in the future. I'm sure he was spending it all in the poker games the Negros held each night in the flat cars anyway, so after a while he probably figured, why bother?

One morning he didn't come, and I shifted that cage on my lonesome. I got used to working alone, and before long it got so those two hours were my favourite, as it's quiet before the rubes come and I've always found things look simpler and peaceful when there's not a lot of noise going on.

I started training my best jumpers, Boston and Beauty, to leap through not one but two burning hoops. Then I got the wagon superintendent to build a see-saw with tiger-sized seats, for I was thinking it'd be a sight to see a pair of adult Bengals—I had Ruggles and Rowdy in mind—frolic like children in a playground. Plus around this time it first hit me that with Pasha's sense of balance I might be able to tempt her to walk across a pair of thick ropes held off the ground. And if that went well, who knows, I might even be able to take one of those ropes away.

What I'm saying is for the next month I did nothing but eat, sleep and breathe my act. The tricks were progressing at a snail's pace, though given how difficult they were the fact they were progressing at all made me feel like maybe I was on to some new kind of training. Was exciting and nerve-wracking at the same time. Course, there was no denying all that work had the added benefit of keeping my mind off my other problem, that being my husband. One night, when my mind *wasn't* off it, I sat down and wrote letters to the Women's Christian

Temperance Union, the Anti-Saloon League *and* that lunatic Henry Ford, complaining how they were to blame for my misery: goddamn prohibition, I wrote, has made salooning so profitable you couldn't swing a dead cat without hitting one and God knows how weak men are when confronted by temptation. The next morning I woke up and saw how desperation had warped my logic. I ripped the letters up and worked twice as hard that day with the tigers as I'd worked the day before. Was my way of promising myself I wasn't going to think about my latest in a long list of husband problems till season end, a promise I was more or less successful at keeping.

Until.

Here I'll put the circus in Denver, for I remember there were mountain peaks in the distance and a freshness of air found in no place other than the Rockies. I also seem to remember seeing women as well as men dressed in flannel shirts, a sure sign you're either in Colorado, Wyoming or Utah. Shortly after set-up, I was walking along the backyard thinking I'd put Rajah on a leash and take him for a walk and then get him back to the car early enough so I'd have some time with the Bengals before the show, the whole time making sure I stayed clear of the red car where my good-for-nothing husband stared at books all day. I had a whole stew of things simmering in my mind, so that when I heard my name called it was like being sucked through a tube.

I stopped and looked around and realized I was standing next to Lillian Leitzel's private dressing tent. Naturally, it was both the biggest tent and the tent closest to the performers' curtain. Leitzel was sitting outside on a divan, smoking a cigarillo. She waved her left arm, the one gone meaty from all her planging, and called again. I went over. Her two bulldogs, Boots and Jerry, were snoring at her feet. Her tent was filled with flowers, courtesy of John Ringling, who had a devotion to her nobody quite understood except that it bordered on the slavish. Like most people I didn't like Leitzel but felt good when she paid me attention.

"Good morning, Mabel," she said. "Vood you like to join me for a cigarette?"

She offered me one of the thin dark things she was puffing on and because I didn't want to seem ungrateful I accepted. Lillian then passed me a Ronson, and when I lit up it was like breathing bark smoke. I worked hard to keep my face from roiling. Meanwhile Leitzel smoked and let a smile form around the spot where her lips held the cigarillo. After a few seconds, she took the cigarillo from her mouth and motioned with it toward the empty divan beside her.

"Sit," she said. "Keep me company."

The imperious way she said it made me want to slap her but by now I was so curious I reacted as though it was a kind invitation. So I sat down and smoked with her while we both watched the busyness of a circus lot only halfway put together. We could hear Negro canvasmen chanting as they pounded in the tent pegs, and we could hear someone warming the calliope.

"I vatched your act ze other day," Leitzel finally said. "It really is somesing, how much control you have over ze tigers. I hope you vill be on the show a long time. I know Mr. John, vell, he speaks very highly of you. Alfred and I dined with him just before he vent to Sarasota and he told me so himself. He said, 'You know, Lillian. Hiring Mabel Stark avay from Barnes vas one of ze smartest moves I ever made.'"

"Really?"

"Oh yes. He told me he vass going to be looking at some more tigers for you. He'd like to give you ze biggest tiger act in ze country."

"He said that?"

"Oh my vord, yes."

"I'm ... I'm surprised. I was beginning to think ... well, it's just that you never see him."

"No no no. He vas insistent. He ask me to ask you if you prefer cage bred or jungle."

"Don't really matter to me, so long as they're tigers."

"All right, zen, I vill tell him."

Just then, Con Colleano sauntered by and the two started chatting away in Spanish, Leitzel having picked up the language from her distempered Mexican husband. After a minute, Colleano and Leitzel said *adios* and Colleano walked off, his gait stiff-legged on account of his toreador pants being so tight and thickly spangled.

"Ah ... zat man. He is enough to make you want to forget your husband and be foolish, is dis not right, Mabel? Are not ze Spaniards ze most vonderful? Spaniards and Russians. Both emotional as hyenas, only difference being ze vay dey show it, hmmmmm?"

Not really sure what she was getting at, I murmured something that was neither a yes or a no. Leitzel looked around.

"Speaking of husbands. Vell. Zey *can* be a trial, no? Zey can be something us vomen put up with, no? Such boys, zey are."

"Lillian," I said. "Exactly whose husband are we talking about?"

"Yours, mine ..." Here she waved her muscle-bound arm in the air and smiled. "Does it matter?"

Suddenly my hopefulness evaporated and I eyeballed Leitzel and spoke in a way that wasn't my place given how rich and famous she was and given how strict the class system in the circus was. "Lillian," I said through teeth barely parted, "you got something to say, say it. I've got tigers not yet fed. What I don't have is all day."

She let out a hiss of smoke and looked at me narrow-eyed. Then she butted out her cigarillo and sat back in her divan and stared forward. Her voice was smoky and low and indignant.

"Mabel," she said, "vould you listen? I am trying to help you."

Then she told me what was obvious to everyone on the circus but me.

The sound some words can make: was like she'd taken a four-hundred-pound copper bell and rung it, her words reverberating for a full minute afterwards. I could practically hear those words pushing the air around, clanging over and over. Thank God the two Ringlings had been down in Sarasota for the past three months watching their palaces get built.

"Thank you," I said weakly.

I took a short cut through the half-risen big top, the canvasmen yelling words of caution and me not listening, till I hit the connection and turned right and then half walked, half ran past the Congress of Freaks until I reached the red wagon parked next to the main entrance. I turned the door handle and found him in there, alone, so I started hitting him and slapping him and punching him and yelling, "You've got to put it back, Albert! You have to put it back! You know what they'll do to you if you get caught!"

Through a lattice of fingers he cried, "Calm down Mabel put what back?!" and it was the fake innocence of this made me double-time my hits and slaps and yell, "Don't play dumb with me, Albert! You're stealing from the Ringlings which is bad enough but you're also my manager. How do you think that looks!"

Albert then had the nerve to cry, "Honest Mabel I haven't any idea what you're talking about!" This made me see red; I actually picked up a big metal three-hole punch and bonked him a good one on the head so he fell to his knees and gripped his noggin with two hands. Suddenly, he was all ears.

"Listen to me. You have to put the money *back*."

"All right," he whimpered, "all right. I will. All right. For Christ's sake, Mabel, I will...."

I dropped the three-hole punch to the floor and it hit with a wood-chipping thud. Then I stood breathing hard, wishing there was such a thing as killing a man without repercussions or feelings of guilt. After a time, Albert got up and sank back in his office chair and closed his eyes, still holding the pummelled portion of his forehead. I'd left a bump that'd swell to the size of an Easter egg, and I pitied him the headache that'd soon set in, though not enough to stop me from saying, "Find someplace else to sleep tonight, you cheap excuse for a man."

Then I walked out, hoping that maybe a good bonk on the head might've knocked some sense into him. Course, this was wishful thinking, for making a man feel battered and ashamed only feeds the flames of his compulsion, particularly if that battering and shame comes at the hands of his wife.

To make a long story short, Albert moved out, setting himself up in hotels until space opened in one of the office-staff Pullmans. He kept gambling too. Now that he was out of my life, I found I could tolerate keeping my ears open for the whisperings and rumour and gossip. Just goes to show you how stupid Albert was, for he'd always head to the best speak in town, and with two thousand people in the circus was a sure thing he'd be spotted by someone out for the evening. There was talk of him playing poker till all hours with mobsters; of him playing roulette, winning hundreds on one spin and losing it all the next; of him playing blackjack, one-armed bandits, even baccarat, which shows how talk gets exaggerated for there was no such thing as baccarat in America at the time. Still, there was no denying he was out of control. Worse, there were still times when I felt it was my job to save him, for you could practically hear the hey-rube boys dusting off their blackjacks while waiting for the word from Mr. John or Mr. Charles.

Three-quarters of the way through the season, with the circus heading east, I got a message that the Ringling manager, Charles Curley, wanted to see me. I was walking Rajah so I took him along to Curley's office, a tent set up next to the one that would've been occupied by Charles Ringling were he not down south.

"Mabel," Curley said, looking solemn.

"Charles," I said, taking a seat in one of the chairs opposite his desk. Rajah sat in the other, licking his chops and looking pleased.

"Suppose you know why I asked to see you."

"Can't say I do, Charles."

"It's about your husband."

"Ain't no husband of mine. I'd make it official but there's no time on tour. Believe me, my lawyer's on standby in Bridgeport. Moment we get there I'll be Mabel Ewing no longer."

Here Charles's face looked like a shadow had fallen over it. He peered down at some ledger books on his desk and said nothing, though he did take a big breath, which he let go of in the form of a sigh.

With a dry mouth I asked, "How much is it?"

"About $7,000, Mabel. That's not inconsiderable."

There were a few more seconds of silence. For $7,000 they'd red-light him, a punishment involved getting thrown off a moving train, your limbs scattering for miles and the cops so puzzled they wouldn't even bother trying to fit the bits and pieces back together.

"All right. I'll see what I can do."

Which turned to be: pretty much nothing. I saw Albert in his suite that night, only to find it's pretty difficult to get your point across when neither one of you is talking. Finally, I just up and outed with "For Christ's sake, Ewing, the least you can do is run. You might stay healthy that way."

This made him spitting mad. He got on his feet and started ranting, "For the love of Mike how many times do I have to tell you? I haven't stolen a penny. I'm the show *accountant*. I have rearranged some accounts on a short-term basis so that certain high-ranking Ringling employees have some operating capital. I'm *allowed* to do that, Mabel. It's *in* my contract. The books will balance at the end of the season, though I cannot for the life of me see how it's any of your concern so why don't you go off and play with your cats seeing as how you love them so much...."

He went on and on, his true feelings about the value of my profession coming out in great big dollops, for which I was thankful as it made getting up and walking out easier. Course, he kept right on gambling. As far as I can tell he gambled even heavier, no doubt desperate to put back the money he'd borrowed and feeling the whole time that's what he was going to do. I started hearing rumours the figure had grown to $8,500, and by October an even ten.

Then John Ringling rejoined the circus.

I never saw him, what with his sleeping all day and working all night, though I didn't have to. You could sense his presence. Everywhere I went, I heard chatter that Mr. John had been speaking to so-and-so, or that he'd been seen doing this or that, or that someone had passed his Pullman late at night and heard his voice, booming and rich, hollering at the stock ticker. Plus there were changes in the operation of the circus. Performers sharpened their acts and smiled more in case Mr. John's private box got used. The animals looked better. Though the band always played during mealtimes, they started playing songs designed to please Mr. John in case he was in earshot. The day he came back they played "For He's a Jolly Good Fellow" at both lunch and dinner. Days passed, though not enough to make a week. I wasn't sure what Albert was doing and convinced myself I didn't at all care. One night after the show I was in the ladies' side of the dressing tent when one of the spec riders came in and said, "Someone's outside for you, Mabel."

So I went outside, still in my leathers, and found Bailey; he was standing close enough to a light I could see his hangdog face was even more hangdog than usual. I said three words only: "Where is he?" to which he answered, just as simply, "Da trains, Miss Stark. He at da trains."

As the rail yard was close that night, and the transport wagons wouldn't start going for another twenty minutes, I started running. After a hundred feet or so I remembered my abduction in Bowling Green so I turned and ran back to the menage and got Rajah and we set out together, Rajah thinking this running across a field in the middle of the night was some kind of game and enjoying himself because of it.

I was out of breath by the time I could make out the station light in the distance. As we got closer I saw something that would've horrified me if I'd stopped and let it. Hanging from the mail gantry was a bag, and judging from its size it sure wasn't mail inside.

I got there and sure enough it could've only been a body. I was afraid to open it, figuring him for dead or near to it, so instead I stood there, shivering. Fond memories surfaced, though it's true I had to go all the way back to that night in the back of a chauffeur-driven car and Albert not being able to take his eyes off my left leg. At this thought I sniffled loudly, causing a muffled sound to come from inside the bag— was a *mmmm mmmm, mmmmm mmmm mmmmmmmmmm* ...

I looked down at Rajah, confused, and he looked up at me with ears cocked. I reached out and unzipped the bag. Sure enough, Albert was inside, face beet-red, hanging upside down and naked, wriggling to beat the band and trying to talk through the adhesive tape stretched over his mouth. His body had been blackened somehow, and for one second I thought maybe the rube-boys had burnt him to a crisp. This thought persisted for less than a half-second, however, for Albert was wriggling and swinging and doubling up so frantically you'd swear someone was tickling the soles of his feet with a feather. So I reached out and pulled a forefinger down his midsection. It came away damp with motor oil.

There's one other thing worth mentioning: stuck to all that oil was feathers. Hundreds and hundreds of little feathers—chicken, most likely. It looked like a good old tar and feathering, a traditional punishment for grifters, card cheats and confidence men. The only difference was oil had been used instead of hot tar (which had a habit of leaving burns so bad a man could die later of infection). All in all, it showed John Ringling had both a sense of humour and a respect for yours truly.

I said a little prayer of thanks and started laughing, something that seemed to enrage Albert for his eyes popped open and he started *mmmmm-mmmmm-mmmmm*ing in a girlish pitch. The frenzy in his voice made me laugh even harder, so that after a few seconds I had to lie down and hold my stomach and laugh away all the pressure of the past year. Fact is, I laughed so hard tears were rolling down my face and I couldn't catch my breath and my head was exploding though in a good way. Rajah started arfing, concerned maybe I'd gone crazy. This went on and on, Albert squealing and me laughing and Rajah arfing. Around the time the first wagons started coming from the lot I got up, collected myself and walked off, leaving Albert and his privates dangling upside down for every performer, groomer, menage man and stake driver to see.

Next morning, he was gone for good.

That day, I caught up to Charles Curley walking down the connection and said, "I've got to see Mr. John."

He stopped and looked at me and said, "He's busy, Mabel. It's season end ..."

I put my hand on his forearm and communicated how serious I was by saying, "Charles ... please."

He nodded.

Course, this took some doing. John Ringling didn't get up till ten in the evening and refused to conduct any business till after breakfast. By that point, the train was moving and the only car connected to his was his brother's, who was still in Sarasota making sure the palaces got built right. So I had to wait until the next Sunday, a night called insomnia night because the train didn't move and everyone had trouble sleeping without a lot of clacking and jostling underneath. I was told to go to the Pullman around midnight, by which time he would've finished eating what he ate every day for breakfast: corned-beef hash washed down with Old Curio.

I knocked on the door and wouldn't you know it the man himself answered, cloth napkin still tucked in his shirt collar.

"Mabel!" he cried, as though I was in the habit of dropping by on a regular basis. "How nice to see you!"

He held out his hand and I shook it, my little white paw completely disappearing inside his meatiness. He shook my hand so long and so heartily it was more a case of my extracting it than him letting it go.

He offered me a seat and I took it while he, for some reason, remained standing behind his desk. A waiter in black pants, white shirt and a red velour vest was putting Mr. John's dirty plates on a silver tray, Mr. John wiping his lips and then tossing the dirty napkin on top of the dishes. I waited for his valet to go back into the private kitchen at the end of Mr. John's Pullman before I said, "Mr. Ringling, I just want to thank you for the way you handled the situation with my husband. What he had coming was way worse than what you gave him and even though he's a snake in the grass I still want to say how thankful I am and that I hope what he did won't affect your opinion of me."

He lit a double corona, so I wasn't sure whether cigar smoke or the unseemliness of my apology made him squint. When he was finished, he shook the match out by waving it in the air, though at the same time he seemed to be waving away the conversation topic. From where I sat he looked about ten feet tall.

"How *are* you, Mabel?"

"I'm good, Mr. Ringling."

"And the act? How's the act coming along?"

"Fantastic. Been working hard on some new tricks. By next season we'll have a double flaming hoop jumper and a pair of tigers riding a see-saw and with any luck a tightrope walker."

Here John Ringling's eyes widened.

"A tightrope-walking tiger? Really? Mabel, you have to be kidding me? Which one is it?"

"The Himalayan."

"My God, she's a beauty too, isn't she?"

"All my cats are beauties, Mr. John. It's not hard keeping them that way on this show."

"Oh no, I won't hear it, Mabel. If those cats are healthy it's your doing and your doing alone." Here he finished a half tumbler of Old

Curio—just picked it up and threw it down his throat like it was punch. Was when he placed the glass back on the table I noticed his hand was puffy and a little pink.

"Now listen, Mabel, I know I promised you a twelve-tiger act when I hired you off the Barnes show and you've been very patient and I want to reward that patience. I've got my eye on fifteen tigers a game warden's got himself in India. Once he figures a way to, uh, extract them from the country, they're yours. It's only a matter of time. Think you could train a twenty-two-tiger act, Mabel?"

"Oh Mr. John could I!"

"Well, good. *Good.* I thought you'd be pleased. I hope to get them by the start of winter quarters. Would that give you enough time to train them before next year's opener?"

"I'll make sure it does!"

"I figured you'd say that too. Good. It's settled. You'll have the biggest cat act in America. How's that sound?"

"Wonderful, Mr. John. Absolutely wonderful!"

"Good, good, good, I thought you'd say that...."

A few minutes later I left, John Ringling pleading he had a full night of work to attend to, and we must really get together another time soon. It'd been my second meeting with Mr. John, and for the life of me I couldn't figure out how he'd gained a reputation for being so hard-assed and fickle, for it seemed like every time he butted his nose into my affairs my life improved in a way was nothing but dramatic.

Four days later we pulled into Bridgeport, most of us feeling sickly and green from the last night's party in Richmond, Virginia. Three days after that, I awoke early and took Rajah to the corner store, Bridgeport being the one place on earth I could take Rajah for a walk without raising a stir. Bought myself a *Billboard*, and would've got myself a *White Tops* as well except they hadn't been delivered yet. I sat at the soda bar with Rajah on the stool beside me, the soda jerk barely noticing. I ordered a float and looked at the front page.

Suddenly I couldn't draw breath. Read the words over and over and though they made sense at the same time they didn't.

Seemed John Ringling was cancelling all cat acts in his travelling show, citing danger to the trainers and the recent picketings by Jack Londoners. Seemed he'd always felt the cat acts caused a flow problem, what with the awkwardness of the steel arena. Seemed it was an effective cost-cutting measure, the Ringling Brothers Barnum & Bailey Circus being the most expensive bit of theatre ever produced in the history of mankind and one that lost money each and every time a ticket got sold. Seemed he'd still have a wild cat display, but only at the arena shows in New York City and Boston, and it seemed the display wouldn't be the one by Mabel Stark, world's best big-cat trainer, but the one by a tousle-haired newcomer borrowed away from Hagenbeck-Wallace.

Seemed the kid's name was pronounced "Baytee" and not, like everyone thought, "Beety."

CHAPTER 11

JUNGLELAND

IT HAPPENED. KNEW IT WOULD ALL ALONG, AND YET, WELL, you hope. Deep down you think, nah, all my fretting's enough. All my worrying's plenty. You imagine a big scale in your head—bronze, with fine links and gleaming plates and an overall fineness—and you figure if you weigh it down on the bad side yourself whoever's in charge will take this into consideration and won't weigh it down even more. It's a thing we do for order. It helps us pretend things don't happen at random, which is a pretty frightening concept and the reason people get nervous when things go well; in all that quiet they can practically hear it—disaster, lurking around the corner, breathing heavily, waiting to pounce. Art once told me the Eskimos have a word for the sensation sets in when you're positive your kayak's going to tip, even though the waters are calm and there's no wind and not a dark cloud in the sky. When struck with this suspicion they dump their kayaks on purpose, the idea being the gods won't then hit them with something worse.

What makes the whole thing even trickier is I'm starting to believe the powers above have interesting ideas about how the scale balances itself out. Though my mother wasn't a believer my father was Catholic to the core, and when I was little he used to gather me up on his lap and tell me stories from the Bible. Was lovely, just being that close to his body, listening to an accent that soft and soothing. On special occasions—Easter, say, or the Sunday before Christmas—he'd take me all the way to Louisville so I could confess and hear a proper mass. It was during those trips I learned how belief in a higher order can help calm you, can help you forget blue mould and early frost and excess rain and everything else that'll kill a tobacco crop. But then, after my mother's passing, I got shipped off to my aunt, who was about as stern and Presbyterian as it's possible to be: black dress, black granny shoes, pins in her hair the length of fingers, neck as brittle as a twig left to dry. To her, religion meant thunder and hard words (whereas to my father it'd meant grace and poetry, proof positive religion is one of those things that can only give you what you're able to receive). She sent me to church every Sunday, all day Sunday, and when I came home from school during the week I had an hour of Bible study besides. That's why I know the Good Book inside out and that's why I can say with conviction you'd be hard pressed to imagine a book more chock full of mayhem, venality, salaciousness and sin. At the same time, it's a book full of words like *judgment*, *atonement*, *reckoning*, *just deserts*—I could keep going. After a while, it's not hard to figure the two concepts must go hand in hand, so as to even things out in the end.

Remember: I spent my adolescent years in that house of piety, and I admit there were times I took that book to bed with me and read the juicier parts by candlelight, and if that was wrong I'll apologize now. Still, I didn't think it was wrong at the time, for it was something my aunt never objected to, which I always considered strange as she *did* object to pretty much everything else, including dancing, ribald storytelling and talking above a certain volume. At the same time, she didn't mind me reading a book with an entire chapter devoted to the goings-on in Sodom.

Naturally, the Sodomites got smited, which I suppose was fair, given how dirty and foul and overrun with vermin the place was getting. Fun's fun but there are limits and I understand that. What I've always had trouble understanding was the times the innocent were smited just so their faith could be tested. Here I'm talking about locusts or frogs or dust storms so bad they'd blind you, or some weird disease that killed infants by the score. The point is, just what had they done to deserve it? Some past sin the Bible skips over, due to its distastefulness? (Hard to believe, given what's already in there.) Or was it sin enough just being mortal? If so, that's pretty harsh. Reading those stories, I'd always imagine how *I'd* feel after a blighting and I tell you: once those locusts and frogs and dust storms and baby-killing scourges finally got called off, gratitude might not've been the thing I'd be feeling. Instead, I'd be feeling nervous.

Instead, I'd be thinking, *Just how in Sam Hill does this system work?*

Like all buildings on JungleLand property, Jeb and Ida's office was made to look like a thatched hut in Africa. It looked real in postcards, but that's about it.

I went inside. Ida, Jeb and my press agent Parly Baer were there. I sized up the competition. Parly was an old friend and would be on my side no matter what. Ida was a snake in the grass and would fang my eyes out were it not contrary to the laws of California. Jeb was the question mark, for he and I had always got on, seeing as how he'd always had some appreciation for who I was and had always treated me accordingly. So it was hard to say where he'd come down on the Mabel Stark problem. Yes, Ida was his wife and had undue influence for that reason. At the same time, he understood I'd been centre ring on the Ringling show of the twenties, and to fire me would be a slap in the face of the circus at a time it sure didn't need one.

Course, this was straw grasping, there being nothing but silence when I sat down and said hello to the three of them. Ida was smoking a menthol, the smell of which made me want to sneeze. Jeb and Parly kept shooting glances at each other. Finally Parly spoke, though when he went to use his voice it came out as a croak so he had to pretend he'd been intending to cough. He started all over.

"Mabel," he said, "it's not just you. It's Chief and Tyndall as well. It's your age, Mabel. Damn insurance company thinks you're too much of a risk. Chief and Tyndall, too. Besides, Mabel, you can't work your whole life. You have to stop one of these days. You have to take a rest sometime."

At this I pretty much went hysterical, something that involved standing and leaning over the desk so my face was in Jeb's and spouting he was a goddamn two-faced liar and if he or Ida ever, *ever*, tried to take my kitties away from me I'd come back and let myself in the steel arena and challenge one of the meaner ones, Mommy or Tiba, say, over a hippo steak. Hearing this, Jeb sputtered and spurted until Ida hissed a plume of smoke and said, "C'mon Jeb, we don't have to listen to this."

They both stood and walked out, though Jeb did say, "I'm sorry, Mabel," before having his elbow yanked on by his wife. Just sat there crying, I did. Crying and crying and crying. Parly came around the desk and pulled up a chair and said, "Listen to me, Mabel. Jeb and Ida, well Ida mostly, they wanted me to escort you out of here today. This minute. I told them no way, uh-uh, we're talking about the greatest woman big-cat trainer ever lived, maybe the best period, and if word gets out you treated her this way you'll regret it. You *have* to let her say goodbye to her cats. You've got to let her clean and feed and water them tomorrow. I argued for it long and hard, Mabel, for Ida was dead set against the idea. She said you'd vandalize something, or hurt one of the tigers, shows you how much she knows. So you're not helping with all this talk about killing yourself with the tigers. You're not helping one bit. You've got to tell me you'll behave tomorrow, so I can go tell Jeb and Ida you can be trusted to have one last morning with them. Can I tell them that, Mabel? Can I?"

A numbness set in, the same numbness I first knew way back when with my Hopkinsville tubbings, the nerves firing until they couldn't fire any more and then a calm that feels like cold exhaustion takes root. Suddenly I didn't care. About me, about JungleLand, about the tigers. I didn't care one whit. I'd done nothing but care for the past sixty years and now I was worn out and in need of a lie-down.

"Yes," I told Parly. "You can."

Parly drove me home, parking my big old Buick in the spot behind my house and then asking if I was sure I'd be okay. I told him yes, I'd just been talking it up back in Jeb and Ida's hut, though before he'd let me go inside I had to promise not to do anything stupid or rash. I was in such a daze it never even occurred to me he had no way of getting himself home, and to this day I'm not exactly sure what he did. Probably went to one of the neighbours', I suppose Pauline the cook, and called himself a cab.

I went inside and got a Hamm's and sat in my easy chair. Just sat there admiring the inside of my house—curtains, sofa, framed needle-works on the walls. Funny. It was the worst day I'd ever had and all I could think was how satisfied I was with the colour I'd picked for my wallpaper. A lot of people don't like green, but I think a nice light shade's restful on the eyes. Makes you think of forests, or tended lawns, or tiger eyes.

So I sat there for the longest time. Not so much thinking as mes-merized by the wallpaper. Time passed and there was a ring at the door and I got up and Pauline was there holding my supper. Steam was ris-ing between the gaps in the tinfoil and dampening the underside of her chin. She took one look at me and started sniffling, her eyes filling with water the same way Parly's had in the meeting. I ended up inviting her in and sitting her down and giving her a cup of cool water and telling her that, really, it was all for the best, it's true I was upset before but I'm okay now, besides who ever heard of a woman my age doing what I did for a living? Was a blessing, I told her, for it'd give me time to do some knitting and some gardening plus I had a whole bunch of *Billboards* and *White Tops* and Bob Denver fan club newsletters to get through.

After a while she left, though not before I'd given her more of the same don't-worry-I'll-be-fine assurances I'd given Parly. My head felt foggy. I didn't feel like eating even though she'd made my favourite, beef stew with tea biscuits to sop up the gravy. Wasn't a coincidence, I figured.

Instead, I got another Hamm's and watched *Gilligan* and never laughed harder. Tears were rolling down my cheeks and I was holding my stomach, I thought it was so funny. After that, I took two of Dr. Brisbane's pills and slept like a log, and the next morning I took another couple to see me through what I had to do that day. I ate my corn mush squares and my bacon and my black coffee and, like any other day, backed that big old Buick of mine into traffic. Pulled onto the Ventura freeway, sticking to the slow lane, for one thing I've never really liked is driving and in particular driving fast. That's the reason I drive a car as long as my house is deep—it makes me feel protected.

Got into work at exactly 6:20. It hardly seemed possible this was going to be my last day with Goldie, Tiba, Toby, Ouda, Mommy, Prince and Khan. Thinking about this, I felt a twinge of loneliness for old Dale, a magnificent cat with a head like a bear's, who'd died about a year previous. Course, Roger's car was the only other car there; I went inside for the last time and he was waiting at my cage line, fretting and reminding me of Dan the educated valet, the way every thought that ever went through his head was splashed across his face. First thing he did was rush up and say how sorry he was and that firing me was a disgrace and a situation somebody ought to do something about. Then he stopped and came a little closer so he could be heard in a lowered voice, something that struck me as unnecessary seeing as there wouldn't be another person around for at least another hour.

"Mabel," he said, "you won't ... I mean ... you're not really thinking ..."

I looked at him sternly and said, "Oh for goodness' sake Roger. What's wrong with everybody? It's high time you remember I'm an old lady and old ladies have a habit of blowing off steam once in a while. It's called crankiness, Roger. It's called sore joints and bad sleep and indigestion. It's called knowing the best's so far behind you it might as well never've happened. It's called *not having a man since 1932*. For heaven's sake I'll be fine."

By this point he was laughing, and though amusing him hadn't been my intention I didn't mind that it had. We went to work. I took out my tools and put Goldie in the exercise pen and put Toby and Tiba in the ring and started sweeping cages, moving tigers as we needed. As we'd done a hundred times before, we cleaned the wheelbarrow at seven and started feeding, making sure Goldie got her shoulder blade and Mommy her shank. While the animals ate, we scrubbed the blood gutter, leaving everything spotless and then having ourselves a cup of coffee, Roger telling me what he thought of last night's episode as he'd made himself a fan of *Gilligan's Island* just to please me, and damn it if I wasn't sitting there, chatting with him as though this day was the same as any other.

At 8:45 we boned out and by nine I was watching my tigers settle down to sleep, thinking, *Never ever again*, though at the same time feeling like it was someone else who was having these thoughts. Maybe it was my mother's voice, forcing me not to feel anything, or maybe it was Dr. Brisbane's pills, which forced me not to feel anything as well. Either way, I was looking at claws and whiskers and tails and beautiful black-and-orange coats and wet pink noses, and none of these features were adding up to tiger. Whether I was cheated or whether I was spared is hard to say.

Some time went by, how much I couldn't honestly say, though after a bit I noticed Roger was standing on one side of me and Parly was on the other side of me and maybe a dozen feet away were JungleLand's carny owners, just looking on, grim-faced.

In other words, it was time.

"Mabel," Parly said, "we thought maybe Roger and I could see you got home safe and sound."

"Yes," Roger echoed, "safe and sound," and when I agreed I was happy at least there was a little forethought this time around, Roger driving my car and Parly following behind in his Ford. We got to my house and they both looked so worried and sheepish I thought, *Ah what the hell they might as well come on in.*

"You boys like a Hamm's?"

There must've been something unusual in the way I said it for they peered at each other, all surprised, before looking relieved and saying yes. To tell you the truth, it *was* unusual, for it's been my policy for the past thirty-six years to keep a manless house. A lot of my neighbours are ex-circus but at the same time a lot aren't, and the last thing I need is them seeing men traipsing in and out and getting wrong ideas about the old circus woman at 3076.

Roger and Parly came on in. They looked kind of nervous, like they'd stepped inside a museum, until I told them to take a load off. I gave them each a can of beer and watched as they pulled the tabs and slurped. Then I opened a bag of Cheezies and it was like we were having a little party, only one without much in the way of talking. If they'd been women, I suppose they would've given me a pep talk, or maybe they would've sobbed a little on my behalf, or one would've gone off and come back with a Bundt cake and coffee. They weren't, however, meaning they just sat there, looking glum and taking glugs of beer and making grim small talk about the weather and baseball and the general state of the circus world. Though they meant well, it was depressing as hell, so when they'd both finished their beers I stood and said, "Well, boys, was great seeing you but I suppose things're busy at JungleLand. Suppose you've all got a lot to do."

They looked at each other, stunned. Parly said, "You don't want us to stay a little longer? Maybe help with the dishes?" to which I said, "And what dishes would those be, Parly? The bowl holding the Cheezie dust? C'mon. I'm an old woman and I may not have a job but I've got my health and I've got my marbles and that's a lot more than a lot of ladies my age have. Tell you what. You don't feel sorry for me and *I* won't feel sorry for me, deal?"

This made them confident I wasn't about to do anything rash, so they put on their jackets and it was a moment in which it would've been appropriate for them to each give me a hug or a kiss. It was also a moment in which I regretted the guard I'd built up over the years, the one communicating to the world Mabel Stark doesn't accept humanly contact. So instead I saw them to the door. From my stoop I watched them each give a little wave before getting into Parly's Ford and driving off.

What happened next was this. I went inside the house and I turned on the TV and I turned on the radio and I opened windows so I could hear lawnmowers and gamboling children and the rushing noises made by the nearby freeway. Then I plunked myself down in my Laz-E-Boy and closed my eyes and let my head fill with noise.

It took about three days of feeling sorry for myself to start figuring activity would be the best tonic (or leastways the only one I could think of), so I drove out to the garden centre and when it opened I bought myself a shovel and a trowel and some annuals and a bag or two of planting soil. I came home, unloaded the stuff myself and carried it all out to the little square of backyard I keep next to my parking spot. I'd been looking at that backyard for close to thirty years, and had always thought planting some flowers come springtime might be pretty, a chore easier said than done when you've got kitties that need tending each and every day, weekends no exception. With that excuse out of the way the time had come. I went out back and started rooting. Wasn't sure exactly what I was rooting *for*, so I just kept at it, copying what I'd seen my neighbours do, which was digging up weeds and tossing in soil and basically moving earth from bottom to top to back on bottom again. Eventually, the bed looked churned and black and ready, and I had memory scents of West Kentucky come planting season. Raked it out nice and smooth. Got on my hands and knees and planted the petunias and when I was finished went into the kitchen and got myself a Hamm's. Then I went back outside and stood in the backyard admiring my handiwork. Was then I checked my watch. It was 10:30 in the morning.

Now this truly was a shock, how slowly time can pass when a mind and body's unoccupied. A minute passed, and I started feeling mouth-dry and fearful, which is how it always begins. I closed my eyes and rubbed them and none of it if helped, for it was all there, in my mind's eye, refusing to leave me alone: pelting rain, the green of springtime, smoky mountains and that knock on the door because May Wirth was sick and maybe I could help seeing as I was a nurse and all. Half crying, I choked down the Hamm's and got myself another one and took two of Dr. Brisbane's pills just to take the edge off. Then I got Parly on the phone and said, "Goddammit Parly. You're my agent now get me some work."

He sounded delighted. "You bet, Mabel. Just you wait and see. You may not be working the tigers anymore but no one's going to hold that against you. You're still Mabel Stark. You're still the tiger queen. I was thinking something along the line of personal appearances. How does that sound to you?"

"Will it get me out of the house?"

"Yes."

"Then it sounds good to me."

I hung up and commenced to wait. Fell asleep and woke up and made myself some corn bread that wasn't as good as Pauline's and I watched the channel six daytime rerun of *Gilligan* I always used to miss: a spider the size of a hippo trapped them all in a cave and it looked like curtains until Gilligan accidentally tripped over it, accidentally kicking what the Professor figured was the spider's sensitive spot and killing it. When it was over I played solitaire. Went shopping. Buffed my corns. Oiled my scars, a practise making them more supple and less likely to bind. Later, I visited Pauline the cook and we had coffee and while I was sitting there passing comment on stupid things, like sewing and daiquiri flavours, I kept thinking, *This is what women do? This is what keeps them busy?* A day later I was standing in my garden, drinking a Hamm's and thinking I might rearrange the petunias just to keep me busy and stop my memories from kicking in, when the phone rang. I raced inside, or leastways moved as fast as a woman my age has a right to.

Was Parly.

"Good news, Mabel."

"How's that?"

"You're working again."

"Thank God."

"Now don't get too excited, Mabel. I'm telling you right now it's not much. In fact, I almost turned it down, thinking you might be too proud to take it. But it's a start, Mabel. But it's a matter of you not having done appearances before and having to build up a track record. You understand?"

"Course, Parly. You don't go from groomer to trainer overnight. I understand that. Whatever it is I'll take it."

"You're sure?"

"Surer than sure."

"Then be at the Exhibition Center by nine."

"I need to bring anything?"

"You still got your old costume? The one people think of when they think Mabel Stark?"

"It's upstairs in mothballs."

"Wear it."

That night I didn't even need one of Dr. Brisbane's pills for I felt better than I had in a long long while. Went to bed at my normal time, just past 7:30, and as I drifted off I got to thinking maybe it really *was* ridiculous a woman my age training tigers, and that my whole dust-up with Ida was going to turn out to be a blessing in disguise. *Personal appearances.* I said it over and over again, as though rehearsing what I'd say when people asked me what I'd been doing since JungleLand.

When I awoke the sky was just starting to lighten in the east; I had time so I took my coffee into the yard and watched the sun turn from a thin band of violet to a deep red band to a low-hanging orange drape. I had my breakfast and headed up to the attic and dug out one of the old white leather costumes Rajah had liked to rub himself against so much. Course, I was nervous it wouldn't fit: as I've told you I'm itty-bitty, and given the chance weight just falls off me. In fact, my weight is the reason I drink at least two cans of beer a day; Dr. Brisbane once told me I needed it to keep my girth up, though at the time I wondered if he was just using my slightness as an excuse to tell an old woman what she wanted to hear.

In other words, I was worried the damn thing would droop in all the places it used to grip and that I'd look like a fool as a consequence. I went to the bedroom and drew the curtains, looking at myself in the mirror being something I've always preferred to do when the lights are low. Then I took off my clothes, which at my age doesn't get done without a certain amount of creaking and cracking and grunting little expressions of breath. Pulled on the damn suit. Looked at myself in the mirror. Goddammit if I didn't look like a snake getting ready to shed.

The overall looseness of the thing inspired a sudden withering of my enthusiasm, for the one thing I wasn't prepared to do was have others laugh at me. I was about to phone Parly and tell him the whole thing was off when a plan occurred to me. I peeled off the suit, enduring more creaking and cracking and grunting, and hunted through my chest of drawers for some old leotards and a sweater. Pulled those on and pulled the suit on top, and though I looked a little like a stuffed chicken I didn't look as ridiculous as I had earlier, so I figured, ah what the hell, if they can't handle a granny-aged woman dressed in leather, they don't have to look.

Was then a funny thing happened. I walked away from the mirror to get my keys from the dresser. With keys in hand I turned, and saw my reflection from across the room. Remember: the lights were low and my eyesight's just starting to weaken and I was a fair distance from the face of the mirror, so that when I looked at myself my reflection was dim and slightly fuzzy. Suddenly it hit me: how I must've looked when I first wore my body suit. Saw it clear as day. Also saw it for the first time, for whenever I'd looked at myself in my prime it was with a self-judgment that made me think I was frumpy and plain and just a poor old thing from Kentucky. Well, I stood there for minutes and minutes, couldn't take my eyes off it, the thing in the mirror like an apparition from another time. Truth to tell, it looked like a ghost picking that moment to answer a question that'd always plagued and perplexed me.

Well Jesus Christ no *wonder* so many men had wanted to fuck me.

With this thought reverberating I jumped in my big old Buick. I got to the Exhibition Center early, really early, in fact, just me and my big old car sitting in the parking lot, though after a bit vans started pulling up to the loading docks, and men in overalls began hauling out stuff in brown cardboard boxes. It was just before seven in the morning. The only other vehicle parked in the lot was a truck supporting a Pixel sign flashing the words "Conejo Valley Home Show" followed by a platoon of marching exclamation marks.

The parking lot got busier and busier and I just sat there watching the activity, butterflies in my stomach. Finally, around eight o'clock, Parly showed up and parked next to me. He got out and I got out and good-mornings were exchanged. Parly had some kind of pass card that admitted us to the building, where workingmen were running wires and tacking down indoor-outdoor carpeting and hammering together displays. We set to walking through the hall, past booths advertising vacuum cleaners, blenders, hair dryers, floor polishers, car waxers, grout eliminators, pot holders you could wash under a tap, stereophonic sound systems, electric salad mixers, battery-powered wood polishers, even a whirring shoe-brush contraption that charged up when held under incandescent light. Seemed the more I looked around, the more I spotted devices existing for the simple reason people have to spend their money once it finds a way into their pockets.

"Here we are," Parly said.

We were in front of a table with some sort of contraption sitting on a red-and-white-checkered tablecloth. Behind was a gallery of photos stuck to what looked like a bordello screen: a bunch of me from my Ringling heydey, plus others from the Barnes show, John Robinson, the Mills Circus of London. They were all arranged around a sign that could've come from the mind of old P.T. himself: "The Queen of the Tigers Meets the Queen of Food Processors—Mabel Stark Presents the All-New Stainless-Steel Slicing and Dicing Ronco Miracle Kitchen Whirrrr."

I stood eyeballing the Kitchen Whirrrr, a big plastic doohickey with a blade somewhere inside, while Parly looked around for a hint of assistance. It finally came in the form of a woman wearing a green pantsuit and cat's-eye glasses, who rushed up and breathlessly shook our hands. Hers was waxy with cream.

"Oh hello," she said. "I'm so glad you're here. I'm Theresa Gains, Ronco product representative."

"I'm Parly Baer," Parly said, "and this is *the* Mabel Stark."

This triggered another round of handshakes, though when Miss Gains realized she'd already waggled our hands, she flushed and got even shorter of breath. By this time someone had come by and dropped a white plastic basin, the kind busboys use in diners, beside the Kitchen Whirrrr. It was heaped with tomatoes, potatoes, lettuce, turnips, carrots, onions, rutabagas—pretty much every vegetable you could think of.

"These are for demonstration purposes," Miss Gains said. "My advice is you familiarize yourself with the device and put some sliced vegetables on one of the presentation trays you'll find beneath the table. I'll check on you a little later."

She turned and was gone.

Parly and I looked at each other, amused, until Parly said, "Well, you heard the lady, Mabel. Let's do some slicing and dicing."

We inspected the machine. On the front was a button labelled On-Off. Beside this button was a big dial, with settings marked: Thick, Medium-Thick, Medium, Medium-Thin, Thin, Wafer, Paper. It was set on Thick, Parly saying Thick was fine by him so long as I didn't have any objections. I didn't, so he reached out and turned the thing on.

Now it'd be an exaggeration to say the thing started chugging, though I'll use the word anyway, for the Kitchen Whirrrr hummed so much it shook itself slowly around the table. Parly grabbed it and held it in one spot, something made his cheeks waggle. "Feed it a tomato Mabel and we'll see what happens."

I picked up a fat one and dropped it into a clear plastic chute that stuck out the top like a chimney. A second later came a sucking noise, like a drain unclogging itself, and a second after that three inch-thick tomato slices plopped onto the table in a pool of pulp and seed.

"Well anyway it works," Parly said. I put the three slices on a tray and wiped away the tomato guts and suggested we try one of the other settings. Parly put it to Thin. This time, the machine started to whine, and it tried to skip across the tabletop as opposed to slowly lumber. Parly held it with two hands, and I dropped in an onion. Instead of a pained sucking noise we heard what sounded like an axe swiping air, the onion slices jetting from the Kitchen Whirrrr in an arc that could only be described as rainbow-like.

"I'll be goddammed," Parly said. "Best keep it on a lower setting, Mabel. We're liable to hurt someone with this thing."

I agreed this was a sensible idea, and with Parley's help I sliced up a bunch of vegetables, all of them done Thick or Medium-Thick, and then arranged them accordian-style on the tray in a way I thought looked nice. Around this time the home show opened, and people— well, women and their children—started to wander in and look at the tables. Parly checked his watch, and we both decided it was time for him to go, my never having been a woman who needed a lot of hand-holding.

Standing there and smiling was slow work, slower in fact than I would've thought possible. Seems the Kitchen Whirrrr wasn't the only slicer and dicer at the Conejo Valley Home Show, and so it wasn't drawing people the way everyone had hoped. (Leastways this is what Theresa Gains told me on her next visit.) Still, every once in a while someone would come up and ask for a demonstration, at which point I'd thick-slice some cucumber or maybe some honeydew melon. If the woman was holding a toddler, I'd hand a slice to the child and say, "Here you go, sweetheart." Usually this would be followed by a question about whether I'd really been a circus star, to which I'd answer, "Sure as I'm standing here, I was on the Ringling show back when that meant something." Hearing this, they'd nod and then ask how much a Kitchen Whirrrr costs despite there being no fewer than three signs on the table saying "Yours for the Incredible Low Introductory Price of $19.99, All Blades Included."

It didn't take long to figure out the women at home shows come because there's free child care at the back of the building along with food samples you don't have to pay for. In other words, none of them were old enough to know who Mabel Stark was and if they knew the name Ringling at all it was only in a vague unappreciative sort of way—the same way I knew the names Copernicus or Ponce de León, say. Hours went by. Hours made all the more agonizing because Alan Hale himself, the Skipper from *Gilligan*, was two aisles over hawking some sort of carpeting that didn't stain even if you poured paint over it, which from what I heard was exactly what he was doing. At first I wanted to go over and meet the man and tell him how much I liked his work. I also wanted to ask him how the Skipper had felt being the only man on the island without a love interest, Gilligan having Mary-Anne and the Professor having Ginger and Mr. Howell having that fussy old prune Mrs. Howell.

I never did go over, however, for after a bit I heard he was drawing quite a crowd, bigger even than Eve Plumb, the middle daughter from *The Brady Bunch*, who was flogging a hair flattener you plugged into a car lighter. I was hit by a wave of jealousy, and my desire to shake Mr. Hale's beefy hand got put on the back burner.

Plus I was hot. Remember: I was wearing leather head to toe along with a leotard and sweater underneath. This was too much, seeing as I was standing under lights designed to make the Kitchen Whirrrr gleam. Course, by ten in the morning, the Kitchen Whirrrr was starting to crust with tomato pulp and cucumber innards, and my hands were cramped from wiping.

I felt myself start to turn resentful, and unfortunately I've always been the sort of woman who has trouble fending off the arrival of a bad mood, no matter how much warning it gives me. Sometimes I think I even go out of my way to welcome it. I was getting hot and grumpy, and as the morning wore on I wanted nothing more than a can of Hamm's and a Snack Bar Annie leaned-on burger. As lunchtime approached the crowds thickened, all those bodies pushing against one another making the Conejo Valley Exhibition Center an even warmer place to be. I started smelling whiffs of game escaping from the tight collar of my uniform. By one o'clock my stomach was growling something fierce, and I started getting mad at Parly and Theresa Gains and the makers of the Miracle

Kitchen Whirrrr for allowing an old woman to get so hot and foot-sore and hungry. It was practically inhuman, the way I was being treated.

Then. Around a half-past one, and like I say I was hot and bored and hungry and starting to miss my life with tigers. A woman came by who'd obviously had a morning as bad as I'd been having. She was baggy-eyed and pale, her hands full of what was no doubt causing her exhaustion: an evil little monster of a boy, maybe two and a half years old, who kept slapping the side of her face and screeching. His face was messy with what looked like chocolate pudding, and because his nose was running pretty much non-stop there was a stream flowing through the pudding, over his chin and down his neck into his baby suit. Apparently he liked the taste of it, for in between hollers he kept sticking out his tongue and taking a big swipe of snot pudding and then returning his tongue to his mouth. In other words, he was a child put on the face of the earth to make bystanders tut-tut and comment on what a handful boys can be.

Meanwhile, he kept slapping his mother on the side of the head and shrieking. Apparently he'd been doing it so long she'd given up trying to stop him, for she just stood there, having her head pounded and her ear screeched into, the whole time trying to get the hair out of her face by jutting out her bottom lip and blowing. I felt sorrier than sorry for her. In fact, I wanted to take the brat off her hands and teach him some manners while she went and had herself a coffee and dealt with her hair problem. Was a sympathy that disappeared the moment she opened her mouth.

"I want to see the damn thing work!" she yelled over the screeching.

"Certainly, ma'am."

I'd developed a technique: whenever I turned on the machine I'd let one hand rest on it as though was just a natural place to let a hand take a rest, disguising the fact the Kitchen Whirrrr liked to take a stroll when switched on. With my free hand, I picked up a turnip, thinking this might impress her for turnips are tough little customers and much opposed to being cut into bits. I dropped it in, heard the sucking noise and out popped four turnip slabs glistening with juice. For a brief second I was actually proud of the Kitchen Whirrrr and my role promoting it. The boy shrieked and wiggled and slapped, and the woman stared regretfully at the turnip sections as though I'd done something to offend her. She didn't even take her eyes off them when she asked, "How much?"

"It's $19.99."

"Damn rip-off, that. The Slice-Master over in the corner's only $17.99, and I like the colour better."

"Does the Slice-Master come with a purée blade?"

"Uh, don't know."

"Well, see, there you go. You're obviously a woman with children, and believe me a purée blade'll come in handy."

This set the woman to thinking, which she seemed to find hard, either because she was naturally stupid or because she had a thirty-pound toddler smacking the side of her head.

"Plus," I said, "how many settings does the Slice-Master have?"

"Uh, I dunno. Three?"

"Three? Three settings? Far be it from me to tell you which processor to buy, madam, but most housewives find three settings inadequate for even the most basic chopping requirements. The Kitchen Whirrrr, as you can see, has seven: Thick, Medium-Thick, Medium, Medium-Thin, Thin, Wafer, Paper."

Here I motioned like a twit and smiled brightly. Halfway through my arm sweep I realized what a mistake I'd just made.

"Lemme see," she said.

"Let you see what, madam?"

"I wanna see the Paper setting. Graham only eats his carrots if they're so thin you can see through 'em, isn't that right Graham?"

At the sound of his name the boy stopped howling and pounding the side of his mother's head long enough to wipe the back of his arm against his nose, smearing all that snot and dried pudding into a smudge that ran diagonally over the bottom half of his face. Turned my stomach, he did. Having had a momentary break he started screeching and slapping with renewed vigour.

"I'm afraid I'm out of carrots, madam."

"Well, spuds then. I like to get them thin before I fry 'em."

"Of course, ma'am, right away ... oh, darn, the Kitchen Whirrrr works best with peeled potatoes and I don't seem to be able ... where *did* I put my peeler?"

Her face went stiff. She grabbed both the brat's hands, which caught him off guard and shut him up. Then she looked straight at me for the first time since she'd showed up at the table.

"Listen, lady," she said, "you jerking me around for any specific reason or is it just your nature?"

I set the Kitchen Whirrrr to Paper, turned it on, took hold, stuck in an unpeeled potato the size of a football, and aimed. Caught the ugly little goblin right in the eye. I don't think he even got his lid closed in time, for his eye turned pink and drippy and he started screaming in a way that made his previous yowling seem calm by comparison. The woman got mad as a furnace, and through a curtain of greasy hair yelled, "What did you do?"

"Taught your brat a lesson you trashy excuse for a human," I replied, and from there our salesman-customer relationship deteriorated. A commotion ensued, until finally there was a crowd around the All-New Stainless-Steel Slicing and Dicing Ronco Miracle Kitchen Whirrrr, though not for the reasons the Ronco people might've hoped for. My day ended with my telling a spitting-mad Theresa Gains what she could do with her crappy processing machine. Then I stormed out, feeling like exactly what I was: a useless old lady wearing a silly costume fifty years too young for her.

The weather was the way it always is in March in southern

California: hot and beautiful. I forced myself to concentrate on the way the sun warmed my face and on the coolness of the breeze blowing over the parking lot and how that coolness is so often a feature of the coast. At the same time, I forced myself to think how lucky I was to live in a place that wasn't freezing cold nine months out of the year. Then I forced myself to consider my health, my house, my big old car, my memories of criss-crossing this big old glorious country called America so many times I know it the way most people know their own bathroom.

Had to.

I stayed reclined for the better part of a week. Only got up to pee and drink down the occasional Hamm's and swallow my sleep medicine. If the phone rang I let it go on ringing, and if someone came to the door I let their knuckles get raw. I even moved the black-and-white into the bedroom so I could switch on *Gilligan* or the news if the mood hit me. Generally, it didn't.

Finally, one afternoon I awoke and instead of feeling listless and wan I felt raring to go. Vengeful, you might say. This presented two options. The first was getting up and doing whatever it took, no matter how desperate, to get my kitties back. The second was to roll over and wait patiently for another neurasthenic lapse. Both had their attractions and their drawbacks, but after a few minutes of staring up at the ceiling I figured I better pursue the first—if I lay around much longer my muscles would start to go, and then doing anything requiring the slightest bit of vigour would be permanently out of the question.

So I pounced. Threw back the blankets and jumped to the carpet. It felt good moving my body again, so I gave a little whoop along with it. Then I dressed in clothes befitting a woman my age and jumped in the old Buick. Tore onto the Ventura Freeway, and for the first time in my life took the center lane instead of the slow lane, all the while thinking, *You've got to strike while the iron's hot.* Plus I figured driving faster than normal would keep my mind off the fact that I didn't have a plan, or leastways not exactly.

What I did have was possible courses of action. The first was barging into Jeb and Ida's office and demanding they give me my tigers back. While it's hard to describe why I thought this might work, it has to do with my having been adulated once. Another was getting Jeb alone and then out-and-out begging, something that probably wouldn't work either and had the additional drawback of being a humiliation. The other idea I had was somewhere in the middle: I'd find Jeb or Ray Labbat and I'd say, all right, you win. You hire me back and I'll sign on legit and any increase in your insurance premiums you can deduct straight from my salary. That'll make me happy and that'll make the Omahamians happy and you can keep on advertising you've got yourself the oldest living tiger trainer, two shows daily.

Yet as I tore along the freeway, the needle on the senseless side of seventy, I willed myself not to make any decisions. Sometimes when you enter an arena full of animals made grumpy by weather or bad hay it's best to let instinct get you through. If I had a definite plan, it was only to put myself in the moment and then see what determination and a talent for survival would do for me.

So I pulled into the JungleLand parking lot and immediately got mad when I saw someone else parked in my favourite spot beneath the big oak tree. Instead of calming myself down, I let myself get good and enraged, for *that* car being in *that* spot was a part of the moment, and if my being mad as a polar bear was part of the equation, then so be it. So I hit the steering wheel and leaned heavily on the horn and cursed out the window. When this didn't accomplish anything other than make me go hoarse I parked in the grass lot used on busy days. Walked all the way across the lot, and when I reached the entrance Wanda the ticket girl got all wide-eyed and curious about the details of my life since retirement.

"Mabel!" she said. "How're you doing?"

Though Wanda was a decent person with problems that merited sympathy—her son was in prison, and over the past year her husband had bloated with gout—I lowered my chin and held up my palm as if to say, Sorry, Wanda. Not right now. Then I walked on in, feeling relieved she hadn't asked me to pay admission.

For a second I stood in the midway, getting my bearings, feeling the way you do when you return to a place you once belonged—i.e., awkward. Which is not to say people weren't coming up to me and asking me how I was doing. They were, only I was feeling stupid being on the lot without any work to do, so I used body language to indicate I was too busy for idle chat but I'd come by later for a proper hello.

Mostly I wanted to keep up a good head of steam. Though I still had no idea what I was going to do when I finally tracked down my old bosses, there was a better than even chance I'd do it in a voice gone sharp as a mowing tine. I stormed past the games of skill and the coin rides and Annie's hamburger shack. Pigeons cawed and fluttered into my face. (Who did they think they were, saying *I* was too old?) I turned a corner onto the connection leading to the menage. Pulled up. Was as if some furious god with big lungs had taken the wind from my sails with a single sharp inhale.

Henry Tyndall, doddery as ever, was leading Daisy the Dromedary to the show arena. He moved so slowly it was more like the damn camel was leading him.

So. My heart pounded, my eyes brimmed, my stomach went fluttery and I suffered a sudden weakness in whatever muscles decide whether you do or do not go to the bathroom. Seeing Tyndall was something I wouldn't've predicted in a million years. Instead of reacting and being in the moment and running on instinct and doing all the things I'd pictured myself doing, I stood there thinking, *Why? Why me?*

Seeing as there's no more stupefying a question, I knew my first priority was to make it stop bouncing around my head. In other words, I got my legs going before I figured where it was they were going to go *to*. Meanwhile, I sort of left my own body and imagined how I must've looked trying to run, and that way was: arms crooked and tensed, fingers splayed, head stuck out like a turtle's, splinted legs moving at the hips, a stiffness caused by the fear of breaking something. An expression hoping for dignified but not quite making it. I don't think I'd ever been madder at my own self for getting so old.

I'd travelled a few dozen steps when I figured out I was heading in the direction of the monkey house. I kept on going. The monkeys were inside that day, so when I pulled open the door I was met with a steamy rankness. Fought my way through schoolchildren all pointing at the king gorilla, who was fond of vomiting into his hands and then slurping it right back up again, something he was doing that very moment. There was a stretch of daylight between the gorillas and the orangutans, at which point there was another cluster, Gerald the papa orang giving a show by twirling his privates with a forefinger and grinning like a pervert.

By the time I made it to the chimps, I was sweating like a ewe on slaughter day. For a second I stood with my eyes down. I couldn't look. Couldn't even bring myself to lift my head—just sort of angled my eyeballs upward and felt my throat seize tight. Sure enough, that old Indian chief was in there, hunched over and sweeping pellets, his face a thousand red nooks and crannies and crevices.

Had to've been ninety if he was a day.

I put my head down and walked quickly out of the monkey house and if anyone called out, "Hi Mabel how you doing?" I ignored them and kept going. Shaky with regret, I was, and that's a bitter way to feel: even the dumbest eighteen-year-old elephant groomer knows enough to be nice to the boss. Truth was, I'd been too big for my britches. I'd deserved everything that'd come my way, and here I'm talking about more than my firing from JungleLand.

By the time I stopped at Snack Bar Annie's I was pale and shaky and sweaty.

"Jesus Christ, Mabel," Annie said. "You look like you seen a ghost."

"Hamm's."

She gave me one and I popped the pull tab and drank it straight down while she watched. I slammed it against the tabletop, scaring some flies huddled around spilled ketchup.

"Another," I said, and repeated the process. By the time I finished Hamm's number two, I was light-headed and wobbly, two shotgun beers being a lot for an old woman whose weight and age are closer than she'd ever care to admit.

"Thank you kindly," I said. Then I stumbled off and made the entrance and when the ticket girl Wanda said, "Nice to see you again, Mabel," I waved a saggy forearm without looking at her.

I got in my big old Buick. Backed out and made sure I took out the headlight belonging to the car that'd had enough nerve to occupy my spot under the oak tree. Then, so my final departure would be dramatic, I did something I'd heard one of the cage boys brag about once: I pushed my left foot against the breadloaf-sized brake pedal while revving the engine hard with my right.

Understand, my Buick has a fair-sized engine, 425 cc to be exact, and though this doesn't mean a whole lot to me I've been told that's a sizable bit of liveliness under the hood. The engine roared like a lion wanting to fight. I let my left foot slide off the side of the brake, the pad springing upward with a thwock. The tires spun like a son of a bitch, the front of the car staying in one spot while the back swung in a sideways arch. It came crashing against a big old woody station wagon that'd been parked next to the car in my spot. There was the sound of breaking glass and crumpling metal and screeching tires. The air was filled with black smoke. The smell of rubber was something awful. I drove slowly on out.

A minute later, I heard sirens. Was another minute before I realized they were after yours truly. So I took an off ramp and parked on a side street.

A tall, lean cop got out of the cruiser. Immediately I knew I wasn't about to buy my way out of this one, it being a strange truth the skinny ones are rarely crooked. Sitting there, I pined for the days when cops barely got paid and appreciated a gratuity from time to time.

He stepped up to my side as I was rolling down the window. I was just about to hit him with the "Is there anything wrong, Officer?" when he proceeded straight to the "Step out of the car, ma'am."

We were in a black neighbourhood. While he looked at my fake driver's license, which bore a picture of me taken in 1952, I had myself a look about. Behind me was a little strip mall with maybe four or five storefronts, three of which were papered over. Still in business was a liquor store with the word *Michelob* flashing in neon blue, and of all things a creole shack. What a creole shack was doing two thousand miles from the bayou was anybody's guess, but I can tell you at that moment it hit me I hadn't eaten in the better part of a week and would've killed for a hot ladling of étoufée. Goddammit, how the circus used to cheer itself up whenever we crossed the Louisiana state line, and believe me it wasn't the humidity or the gators or the French whores or that funny squeeze-box music they had down there. Uh-uh. Was the *food*.

I was planning to ask the officer if he could spare me for a minute when he told me to stand on one foot and close my eyes and touch both fingers to my nose.

I practically laughed.

"Might as well ask me to flap my wings and fly, sonny Jim. You're looking at an old lady, and old ladies have trouble staying upright on *two* feet."

He stewed on this a second. I even saw a flicker of sympathy cross his face, something that made me think he'd never last.

"All right," he said, "count backwards from a hundred by sevens."

Again, I had to laugh, this being a test as old as the hills. Back in the days when the Ringlings were hiring Pinkerton agents to help thin the grift a little, there were a few months when John Ringling's fastidious wife, Mabel, decided she wanted to rid the circus of alcohol too. This made us all snicker, Mabel Ringling having a husband who drank schnapps all day and who never went to bed without having a dozen pints of German lager. Course, maybe that was the reason she was so keen to see the circus turn temperate: she was worried her husband's drinking would kill him, which of course it eventually did. In the meantime, she'd stand near the workingmen's train on nights off, bushwhacking those on their way back from the blue car and asking them to count backward from a hundred by sevens. Was about as unfair as unfair gets, seeing as a typical workingman'd never made it out of grade school and couldn't have done it sober. They'd fluster up and cipher in their head and usually go mute with nerves. Then Mabel would fine them 50 cents, an amount the front office boys never bothered to collect, seeing as they were the ones who sold them the beer in the first place.

Though I never got the test myself, I knew enough to practise. It wasn't hard, once you got the hang of it, so when that officer asked for it I knew I had him licked, the sharpness of my mind being about the only thing I still took pride in.

I started.

"One hundred," I said, proceeding by memory to the next step, "ninety-three" and the next, "eighty-six."

Now here a distressing thing happened. I couldn't recall what the next number was, though this didn't overly concern me, for it'd been more than forty years since I'd practiced Mabel Ringling's sobriety test. No problem, I told myself. I'd just figure it out. Problem was, by this point I seemed to have forgotten the number I'd just said, so I had to go back and repeat the count in my head: *One hundred ... ninety-three ... oh, right, eighty-six*. Once I got the eighty-six back, I had to minus the seven, though I found pulling the number out of thin air was like pulling teeth: instead of just landing on the number like I would've years earlier, I had to count backward from eighty-six, embarrassed the whole time my lips were moving.

"Seventy-nine?" I said weakly.

You could see by the hopeful expression on the young man's face he was rooting for me. I guess he figured if a woman as old as me could handle this test then maybe old age wasn't so fearsome after all. His eyes widened and his lips parted. I thought he was even going to mouth the next number. Course, he didn't, and by that point I'd forgotten what I'd just said, so I had to start all over in my head, stalling at eighty-six, counting my way down past seventy-nine and losing my place somewhere in the mid-seventies. Meanwhile, my stomach was growling and my head was hurting and sun was getting in my eyes so I decided I'd take a guess.

"Seventy-four?" I croaked, my tongue seeming to quit on me as well.

The young officer immediately looked guilty as a sinner. Was like *he* was the one who'd smashed a few cars in the JungleLand parking lot.

"Ma'am," he said softly, touching my sweatered elbow with two fingers.

In this way he led me to his squad car. He opened the front passenger door and I got in. When he got me home he said he wasn't going to press any charges but that I wasn't about to drive again either; to emphasize this fact he took my old forged license and slid it into an inside jacket pocket (which didn't bother me unduly, as I had four or five others sitting in one of my kitchen drawers). After promising him I had someone to look after me, he nodded and drove off. I went inside my house and immediately hated the green, the garden, the little kitchen, the me-ness of it. Believe me—it wasn't possible for a person to feel lower than I did at that moment. I knew I couldn't be alone—in fact, I could practically feel my memories reaching from the walls and trying to grab me by the throat and it surprised me when I realized there was only one living person in the whole world I wanted to see. I picked up the phone and dialled the JungleLand cathouse. When I got through I asked for that little Okie job-stealer Roger Haynes.

"Mabel!" he said. "How in Sam Hill you doing?"

I let a pause go by.

"Better come, Roger. Better come."

He got there shortly after the supper hour. I didn't answer the door, seeing as I couldn't hear him over the TV and two radios blaring. Luckily, he had the smarts to come on in, finding me on the living room sofa.

"Jesus."

First thing he did was run around and turn off all the racket, and then he galloped into the kitchen and grabbed me a glass of water and a hunk of Velveeta. Though I pushed them away, he insisted, and figuring he was a guest in the house I eventually became amenable to getting something in my system.

First thing I said to him was, "Oh, Roger, why in the hell didn't you tell me Chief and Tyndall were still working?"

"I was afraid to, Miss Stark."

"Goddammit, Roger. I feel like a fool."

"Plus I figured Parly was going to."

"Well, maybe he should've."

After that, it got difficult to communicate. Roger mostly kept his eyes fixed on the carpeting, and he kept rotating his wedding ring, something he tended to do when nervous. Course, I wasn't helping, which was strange given a few hours earlier he was the only one on earth I figured could stop me from doing something desperate. Maybe it was my last shred of dignity talking.

Roger's face lightened and the corners of his mouth sneaked

upward. "Miss Stark. I was wondering if you might let me show you something."

"Depends what it is."

"If you're curious, you'll just have to wait and see."

Here I asked him a few more questions about the nature of the surprise. Roger wouldn't answer any of them; instead, he rose to his feet and kept shaking his head and saying, "No no no, Miss Stark. You're just going to have to trust me. We'd better hurry or we'll miss it."

Here I figured if I couldn't trust a person like Roger then there wasn't much point in trusting, period. Getting to my feet was difficult given all the Hamm's I'd poured into myself, though once I did I let Roger guide me outside the house to his car. Course, he did this by putting two fingers on my elbow just like the police officer had.

We got into his car and headed northeast on Highway 5. Roger drove faster than the speed limit, which I ordinarily wouldn't've tolerated. After about half an hour, we got so we could see the foothills of the Tehachapis, which I knew well for I'd crossed them every year I was on the Barnes show. We drove a bit more, neither one of us saying anything. Then Roger made a right onto another smaller road, this one unmarked and gravelly, like the kind ranchers use. Only you could tell this one wasn't in use anymore, for the space between the tire ruts had grown over with weeds and chaparral. Probably the land had been bought up by developers willing to let it sit idle until the value went up.

"Roger, where are we going?" I asked.

Instead of answering the question he looked at his watch and said, "Oh good, Miss Stark, we're here right on time." It was dusk, the shadows lanky.

We followed along the little path as it inclined a drumlin. I pretended to be cranky, saying, "Jesus Christ, Roger, you're going to get a tire stuck," though I was doing it mostly to hide the fact my curiosity had been pricked and pricked good.

Roger stopped the car just as the lane turned into a footpath. We were parked before a split in the drumlins, and the path seemed to lead up between the two of them. I peered up it, squinting for effect, and said, "You can't possibly expect me to trot on up there like a mountain goat, Roger. I've had me a long day."

Fortunately, by this point he understood I was just being disagreeable out of reflex. He grinned, and came around my side of the car to let me out. This time when he took my elbow, I shook his hand away, saying, "Good grief, I can manage."

So we walked up the path, Roger leading the way. As I'd thought, the path split the two drumlins but instead of leading back down the other side it stopped on a ridge. Roger invited me to sit on some boulders and we both looked out over a valley.

"Roger ..."

"Shhhhhh, Miss Stark. It's just about to happen."

Roger pointed, and I realized he was pointing at the sun, which was getting ready to dip below the mountains on the far side of the valley. As soon as it did, it started to turn colour, filling the valley with a thick golden light.

Then it happened. My mind's eye and that valley blended into one and I saw things, floating and shimmery. Like Rajah's face. Like Al G. Barnes's mischief grin. Like an audience on its feet with the lights turned up.

Like: Art.

After a minute or so, when the gold had downgraded to a rusty copper, Roger turned and said, "Well, that's it."

"That was something, Roger."

"I'm glad you liked it. We might as well go."

"Might as well."

We left the ridge, and because it was getting a little on the dark side I didn't shake Roger away when he took my elbow. We got in the car, and Roger headed back to my house in Thousand Oaks at a speed aimed to calm. I kept on looking out the window at the city lights in the distance.

"Roger?"

"Yes, Miss Stark?"

"You ever wonder why things happen?"

"What do you mean?"

"What makes the things that happen, happen? God, you figure? Or is it all just luck? What do you think, Roger? If it's God running things, I could live with that, but pure dumb luck? I'm not sure how wild I am about that...."

He looked at me, his lips slightly parted and the rest of him white as a halibut. "I don't know what you mean, Miss Stark."

I let the matter drop, figuring he was a young man and it was a mistake bothering him about an old person's concerns. Still, was no denying I felt like gabbing.

"Tell me something, Roger."

"Uh-huh?"

"You got yourself a baby at home."

"Yes, Miss Stark."

"Then why work so hard? If I had little ones I'd put them before tigers, believe you me."

He didn't say anything, and I felt bad about turning naggy.

To make amends I said, "Roger?"

"Yes, Miss Stark?"

"That sunset. It helped. It did."

"Don't mention it."

"Well, just so you know."

"You're welcome, Miss Stark."

"Helped put my head on straight. I owe you one, Roger. Maybe I'll knit that little gaffer of yours a sweater. I'll bet she's a sweetie. How come you never brought her around?"

"I never thought you'd be interested, Miss Stark."

"Well, I would've."

There was a pause.

"Well, just so you know, Roger. I feel better."

"I'm glad."

"No, really. I feel like a new woman."

This went on and on, my thanking the boy but never telling him exactly what it was I'd decided while watching that sunrise. It felt good, finally having myself a plan I knew, without a doubt, I could make happen. For the truth of the matter is, there's something about gazing on majesty that makes the big decisions seem so small as to barely be decisions at all.

CHAPTER 12

THE NEW MENAGE BOSS

HE WAS: DRESSED IN DUNGAREES AND STEEL-SHANKED BOOTS and a heavy cotton work shirt, rolled to the elbows. Maybe fifty years old, with a thick grey-flecked moustache veering toward walrus but not quite getting there. Cheeks red, and latticed with little burst veins like cinnamon-coloured spider webbing. Left leg afflicted with a limp, the inside of his left shoe worn down to a thinness, so that as he came toward me he made a brushing noise against the earth (such that even now, an eternity later, I recall that brushing noise, and it feels so real I have to stop myself from looking around on the off chance his ghost has decided to make an appearance). Hunch-shouldered, perhaps through worry, perhaps through years of hard lifting, his arms bent slightly at the elbow and swinging slightly with each step. Cigarette parked at the corner of his mouth, his natural breath drawing an infusion of smoke that was constant. An anchor-with-rope tattoo on his forearm that'd faded to the colour of kelp.

He was only a few inches taller than me, though he looked like anyone would have a time trying to knock him down. His hair was ample and slightly reddish, and it swooped off wavy to the left, which made me think he straightened it by using the fingers of his right hand as a comb. His eyes were a pale blue grey, a shade below robin's egg, and his skin looked like it'd seen more than its fair share of the sun: baked and wrinkly, though with enough of a reddish hue I had to wonder if he had a little Indian blood in him. His arms were gristly and criss-crossed with ligaments. Plus they were oddly shaped: narrow as a woman's at the wrist though widening to the size of a horse hock at the elbow, the whole effect being practically vase shaped. His back he kept stiff as a board, which looked out of place atop his odd, hiccuping gait. His legs and butt were skinny, his pants saggy and riveted with the dirt an animal boss can't help but pick up by nine in the morning. But his most remarkable feature was his fingers: dry and stubby and covered with little nicks and scars, the nails coated with a shade of polish that wouldn't've looked out of place against a summer sky.

He stopped in front of the cage belonging to a two-year-old menage lion named Betty. It'd been stormy the past couple of days, the skies chunky and dark. Like always, the change in atmosphere affected some of the animals, the menage filling with the sound of females announcing themselves with loud, heartfelt bellows. So it was with Betty. A day or two earlier she'd gone into heat with a vengeance, which would've been fine except it was causing a commotion among the males: the pungency of her spray and the generally pink and inflamed condition of her privates was giving them ideas that conflicted with the existence of their cages. The danger, of course, was they were going to hurt themselves while trying to butt their way through the bars.

"Good day, Betty," he said in a voice deeper than I expected on a man wearing nail lacquer. "I hear tell you're a little rambunctious these days. Not to worry, sweetheart. It's the weather to blame, not you. Psssssst psssst psssst...."

Betty perked up her ears and looked at him. Then she arfed, a signal she had no immediate plans to move from the back of her cage, where she'd spent most of the past two days rubbing herself and looking aggressive. Her entire underside was gummy with laid-down straw.

Meanwhile, he cooed, "It happens to the best of us, darling. Nothing to be ashamed of. If you could just come this way old Art might be able to offer you a little relief...."

He placed his right forearm through the bars, anchor side up.

"Here, sweetheart," he said, "come to old Art. Come on, girl. That's good. Pssst pssst pssst. Don't be wary...."

Betty kept looking at him as though he was a crazy person, while Art kept making *pssssst pssssst pssssst* noises, eyes glinting the whole time. Finally, it worked. Betty lifted the front half of her body, and then the rear half of her body, until she was wholly standing. As she lumbered toward the front of the cage, goop dripped out of her hindquarters.

When she reached the bars she sniffed Art's forearm, something that made my heart thrum: though she was a good lion what Art was doing was foolhardy and nothing but.

Still.

Betty sniffed daintily, as though his tattoo released a pacifying scent, which was remarkable seeing as how any calmness she may've once had had pretty much disappeared with the change in weather. Art just let her, offering such encouragements as "That's it, Betty," and "You have yourself a good long smell, sweetheart." After a minute of sniffing she seemed to be satisfied, for she turned herself right around and lifted her tail, letting him press his forearm into the oozing pink furrow that was her vulva.

"That's it," Art said. "Now you go ahead and have yourself a nice long sit."

Betty's eyes closed, and she started rubbing herself, slowly and deliberately, against his forearm. After about a minute or so she stopped and gave her torso a little side-to-side shimmy, a motion causing her crevice to accept more of Art's vase-shaped arm, till it disappeared so fully it looked like he had an elbow and a fist with nothing in between. She purred and licked her lips and produced a big lion grin. Then she resumed her slow, sawing motion on his arm. After a bit, she picked up the pace a little, and after another bit she picked up the pace in a way that was nothing but wanton. Her chin was pointed to the ceiling and her tail the same. Her eyes were squeezed shut and her forepaws were rigid as tent poles. Meanwhile, she pistoned—no other word for it— her torso hammering against Art's forearm, his arm probably getting chafed something awful for the inner folds of a female cat are leathery and rough no matter *how* lathered up. Meanwhile Betty was growling and howling and spitting and screeching and shrieking and generally making sounds like she was getting murdered. After about thirty seconds, she finished, let out a hiss that sounded like a venting steam valve, and in one smooth motion turned and took a lethal swipe at the arm that'd just pleasured her.

Art must've been expecting this, for he snapped his arm back through the bars and then held it out for her to look at. He was smiling. This caused Betty to growl and slink off to the back of her cage, where she had her first real nap in days.

As the cat dozed, he started whistling while he rolled his sleeve down. Forty-three years later, I remember the name of the tune, it being the sort of detail that makes up for its lack of significance by refusing to ever die: was "Farmer in the Dell." He finished rolling down his sleeve, though when he did he didn't move on. Or at least he didn't move on right away. Instead, he whistled the whole song, start to finish, throwing in a lot of warbles and flourishes for good measure. Only when he finished did he clear his throat and get to his feet and walk straight over to where I thought I'd been hidden.

"Hello," he said.

"Hello."

"You're Mabel Stark, aren't you? *The* Mabel Stark."

I nodded.

"In that case I'm going to say something and I hope you don't find me out of order saying it. What they're doin' to you on this circus is a crime. A waste of God-given talent. I just want you to know I *know* that."

I gave a good long look at this strange little person. He had the sort of bearing that men who've been coddled don't have, by which I mean beaten down yet hopeful as a child. Plus he had those colourful fingernails, set against a criss-crossing of nicks and scars, the contrast of which was so odd I had to force myself not to stare. Meanwhile he stood there smoking, the pause dragging on long enough he started to look a little wounded. Was then I realized I didn't like the thought of him wandering off so soon.

"You sitting?" I asked.

He hitched up his trousers and lowered himself with a grunt to the hay bale next to mine. After lighting his next cigarette off the old one, he tossed the butt into tanbark. I didn't say anything, for he'd reminded me how upset I was at my general state of affairs: after the Ringlings pulled their cat acts I'd been thrown in the High School display, horse riding being something I'd learned to do poorly way back on my first season with the Barnes show. It was also something I hated about as much as it's possible to hate anything, High School riding being a prancing, finicky business, better suited to schoolmarms than real performers.

In other words, I was brooding so hard I'd almost forgotten the new menage boss had taken a seat beside me.

Art finally broke the silence. As he spoke, smoke billowed off his cigarette and out his mouth and through his nose, his face looking like a little smoke factory.

"I saw your act last year in Baraboo. Marvellous. Just marvellous. That group sit-up—each head cocked at exactly the same angle, why you could've run a tightened string in front of their faces and each nose would've touched. And the rollover. I don't believe I've ever seen a group rollover when every cat comes back on its pads at exactly the same time and at exactly the same speed. I honestly don't know how you do it. I honestly don't. You, Miss Stark, have a one-of-a-kind act, and believe me when I say I'm not a guy who exaggerates to make his point known."

"Thank you," I said, feeling honestly pleased: those touches he talked about were the product of early-morning training sessions and sessions conducted at night when you were so tired you swore you'd fall asleep on your feet. I was never quite sure why I bothered, seeing as no one ever seemed to notice, my only rationale being that goals and standards have a way of making life feel more meaningful.

"Funny," I said. "You're talking about the group act when the thing people always remember about me is the wrestler."

He grinned, and where his lips separated smoke tumbled out.

"The wrestler. His name's Rajah, yes? Sure. Sure. That's a good act too."

Though he'd just paid me another compliment, his voice didn't sound as enthused as when he was talking about my group act, all of which was cockeyed seeing as how Rajah was the one who'd made me a household name.

"You sound like you liked the group act better than the wrestling act."

"Well, of course. Don't you?"

I looked at him, an eyebrow cocked.

"Now, don't misunderstand me. I like a wrestler as much as the next guy. But it happens. It happens. You get a cat when he's young and spend all your time with him he *will* start thinking he's more human than animal. And because he thinks of himself as human, he *will* start thinking you're his bride. It's called nature, and while it's impressive you caught that bit of nature in a ring that doesn't mean nature is always beautiful. Fact of the matter is, nature can be a little brutish when it has a mind to, and here I'm talking about the way he used you as his own personal rubbing post. All that bellowing and drooling. It's a hell of a trick he didn't kill you in the process, but you have to admit it was still a trick. But the *group* act. Christ. The first time I saw it I got goosebumps."

This was a whole lot to digest (though later I'd learn this was usually the case with Art's take on things). So I just sat pondering, the mad gone out of me, thinking, *Who* is *this little man?*

"So," he said after a bit, "the question is, How're you going to get back in a tiger cage where you belong?"

Was a question made my situation come rushing back. I sighed and said, "It's a problem."

"*Every*thing's a problem. That's hardly an excuse not to do anything about it. That way when the next problem comes along you'll only have the one problem to deal with instead of two. The way I see it, the Ringling Brothers don't want a cat act, but they also don't want any other circus drawing with your name. Am I right?"

"You're right, all right."

"Well, maybe they need a little convincing."

"They," I said, "are never around. They're always gallivanting around Europe, buying up art or violins, or they're down in Florida building homes the size of Rhode Island. They're impossible to get to."

"If they were easy to get to it wouldn't be much of a problem, now would it? Listen, I got an elephant who needs a little TLC. You want to come?"

I thought about this a second, said yes and followed Art out of the menage toward the bull yard. On the way, Art picked up a newspaper and a thermos of coffee. Meanwhile, he talked a blue streak.

"I'll tell you something. They weren't a second too early hiring me. The condition of this menage—terrible. *Terrible*. I thought things were bad with Hagenbeck, but this! When I took my first look

I practically called up those crazy Jack Londoners just to tell them what was what. Take a look for yourself." Here he motioned with his arms. "Cockatoos losing their feathers, chimps with cage fever, distempered camels, hyenas so depressed they've quit laughing, poxed lemurs, scurvied wombats, there's a Sicilian burro I swear has psoriasis—the poor bastard's practically standing in a hill of his own dandruff. Plus Zak—Zak being a llama they'd painted red and attached horns to so he'd look suitably hell-sent during the new spec, "The Wrath of Moses"—you had a look at him lately? All that paint has clogged his pores so he doesn't sweat properly. It's no wonder he's been so draggy of late. No, I'll tell you the truth. If those Ringlings had waited just a little while longer they wouldn't have had a menage for a new menage boss to take care *of*."

We reached the bull pens. Art began walking down the aisle separating the rows of enclosures, looking for the elephant that concerned him. He stopped in front of the space holding Tony, a big African bull who three years earlier had gotten loose during parade and had sat on a knockwurst stand, killing no one but causing so much damage he might as well have. He was about to be shipped off when John Ringling, feeling drunk and silly, noted Tony's actions as being patriotic and deserving of a spot in the menage. Since then, the old elephant had spent his time scaring children and trumpeting aggressively. Each of his feet were shackled, something the bull men did with bulls gone rogue.

"You'll need a section of newspaper," Art said in a voice lowered but not quite a whisper. "Here, take the front. See that hay bundle there? Have a seat so you're sideways to Tony, and start perusing. Don't look straight at the bull or he'll be liable to get riled and lean over and squash me. This shouldn't take long."

I did as I was told, feeling the sort of curiosity that makes your heart speed. I tried to focus on the newspaper, at the same time peering out the side of my eye, fascinated by what Art was up to.

Which was: after unshackling the juncture electrifying the enclosure wires, he stepped inside Tony's area. He never once looked at the animal. Instead, he sat on a little chair that'd been placed in the most dangerous spot imaginable, by which I mean right beside the elephant, in a prime spot for a squashing. Was the stupidest thing I'd ever seen anyone do, though it didn't seem to bother Art. He slowly unscrewed the top of his thermos and he opened the sports pages and he leaned back and acted like he was enjoying a coffee break, which in a way I suppose he was. (For the record, he crossed his legs at the ankles and not at the knee, thank you very much.)

Tony couldn't take his eyes off this strange fellow with the newspaper. His tail was snapping at flies so hard it was making little slapping noises on his haunches. By the same token, he wasn't trumpeting or sweating profusely or doing any of the things that indicate an elephant's in distress. He also didn't try to teeter himself on top of Art, something rogue elephants are fond of doing and a plan of action that must've crossed his mind at least once or twice.

He seemed content to keep an eye on what Art was doing, which to my mind was not a whole lot. He just sat there, reading and taking sips of coffee. You want to know the truth, it was sort of boring, watching Art gentle an elephant, the only action coming when Art turned a page. After a bit, I went back to my own part of the paper.

Finally, and I mean finally, for I'd been sitting on that bale long enough my underside was feeling pins and needles, Art swallowed the last of his coffee. He made the sound people make when they're happy and satisfied—an exhalation of breath with a hint of rasp tossed in—and he carefully screwed the thermos top back on. Then he folded his newspaper and placed it next to the thermos, which was a little tilted due to the unevenness of the bull-pen bedding.

He got up and walked to the front of the elephant, held out his hands, and God strike me dead if Tony didn't calmly place the tip of his trunk in Art's hands. Every part of that elephant went completely still, the exception being the tip of his trunk, its movements so much like that of a caterpillar I couldn't help but marvel at the similarity. After a bit, Art lifted Tony's trunk end and placed it to his lips, and to this day I'm not sure if he whispered something or simply breathed out warm air. It was probably the latter, seeing as elephants can't hear out of their noses, though with Art you never knew: he was the type of guy who could tell you elephants can *too* hear through their noses, and because of the Indian in him you felt narrow-minded and stupid insisting they couldn't.

This went on for ... what? A minute? Two at the most. When he was done, he held the underside of Tony's trunk in his right hand while stroking the top with his left. Throughout he kept saying, "Good boy, good boy. That's it. We'll have no more trouble out of you, am I right or am I a man gone crazy?"

That night, Tony rejoined the team of elephants used for tearing down the big top, his immense size coming in handy with the centre poles.

The next day, I saw Art eating alone in the cookhouse. I asked to join him, his face brightening when I sat. I took my first bite of roast beef, and while I was chewing I noticed yet another curiosity about Art Rooney: heaped on his plate were mounds of vegetables without the slightest bit of meat in sight (which is something the hippies do all the time now but back then raised eyebrows more than the fact he wore makeup). We chatted about animals and my act and what I was going to do about it. When we were near being done—which took close to an hour, Art having a theory that food digested better if you chewed each bite until there was nothing left to chew—I told him about Rajah.

"Ever since I stopped working him, he's turned a little surly. Started growling at strangers, particularly highfalutin ones. And I've noticed his gums are a little bloodied in the mornings."

"What's his age?"

"Seven."

"You feedin him innards?"

"I am now."

"His coat's fine?"

"Thin, in places."

"Well. I gotta say it doesn't sound like he's sick, which leaves only one other possibility."

I had a feeling he'd say that.

"But don't you think if he was going to go rogue he would've done it already?"

"Not always. I figure animals and humans are alike, in that most of them all do the same thing the same way, except for the odd few who march to the beat of a different drummer. Now *they're* the ones I usually take to and vice versa. Fact is, I'd very much like to meet your Rajah. I've a feeling we'd get on."

I hesitated, but only for a second.

"Take our coffees?"

Seeing as the lot was close to the trains, and it was a nice cool sunny day, we didn't wait for a service wagon. Course, we got plenty of side-long glances during the three-block walk through town, partly because I was wearing my riding costume (long divided skirts, English jacket, white tricorne hat) and partly because Art was wearing lipstick that made him look like he'd been sucking on an orange. We reached the yard and found the performers' train.

As Art and I walked along the cars you could tell he was impressed by how far up the train I was: Colleano, Pallenberg, the Christensen horse family, Bird Millman and May Wirth all had their staterooms around mine. A little farther up was the Pullman occupied by Lillian Leitzel and Alfred Cadona, and beyond that were the opulent private cars occupied by John and Charles Ringling when they travelled with the circus.

I knocked to let Rajah know I was coming in and pushed the door open. Art looked at what little there was to look at: dresser, bed, washbasin. Above the bed was the only piece of art in the room: the gold poster Al G. Barnes had made when he was courting me so I wouldn't leave his circus. I'd framed it and put it behind glass so it wouldn't yellow.

Rajah was in the corner, groggily licking his lips and coming awake.

I didn't think twice when Art moved over to make Rajah's acquaintance, Art having the gift and Rajah looking completely at home with the idea. His head was resting on one of his paws and he was licking a stretch of fur.

Art kneeled in front of Rajah and said, "Good boy, good boy," and he followed this by scratching Rajah's ear. Rajah yawned, and resumed licking himself. Art was turning his head and saying, "I think he likes me," when it happened: without a sound, Rajah swiped a nail along Art's forearm, removing a considerable chunk of flesh.

Art howled and jumped to his feet. I rushed over and batted Rajah on the nose. Then I turned to Art and apologized like a ninny.

"Don't worry," he said through gritted teeth. "It's nothin'. A scratch. I guess I shouldn't have been so forward."

"Let me see."

Art was reluctant to pull away his hand, though when blood and goopy orange started seeping up through his fingers I insisted, peeling back a pinky to promote the idea. A sizable chunk of arm had been torn out and was left in place only by a flap of skin up toward the elbow. He'd have some nasty mashed potato scarring, though my concern at that moment was his nerves, so I asked him if he could make a fist. He could, though when he did he winced and a bubble of orange geysered up from the wound. Seeing this, I grabbed one of my riding blouses and told him to clamp it hard over the entry.

"It isn't bad," I said. On our way out I flashed Rajah a glance that said he'd have a talking to and maybe more when I got back.

We stepped outside, Art hunched and holding his wound, our immediate problem being I wasn't sure he could walk the three blocks back to the lot, given his eyes were tearing and his nose was snotting and if he wasn't feeling light-headed he would be soon. Just then, a wagon pulled up with a bunch of spec aerialists, all of whom gasped when they noticed the rag on Art's arm was soaked crimson. The driver shooed them off and helped me get Art into the wagon cab. He drove back to the lot quicker than normal.

"Now don't you worry," I said on the way. "I've been bitten a lot worse so I know what to do. I'm not saying it won't smart some, but you'll be okay. I knew it as soon as I saw your fingers wiggle. Trust me. It'll be more of an inconvenience than anything."

The driver dropped us in front of the infirmary tent. Of course the doctor was out somewhere so I laid Art out on a gurney and put his arm over a bowl and I cleaned the arm with cloths dipped in boric solution. Then I let it drip. After a while Doc Ketchum heard he had some business and came hustling over and agreed it looked about as good as a wound oozing pus has a right to. Art slept while I went off to do the matinee. For dinner I spooned him some soup along with some reassurances, and it was around this time Doc Ketchum and I decided his wound had drained enough to be bandaged, there being no defined cut or place to do any stitching. The evening show started and shortly after that some workingmen showed up, wanting to take down the tent, so we had to gingerly load Al back on a gilly and take him to the rail car reserved for those recovering from sickness and injury. When we finally got him settled, he looked tired and a little pale, all of which was understandable given the day he'd had. I left him dozing and made it back to the lot in time for my High School display.

Believe you me, as soon as the show was over and I'd gillied back to the trains I went to have a word with Rajah. Soon as I entered my stateroom, I trod over and slapped him on the nose hard and said, "Naughty boy." Being a smart cat, he knew why he'd been smacked and he whimpered. Then he rolled over to face the wall, his body quivering a little.

"Now you listen here," I told him. "I've had myself a total of four marriages and my one-nighter with Al G. and each one's been a disaster. You get so you want to swear off the opposite sex altogether and maybe with Art that's what I'm doing. Truth is, Rajah, this is a tough time for me and some human company would help. I know he's unconventional but I don't exactly fit well with conventional men and remember, I'm technically a bigamist and a fugitive and a woman who's been locked up for nervous problems so I'm hardly one to be picky. What I'm saying is this: I think I'm going to be giving Art a go, and I don't care that you're a tiger and bred to get your way. Get used to the idea, is my advice."

He shook but didn't say anything beyond a whimper.

"Rajah? You hearing me, Rajah?"

I had a feeling he was sulking.

I checked on Art whenever I could over the next day. His wound didn't reek or fester, so the doctor said he could stay on the show. Art's only complaint was the jiggling of the train made his wound throb, something I told him I knew all about.

On the third day, the doctor said Art was recuperating fine and could go back to his stateroom. I looked at Art's wound and since the bandages weren't green or red and the wound wasn't excessively painful I told him the doctor was probably right. The bandage stretched from the middle of his upper arm right to the wrist, making it hard to bend at the elbow.

"Does it hurt bad?" I asked.

"Nope," he said, by which he probably meant some.

So I took him by the good arm and walked him back up the train, though we slowed when we got to the stateroom he shared with a cookhouse boss, the pad-room boss and some guy who kept the electricals going.

"Why're we stopping?" he asked.

"You live here, remember?"

"No, uh-uh, there's something we have to do."

He saw my confusion. "We can't let that cat get the better of me, Mabel. You know it as well as I do. He and I need to have another eye to eye or he'll never respect me, and a lack of respect is something I do not and will not tolerate in an animal."

This was true enough, so even though I didn't like the idea I agreed, for the last thing I wanted was Rajah thinking he could push Art around.

It was midmorning, the train lot deserted. We continued along the length of the train, Art whistling and smoking and looking not at all nervous. It was late in the season, and we were somewhere in the east, winding our way back to Bridgeport; I remember the ground was covered with damp, fallen leaves. On either side of the trains were suburbs, something we were seeing more and more of. I could hear lawn mowers and kids crying and men repairing fences, all of which were noises that tended to make a trouper break out in a nervous sweat.

We reached my suite. I took a breath, prayed things would go better this time and went inside. Art stepped in as well, still whistling, though he stopped when Rajah's head perked up and his ears tucked back and sputum rattled in the back of his throat. A second later, he sprang at Art. Would've got him, too, had I not thrown myself in the way and wrapped my arms around Rajah's shoulders and yelled "No!" into those emerald eyes gone reckless with jealousy. My full weight seemed to slow him a little, and I got dragged a few feet along the stateroom floor, Rajah stopping only when he saw Art hightailing it outside.

I let Rajah go and he sat up on his haunches and licked his lips and generally tried to regain his composure. I was panting and noticing the sleeve of my costume had gotten ripped.

"All right, mister," I said, "that is *it*."

I stood up and got his leash and snapped it on his collar and barked, "Let's go!" He must've known what I had in mind, for he whimpered and cocked his face to one side and made his eyes go round and blinky.

I started to pull on Rajah, something that didn't work for he centred himself on his haunches and dug his forepaw claws into the floor beams and refused to budge. The collar dug into his jawbone.

"God*dammit* Rajah!" I said, and to show him I meant business I let the leash go slack and socked him hard on the nose. I yanked again and this time got somewhere, Rajah taking little tiny steps toward the stateroom door. Once he got outside he blinked into the sun and became more agreeable, letting me gilly him down to the lot, though he whimpered and arfed mightily throughout the ride. When I dragged him into the menage he really started complaining and spinning his paws against the tanbark and generally pleading with me to reconsider. The fact I *was* starting to weaken made me even madder, so I closed my eyes and got the job done, heaving Rajah into the empty cage next to the twolings Boston and Beauty.

I slammed the cage door shut and suddenly felt guilty as hell.

"Come here," I said, and when Rajah did I cradled his gorgeous face through the bars and said, "Now this isn't permanent, sweetheart. Soon as you figure no man is ever gonna replace you, well, you can leave the menage and live in the stateroom again. So I recommend you spend this next little while doing yourself some thinking. Maybe I'll do the same."

Rajah burped and I walked away, feeling those green, green eyes on me.

That afternoon, between the matinee and evening shows, I caught up to Art Rooney. He was sitting beside Rajah's cage, turned sideways, reading a newspaper, while Rajah lay panting and eyeing Art venomously. I asked him what he was doing.

"There's no reason this can't be worked through, Mabel. Rajah and I, we got off on the wrong foot, that's true, but I've always found some of the best friendships can start with some pretty serious dust-ups. Sometimes a good locking of horns will actually lay a foundation of respect and mutual admiration, and I figure once old Rajah gets used to the idea of me that's what'll happen. We're going to be the best of friends, just you wait and see."

I looked at Art. With him it was always the same: you didn't know whether to laugh or shake some sense into him or say, Gee, now that I think of it, you may be right.

Instead, something else blurted out of me: "Have dinner with me tonight, Mr. Rooney."

The evening show went a little over that night, so when I rushed back to the train I found him having a smoke by my stateroom door. Inside, I made him a vegetable fry on my gas cooker. I even served supper with lacquered chopsticks bought in San Francisco, it not surprising me in the least that Art knew how to use them and use them well. (He said they were better for the health, as they slowed eating and promoted digestion.) We ate by candlelight and drank red wine that Art had brought, though I noticed he had no more than a few sips himself. Afterwards, he had himself a smoke, and when he offered me one I helped myself. I suppose you could say everything was right out of a romance novel, what with flowers on the table and violin music playing on my cylinder, the only difference being Art wore lavender fingernail polish and rouge highlighting his cheekbones.

But the best thing about having a private meal with Art Rooney was I knew he wasn't going to be much in the way of manly desire afterwards, meaning I didn't have to worry so much about what was going to happen next. I relaxed totally, and the next thing I knew *I* was starting to feel desirous, something I never expected and surprised me so much that for the first minute or two I thought maybe my tingling was the result of something yeast related. But there was no denying what was happening. My cheeks flushed till they were as rosy as Art's, and my pulse quickened and I could feel my groin complain, much in the way a stomach does when empty.

So instead of getting dessert, I stood and said, "Well, Mr.

Rooney, you might as well understand the situation. I'm keen on you and that's something I've never felt for a man before, which maybe explains why I've been to the altar so many times. Now I can't have babies, you might as well know that, seems my womb isn't quite where it oughtta be, though at your age I'm hoping your impulses toward fatherhood might be dulled somewhat. So there you have it. Cards on the table. I'm a direct person and getting directer every day. How's about giving us a kiss?"

He nodded, so I went over and sat on his lap, wrapping my arms around his head and clutching him to my heart and feeling his warmth and damn it if a safe, happy feeling didn't set in. We kissed softly, and it wasn't at all bad, so after a bit more smooching I took his hand and led him to the bed. He was trembling and his skin was clammy, so I sat him on the edge and asked him if he was sure he wanted to have a go at this. He said he did, badly, so I said, well fine then, and after necking like teenagers we got to seeing what was what.

It took about ten minutes before I realized no amount of touching or tugging or caressing or stroking was going to get us past half mast. So I said to myself, *Well, if that's going to be it, there's no point in complaining,* so I sort of climbed on top and stuffed him in like sausage into a casing. Art was looking pleased with himself, and to make what we were doing feel more authentic he reached up and caressed me and said something loving.

Was when I started to move I realized we had ourselves a problem. With any decent-sized buck or canter Art tumbled out, and I'd have to stop and stuff him back in again, something that began to lose its novelty after the third or fourth time. Plus Art was getting flustered, I could tell as he was wincing and the ends of his moustache were quivering and the rest of his face had gone the colour of his cheekbones. So I reverted to plan B, which was to slide myself back and forth rather than ride up and down. After a while this presented its own problem, namely that it felt like a pale imitation of the real thing and therefore silly. It didn't take long before Art was as soft as an oyster. So we stopped. I lay down beside him and told him I didn't care, that I'd never been much for fornication, that what I really needed was a closeness and just laying side by side with the feeling I had at that moment was fine enough for me. After Art mulled this over for a few seconds, I added that I could easily do without the sex, especially since I knew a baby wasn't going to come from it.

Art smiled, looked over and held up the arm that wasn't in a bandage. For a second, I thought he was picking that moment to show me his anchor-with-rope tattoo.

"You know," he said, "there *is* more than one way to skin a cat."

Well.

I've heard it said that necessity is the mother of invention. I'd say it's more the mother of improvisation, and believe me we had ourselves some improvising that night. The things that man could *do* with a stretch of arm—was as though the ropes popped out of his tattoo and lassooed themselves around my interior, refusing to let go until there was a whole symphony of sounds undignified. Suffice to say I straddled that arm until late and the train was running. We both lay back and listened to the clacking of the wheels. For the longest time we didn't talk, the sounds of lovemaking conveying information far more important than is generally handed over with words.

Nevertheless, the train had been moving for about forty minutes when Art blurted out something confessional.

"You know, I shot a man once."

I turned and looked to see if he was serious. "You telling the truth?"

"Always do."

"Well, why then?"

"Jealousy."

"I see. I think."

"It happened in Laramie, Wyoming, which is about as stupid

a place as you can find to draw on someone. I was still drinking in those days."

"And you shot him because you were jealous?"

"Yep. That's right."

"Interesting reason."

"Only *good* reason, far as I can tell."

"He live?"

"Sure did. I'm a terrible shot."

"You sorry you did it?"

"Yep. Son of a bitch shot back. That's why I walk with a lurch. I went to jail, too."

"How long?"

"Long. And it would've been a whole lot longer except I was injured worse than my victim. Still, I guess I can't complain for I got myself straightened away in jail, which I can tell you doesn't happen often. When I got out I took the only job I could get."

"You were a workingman?"

"With Hagenbeck. For almost four years. Finally they made me a groomer, and then when they saw my way with animals they made me a cage boy."

I digested this information, thinking it was sort of funny, the way even the gentlest of men can turn out to have been wildcats when young. In fact I practically giggled, thinking about the silliness of men, when information of my own came bubbling out of nowhere. At first I fought it, thinking, *Don't say it whatever you do* when it just sort of popped up all on its own: how I should've stopped my mother from tracing up that crazy old mountain horse, Tom. How her absences and loony behaviour had been annoying me so much I was half hoping something would go wrong when she headed out the door. How when she left that day I was wishing her ill and nothing but. By the time I was finished unburdening myself, I was feeling misty and weak.

"Mabel," he said, "listen to me. That wasn't your fault. It just wasn't. If it was anyone's it was your mother's for it sounds to me like maybe she didn't mind the idea of having a bad accident, which was nothing but irresponsible given she had a girl to take care of. Trust me. If you told that story to a hundred people, a hundred people would tell you the same thing. *You* were wronged. Not her."

I lay there enjoying the rare sort of weakness that feels good all over.

"You think so?"

"I know so."

I looked at him like he was crazy. What he'd said was like telling me up was down and down was up. Art looked over, so we were staring eye to eye. Then he gave me one of those sly little grins that in Art-talk meant, Just you wait.

Just you wait and see.

That winter we rented the same house I'd had the year before. Art sewed curtains and crocheted sofa-arm protectors and painted the kitchen a shade of yellow veering closely toward peach. With no High School act to perform or cats to train, I now had plenty of time to spend with Rajah, taking him on walks and wrestling with him and just letting him know he hadn't been thrown over. This helped; by March his surliness and his gum problems eased, though he still couldn't be let anywhere near Art, his aversion to the man smell-based and difficult to overcome.

In April, the circus opened its week-long stint at Madison Square Garden. This meant I had to watch Clyde Beatty spend a full eight minutes getting a single cowed lion to do a sloppy sit-up (and then almost get himself killed before emerging sweaty and shaky and bathed in applause that rightly should've been mine.) The only thing that made it bearable was having Art beside me, tut-tutting and shaking his head in disgust. Afterwards he brought me flowers and massaged my feet and cooked me omelettes.

"Don't worry," he told me more than once. "History has a way of figuring out what's crap and what isn't, and I got a feeling one day history's going to be mighty accurate when it comes to the subject of Mabel Stark, tiger trainer."

"The only problem," I'd respond, "is there's nothing history can do for me now."

That year the circus took its normal route, skirting the lower half of the U.S. during the spring and then wending its way north for the hotter part of the year. Business was good, it being 1926 and people having money to spend, though it would've been better were it not for all the circuses owned by the Ringlings' main rival, Jerry Mugivan, by which I mean Hagenbeck and Cole Brothers and John Robinson and a handful of others. That year John Ringling decided he'd buy an albino elephant some trapper had taken in Siam. It was the only known albino bull in existence, so the cost was high: $100,000 American. Ringling put him in the spec and the menage, where for a while he earned his keep. Shortly thereafter, Mugivan began displaying albino elephants as well, though his were regular elephants covered with whitewash. This worked until one day a rainstorm hit. While it embarrassed Jerry Mugivan, what it did to Ringling was worse: every Tom, Dick and Harry now believed *his* white elephant was fake as well, a $100,000 bull suddenly worth no more than a circus lot mongrel.

When what was happening sank in, it's said John Ringling flew into a rage, tossing furniture and throwing lamps and smashing sculptures worth almost as much as his white elephant. Meanwhile, his solemn and brooding brother, Charles, looked on. Around this time rumours started that the Ringlings were trying to buy the Mugivan shows. This sounded too extraordinary to be true, for it'd mean the Ringlings would own every decent-sized circus in America, and it was impossible to imagine any two men having that much power. Mostly the rumours were dismissed. I know I didn't pay them much attention, mainly because I was busy with my own concerns, such as was I or was I not going to get my damn cat act back.

About two months into the season, the circus was someplace south, Mississipi or Alabama I believe. Hot, I do remember that. I was in the menage, filling water pans toward the end of the day, feeling depressed my tigers were starting to look like run-of-the-mill menage creatures, by which I mean flabby and lacking in gumption. I heard whistling, and when I turned I saw a trail of smoke rising above the cages one aisle over. Art turned the corner and gimped up quickly. When he spoke he was practically squealing.

"Mabel! Charles Ringling is on the show!"

"Well, good for him."

"No, no, you're not listening ... he wants to meet me. He just sent for me. He wants to hear how the menage is doing."

"Well, good for *you*."

Here he grabbed me by the shoulders and spun me around and I saw he was beaming about something.

"Mabel," he said, *"you're* coming."

"Me? Coming?"

Art nodded and that did it. I was off, Art struggling to keep up. I stopped outside the flap of the manager's tent and caught my breath and then whispered to Art, "Oh my God I'm so nervous I don't think I can do this."

"You can. You *can*. Just let me go first...." and with that two things happened. First, Art stepped inside the tent and said, "Hello, Mr. Ringling." Second, he reached back through the tent flap and grabbed my forearm and yanked me on in.

Charles Ringling's face was just as jowly and round as Mr. John's, though less prone to expressions of pleasure. When I stepped through the tent flap he was lifting himself up from a chair parked behind a desk on the other side of the tent. The exertion seemed to be taking all of his attention, so at first he didn't notice me. Finally, he made it to his feet, though he was puffing and leaning over and supporting himself on his hands. He looked up and spotted me, a step behind Art.

They say that John Ringling always kept people a little off guard by refusing to sit during business meetings. With Charles it was that mug of his: sour, as though he'd just swallowed borscht turned to vinegar. He sighed and sat back down with a huff, a way of signalling he was no longer going to shake Art's hand given the inconvenience he'd brought along with him. Instead, he held up the ring and middle fingers on his right hand and gave them a waggle, indicating we were supposed to approach. Was like something an emperor of Rome might've done, and I admit my initial reaction was to comment on his rudeness by turning and walking out. Fortunately, Art still had a hold on my forearm, and he led me, half against my will and half not, to the two chairs in front of Charles Ringling's desk. I took one, Art the other.

Mr. Charles had returned to his work, signing paper after paper after paper. Even this made him lose his breath. I noticed his hands were slightly puffed up and that he had the pallor of a gecko's belly.

He spoke without looking up.

"I don't recall issuing an invitation for two."

He stopped scribbling. The silence that followed made my stomach quiver. He leaned back, his chair squeaking. Then he gave a little grin, though it was a grin designed solely to intimidate.

"I'd heard the two of you were friendly," he said while looking straight at me. "To what do I owe the pleasure of your company, Miss Stark?"

"It's about, well, the upshot of it is, sir, well, it's about my being in the High School chorus. It's just that I'm not a particularly good rider, though I am a good cat trainer."

He arched the bushier of his eyebrows. "Your point being, Miss Stark?"

I started sputtering so Art took over.

"You see, Mr. Ringling, now that cat acts are a thing of the past, Mabel here is riding High School chorus, which seems a waste of talent and an undue frustration for a committed cat trainer like herself."

"Rooney," he snapped. "Of *course* I'm aware of the situation. It was my brother's decision. Are you saying my brother and I don't talk?"

Was then I saw something I wouldn't've thought possible. Art's mouth dried up, the only noise coming out of it a poorly pronounced "oh" that sounded more like a pop bottle cap coming off than actual speech. He went still, too, the only motion the quivering of his moustache. My heart sank and sank deep. The three of us sat in silence, Art and I looking like a pair of dimwits while Charles Ringling's brow grew more and more furrowed. At least ten seconds passed, and believe me that's a long time under such circumstances. Finally Mr. Charles's face lightened and his brow unfurrowed slightly and the formation of his lips approached a condition that was almost a grin but not quite.

"You're right," he said. "It was a stupid idea. That brother of mine can be a real horse's ass sometimes. I'll make a call or two tomorrow and get this foolishness taken care of. The menage doing fine?"

After rushing to tell Rajah the good news, Art and I celebrated cautiously, having a fish dinner in town. Had it been Mr. John, we probably wouldn't have celebrated at all, what with his reputation for forgetting promises one minute after issuing them. Mr. Charles, though considered a hard-nosed bastard, had a tendency toward doing what he said, unless of course what he'd said had only *been* said to get him out of a sticky situation, which wasn't the case with us. I suppose *guarded* is the word describing how we felt.

The next day Charles Ringling died bloated and pale, a victim of the same thing that killed every last one of the Ringlings: heart attacks related to high living. It rained that day, though you wouldn't've known it, given how well paraffined the big top was. Flags flew at half mast, and the ringmaster, Fred Bradna, dedicated that evening's performance to Mr. Charles. John Ringling, who had trained in from

Florida or some damn place, snuffled throughout in the owner's box. During cookhouse the orchestra played sad, slow music, like the kind you'd hear during the first half of a Dixieland funeral. The next day, rumour had it the last surviving Ringling was carried blind-drunk to his private rail car and taken to Cape Cod for an application of sea air.

Course, no one mourned more than me. When I heard the news I went to the menage and I leashed up Rajah and we took a long walk; he seemed to sense my deflated mood, and was kind enough not to snarl or air swipe or micturate at anyone. When we'd wandered far from the lot, I let him off his leash and we rolled in the earth and I nuzzled his pleasure spot, making him purr. After that, he lay on top of me. I felt safe and warm under his full weight, the world totally blocked out. Honestly—if I had to choose between a few Hamm's or a tiger lying full weight on my back, I'd choose a tiger every time. The two of us were out for a full hour that day, having the sort of sad-hearted fun you have when trying to fend off hopelessness. At the end of it, I wished I didn't have to put him back in his cage.

Basically, it felt like I had shoulders so the world would have some-place to rest. Knowing this, Art was nicer than ever. He brought me roses and gave me a box of chocolate macaroons. That night, he put my feet in a tub of water mixed with peach-scented bath oil, and as he rubbed them he assured me everything was going to be all right and one day I'd get off the Ringling show and I didn't have a thing to worry about. Afterwards he read to me, Art Rooney being the sort of man who owned poetry books. When I told him all that flowery language was making me feel romantic, he moistened up his forearm in the same peach-scented oil I'd had my feet in. Then he was as loving as is possible for one human to be. Afterwards he slept with those muscular vase-shaped arms wrapped around me. Having never been with a kind man before, I had to wonder why I'd always been so dead set against the notion.

I had a fitful night, waking over and over to noises that ordinari-ly helped me sleep, like whistle stops and clacking. I slept late. When I opened my eyes, I was surprised to see Art still in our stateroom, for he was usually up and out the door early to oversee the animals being unloaded. Instead he was sitting at my desk, hunched like a dwarf, reading something. I got up to see what he had. This proved to be difficult, for it looked like he'd been at it for quite a while, his back having hunched way over, so that he now completely covered whatever he was working on. In the end I just asked him what he had.

He sat up, stretched and peered at me through eyes gone blurry.

"This," he answered, "is your contract."

For the next week or so, most of my time was spent fighting off old demons. I found making full sentences a trial, and if I didn't so keenly understand what can happen to woman if she weakens and shows what sadness has done to her, I think I would've given up talking altogether. I forced myself to keep going, making mistakes where I made them. During High School one day, I forgot where I was, and while making a turn my body went one way and my horse the other. I stayed mounted only by grabbing poor Alvin's mane, which made him whinny loudly and lose step. It was an inelegance that disrupted the act and earned me an earful from the equestrian director. Mostly I was worried my old friend neurasthenia was paying another visit, the stress of this realization not helping in the least.

Art, however, had reacted to Charles Ringling's death with a shrug and the comment: "So it's a setback. Pretty much everything in this world is. We'll think of something else. Mabel, you mustn't *worry* so. Believe me it's unhealthy."

Basically he was looking for a loophole. Seemed every time I saw Art he was carrying my contract, a dictionary and a magnifying glass for the small print. The document was twenty-seven pages, crowded with subsections and subclauses and legal gobbledygook, so poring over it was taking some time. I'd see him in the pie car, his coffee long stopped steaming beside him, puzzling over the meaning of every section, forehead supported by a clawed, hammy, nail-polished hand. One day I found him in the menage, sitting next to the distempered yak. He was turned sideways and craned over reading, contract in one hand, legal dictionary in the other, magnifying glass at his feet.

He read through it once, just to understand it, then he started in on it again, this time looking for what he called "areas of interpretability." Soon the document picked up animal stains and began to look dog-eared. When the staples went, he started keeping it rolled up like a scroll, the whole thing bound with a thick elastic band.

Six days into the project he found me in the female change tent. He just walked right on in, despite there being half-dressed ladies present. None of them shrieked, however, seeing as it was only Art.

He came over, the contract opened to page sixteen. He pointed to a line he'd circled. My mouth fell open as he said, "After the matinee, I do believe we'll pay Mr. Curley a little visit."

I was so eager for my display to end I kept spurring Alvin to move through his steps a little faster, hoping the others would follow my cue and get the thing over with faster. Course, this didn't work, Alvin being the one in charge and the two of us both knowing it. When I finally rode out through the blue curtain, I dismounted and practically ran to the change tent where I met up with Art. We strode over to the tent belonging to the Ringling manager, Charles Curley.

Now, I'd had meetings with Curley already, and he'd seemed genuinely sorry I was a cat woman having to work with horses. By the same token, he always told me a contact's a contract, and though he felt for me there was no way he could farm me out without talking to John Ringling, who quite frankly had bigger fish to fry.

We barged in. Found him seated at the same desk where we'd encountered Charles Ringling a week earlier. Art slapped the contract on Curley's desk and pointed to the circled sentence.

It read: "Under no circumstances, during the duration of the contractee's tenure with the contractor, will the contractee have the option, right or freedom to perform or otherwise labour or otherwise appear, in any capacity, for an American circus, vaudeville, carnival or theatric troupe other than the one owned and/or operated and/or presided over by the contractor."

Curley read it. From the looks of it, twice.

"What's your point, Rooney?"

Art pointed at the part of the sentence most germane to our little visit.

"American circus? So what? That's something people just say."

In a way he was right; back then the phrase *American circus* was as apt to roll out of people's mouths as the single word *circus*. Art, however, wasn't put off.

"Now you know as well as I do when it comes to lawyers there's no such thing as 'something people just say.'"

Curley looked at the phrase in question again, this time holding it up for closer inspection. For a few seconds his face was hidden. I heard a sigh and he put the contract back on his desk. Then he grinned.

"You might just have something here, Rooney."

A week later, Art and I said goodbye on a platform next to an idling train that was about to take me all the way to New York City, where I'd board an ocean liner to England. There, I'd do my wrestling bit for an outfit called the Mills Circus of London. Rajah was in a crate in the baggage car, sleeping the sleep of kings, owing to a tranquilizing pill he'd had with his horsemeat that morning.

Art kissed me, and it was one of those moments when equal parts joy and sadness mix together and make everything feel right. His arms were wrapped around me, and I was dampening the front of his flannel shirt. We stood that way for the longest time, Art dripping tears on the top of my head and me snuffling. Finally, we gave each other a little shove and I turned and mounted the train. He followed along the platform as I looked for my seat. As the train pulled out, I waved and blew kisses and soggied a hanky. I stopped to wipe my tears with the back of my hand, and by the time I was finished the train had pulled out of the station. I sat back, took a deep breath and marvelled at how pulling away from a place makes you think hard on the things that make life worth all the problems. A few minutes after *that* and I was slumped in my seat, feeling warm and drowsy and not at all bad to be me.

CHAPTER 13

ART

THE THING THAT SCARES ME THE MOST? THE THING THAT makes me jittery, that makes me dart for one of Dr. Brisbane's pills, that makes me contemplate rash actions? What if neither God nor luck has anything to do with it? What if we make our own luck? What if everything that happens to us happens because we wanted it that way?

I need you to understand this totally, so just this one time back up with me and recall that head doctor in Hopkinsville, the one who used three slightly bent fingers to push away a wet spindle of hair when a single straight one would've done fine. Before, I described him as one of the kindest men I've ever come across, it's true, but as I dig deeper and deeper into this thing called my confession it's starting to occur to me maybe he wasn't. Fact is, the more I think of it, the more I start thinking he was the cruellest of the lot, for there was this one tubbing when I was complaining bitterly about all the bad hands fate had dealt me and wondering what I'd done to deserve it all and feeling as sorry as sorry gets for myself in the process.

"I swear, Doctor," I told him, "if it weren't for bad luck I'd have no luck at all."

Here I expected him to say something encouraging, like he usually did, like "Don't worry, Mary, you're an intelligent young woman and once you put all this behind you, your life will work out fine." Instead came the sound of him breathing heavily through his nose, a sign he was going to tell me something I might not particularly want to hear. What he said was "It's true there is such a thing as bad luck and there is such a thing as good luck. But there is also a third type of luck, Mary. There is also the sort of luck we create for ourselves. There is also the type of luck we think we deserve."

I didn't pay much attention to what he'd said then, answering with my usual, "Yes yes, Doctor, I see what you mean." Still, what he said stuck with me, and it's starting to make more and more sense, and as it makes more and more sense, one particular thought concerning the good Dr. Levine keeps bubbling to the surface.

How dare he?

How dare he make me understand that?

The answer, of course, is he loved me, and there's nothing like love for turning you mean. There's nothing like love for picking you up and turning you crazy and in that craziness there's a loss of control and when people lose control?

Well. They're capable of pretty much anything, has been my experience.

After six months of drinking warm beer, of deciphering Cockney accents, of visiting crown jewels and famous bridges, of writing letters every day no matter what, of suffering from the emptiness spurred by homesickness, of getting used to my food either deep-fried or baked into the shape of a pie, of riding on the top deck of buses for the sheer novelty of it, of almost getting run over every time I stepped off a curb because traffic all ran the wrong way, I turned around and came home happy. My return was to a greeting of flowers, tears, embraces, a home-cooked meal and a dose of affection that veered toward the frantic and maybe even beyond. Afterwards, Art announced he needed a walk, and he left me lying in bed. About a half hour later, there was a commotion outside our stateroom, so I pulled back the curtains on the Pullman window and had a look. Couldn't believe my eyes. One of the gold Roman chariots used in the opening spec was hitched to a pair of Friesians. Inside the buggy was Art, holding a whip and wearing a top hat, livery boots and white cotton jodhpurs. People were milling and mulling, gawking and chattering. Poodles Hannaford was standing on his hands. Bird Millman's parrot announced it wanted a cracker. I even saw Leitzel on the sidelines, smoking and trying to look unimpressed, which wasn't easy given Art had highlighted his cheeks with a powder that could only be described as sparkly.

"Your chariot," he said with a sweep of his right hand, "awaits."

So I got in, giggling, and he clicked his teeth and the horses trotted us away and down a country lane leading from the rail yards. Art stopped by a creek he must've scouted out earlier that day, for it was lovely and moonlit and trickling. He jumped out and went around the other side of the chariot and helped me down by taking my hand. He led me to a tree stump and motioned for me to sit. He went down on one knee, though not in the way you're probably imagining, for instead of facing me straight on he knelt sideways, such that I was looking into the side of his face.

"Mabel," he said, "it's about time I explained my theory of life, love, animal training, the pursuit of happiness, the reason we choose to be alive and last but not least what we mean when we yammer on about God. You might call it Art's Theory of Absolutely Everything, or you could call it a damn fool's take on things—that's up to you. Either way, it goes like this: *I* believe if you see something and it immediately strikes you as the most beautiful thing you've ever seen it probably ain't. What you're seeing is flash or dazzle or razzmatazz, or even more likely what you're seeing is what everybody around you *figures* is beautiful. And while there's nothing wrong with that it doesn't mean what you're seeing is beauty of the truest sort. Beauty, and I mean the real McCoy, sneaks up on you. It bushwhacks a fellow. It's the sort of thing you don't notice at first, until one day it appears in the corner of your eye and you turn to look and you say, by gum, why didn't I notice that in the first place? You understand, Mabel? You see what I'm driving at? Mabel Stark, I do believe you're the most beautiful person I've ever seen in the whole of my life, and I'm not talking about your blond curls or your shapely figure or your natural pluck. I *am* talking about what's inside you, and what allows you to do the things you do with tigers."

Here I swallowed, which was no easy feat as my voicebox was swollen to discomfort.

"Will you marry me, Mabel Stark? Will you be my wife forever? And before you answer, I encourage you to consider that forever is a long stretch of time."

He finally turned his head toward me, looking as hopeful as a child wanting seconds on dessert.

Mostly I answered by blushing. Blushing and folding my hands between my knees. Art rose and went to the buggy and with his back turned said, "Mabel, close your eyes, I have a surprise." I did as he asked and listened to him rummage around. When he neared he said, "All right, now, hold out your hands," and when I did I guess I was expecting him to drop in a ring of some sort.

Instead I felt something square and cardboard, about the size of a box of chocolates though heavier, lowered into my hands.

"All right," Art said. "You can open it."

What I had was an album of some sort, covered with two pages of decorative cardboard, the whole thing bound with yellow ribbon. My stage name was inscribed on the front.

I looked at Art, mouth agape.

"Open it," he said. "Go on. Have a look."

I opened the cover. On the first page was an old *Billboard* article. It was small, maybe four paragraphs on a single column, surrounded by stretches of white border, and it was reviewing that first mixed act I did on the Barnes show way back when. I turned the pages. There were articles, reviews and write-ups from *Billboard*, *White Tops* and local papers, recounting every step of my career. All the highlights were there—my balloon act with Samson, my being the first to train Sumatrans, my debut with Rajah, my battle with Nigger, along with a hundred lesser moments.

I closed the album and held it to my chest and felt myself go weak.

"Thank you, Art," I said.

Seemed he wasn't out of surprises yet. Instead of saying you're welcome, he reached out and slid the album from my grip and walked back to the buggy.

"This," he said, "is not for you. Leastways not yet."

It was all so utterly confusing I didn't even ask him what he meant. Instead I contented myself with watching him walk back to the chariot and return the album to a canvas sack, handling it the whole time like it was treasure. When he came back, he knelt and plucked a dandelion from the earth. He pulled off the flower and twisted the stalk into a little ring. I held out the right finger and he slipped it on.

"Mabel Stark," he said solemn as a judge, "with this ring I thee—"

He couldn't continue, my arms being around him and our lips pressed firm.

We decided we'd hold out till winter quarters in Bridgeport. Art suggested mid-November as a date, specifically his birthday, and as I figured this was as good a day as any, I agreed.

Hearing this, Art got so pleased he hopped up and down, those big hands doing an air dance in front of him. After that, his spare time was busied with preparations, even though there was precious little we could do before getting to winter quarters. Still, in every town he'd go downtown and look at dress shops, florists and male clothiers. Ideas, was the way he justified these outings. "I'm just getting ideas, Mabel. I'm getting the creative juices *flowing*. By the way, what do you think of lilies of the valley?"

He'd also poke around in churches. Neither one of us was particularly religious, so Art figured we'd marry into a faith with, as he put it, "an appreciation of grandeur." Roman Catholic, Anglican, Presbyterian, Lutheran, United, Seventh Day Adventist, Methodist, Jehovah's Witness, Evangelical, Buddhist, Confucian—he even went to the odd Baptist service on the wrong side of town, the only white man in a congregation of heavy-bosomed black women speaking in tongues. In the end he said he favoured the Catholics because of all the stained glass and expensive wood. I told him no way any priest worth his salt was going to marry a non-devout circus performer about to take her fifth husband. This made Art pout for the rest of the day, though the next morning, in Athens, Georgia, he got up and went church hunting with renewed vigour. That day he started hinting Unitarian might the way to go.

Was one other thing he started work on. Though he knew about my first two marriages, he considered them mistakes made long ago when I went by a different name and besides I'd never even screwed James Williams so that one didn't count. Albert Ewing was a different story. Ewing was known on circus lots, and it was known I'd been married to him. Marrying Art without divorcing Albert would be bigamy pure and simple, if only because everybody would know about it.

Problem was, Albert had dropped off the face of the earth. No matter how many people Art talked to he always heard the same thing: the last recollection they had of the man was watching him dangle from a mail gantry, his privates pointing at his chin. Art sent letters to all the major circuses and a few dozen smaller ones besides. The answers all fell into one of two categories. The first was "Heard about what he did to the Ringlings, no way he's working here." The second was "Who?"

After two or three weeks of this fruitlessness, Art decided we should run a small ad in *Billboard*. It read:

> *$100 Reward!*
> One hundred dollars paid to anyone able to furnish information regarding the whereabouts of one Albert Ewing, former Ringling accountant. Cash upon location, all information confidential, no questions.

Turned out this didn't work either, not because we had no responses but because we had thousands, every last one from hysterics, the Ringling postmaster coming to our stateroom one morning and hinting he wanted cherry pie for handling all our mail. Looking into all the leads was going to be impossible, so we didn't look into any, Art deciding we'd best talk to a private eye. Charles Curley helped out by calling up Pinkerton's, the agency Mabel Ringling used when she thinned the grift on the circus back in the earlier part of the decade. They sent someone over, and we all met, and two weeks later we had a second meeting.

Seemed my husband was living in a hotel above a betting parlour in Cincinnati, Ohio. He no longer had anything to do with circuses, and was now going by the name Al Driven.

(Me: So how's the little bastard?

The Pinkerton's agent, a small mountain of a man with tiny eyes and a nose flattened to one side and ears like flaps of romaine lettuce and a chin as big as a lunchpail: Hmmmmmmm.... Not so hot.)

There was one other critical piece of information. Albert would grant me a divorce if I gave him a cheque for $1,000. Hearing this, my thought was *no blessed way*, Albert Ewing being a sneaky little cheat, and if anyone was going to get a thousand dollars it by all rights should be me, considering all the grief and embarrassment his shenanigans had caused me. Truth be known, I was getting all worked up, though when I looked over at Art he gave me a soft, raised-eyebrow expression that could've only meant one thing.

Consider it sideways, darling.

With that finally settled, Art sat down and got a nib and ink and drew himself up an invitation, one festooned with curlicues and hearts and cupids firing arrows at one another.

"Art," I said, "who're we going to send the invitations *to*? Neither one of us has much in the way of family, and we're not exactly crawling with friends here on the show."

This made him puzzle. But you could tell he was looking for solutions instead of reasons to have a drink or a hand of cards, and if you want a reason for my loving Art Rooney that could be it right there. After a few seconds, his eyes brightened.

"The workingmen," he said, and it was the sort of thought that makes you recoil before the reasonableness of it sinks in.

I said, "Well, they're thieving and unwashed and most of them are on the run from something, but it's true they're the only ones I seem to see eye to eye with these days. Plus you're an ex-workingman so it seems fitting. We'll give them a ham-and-potato-salad buffet. They'll like that."

It was settled. I'd become Mrs. Art Rooney on Friday, November 20, in the city of Bridgeport, Connecticut, the guests in rented suits and too-tight shoes and no doubt trying to control their shakes. No one had ever had a wedding like that, which I suppose is why the idea had occurred to Art. There'd be lilies of the valley and streamers and spruce garlands. Sounded perfect. I couldn't wait. I went down to the menage and told Rajah, who took the news about as well as could be expected from a cat gone irascible with age and jealousy.

That fall, the circus wound its way up through the southern states toward the last dates in Virginia. By the time we hit the Carolinas it was getting cool during the evenings, the flyers warming their hands over Bunsen heaters so they wouldn't miss a pass due to numbness. I started working my tigers again, letting them in the ring and practising their old tricks, which should tell you something about my mood in general. Seems life travels in ups and in downs and this was an up, for way down south in Florida, in the basement of a mansion called House of John, one of the richest men in America was opening himself a package.

It's true I wasn't there. It's also true I didn't know the man well, except to say whenever he came in contact with yours truly my life either got a hundred times better or a hundred times worse. But with his riches came fame, and with fame came a general broadcasting of the way he lived. So I can imagine. I can picture how it happened.

His day starts at ten in the evening. He has a breakfast of corned-beef hash and eggs washed down with tumblers of Old Curio. Then he takes his meetings, which goes to show if you're one of the ten richest men in America you can schedule a meeting for midnight in a town didn't exist ten years earlier and still expect people to show up. While his wife sleeps his servants stay up, for someone has to serve him sherry glasses filled with the German schnapps he has bootleggers drop in the bay outside his home.

Throughout the night, he works and he broods and he wishes, vaguely, with no real conviction, that he could take a vacation from being John Ringling. Decisions, are the root of it. Decisions, decisions, decisions—if only they'd stop coming for one blessed minute. Railroads, oil fields, stocks and bonds, real estate, an art collection worth millions, the circus—all of it needs tending. While it's true he'd once felt energized every time he dashed off his signature, that was back when there'd been five of them and an empire a fraction of the size.

So he wanders. Thinks. Broods. Admires his art. Watches the sun rise from the cliffs outside his mansion. If he comes across a servant, his manner changes and he's John Ringling again, smiling and saying good-evening and maybe having a little conversation about nothing. The evening wears on. The whole time he fights the urge to get on a boat bound for Europe in the morning, a place where demands and decisions have a tougher time finding him, though in the end he doesn't, for he's smart enough to know the thing that's chasing him is the same thing chasing all successful men, that being the fear that in some elementary way he isn't good enough. So he drinks. He sighs. He wishes the world weren't so damn beautiful all the time. In his spare moments he attends to business matters in the same way a gun treats a scatter of shot—without order, reason or even a care about the results. When something occurs to him, he scribbles his wishes on a little flip-over notepad he keeps in the breast pocket of his robe. Come 9:00 a.m. he hands off the day's pages to a handler, whose job it is to make sense of the scrawl and dispose of the more lunatic ideas.

Then, to his private room in the cellar, where John Ringling pours the first of twelve pints of German lager he has every morning. His mail is brought there, in a pile next to his desk, thousands of letters and bills and demands and decisions. Much of it he ignores, some of it he answers, the bulk he sends straight to lawyers or accountants. This morning there's a package, wrapped in string and brown paper, near the top of the mound, tweaking his curiosity. The big man tries to unwrap the package with his fat, jointless fingers, in his drunkenness finding it hard to manage the tightly wrapped string. A flash of frustration. He grabs a letter opener, the one with the handle made from Kenyan ebony and finely honed Pennsylvanian steel, and jerkily rips the package open.

It is: an album of some kind. Mabel Stark. Hmmmm, name sounds familiar, though he can't remember from where. Opens the pages. A tiger woman of some sort and not a bad-looking one at that, what with those schoolgirl locks and those tight leather bodysuits. Got to keep the fathers interested though what I wouldn't give for a good old-fashioned flat-out cooch. Hmmmmmmmm. Stark. Stark, Stark,

Stark. Of course! Mabel Stark—little blond wisp of a thing, back-woods way of talking, had a good wrestling act and if I'm not mistaken a bit with a jaguar. Hmmmmmmm. Where *did* I see her? What show *was* that? Broke the cats herself, if I'm not mistaken. Jesus, Mabel Stark. Now there's a name from the past.

Wonder whatever happened to her?

Seems John Ringling got on the telephone and had a conversation with his circus manager, Charles Curley. It also seems John Ringling flew into a rage when told I already belonged to his circus and that I'd been demoted to riding High School, despite it being a decision he himself had made. By the time Charles Curley called me to the ticket office, he looked tired and fed up, a way people often looked when dealing with John Ringling.

"Mabel," he said, "have a seat."

Curley rubbed his temples. "I've been on the phone all morning, making some arrangements."

Here he paused, giving no indication whether those arrangements were for my benefit or detriment. Could've been either. His fingertips moved to his eyes, and they had a good pressing as well. He spoke through his hands.

"Next season you'll switch to the Robinson show. He's got eight tigers that are going to need a new trainer come July. Rajah gone rogue yet?"

"Uhhhh ... no. No sir. Not at all."

"Then he's going with you. The Ringling cats, too."

I left feeling tingly. Found Art in the menage, where he was singing a lullaby to a chimp who'd taken to tearing at sleeves through the cage bars. Art noticed me and nodded, still in mid-song.

I came up behind him and wrapped my arms around him, settling the side of my face into flannel. I took a deep breath and closed my eyes and a picture came and what I saw was ...

Well.

Was pleasing.

One week prior to season end, on a day off, with the trains parked in a rail yard outside Columbia, Art returned, whistling, to our Pullman suite. He had with him a cardboard box, which he plopped on our fold-down table. Then he handed me a pair of scissors and said, "Take a look, Mabel."

I snipped the string holding the box flaps and pulled out one of the invitations. Art's fancy writing was printed, embossed and silver, on linen paper the colour of *crème fraîche*. The envelope closed by slipping the pointed tip of the upper flap into a little silver sleeve built into the lower flap.

"Art," I said, "how many of these things have you made?"

"How many workingmen are there?"

"About six hundred."

He grinned, and I had my answer. We spent the rest of that afternoon slipping invitations inside envelopes, which at first was giggly work but after a bit became chore-like, and a bit later still downright onerous: I remember my hand muscles getting sore and my finger joints feeling like they'd been tromped on. Throughout, Art kept me entertained with songs from that time, like "Bye, Bye, Blackbird" and "I Found a Million-Dollar Baby in the Five-and-Ten-Cent Store," which he sang in a voice more than capable of carrying a tune. Finally we finished, and I asked when he planned on handing them all out.

"No time like the present. Got to strike when the iron's hot. Never leave for tomorrow what you can do today. *Carpe diem*, as the Romans said."

In other words, we headed off to the sections of train containing the workingmen cars. They were at the rear of the fourth section, meaning it was a bit of a walk, and throughout I couldn't help smiling at the ridiculousness of it all. "I know you suggested we have a ham-and-potato salad buffet," Art was saying, "but I think maybe we better get some chicken slices as well. Not everyone likes ham because of the salt. And macaroni salad. Lord love a duck but sometimes I like a nice helping of macaroni salad. Of course, if you're going to have macaroni salad there's no point going without a vat of gherkins...."

On and on he went, regaling me with the finer points of buffet eating, and I was just about to impart my feelings on devilled eggs when we reached the workingmen compartments. As always, most were sitting around outside, playing cards on overturned trunks, the makeup of their foursomes indicating the division that existed within their trains. There were the Negro workingmen, most of whom drove stakes or otherwise helped with the big top. These were the ones I felt the most sorry for, seeing as how their only problem was the fact they were poor and southern and saddled with the wrong skin colour for that particular time in America. The rest were white workingmen, who were groomers or train builders or maintenance men or cookhouse help. Unlike the Negro workingmen, who were beaten down more than anything, the white workingmen seemed to suffer from a smorgasbord of afflictions, the most common ones being alcoholism, craziness, syphlitic diseases or criminal obsession, a good many of them suffering from all four.

When fights broke out, it was generally between these two groups, for when misery wells up and makes men hunt for an excuse to fight, a difference in skin tone works about as well as anything. The one thing they all had in common was the fact they were taken advantage of. Because circus workingmen weren't generally allowed in local bars, and wouldn't've had the time to go drinking if they were, management sold them beers in the blue car against future wages. The theory here was by the time payday rolled around, their money would already be spent, and a broke workingman was far less likely to run off than a workingman with two weeks' worth of breathing room jangling in his pockets. On top of it all, they were looked down upon, the common wisdom being they deserved their lot seeing as how they were lacking in imagination. Course, this was something I never held against them, for it's always been my belief that when your imagination can't so much as picture a way out it's probably better just to shut the damn thing off altogether.

So.

Art took four envelopes out of our box of invitations and headed toward the nearest group of card players. All shuffling and dealing and betting immediately halted, for if a boss or performer approached a workingmen it generally meant one of two things. Either the workingman in question was going to have to do something hard and distasteful—hosing the latrine cars, for example—or he'd been caught out doing something wrong, and believe me when I say that damn Mabel Ringling had rules forbidding every last workingman pleasure, from fighting right on down to stealing shirts off townie clotheslines. Even gambling was technically against the rules, though seeing as the workingmen bosses all partook themselves, the rule generally went unenforced. Still, every once in a while Mr. John's wife would come down and there'd be a sacrificial lamb, which explained why all four card players went wide-eyed and stiff when the menage boss approached. Their body language would've even been funny had it not indicated their defeated stations in life—the closer he got, the more they angled their shoulders away from his general direction, so that by the time he reached their overturned crate at least two of them looked like they were leaning into a curve.

"Good morning, fellas," Art said, beaming.

"Morning," a few of them grumbled, fearing the worst, those fears half confirmed and half not when Art dropped those funny-looking envelopes in front of each one of them. For a time the cards just stayed there, untouched, the four men in a clear state of agitation tinged with curiosity. I watched them mull over possibilities. Meanwhile, Art confused them by smiling and not offering up any clues. Finally, and I mean finally, one of the workingmen reached out.

I remember his nails were dirty, and a scar ran crossways over the tendons and veins on the back of his hand. He took the envelope, opened it and pulled out what was inside. He turned it over a few times before narrowing his eyes and spelling out the words. Judging by the movement of his eyes and lips, he read it a second time and then a third time for good measure. Was then a look of relief passed over his features, though you could tell he didn't want to surrender to it totally in case he'd somehow gotten the meaning wrong during all those read-throughs.

"What is it?" said one of the others.

The workingman looked up at Art, and then back to the card, and then up at Art again, before letting the corners of his mouth creep up toward his eyes. Then he looked at the others.

"I think," he said, "we're going to a damn weddin'!"

On November 17, 1926, the Ringling Brothers show pulled out of its last date, in Richmond, Virginia. Art and I skipped the last-night party, preferring to stay in, reading books and talking. The next day, the trains pulled into winter quarters. While normally the workingmen would've scattered to all four corners of the country, this time they hung around, camping down by the rail tracks, sleeping under railway bridges, having three-day-long games of poker, scurrying about parts of the city the clean and respectable citizenry of Bridgeport probably didn't know existed.

Three days later, on November 20, I woke up in my Pullman suite, where I'd spent the night not with my fiancé but with my grumpy old cat, Rajah. Upon waking, I rubbed his muzzle and tickled his underbelly, which normally would've brought him awake happy to be alive. Instead, he burped a cloud of meat-smelling air in my face and growled and moved closer to the edge of the bed, all of which I took to mean he was not in any way pleased with what I was about to do that day.

The wedding was at eleven. I spent the morning relaxing and

sipping coffee and getting into my wedding suit, gowns being something I'd never been a fan of, seeing as they're fussy and expensive and not even comfortable to sit down in. Still, was a lovely few hours, for it was the first of my five weddings in which I hadn't misgivings beforehand, something I'd always made the mistake of attributing to nerves. Around 10:30 my cage boy, Bailey, knocked; he was wearing a brown suit that strained at the buttons, and his hair was slicked back over the top of his head.

"Morning, Bailey," I said, to which he smiled and backed away and proudly gestured at a car he'd gotten somewhere. I got in, and he drove me to a community hall Art had rented downtown, Art's dream of being married in a church having died when we found out how much it cost to rent a church large enough to seat every workingman on the Ringling Brothers Barnum & Bailey Circus. Instead we were being married in a windowless cube of a building, with clapboard walls and a flat roof, the words Polish Welders Association Hall splashed across the front.

I was about to open my car door when Bailey barked, "I'll do it!"

I leaned back and smiled and said, "All right, Bailey. You just go ahead." He turned the car off, staying put while it rocked and jiggled, after which he hustled over to my side of the car as fast as he was able. Beaming, he took my arm, and walked me to the front door of the hall, where we stood waiting till we heard organ music, though in this case it wasn't organ music but the groaning breathiness of a calliope.

"Are you ready?" he asked.

"I am at that," I answered, after which we walked on in, causing six hundred heads to turn. *Jesus*, I muttered under my breath, and if I'm not mistaken I heard Bailey mutter something similiar, for each and every one of those poor workingmen had somehow managed to get himself into a jacket and tie. As I scanned the room, I saw jackets with frayed lapels, with unravelled stitching, with buttons missing, with stains as big as squirrels, with pockets torn clear off. I saw jackets straining over shoulders clearly too big, and I saw jackets draping off shoulders way too spindly. I even saw nice jackets, for there was one table with workingmen dressed in fine wool suits, meaning a men's clothing store had probably been broken into the night before.

The other surprise was each and every attendee had cleaned himself up—those were polished foreheads giving me little nods of recognition, and those were clean hands giving me little waves, with clipped nails and bandaged cuts besides. Many of them had had haircuts, and the ones who hadn't had combed their hair, many of them pomading it to one side. Far as I could tell, every last beard had been trimmed, which is saying something seeing as how all workingmen wore beards. I'll tell you it was a sight, all those smiles as I walked down that aisle, showing teeth that, while not exactly white, had been baking powdered to a state just this side of clean.

In other words: I was a touched Miss Mary Haynie from the earthy part of Kentucky, and crying enjoyably because of it. Art was waiting for me at the front of the room, and of course he wouldn't be Art if he didn't have a surprise in store: his best man was none other than a tiny little elephant we all called Baby. Seeing this, I laughed through my hiccuping tears, the workingmen seated nearest the aisle laughing along with me. When I reached Art he held my hand with the one not holding on to Baby's leash.

With that, the ceremony started. The minister was Unitarian, and as a result didn't wear a robe, just a normal everyday church-going jacket. When he started in on the service I faded out, for I'd heard those words—the ones starting with "Ladies and gentlemen, we are gathered here today" so many times I practically knew them by rote. To pass the time, I let my mind wander and I started thinking about how absurd life is, my being the only woman at my own wedding and marrying a man most wouldn't describe as being particularly male and still my being pleased about every last bit of it. I came back to the here and now around the time the minister told Art it was ring time. Art whispered something to Baby, and Baby raised the tip of his trunk. It held a little powder-blue box, which Art took and opened. I gulped. The ring was emerald, and what's more I knew the reason why: I'd once mentioned to Art the most beautiful colour on earth was the colour of Rajah's eyes. By now I was really crying—try wanting something for your entire adult life and finally getting it—so to a background of whimpers and sniffles I heard that Art was to kiss the bride. A second later Art's hands were on my waist and his lips were on my lips and his moustache was tickling the underside of my nose and I was officially Mrs. Mabel Rooney, Bridgeport, Connecticut.

At which time lunch was served.

Art had hired a bunch of local teenagers to tend to the food, and they came out with bowls of potato salad, macaroni salad, ham slivers, chicken pieces, turkey hocks, cheese cubes—you name it, we served it—and they set them on a series of buffet tables against one wall. Art and I served ourselves first, after which we sat and ate and watched the workingmen line up, not a hint of pushing or elbowing or name calling, only a lot of smiling and jovial talk. With such orderliness it wasn't long before they were all back in their seats, plates heaped high with food, a plastic rose in front of every third man, and oh was it comical watching them try to eat turkey hocks with cutlery instead of their bare hands. Throughout, there wasn't any swearing or bawdy joke telling or fights over who did or did not pass the salt. Prior to the big day, Art and I had talked long and hard about whether we should give them beer, our decision being we'd put enough for two each in big ice buckets around the room. Turns out we needn't have. Not one workingman had a beer. Most wouldn't even look in the direction of the tubs, sticking instead to the pitchers of water and iced tea on the tables. Was as though they'd all gotten together and voted not to go near anything containing even the smallest amount of liquor, which I later learned was exactly what happened.

Mostly, it was what I call a nice sociable event, a lot of pleasant chatter without all the fussing, dust-ups and fornicating that tend to come along with circus parties. Since we'd started first, Art and I finished eating before anyone else, so we went from table to table, thanking them all for coming, and I can tell you they were all a hundred times more appreciative than any of the performers would've been. We'd done a good thing, inviting those poor men. We just *had*. When we were done our little tour, Art and I found ourselves standing by the door to the Polish Welders Association Hall. Art looked at me, giving me that Art grin.

"Well, Mrs. Rooney?"

"Well, Mr. Rooney?"

"I suppose we should go."

"Yes, I suppose we should."

He pushed open the door and we stepped outside. Was a coldness to the air, but not a bad one, owing to the sun in the sky and the clearness of the day. The car Bailey had squired me in was parked outside, the keys in the ignition and our packed bags in the rumble seat. Art helped me into the car, and by the time he got in himself some of the workingmen were coming out and making the first ruckus of the day, though was a ruckus more along the lines of whooping and hollering and wishing us a great honeymoon. We drove off, waving and feeling like royalty. As we made our way through town, other drivers honked when they saw the "Just Married" sign roped to the rear fender. Pedestrians waved and a friendly cop, seeing the carnations glued to the headlights, directed us around a broken water main.

Ten minutes later, Art was hoisting both our bags onto a train that, believe it or not, didn't belong to John Ringling. As we sat and waited for the train to leave, some of the workingmen showed up on bicycles and began waving and being generally boisterous outside our compartment window. A few turned cartwheels, and one made swimming motions in the air for no clear reason I could think of. We laughed anyway and waved and generally felt light as feathers and eager for travel. After a few more minutes a whistle blew, and blew again, and the train started to jostle, my not bothering to ask Art where we were going because I knew under no circumstances would he tell me.

Four days we were on that train. Normally when I travelled, I had a hundred things on my mind—which tiger had a toenail problem and which tiger was suffering from a churny stomach and which tiger was balking on a rollover and which tiger was showing testiness during the tunnel-in. With my mind so occupied, I often missed what went rolling by my Pullman window, the fact the Ringling show travelled mostly at night not helping. This time, with no tigers to worry about and my mind eased by my new last name, I had a chance to take a good long look at the countryside. In other words, I felt like I was seeing it for both the thousandth time and the first.

Just outside the Connecticut state line, the train veered close to Manhattan Island, close enough I could see office buildings and the Brooklyn Bridge and, looming over them like a watch mother, the Statue of Liberty. (Was always my opinion New York City was crowded with tall buildings so that those arriving would see them and be impressed and think, *Jesus, what must go* on *in this country?*) After chugging through New Jersey, we travelled through the steel towns of Pennsylvania, the industry of which impressed the part of me valuing hard work above all. Next stop was Washington, the nation's capital and regal because of it, Art and I having just enough time to get out on the platform and eat a vendor frank and wish we could visit the government buildings. We reboarded, and for the next long while there wasn't five minutes in which the train was heading in a straight direction; was nothing but curves and inclines and declines, the train making a potpourri of noises, from the locomotive straining up the side of a mountain to the brakes rushing air to stop the train from hurtling down the other side to the screech made when train wheels cornered on worn-out gauge. Every once in a while, as I peered out the window, the forest would break, and

I'd see a mountain peak and someone else would see it too and say, "Look, there's Mt. Mitchell" or "Hey, whaddaya know—there's Sassafras Mountain, will you get a load of the mist no wonder they call them the Smokies."

Took us a full day and a half to get through Virginia, North Carolina and Tennessee. We must've seen a hundred little logging towns, the houses all made from wide-bore timber, smoke pouring out of each and every stone chimney. On the station platforms, little white children with close-cropped hair would try to sell us packets of sap gum or homemade string-with-ball toys, waving at the train as it pulled away to the next little mountain town. By the time the terrain turned swampy, the trees dripping moss and the land cloaked in the mystery poorness causes, I knew we were skirting the tops of Alabama and Mississippi. Suddenly the children greeting us at each whistlestop were black and so wanting for nourishment it made the back of my throat ache: they were dressed in rags, and living in houses made from tarpaper. In one town—I forget the name, Holly Springs maybe—Art bought a bag of apples from a station vendor and started handing them out, though he stopped when the older kids started pushing down the younger ones to get more than their fair share.

The train picked up speed when we hit the wide-open spaces of Arkansas and Oklahoma. And while I won't say those states are as lovely to look at as other parts of the country, I will say there's an impressiveness in the ability to remain unchanging. As we gazed out our compartment window, watching all that scrub roll by, the eye got drawn to simple things it wouldn't've noticed in the mountain states. A lone homesteader shack, still in use. A cow getting branded. A vulture sitting lazily on a fence post, nothing around him for as far as the eye could see. Funny how a little hill, one that would've looked no bigger than a pimple in the Appalachian states, can be a source of fascination and meaning when it's all alone and surrounded by flat space.

During those two days or so, with nothing must-see on the far side of the window, Art and I did most of our talking—was a lot of handholding and baby voices and blabbing about the future, till finally I asked one of the many questions I had about the origins of Arthur J. Rooney.

"Art, I want you to tell me something. Do you, or do you not, have some Indian blood coursing through those veins of yours? If you do, just tell me, because to my mind anyway it's nothing to be ashamed of and I'd really just like to know."

He blinked several times, thinking, before providing his answer.

"Some," he said.

He didn't say anything for the next half-minute or so, which is a long time for a pause in the middle of a conversation.

"My mother was Indian."

"And your daddy?"

Here Art took a deep breath.

"Peddled whisky on the reservations. Or at least I'm told he did. I never knew him. My mother was his best customer. You can probably guess how she paid him, considering I'm sitting here talking to you. Since she was in no state to raise a little one, the other squaws mostly banded together and took care of me. They say every man is a product of his environment, and my environment included ten mothers, no fathers and more confusion than is generally considered beneficial to the welfare of children."

"When did you leave the reservation?"

"When they passed that damn Boarding School Act. I was ten years old when they sent me to a white school. I didn't fit in with the white kids there and I didn't fit in with the Indian kids there, so I mostly spent my time with the workhorses and with some stray dogs the schoolmaster fed with scraps. Without the company of those animals, I think I would've gone crazy. I suppose in a way I did, what with all the fussing I did after I ran away. I did *that* when I was twelve, and I spent the next five years doing whatever it took to keep an Indian boy alive on the streets, none of which I'm willing to talk about, for the appetites dreamt up in some of those frontier towns are unfit for the ears of a good woman like yourself. One day I hitched a ride into Laramie. I figured I'd stay a few days, maybe a week. I ended up staying fifteen years."

Art lit a new cigarette and took a deep sucking drag, which he held so long the smoke all but disappeared.

"Everyone has trials and tribulations, Mabel. Everyone. I've been alive for fifty-three years, and in that time I've learned one thing and one thing only. There ain't a problem on this great green earth helped by feeling sorry for yourself. Nope, not *one*."

Art looked out the window, his teeth moving and his moustache bobbing the way it did when he was deep in thought. Suddenly his face lightened. He clamped his elbows to his sides and gave a little shake.

"It's chilly in here. You know what we should do? We should go to the dining car and get some ice cream. Whenever you catch a chill you should eat something cold—suck on an ice cube, say, or locate a polar bar. It makes the temperature outside your mouth feel warm by comparison, and when you really think about it, warmth by comparison is about the only type of warmth there is."

To which I looked at him adoringly and thought, *Oh, Art*. Please.

Soon after, the train took a turn south and we crossed over the state line into Texas. There was an hour's whistle stop in Dallas, during which we got out and stretched our legs and each had a barbecued turkey leg. We got back on board, and it was outside of Houston that Art stood and started putting clothes into his suitcase. I looked at him questioningly, a look that caused him to grin and stop packing for a second and say, "This is our stop, Mrs. Rooney. I'd get myself ready to go, if I were you."

I hurried to get my things together. When the train next stopped, a Negro porter came and took our things and carried them to the platform, Art instructing him to check them at the baggage counter. When all that was done he tipped the porter, who thanked Art and strode off whistling. Art took a deep breath and had an admiring look around the high glass-ceilinged station.

"Well, Art," I said. "I know you want to keep me guessing, and my guess is since you've checked our bags, Houston isn't our final destination, and that maybe you want to do a little sightseeing before we move on. Am I in the right ballpark?"

"You are, Mabel. I have a little Ringling business to attend to here in Houston, but other than that you're right on the money."

We left the station and Art hired a taxicab and we crossed downtown, Art saying nothing but smiling like he had something up his sleeve. As for me, I'd been to Houston many times previously, and had always marvelled at what an ugly town it was, a reaction I was pretty much having again. I suppose the problem was it was more or less a port, meaning most of the buildings were either warehouses storing whatever came through Galveston Bay via steamship, or darkened hotels frequented by seamen on shore leave. What Houston didn't have was the normal upside to big city life, that being restaurants and markets and theatres and people everywhere. Why this was, I wasn't sure, and the only thing I could think was that Houstonites grew so used to staying put during the sweltering heat of summer they forgot to break the habit when the weather got more agreeable.

After ten minutes or so, we stopped in front of a squat building indistinguishable from all the other low buildings on whatever street we were on, except there was a sign on the door reading "Peterson & Co., Animal Traders." Art rang the doorbell. After a bit, a man answered, his face breaking into a smile when he saw Art.

We all went in, Art introducing me as his new wife and Peterson as one of the most respected men in the animal wholesale business. We were in a giant room filled with animals of every description, and we had to speak loudly to be heard over the noise. The air was thick with dander, and though I found it unpleasant to breathe, Art didn't look like it was bothering him in the least.

Art told Peterson he needed to replace three animals: a camel that'd just died of fever, an elephant who'd passed on from old age and a llama that'd gone deaf and could no longer follow instructions during the pell-mell of the opening spec. Peterson nodded and told him to take a good long look around, and to let him know if there was anything else that caught Art's eye, for most of the animals had just come in and were as yet unspoken for. Peterson wandered off, leaving Art and me to roam up and down aisles crammed with crates and cages and large wooden boxes, each filled with an animal either sleeping or sniffing at the spaces between slats. Truth be told, I found it all a little sad, for the animals obviously weren't getting enough sunlight (or loving, for that matter), and I felt guilty for creating a need for this kind of traffic in creatures.

Art, too, looked a little displeased.

"The shipment must've been from South America," he said, pointing around as if to indicate he wasn't about to find an elephant or a camel among them. He did pick out a llama, saying it was a nice healthy specimen with good-sized hooves and a temperament that could be worked with. Art then invited me to have a peruse, which I was already doing. After a few minutes, I found a crate carrying two ocelots, which interested me because they weren't the local variety but had come all the way from Patagonia, meaning they were smaller and their coats more mottled. Though I couldn't work them, ocelots not being anywhere big enough to thrill a crowd, I did think they'd be an interesting addition to the menage, and when I told this to Art he bought the pair as well. After filling out some paperwork in Peterson's office, we stepped outside. A grey coupe was parked at the curb, and our bags were piled up in the rumble seat.

"Well," Peterson said, "there she is. I just had her serviced, so as long as you don't hit anything you won't have any trouble. You two have a good time and ..."

He said something else, though I didn't hear it because by then

Art had taken the turn and had started the engine and was revving it to make sure the gas flowed properly. I climbed in and we all waved and there were smiles all round and then we were off. Over the sound of the motor ratcheting itself up to travelling speed, Art explained he'd been able to borrow the motorcar because Peterson was not a bad sort and because the circus bought as many animals as all of Peterson's other clients put together. Art then looked at me, blinked, and said mostly it was the second reason.

I smiled, not because of Art's witticism but because I was starting to feel like we really were on vacation: the top was down and wind was flapping our hair and once we got away from the homeliness of the city we started passing cypress trees and pines and live-oaks and it was all pretty, every bit of it. The bay road was mostly sand, meaning we got dry-mouthed pretty quickly, so after a bit we stopped at a tiny little town where everyone wore suspenders and chewed on toothpicks. There was a general store, where we bought glasses of lemonade and jerky for when we got hungry later. Art also had the presence of mind to chat up a local sitting at the counter, who upon hearing what we were doing offered us a pail of water to pour over the radiator.

After another hour or so, we reached a rickety wooden suspension bridge, which we crossed so as to pass onto the island of Galveston. The road led through town. Though it was off-season, there was still the odd person about and the odd café open, so I told Art I wanted to stop and have a look about.

"All in due time," he said. "All in due time, Mabel. First, we have to keep an appointment."

Pretty soon the road banked to the right, and the next thing I knew we were driving along a breakwall, and beyond that the Gulf of Mexico stretched choppy and blue to infinity. I gazed out over the water and felt my body lose its tension, something that happened whenever I fell witness to a vanishing point. I asked Art why he thought this was so and of course he had an answer. "Fear of death," he said without blinking. "It disappears. When you look out over water, and you feel like you can see forever, the mind starts thinking maybe some things really can last forever. That maybe some things really *are* eternal. Once the mind figures that out, it's only natural it starts suspecting maybe the thing that make us *us* is also a thing that has the potential for everlife. And once the mind figures *that* out, well. It's not long before it realizes it's been doing a whole lot of worrying for nothin'."

I looked at him, agog.

"The only trick," he added, "is holding on to that feeling when you're not looking out over an ocean or an undisturbed stretch of flatland. I'll tell you, it's a trick really separates the men from the boys, if you know what I mean."

A few seconds passed.

"Tell me," I finally said. "You make this stuff up on the spot, or do you actually spend time thinking about it?"

"Mabel. I lived in a four-by-eight-foot cell for fourteen years. I had time to think about pretty much anything I cared to and other things besides."

After a bit the seawall gave way, and instead of the waves crashing against piled stones they broke choppily over smooth, light brown sand. Though the weather was nice and sunny and verging on warm, there now wasn't a soul around. We started passing neat little clusters of houses on the beach side of the road, some of them no bigger than huts and all of them painted either pale blue or a sunny yellow. We also passed signs bearing the names of the resorts: "Seaside Cottages" and "Ocean View Suites" and "Sandy Shore Rentals." I started suspecting we were going to spend our honeymoon in a rented cabin on the water, a proposition that suited me fine, for as I've said I've always associated sun and waves with time off and the opportunity to recuperate. I had my suspicions confirmed when Art pulled into the very last set of resort huts on the spit, a tidy grouping of little houses called Sunny Side Cabins.

"Well," Art said, "what do you think, Mabel? We'll have sun, the ocean, all the seafood we care to eat. Most important, we'll have time alone to contemplate our navels, and according to some religions there isn't a thing in this world more important *to* contemplate."

Without waiting for an answer, he pulled up in front of the first cabin in the row, which looked better appointed than the others: lace curtains were hanging in the windows and the garden was tended and there were window boxes filled with late-season flowers struggling to bloom. A little sign reading "Office" was over the door.

Art tapped on the door. We could hear a radio playing inside. Art tapped more forcefully, until we heard the radio being turned down and steps shuffling toward the door. A lace curtain was pulled aside, and though we couldn't tell for the glare we both knew we were being looked at, so we smiled and generally tried to look honest. The door swung open, and we were said hello to by a dumpling of a woman wearing a knitted pink sweater. Her hair was a frizz of grey, and her cheeks were so rosy and round that when she smiled, as she was doing at that moment, her eyes narrowed into slits I was amazed she could see out of. She was so little she had to crane her neck upward to look into *my* face, which was a change of pace for in a typical crowd of adults I'm almost always the smallest.

"Well, hello!" she said in a croaky voice. "You must be the Rooneys. I'm Bertha Wain, the owner. Gosh, you two must be tired. I've just made tea. Would you like to have some?"

Art and I exchanged *sure why not?* glances and followed her shuffling steps into her little yellow kitchen. We sat at a wooden kitchen table and watched as she padded around the room, collecting spoons and milk and a sugar bowl, then pouring hot liquid into little cups bearing the words "Galveston Island, Vacationer's Paradise."

When we were all seated, she turned to me and said, "When your husband contacted me I was surely surprised, for as you can see it's off-season. Normally people aren't interested in coming this time of year—they complain about the wind and the salt spray it kicks up—but your husband said you two were looking for a place where you could be by yourselves seeing as this was your honeymoon and all. Well, I don't think you'll be disappointed. It'll just be you and me and the gulls for the next week, my Harold having passed away seven years ago now, all of which I explained to your husband here and he seemed to think it was just fine."

We talked a little bit more, mostly about our long train trip and the weather that time of year in Galveston, though when we told her we were troupers with the Ringling show her face lit up and she said she was a fan and sure enough she had a thousand questions, mostly about the secret lives of the bigger stars and how on earth we managed to up and move the whole thing every single day. After a bit, I started to get restless. Seeing this, Art waited for the next natural pause in the conversation, at which point he drained his tea cup and said, "I can't wait to see our cabin."

"My oh my of course" was Bertha's response. "And here I am, keeping you two lovebirds from yourselves. Where are my manners? They just flew out the window when you told me you were circus folk, I suppose. Gracious, what did I *do* with that key?"

She got up, a movement involving a lot of chair-leg scraping and the use of her forearms, and then rooted through a half-dozen kitchen drawers, pushing aside egg flippers and potato mashers and meat pounders, until she finally found a key on a looped piece of string. We followed her across the sand, which was slow going, Bertha taking the opportunity to inform us she was a sufferer of lumbago, and that if you happen to have lumbago there's not much worse you can do for yourself than walk along a sandy beach. True enough, her motion was mostly in the shoulders, her back ramrod stiff as she walked.

We reached the last cabin in the row. Just beyond was the end of the cove, the beach turning to light bramble and then a promontory covered in a sparse pine forest. "If you want to make a fire," Bertha said, pointing, "you'll find all the deadwood you can possibly use. Plus you'll find the spit offers a little protection from the wind, which we do sometimes get here in November. Other than that, I think you've got everything you need. I put in towels and bedding and there's a pump out back so you'll have no shortage of water. It's right next to the outhouse, so you can kill two birds with one stone, if you catch my meaning."

She jiggled the key, and we followed her into the cabin.

"This is it," she said. "Home for a week. You like it?"

She was breathing deeply, and while she rested I took a look around. The kitchen was small, holding nothing more than a stove, an icebox, a few cabinets and a table for two. On the table was a vase filled with cut flowers and a bowl of oranges. There was a counter separating the kitchen from the living room, the same counter our hostess was at that moment leaning on, huffing and holding the small of her back and saying how she really had to get over her mistrust of doctors and go see one. The living room was wood panelled, with an oval crocheted rug flanked on both sides by sofas that'd obviously seen better days but at the same time looked comfortable and plump. Behind one of them was a door, which, I presumed, led to the bedroom. Behind the other was a wall decorated with an old oil painting of two children walking in woods.

But the cabin's best feature was the picture window, taking up the better part of the wall facing the beach. Our view was sand and sun sparkling off water and beyond *that* a good long glimpse of nothingness. As I took in the view I'd have for the whole of the next week, it occurred to me if this wasn't a place where I could relax then that place didn't exist, all of which should explain why I acted so out of character and went up to poor old huffing Mrs. Wain and hugged her while saying, "Oh, yes, Bertha. It's wonderful!"

Bertha left and we unpacked and when we were done we stood by the picture window and admired the view, Art saying he had a half a mind to go have a dunk in the surf. The next thing I knew, we were both splashing around like fools, the water cold but not nearly as cold as I would've thought. We got out and the breeze condensing all that salt-water on our skin *was* cold, so we ran shrieking to the cabin, where we towelled off and got dressed again. Then we went into town. While most of the stores along the Strand were closed, there were a few shops open that serviced the locals, including a place for groceries. We stocked up, throwing anything that caught our fancy into the grocery carts, as well as paraffin for cooking and a big bag of ice to keep our provisions from spoiling.

By then, it was starting to get dark, and as we drove out of Galveston the sun was settling low over the gulf. As Art drove I watched, for it was something to see, a fat burning ball fanning bands of orange over the water. Back at the cabin, Art ran around and collected driftwood in the dwindling light, and every time he found something big enough and dry enough to burn he'd give a little holler. He came back inside with an armload and built a fire while I made us a supper of corn, potatoes, salad and clams in butter. By the time I was done the cabin was warm as a bun. We ate by lamplight, the cabin having no electricity, Art giving a satisfied little grunt after every mouthful and at times saying, "My goodness, Mrs. Rooney. If I'd known you were such a culinary expert I would've asked for your hand in marriage earlier." Here I giggled and took a mouthful of clams and I tell you, I might as well have been tasting food for the first time, which is a strange experience for anyone but particularly for a woman with nearly forty years and five husbands under her belt. I took a sip of beer—Art was drinking iced tea—and practically grew maudlin at the thought that someone, at some time or another, had sat down and been smart enough to invent a drink as cool and delicious.

We were just polishing off a big slab of store-bought chocolate cake when Art announced there was something we just had to do. Before I had a chance to ask what that thing was, he was through the cabin door and running around giving excited little whoops for the second time that evening. I turned down the lamplight and tried watching Art through the picture window, his running figure crossing through bands of moonlight. Was then I saw the spark of a match, and before I knew it Art had a bonfire going on the beach. He came back inside the cabin and fetched blankets.

"Well come on, Mrs. Rooney," he said. A minute later we were both out on that beach, lying on blankets next to the heat of a fire, staring upward. There must've been a million stars out that night, of the twinkling, blinking *and* shooting varieties. Art pointed out Orion, the North Star and the Dippers. He pointed out some other constellations with long Latin names, and though I couldn't make them out I said I could just to be agreeable. Then we fell silent and held hands and generally felt good being alive, which is a wonderful and rare experience and really ought not to be disturbed by small talk. Only problem was, I didn't have Art's ability to let my mind go blank. What I'm saying is, a single thought popped into my head, refusing to leave or turn into something different, and it wasn't long before keeping it to myself started to feel like torture.

I took a deep breath, looked into the side of Art's face and asked him something I'd been wondering about for as long as I'd known him.

"Art," I asked softly. "Why *is* it you make yourself up like a woman?"

I looked for signs I'd offended him, seeing as it was a topic he'd never raised himself, another thing that'd always struck me as odd seeing as he was a man who, next to tending to animals, liked nothing more than talking. He looked out over the water. Seemed to me he was taking his time composing an answer.

"Well, Mrs. Rooney," he finally said, "that's the big question, and to answer it I'll have to ask you to remember I wasn't always the man you know now. No siree. For almost forty years I was driven by devils, which is one of the worst ways a person can be but unfortunately one of the most natural. After a while, you get so you don't even notice how tired you are, fighting yourself all the time, and it's this sort of tiredness can cause a person to make mistakes he'll have to think about for the rest of his life. In my case I ended up in prison, and I'm here to tell you it was terrible. Three inmates per cell, guards as mean as mongrels, food so poor you could barely swallow it. One day I decided I'd had about enough, so I went up to this one guard I hated worse than the others and said something long and full of profanity. It got his attention, and when he turned around I hit him as hard as I could in the teeth, just to make no bones about who was crazy and liable to do anything. He and the other guards beat me so bad I pissed blood for weeks. Then they threw me in the hole, where you're supposed to get food and water but since I'd attacked a guard I got nothing. Soon I got so thirsty I even tried drinking my own orange water. Finally, I decided I'd been born rotten and nothing was ever going to change that, so I might as well lie down and die.

"Now this is the sort of decision that frees a man, and allows him to take a good hard look at himself. Or maybe it was the fact I was weak and delirious and still bleeding from the insides. To this day I'm not sure. I only know I put myself on that cell floor and I prayed to the Creator and I asked him to please take pity on me when I came up to meet him. A day went by. Another. I didn't die, or leastways was pretty sure I hadn't. On the fourth day it happened."

"What happened?"

"I got visited."

"Who visited you?"

Art shrugged.

"Hard to say. He was partly man, partly animal and partly neither, though I'd hate to call him a creature for it's a word that implies lowliness and there was nothing lowly about him. What he was isn't important. What *is* important is he had something he wanted to tell me."

"Which was?"

A smile crept over Art's face.

"He told me I am what I am and everything has a reason and the sooner I understood that the better. Then he was gone. I lay there, mulling, coming to conclusions, sizing up life, thinking maybe I'd have another go at it if I ever got out of this hole. I was there another three weeks. First thing I did when I got out was paint my toenails the way the squaws always used to. After that, the fights and the drinking tapered off, till the day I noticed I was no longer a man who fought and drank, you understand?"

I told him I did, though the truth is I was struggling. Like so many of the things Art said, it made sense only if you stopped trying to explain it to yourself with words. Course, this is easier said than done, so after a bit I asked, "You mean you wear makeup so's not to hit people?"

"That's a pretty simple way of saying it but seeing as the simple way's often the best way I'd have to say you're right."

I thought about this a bit longer, though eventually I gave up and asked Art if he felt inclined to get on with the honeymoon. He said he certainly did, so we got up and held hands as we walked away from the sparking fire. Inside we blew out the paraffin lamps and got undressed and crawled underneath an eiderdown comforter. For a time we lay listening to the sound of waves lapping at the beach, though it wasn't a long time for we were both feeling happy and warm and in love. We kissed and held each other and whispered words of adoration. I was about to take hold of Art's forearm when he guided my hand toward the part of a man's body more commonly put to use on the first night of a honeymoon. I whispered his name in a way that posed a question, for he was ready as ready gets and I thought maybe I was imagining things. He answered by slipping inside me, so easily it was as though we'd done it a thousand times previously, and for the first time I learned of a satisfaction that has nothing to do with ardour and has everything to do with a human being's desire for being pressed tight against another body.

Afterwards we snuggled and talked about how we were going to do some exploring the next day. Art fell asleep with a smile on his face. I tried to sleep too, but couldn't, for I was still thinking about what Art had told me. Course, the reason I couldn't stop thinking about that story was I'd seen myself in it; was little use denying I'd spent *my* whole life locking horns with others, and while I could find a reason for each specific battle, I couldn't find a reason why I'd had so many of them, the one possibility being it wasn't others I'd been fighting all along.

No sooner did this thought come than a floodgate opened in my head, and all the reasons why I deserved the way I'd been treating myself came rushing in—everything from the way I felt about my mother to my having cooched in a sideshow to some of the things I'd done to advance my career to the things Rajah and I had done together, in the dark, my mouth pressed into fur so I wouldn't be heard over the clacking of the train. Suddenly, I wished I was clothed. I put my hands over my eyes, the way a child will when trying to make herself disappear. I curled up, if only so there'd be less of me. There likely wasn't a woman on earth who'd sinned worse than me or more often, though it wasn't this fact that had me sobbing deeply and quietly so as not to waken Art. If I was feeling emotional, it was because I was lying next to a man who knew me and knew everything I'd done and still, *still*, had never once thought to hold it against me.

We spent the rest of that week playing like children, which was a way I'd never felt as a child so it was all new and exotic and glorious. Long walks were taken, cookouts were had, evenings were spent under the stars, next to a fire, watching constellations and feeling lucky to have found a place so private. The entire universe might as well have been up there for us and us only. Bertha let us use a pair of bicycles that were property of Sunny Side Cabins, and instead of taking the car we'd pedal into town to buy milk or bread. On the Tuesday morning, we found a drugstore tucked off the Strand, so we stopped and had a soda float each and bought paperbacks. That afternoon the wind kicked up, the sand swirling so fiercely it was unpleasant to be outside, so Art and I just lay around on the two sofas, reading our murder mysteries, listening to the cabin's loose shingles clatter in the wind. This all gave Art an idea, and the next day we cycled back into town where he bought the makings for a kite; that afternoon he tacked it together and it flew like a bird, though when it came time for my turn I got distracted and it slipped from my hands. For all I know, it's still out there somewhere, following the gulf stream to who knows where. We ate mostly seafood, though one night I roasted a chicken. One morning Art got up with the sun, and by the time I awoke he'd netted some mullets from the gulf, which he'd filleted and was frying in butter alongside eggs and potatoes. At night we made love under that eiderdown cozy, something Art was starting to get good at, his theory being the salty air was energizing him in a way he had no control over. I slept well, and if I had any bad dreams they were gone for me by morning.

These, then, were my memories of my honeymoon, my final recollection being the delicious sadness I felt the day we packed our clothes, said goodbye to Bertha Wain, took one last look at the Gulf of Mexico and drove the Ford back to Houston. There we spent a night in a hotel before starting our train ride back, a ride that for some reason seemed twice as long as it had on the way out. Fortunately, we'd stocked up on dime novels to keep us occupied, the only problem being at times I'd feel so excited and happy at the prospect of starting our lives together I couldn't even focus on the words. Breathless, I was, and a little delirious because of it.

The first thing I did upon stepping off the train was go see Rajah, who'd spent the entire week in his cage seeing as there hadn't been a cage boy willing to take him out and walk him. Having not seen him for a week, I took in his appearance with new eyes. He hadn't been worked seriously for five years, so in addition to growing foul-tempered he'd swelled to almost six hundred pounds, a size nearly impossible on a

Bengal. Mostly he looked shaggy and old and huge. I went in and tried brushing him, but his hair was matted and I didn't have the steel-tooth brush. To make matters worse, he kept rolling away from me, a way of showing he was definitely and without reservation pissed off. To appease him I tried stroking the soft spot between his front legs, though he'd have none of it, growling and gently batting me away with the back of a paw. "Rajah!" I said, "What's gotten into you?" and was then he purred and rolled over and sidled up toward me and started rubbing himself against me. I sighed and moved away, something that seemed to wound him even more than being left a full week in a cage. He bellowed, and then roared, and then waved a paw in my face, and I was starting to think it might be smarter if I got myself out of there when a switch got thrown inside Rajah and he turned into a sulky old kitty. He came over and sank his head into my lap and licked my palms. I stayed a good long time with Rajah that day, and when I left it was with the promise things were going to get back to normal and he'd have lots of time outside of his cage and he was not to worry, I wasn't about to let my prize wrestler turn into a skulky old menage cat anytime soon.

Art and I spent much of the holidays opening presents the workingmen had brought to our wedding. A lot of them were things you would've expected: half pints of rye whisky and decks of playing cards and stacks of poker chips. But mixed in were gifts that tugged hard at the heartstrings. One of the stake pounders had his momma make up a recipe book of southern dishes, like ham hocks and black-eyed peas and a few dozen rice-with-okra combinations, all of which I'm partial to. Another gave us a soap carving of a tiger riding an elephant, which was so realistic from a distance it looked like polished ivory. (I'd have it still, except one day I accidentally left it by an open window and rain got at it.) One burly old white workingman, who'd been with the show for years and was therefore called Mayor, gave us a big rusty latchkey, which he'd obviously found in a field somewhere. He'd then glued it to a plaque, above the words "Art and Mabel's key to the city."

By the new year, I'd started spending a lot of time working with the eight Ringling tigers, reacquainting them with the idea of double-hoop jumping and rope walking so they'd be ready to join the Robinson show at mid-season. I also figured I better get Rajah's head around doing his wrestling act again, so early one freezing cold February morning I went and got him, and instead of taking our usual walk through the yard I led him to one of the training arenas. It was cold that day, his breath rolling like San Francisco fog. He took his seat command without a fuss. I turned my back to him, and acted like I was stupid and deaf in front of a howling audience. I whistled, and soon after understood I had a problem, for instead of playfully jetting off his pedestal he growled and dismounted and lumbered gracelessly toward me, standing on his hind legs and hitting me hard on the shoulders with his paws. I hit the frozen ground hard. Rajah flopped on me, and roughly did his business. Wasn't any playfullness or affection or hammy acting involved, just a cat relieving himself on whatever was available and even as I was being rubbed against I knew it'd look nothing but vulgar to an audience of rubes.

That night, Art had a look at the plate-sized bruises on the back of my shoulders. He also helped me wrap bandages around my wrists, both of which were aching.

"Mabel," he said when he was done, "I suppose you know Rajah won't be getting any better."

I sighed. Art was right, rogueness being something that always sets in sooner or later, the bottom line being in Rajah's case it'd happened much later than normal and for that I should've been grateful. Still, it was a disappointment and a sadness, though at the same time it was one I could live with seeing as there was so much good in my life. And when I say good, understand I mean better than good, wonderful even, for there we were, Art and I, a night or two later, nude and warm and snuggling in bed, a place where the truest sorts of conversations take place.

"Mabel," he says.

"Yes, Art."

"I have an idea."

"You usually do."

"The one thing still missing from your life is the squalling of a little one, which is a problem that's not about to go away all on its own and for which I can see only one possible solution."

"And what might that be? Immaculate conception, maybe?"

"Nope. We adopt."

I laugh out loud.

"For Pete's sake, Art. Who on God's green earth is going to give a baby to a pair of troupers, one of who's been in jail and one of who's been in a loony bin, no less?"

"Well, of course it won't be a baby with a complexion anything like yours. But if you can stomach a baby with my ruddiness times a factor of two, I can tell you for a fact there are a lot of Indian toddlers out there who need any kind of parent they can get."

I turned my head, and saw he wasn't smiling or kidding or pulling my leg. We talked a bit more, the tone of our voices lowering in volume and gaining in warmth, and before you know it a plan came together: after Art and I finished the year with the Ringling and Robinson shows, we'd regroup in Peru and head South Dakota way. There we'd scrounge ourselves up an Oglala baby, Art being part Oglala himself and therefore partial to the idea. Just hearing Art's closing words on the subject—"This time next year you'll be somebody's mother, Mabel"—made my heart skitter. So I lay holding myself, knowing sleep wasn't going to come easily, not that night, for I was feeling as breathless as I'd felt on the train ride home, and to make matters worse I couldn't stop thinking how amazing it is that the moment you start thinking a thing can't happen is generally the same moment it does.

Two weeks later, the circus started the season with its annual stadium show at Madison Square Garden in New York. This meant I had the privilege of watching Clyde Beatty's act twice daily, Beatty having added another Nubian who was more ragged and unkempt and bitter than the other four cats put together. Now. When watching his act that spring of 1927, did I get furious at the way he beat his animals? At the stupidity of rubes for cheering him? At the fact it was him down there, soaking up applause, turning famous, being mobbed by *White Tops* reporters and generally basking in the limelight that comes from being center-arena Ringling? A little. I admit it. But the point is only a little, for it mostly felt like Beatty was a joke on a grand scale, designed to show the world that someone up there has a good sense of humour rather than a malevolence about him. *That's* how good I was feeling. (Art, meanwhile, fumed his way through each and every Beatty performance, one matinee actually turning to me and saying, in a voice half joking and half not, "I wish one of those Nubians would use a pistol on *him*.")

After New York, the circus moved to Boston, where we did the other stadium show of the year. After that, we started moving like a real circus, jumping every night, mostly clinging to the eastern seaboard though with the odd, quick jaunt inland. When a circus of that size goes on the move, everyone gets busy, busier than you probably think is possible, though that year my busyness was twofold. I was still riding High School for the Ringling show while trying to get the eight cats ready for the Robinson show and at the same time trying to figure out how I could include big old Rajah in an act without another tiger getting hurt. There wasn't a second when something didn't need doing, when a tiger hadn't chipped a tooth or the hay hadn't gone mulchy in the feed car or my horse hadn't stepped on a piece of glass and needed it pulled from its hoof. Trying to do all this, I slept maybe five hours a night, something that didn't bother me for I was so excited about the turns my life was taking I found I couldn't relax enough to sleep anyway. One night,

around early March, maybe two o'clock in the morning, I was struggling to sleep when I looked over at Art, who was lying there with a
heaviness and a stillness suggesting permanence. A notion popped into
my head, a notion that made my eyes widen even though it was dark in
the Pullman and there wasn't a whole lot to see other than Art's moustache quivering as he drew breath.

    Oh my, was the thought. *Oh my, oh my, oh my.*

    He's here to stay.

The following morning came up smoky, by which I mean cool the night
before though intending to get hotter, causing a puffy haze that dampened everything from the shin on down. The train had pulled in sometime during the night, meaning by the time I got up the lot was alive
with the frenzied, beehive activity that always predicts the putting-up
of canvas. I went to the cookhouse and had coffee and eggs with Art,
who then rushed off to oversee the construction of the menage tent. I
had a few minutes off before they unloaded the tiger cages, and seeing
as I couldn't sit still I thought I'd take my second cup of the day outside
while strolling the connection and watching the circus getting built. By
then the centre poles were up, the big top in the air and wafting, and the
elephants getting ready to work on the half poles. A group of stake
drivers were pounding in the pegs that the sidewall lines would be
attached to. I stopped to watch, for it was always a thing of beauty,
watching the stake pounders do their job: armed with a sixteen-pound
sledge, they'd hit the peg with the full weight of their backs and shoulders and then deflect the head of the hammer in a single smooth strong-
armed motion. A split second would pass before the head of the stake
was hit by the next Negro. Had someone made a mistake, such as glancing off the stake or pulling away the sledge too slowly, hammers
would've collided and the rhythm lost and maybe someone hurt. It
never happened; with five men around a single stake, the sound was
like Tommy-gun fire, the stake sinking not in a series of jolts but in a

motion that was practically seamless, each man taking three hits until only the stake head and the knot of the sidewall line showed above turf. Then all of them would move, in step, to the next stake. As they worked, they chanted, providing a rhythm for their pounding. Working this way, they could sink three or four stakes into the earth every minute, meaning the whole tent would be done in about an hour.

I stood watching, gleeful as gleeful gets, when it happened: a pair of unseen hands descended from the air and clamped themselves around my rib cage. I took a deep breath, only to find I couldn't quite draw in enough air to satisfy whatever urge it is that makes us take a deep breath in the first place. At the same time, I was feeling dizzy and claustrophobic, which is a weird way to feel when you're out in the open. Thinking maybe I'd caught something, I went over to a bench set up next to the after-show tent and I lay on it and closed my eyes. After a few minutes the sensation had decreased enough I could pretend it wasn't there.

Then, two days later, I was standing outside the blue curtain during the performance, surrounded by other performers waiting for their displays, when I felt those hands reach around me and squeeze and not let go. A small puff of air left my lips, causing a quiet gasp, and I looked around to see if anyone else had noticed. I took a deep breath, again found I couldn't get enough air and decided I better do something about it. With my head lowered slightly, I took off down the connection and found the tent where Doc Ketchum dealt with illnesses and injuries. I told him what was happening, and with a puzzled expression on his face he suggested I try breathing into a small brown paper bag, which he then provided. I lay down and breathed into the bag, the paper crumpling and ballooning with each breath, my mouth and air passages filling with the dry taste of brown paper. To help further, Doc Ketchum snuffed out his lamp, making the tent dark and restful.

"Now you keep doing that, Mabel, and I'll be back."

About ten minutes went by before he came back and lit his lamp. He asked if I was feeling any better, and when I told him I was he suggested I carry a brown paper bag in case this ever happened again. "That," he added, "and maybe you should get a little rest."

Right then and there I made a decision to do the bare minimum with my tigers, figuring so what if they were a little rusty when I moved them over to John Robinson. I also pledged to eat better and get more rest and relax more in the evenings with Art, playing cribbage or reading books or shooting the breeze or turning off the lights and pursuing a little married-couple enjoyment. But the odd thing? The thing should've told me trouble was brewing? I didn't tell Art about my shortness-of-breath problem, a fact nothing short of bizarre seeing as I told him everything about everything. Art didn't notice I was acting funny, or if he did he didn't mention it.

Most likely it was the former, for he'd gone out and bought a baby-name book and was spending his evenings poring over it, saying each name out loud in as many different ways as the name could be said, as though trying to unlock the mystery behind the way it sounded. ("Abigail. Hmmm. *Ab*igail. Abi*gail*. Has a nice a ring to it, don't you think, Mabel?")

For the next week I was fine—no dizziness, no tight-chest feeling, no sensation the world was somehow unreal and I wasn't a part of it. Then, late one afternoon, I was walking down the connection when it hit with a fury I can barely bring myself to describe. It was as though those big hands had found their way inside my chest and were applying themselves directly to my lungs. Tears came to my eyes, jiggling my vision. I started choking.

I happened to be passing the menage, and though my initial impulse was to visit Doc Ketchum, I didn't do that; instead, I found myself hobbling into the tent and fighting to pull in lungfuls of dander and elephant smell. I found my way to Rajah's cage. I let myself in and sat down beside him, doing all I could to catch my breath. The remains of a shank—it was split in three places, the marrow scooped—lay beside him, which probably explained why my big tiger was asleep, licking his lips and no doubt dreaming about earlier days. I patted him and felt sorry for what happens to old male circus cats.

"Oh, Rajah," I said in a soft voice. "The problems this world'll think up."

Rajah swept his tail in a wide arc across the floor until it came to rest against my thigh. I held it, thinking of all the times I'd given him bottles of warmed goat's milk in the middle of the night back when he'd been a kitten and Louis Roth my husband, and since it was a memory that made me feel maudlin I was glad to be there, at that very moment, with my baby tiger. Dreamy, I felt, and disconnected, like maybe I didn't understand why fear had to be such a big part of being alive. Without really understanding why, I reached out and took one of Rajah's big paws and petted it, saying, "It's all right, Rajah. It's all right. I don't know how I'll do it but I swear your retirement won't be spent in this awful old cage." I turned his paw over, and ran my fingers over the pebbly underpadding. Doing so made me feel tingly and warm. Again, without really thinking, I found the spot between the pads that makes a tigers' claws pop out, and I pushed with both thumbs. They came into view, not so much popping into sight, but rising slowly, like they were being inflated. They'd grown jagged and sharp, and I swore as soon as I was able I'd give myself a few hours with Rajah to groom his coat and file his nails and clean his teeth. It was a crime the way I'd been treating Rajah, it really was, especially considering all we'd been through. I noticed I was breathing a little better, just being with Rajah, and I placed the inside of my forearm against the tips of his claws, the sharp curving points making an impression in skin. I pulled, opening up the first layer and leaving three straight, bubbling red shallow furrows. As I did, I sighed. It felt wonderful, all that pressure in my chest releasing, a fine mist puffing from the openings in my arm and sifting through the steel arena bars.

A minute went by, with me just watching the blood seep to the surface of my arm, when I popped out of my trance. My head jerked from side to side, to see if anybody had noticed, and a keen embarrassment set in. I unrolled my sleeve and held the material to the three red lines on my arm. Every time I pulled the sleeve away, the wounds looked like they'd stopped bleeding, but then after a few seconds blood would start rising to the surface and I'd have to clamp the material of my blouse to the skin again. It grew sticky and orange in spots, though after a bit the flow was more or less staunched. I fast-walked back to our Pullman suite and applied some carbol and when the whole thing was clean and not bleeding at all I changed my blouse, throwing the other away so there wouldn't be any evidence.

The rest of the day I went about my routine—caring for my cats, doing a little training but only a little, riding High School in both shows, helping to load the tigers onto the flat cars, and then lying down beside Art in our darkened suite at the end of the day. I made sure I undressed in the dark, and seeing as this was a policy I'd always had anyway, Art didn't take any notice. As I cuddled up he started chattering away. "I've been giving some good hard thought about boys' names, Mabel, and to my way of thinking I've got it pretty much narrowed to Michael, Thomas, Wesley, Jake, Leonard, Parker, James, Cornelius, Beauregard, Pete, Julius, Richard, Lewis, Kenneth, Conrad or Frank. Any of those reach out and grab you? Hmmmm, Mabel?"

I didn't answer, my mind a thousand miles away, Art having to nudge me in the side and say, "You listening, Mabel?" Though I told him I was, that all those names were fine, I was really thinking about what I'd just done with Rajah, and how awful it is when life forces you to confront the things that give you pleasure.

The next day, in a town called Harrisburg, Pennsylvania, I stayed away from Rajah altogether, feeling guilty about doing so but figuring I was punishing myself as much as I was punishing him. Two days after that, May 8 and 9, we were in Pittsburgh, and during those dates I felt fine and rested and like I was getting back my grip on things, which turned out to be a dangerous way of thinking for the very next day, in a place called Morgantown, West Virginia, I allowed myself to visit Rajah again, just to see how he was doing and give him a cuddle, never stopping to think why it was I'd brought a clean towel along. We visited a good long time, enough that after a while I started thinking, *Good, there's nothing wrong with me. I barely feel tempted,* so I stood and walked out, giving Rajah a hug and a kiss and that's all.

(Which was not at all what happened the next day, May 11, in a town called Clarksburg, West Virginia, an over-the-hill Mabel Stark sitting down beside a dozing old tiger, and because she'd proved the day before she didn't suffer from any sort of compulsion or obsession she goes ahead and she pulls the same three tiger claws against the underside of her arm, watching blood rise and fine mist sift and all the while she tells herself, *See, it was nothing, I didn't enjoy that, uh-uh, no way, no reason anyone would.*) May 12 and 13 we were in Charleston, where a blowdown hit so fast we couldn't get the big top down in time, meaning everything got blown all over hell's half acre and a fuming Charles Curley left behind a team of workingmen to deal with the mess, all of which involved hiring a private locomotive to pull the section of train he'd had to leave with the clean-up crew. May 14 we were in Beckley and May 15 we were in Roanoke, two little towns where there was nothing to do and if there's anything that'll make a person succumb to their predilections it's boredom. On May 16 we pulled into Waynesboro, where one of the High School riders got thrown from her horse and broke her collarbone so badly she was howling and weeping and bent as a pretzel when they took her out of the ring. May 17 and 18, Richmond, where Lillian Leitzel got her plange count up to 184, John Ringling telegraphing her afterwards with a message that must've pleased her mightily, for the next day she walked around with her nose lifted even higher than normal, and because this didn't bother me one little bit I knew I was happy as happy gets and as a result God's unseen hands were just waiting to get me and grab me and squeeze the life out of me and it was *this* knowledge that kept me fighting the inclination to visit Rajah. May 19, Norfolk, and then on to Virginia Beach, the jump less than an hour. Because the circus pulled in before midnight, the local speakeasies, brothels and betting houses experienced a brief one-night bonanza. May 21, Durham, North Carolina, and a little farm girl from the tobacco end of Kentucky knew she had a problem, but because she was her mother's daughter she refused to admit it to herself, meaning she continued to put her head down and work and pretend everything was like it was before Art's announcement she was going to be a mother this time next year. May 22, Raleigh, and it was there, late in the day, just before the jump, that Art grabbed me in our Pullman and roughly pushed up my sleeves, which I'd been keeping buttoned to the wrist even though the weather had turned agreeable. We both looked down. A silent, miserable few seconds passed. Art's eyes looked jellied. Glancing back down, I saw the underside of my arms as he was seeing them instead of how I usually saw them. Was no denying it. The skin was swirled with scratches, like the swooping criss-crosses bugs make on the surface of a pond.

Art eyeballed me, and I do believe it was the first time I ever saw him look flustered or upset or just plain incapable of handling a situation. It took him a long time to talk, but when he did it came out like a crackling. And though his words probably won't mean much to you, understand they were one of the last things he ever said to me, and that they still wound every time I think of them.

"Goddammit, Mabel," he said. "Can't you just be happy?"

Which brings me to yet another subject we need to hash out. *Words.* Used to be they came to me in sentences, in paragraphs, in sequences. Used to be they came to me in order. Now they come the way time does, though with more of a vengeance. They come to me mixed up, blazing, intending only to confuse, subtle as a hailstorm. They come to me *hollering*, and when they do it's only a matter of time before they get reduced to those five old awful words—*can't you just be happy?*—and they repeat, over and over, till I want to hold my head and yell with the shame of it, for if I'd dealt with those five words when Art first posed them then maybe he'd be an old man today. Maybe it's my age, or maybe it's my medication, or maybe it's me being so upset about the way things're playing themselves out. All I know is my thoughts are a maelstrom, that keeping them straight is exhausting me and that in the centre of that maelstrom is a quiet plan, born on that valley ridge with Roger Haynes. You tell me. How many words do you think I've used in this little confession? Has it been ten thousand? Has it been a hundred? All I know is I've been at it for weeks now and the only thing that's made any sense or given me any comfort is the idea of doing what I'm thinking of doing to myself. Maybe the problem is I'm not done talking yet, and when I finally get out this last little bit all my words'll have added up and given me the things I was hoping to get out of this damn confession in the first place, like calm, like peace, like rest.

Like ... absolution.

On May 23, 1927, the Ringling circus pulled into a place called Laurinburg, North Carolina, a destination only because it broke the jump between Raleigh and Charleston. Since the big top held the whole town, Curley killed the evening performance, figuring it'd been a time since everyone had had a night off that wasn't a Sunday. The matinee went fine, and after doing my riding bit I went to the menage to visit with Rajah and work my other tigers. Then I went back to the train to have a bit of a read and a lie down. When I got up it was already close to five, so I decided to go back to the lot and find Art and see if he wanted to go into town for dinner, a practice customary on Sundays and nights off. As I was pulling on my dungarees there was a knock on my door. I opened up.

It was May Wirth's mother, frowning and wringing her hands

and looking generally perturbed. When she spoke, it was in an Australian accent that hadn't been weakened one iota by her time in America.

"They say you used to be a nurse?"

"A long, long time ago."

"Then come. Please. Help."

I followed her down the line of rail cars. A strong wind had picked up; it was ruffling my hair and swirling paper and when I looked up I noticed the skies were darkening. As soon as we entered her daughter's stateroom I could tell by the smell someone was seriously ill. That someone was May, the riding sensation from Perth.

She was a pretty girl, May, much prettier than Leitzel and a far sight nicer. Truth was, I admired her and wanted to help, particularly when I saw how sick she was. Her face, which was pale at the best of times, had turned the white of chalk. Her hands, which were gripping her bedspread at her throat, had wizened, the skin wrinkly and the joints enlarged. Next to her bed was a pan filled with greenish sick.

I sat on the bed beside her and could feel the sheets were dampened with sweat. Her forehead was hot as a grill. Meanwhile May lay perfectly still, her eyes unfocused and at half-mast. Her breathing was raspy, and a remnant of sick spanned the corners of her mouth. With each slow breath it bubbled up and then popped messily.

"May," I said, "it's Mabel Stark. Can you hear me?"

She nodded weakly, and I was beginning to plan a course of action when she came off the bed, the muscles in her neck and face distending, poor little May leaning over the side of her bed and releasing a torrent of pale green waste into the already filled pan. When she was finished, she collapsed back on her pillow and gave a long, pained moan. She pulled the blanket back up to her chin and I decided to have a look at the whole of her, so I took the bedspread from her weakened hands and, bunching it with the bedsheet, pulled it down. Just as I'd thought, she'd soiled the bottom half of her as well.

"How long's she been this way?" I asked May's mother.

"Two hours, maybe three. It started with pains in her stomach."

I put a cold compress on May's forehead. Her lips trembled for a second and she closed her eyes. If she was any more comfortable, she sure didn't look it.

"I guess it's some sort of flu," I said. "It's best we get her cleaned up."

Again I pulled down her bedsheets, though this time I pulled May's arms and got her sitting, something that inspired another round of convulsions and vomiting. With her mother's help, I pulled off her nightgown and changed her into something with flannel in it. As her mother held her, I cleaned up the lower half of her bed as best as I was able and then covered the wetness with towels and we laid her back down. May took a deep breath and closed her eyes and seemed to fall asleep, though I could see from the droplets on her upper lip and forehead it wasn't so much sleep she was having as the stupification caused by fever. Every twenty seconds or so she'd give the meek, shuddering groan that indicates a person's insides are aching and aching fiercely. I felt for her, I really did, though I wasn't unduly worried for I'd seen lots of people with bad flus back at St. Mary's, and knew it was a rare one a healthy young person couldn't recover from.

"Well," I said to May's mother, "she's sick all right but so long as she gets enough liquids twelve hours from now you'll see improvement. I'm not saying it's going to be pretty, but keep giving her water and she'll pull through."

I stepped outside and was about to pursue my plan of finding Art and having some dinner when one of the elderly Concellos, long past his flying years, came bustling along the train, his old face a mask of worry. Spotting me, he took my hand and pulled me along the train while saying, "Please. Hurry. Please. Is-a Antoinette."

The Concellos were a big family and they occupied a row of staterooms that could be opened up to make one long Pullman. The old

Concello pulled me inside and again I was greeted with the smell of sickness. A whole group of people, flying Concellos all, were huddled around a bed no doubt occupied by the ailing Antoinette. No one turned to acknowledge me, they being too busy fretting and arguing in Italian, so I stood there not knowing what I was supposed to do.

The old Concello took my wrist. "Come," he said. "Dis-a way, please." When he spoke, the other Concellos turned and, seeing I was there, backed away from the bed so I could look at poor Antoinette. Even from across the room I could tell she was suffering from the same pallor, convulsions and ungodly stains. I moved closer. If anything, Antoinette was even sicker, for the smells were fouler and her eyes had loosened in the sockets and were pointing toward her nose. Plus when she vomited she didn't even have the energy to lift herself off the bed, the evil greenness just gurgling out of her mouth and down the side of her neck. Someone handed me a damp cloth and I wiped Antoinette's face. It was then I noticed her lips were so cracked and dry that every time she groaned flakes of dead skin flapped and wavered. This made me sufficiently impatient I turned and barked.

"For Christ's sake, can't you see the girl's drying up? She's got the flu!"

This inspired a hubbub, the Concellos who spoke English explaining what I'd said to the Concellos who didn't speak English. When everyone understood, my diagnosis was met with grim expressions and mutterings. The men turned their backs as I had the women clean up Antoinette, who hung limply as she had her clothes changed and her body sponged. Then I had the women change the sheets and put down towels and return Antoinette to bed. She was shivering and clutching her torso and saying in English how much it hurt and how cold she was. I kept dampening her forehead and mouth, water seeping through the cracked dried crevices of her lips. It was a hell of a flu, this, and though I told the Concellos I'd seen lots of cases like it back in my nursing days, the truth was I was beginning to question whether I really had.

"Remember," I said. "Water. Plenty of it. She gets any more dehydrated that's when the problems'll start for real."

This sparked another burst of yammering and hand gesturing, everyone suddenly so emotional I made it real simple by pointing at my open mouth and saying. "Water. Acqua. Lots of it."

I left the Concello suite and headed back to my stateroom. The winds had turned into a full-out gale, and I had to stoop so's not to get blown over. There I changed into clothes that hadn't been sicked and sweated on. I'd just finished when there was another knock on my door; I almost didn't answer, for I figured it was someone else without enough sense to treat a flu with liquids and clean bedsheets.

Instead it was Doc Ketchum. The long strand of hair he normally kept plastered over the top of his head had come loose and was irritating one eye.

"Mabel," he said gravely. "I could use your help."

I let him come in. He rearranged his hair and then rubbed his eyes hard with the base of his hands.

"Been busy?" I asked.

"I've been at it for three hours."

"Some flu," I said.

"I thought so too."

I nodded knowingly, but then stopped. If my ears weren't playing tricks he'd used the past tense.

"You *thought* so?"

He nodded, tight-lipped. "Then I helped Con Colleano take a piss."

"So?"

"Was blood in it. Mabel. I'm gonna need a good nurse."

I raced out of my room. Ran all the way to May Wirth's and barged in without knocking. May was stirring and moaning, her mother lifting a glass of water to her lips.

"No!" I yelled.

Mrs. Wirth looked up, frightened.

"It's the water. The barrels are bad. Infected." Was then I looked around the room and saw that May, like most of the performers, had a small paraffin stove; I told her mother she had to use it to boil water and then give May that water and that water only.

Mrs. Wirth immediately gained the blinky, weak expression people get when circumstances change in an instant, which is the way she still looked when I ran from her stateroom to the Concellos'. Was a lot of yelling and throwing up of hands and accusations directed my way in Italian, none of which I hung around for: a whole lot of people were going to come down with amoebic dysentery that night if we were lucky. If we weren't, it was going to be typhoid or cholera and a lot of dead piled up by morning.

Seems Ketchum had gotten tired of waiting in my room, for I ran into him just as he was stepping down to the rails. By then the skies were darkening both because of the time of day and the gathering rain clouds. I had to yell to be heard over the wind, which had escalated from a howl to an out-and-out screech.

"WHAT DO WE DO?"

"GET MORE HELP."

I went looking for nurses, Ketchum for orderlies. Amazing, how people will suddenly insist you need a special license to wipe spew off a bedsheet, though after moving through two or three performer cars I discovered who the real troupers were. Here I'm talking about the ringmaster's wife, Ella Bradna; Anders Christensen's daughter Petra; a Loyal-Haganski named Olga; and believe it or not Lillian Leitzel, who I'm sure volunteered just so's she could prove any opinions I had about her wrong.

("So? Haff zee circus is ill? Vell, den. Lillian vill help. Lillian vill help *villingly*.")

We started moving from car to car. The first sick car we reached was the one belonging to Poodles Hannaford, something I remember for two reasons. First, he still had his clown freckles and clown smile on, which looked nothing but macabre on a man bent over naked and retching. Second, the moment the Loyal-Haganski girl caught a whiff of foul odour she vomited all over her shirtfront and skirt. When she'd finished emptying her stomach, Ella Bradna led her, white and shaky, back to her stateroom.

This meant we were down to four, which was fine, for four is about as many as can work in a small stateroom anyway. Together we bathed and stripped and cleaned and formed bundles out of slime-oozing bedsheets and assured relatives gone frantic with worry there was nothing to worry about, only a little bug in the drinking barrels, tomorrow everything would be back to normal, just you wait and see. Ella Bradna worked like a mule, steady and without complaint, at one point telling me she'd seen the same thing happen on a German circus she'd worked on years earlier. Petra Christensen was tentative, a fault of her being no more than sixteen, though once she overcame the embarrassment of seeing people nude and splattered with sea-green muck, she put her head down and worked as quietly and efficiently as Ella Bradna.

Which left Leitzel. Naturally, everything was done with flourishes and sweeping arm movements and sighs meant to draw attention. And while she wasn't particularly helpful in the cleaning department— she held everything at arm's length, meaning she couldn't get much oompf into her scrubbing—I have to admit she did excel in the fear-easing department. When we got to the room belonging to Merle Evans, the bandleader, we found him shivering and coated with diarrhea and frightened his age was going to work against him.

"Vat?" Leitzel exclaimed. "You call ziss sick? Belief me. Alfred is vorse after a night drinking tequila. Now. Let me light your paraffin stove and get ziss vater to bubbling. You need is a little vater and everything is fine."

Slowly we moved from the star cars to the section of train carrying chorus performers and maintenance workers. Things got more crowded, generally four bunks to a room, and that made the work harder. We kept asking the sick which barrels they'd drunk from, though mostly they were too frothing with vileness to answer. For this reason, it was impossible to detect any rhyme or reason for the outbreak. In one car everyone would be healthy and in the next all four would be violently puking and in the next you'd have one or two just starting to come down with it. Yet it wasn't the stench or the sights that got us but the sheer amount of manual labour. Our fingers ached and our elbows got stiff and we all got the deflated feeling that comes from having work that doesn't seem to have any intention of ending. Plus Ella Bradna's back started complaining loudly; I could tell because she'd stop, put a hand on her lumbar and wince. Luckily, we picked up three spec girls who wanted to help so we started doing two cars at once, my dashing back and forth to give instruction.

About an hour and a half in, we got to the workingmen part of the train. There we took a rest outside before the real fun started. By then it was totally dark outside, and the screeching winds had grown chilly; still, the healthy workingmen were all outside, huddled and passing bottles and bearing the weather as best they could. Ketchum was there as well, helping a group build bonfires so they could boil water over flames, the workingmen not having the benefit of stoves in their dorm cars. When he saw us he came running over. I don't know if it's possible for skin creases to deepen in a couple of hours, but it seemed to have happened to him.

"GOT GOOD NEWS AND BAD NEWS!" he hollered over the weather.

"GOOD NEWS FIRST!" I shouted back.

"HEARD MAY WIRTH'S DOING A BIT BETTER. NOT MUCH, BUT A LITTLE AND I FIGURE IF IT WAS TYPHOID OR CHOLERA SHE'D BE DOING A LOT WORSE. IT'S DYSENTERY, MABEL, BAD DYSENTERY AND AMOEBIC SURE AS SHIT, BUT STILL JUST DYSENTERY."

This news went a long way to reducing my numbed, achy-finger feeling. I let my voice rest a minute before yelling again into the wind. "THE BAD NEWS?"

Here Ketchum gestured toward the workingmen's car, squinting against a whipping hair lock. "IT'S BAD IN THERE, MABEL. BAD."

The rest of my nurses all heard this, so we each took a big breath and avoided looking at one another. Then we went in.

In the workingmen's car they slept three to a bunk, the bunks piled three high. Even spread out, there was at least one sick body in every bed and in some cases two and in the odd one three. Every single man in that car was groaning and clutching himself and running torrents from both ends. The aisles ran with puke and diarrhea and urine gone rosy with blood. Though every window was open, the jetting winds outside were no match for the thickness of the stench inside the car; one of the spec girls started to sniffle, and we all stepped back outside feeling horrified.

There couldn't've been less than four hours work in there. Course, there was little we could do without fresh bedding and given they were workingmen it was unlikely many of them would own a spare set. Hearing this, we all decided Ella Bradna would take the spec girls and go up and down the train begging people for spare sheets and drinking water, at the same time trying to recruit more nurses. That left me and Leitzel and Petra Christensen. Seeing as there was nothing left for us to do but roll up our sleeves and do what we could do in the meantime, I headed toward the door of the workingmen's car, which had been left open and was slamming over and over into the door frame.

After taking a few steps, I noticed I wasn't being followed, so I turned. Petra Christensen was crying, I suppose from fatigue and shock, though it really didn't matter for I could tell she was done.

"I vill take her back," Leitzel said, "und return as soon as I am able." They walked away, one stooped and one with her chin up, both with their clothes ruffling in the winds. I knew I wouldn't see Leitzel again, nursing fellow performers being one thing and nursing lowly workingmen being something altogether different.

So I headed into the workingmen's car alone. Now that I'd arrived, they were calling out and holding on to me and saying my name, which was spooky because a lot of them had gone delusional with fever and were calling out the names of wives or girlfriends while others were moaning, "Help me, Ma." Others were panicking, whimpering they didn't want to die a poor circus razorback in debt to the blue car for drinking. I dampened a few lips and foreheads and pulled up a few blankets, which'd get thrown off immediately due to the patient being hot with fever. After a few minutes, I realized there was precious little I could do on my own, so I made a decision: I'd go to the menage, check on Rajah and by the time I got back there'd be help and water boiled and hopefully fresh linen.

So I left. Had to dodge outstretched hands and avoid faces gone slack with dryness. I stepped into the bitter weather and, hunched against the wind, hustled to the other end of the train, which in those days was practically a mile long and travelled in four sections with four locomotives. I half walked and half ran the whole way, reaching the menage cars out of breath but amazed at my own energy. There I saw Art, sitting in a cage, tending to an elephant with a river of green muckiness spilling from a butthole dilated to the size of a basin; it flowed from the cage over the wash-out gutter and into the earth, making a puddle of awfulness I practically stepped in.

"ART!" I hollered.

He waved and yelled back something I couldn't quite make out because of the wind, though I think he said some of his bulls were sick but he'd see me later. I moved on, taking a bit of water Art had boiled next to the bull pens. As I hurried, I ignored the sounds of sick animals: was yaks lowing and camels spitting and gorillas chest-thumping and hippos crying and lions rumbling and a whole lot of healthy animals gone vocal for fear of what was happening.

A big crowd had formed around the prize Ringling akapi, for she was the only akapi in America and had cost almost as much as the albino elephant and if she died someone would have to deal with John Ringling and his temper. I got to the cat section of the train and started hoisting up sidings. Checked every one of my kitties. They were all more or less fine, only Pasha and Boston looking a little peaked and drippy but not too bad, considering. I gave each a little fresh water with a promise of more later. Then I cranked up the siding on Rajah.

I took a look, and it was a case of forcing myself not to fall to pieces.

"Oh baby," I purred, "oh, you poor little baby."

Rajah lifted his head and growled, and as he growled a stream of sick ran between his molars and onto the cage floor. I knew I had to be careful, for a sick cat is a scared cat and a scared cat is always dangerous, no matter how well he knows you. "Oh sweet kitty," I kept saying as I slowly lifted the big metal latch and let the door swing upward. "Mommy's here, darling little kitty," and I took a step inside, offering fresh water, when Rajah mustered all his strength and lunged. Landed his paws on my shoulders and pushed me back up against the bars, and for a moment there was a murderousness in his eyes that made me think I was done for. Then his eyes focused and he seemed to realize who he'd pinned. A softness returned to his look, and his muscles lost their tension. He arfed and laid his head on my shoulder and drew me toward him.

So I put my arms around Rajah and got them messed with vomit. His breath smelled like a sewer and his fur was crusted with awfulness. I just held him tight and told him no way he was going to die, not with me around, it being then I decided there wasn't a chance in hell I was going to care for a $10,000 wrestling Bengal in a filthy cold menage cage. So I wiped him off as best as I was able and gave him some clean water and rubbed his pleasure spot. Then I took him out of his cage,

Rajah shaky and arfing from his aches but not nearly so far gone as a lot of the humans I'd seen that day. Still, it was obvious he was too weak to make it to the performer train, and I was wondering what I was going to do when I saw one of the workingmen driving a gilly loaded with barrels of just-boiled water from the pie car. I hailed him and he dropped Rajah and me in front of my stateroom.

I took Rajah inside and made up a pallet from sofa cushions. I covered it all with a spare sheet and laid him down. For the next fifteen minutes or so, I gave him sips of water and cleaned him with a warm sponge and told him over and over how he was my baby and my best kitty and how he was going to get better and get better soon. When he was breathing evenly and asleep, I left him, glad he was in the warmth and quiet of my stateroom. Already he was looking a little better: as he slept he kept licking his lips, which in my experience means a cat's dreaming of something agreeable—hippo steaks, maybe, or tearing apart an impala.

Just before I left, I looked around for a piece of paper. Course, I couldn't find one, so I took some paper towelling and with a stubby pencil wrote, "Art. Rajah inside. Careful!" After tacking it to the door, I locked up and started making my way back to the working-men's cars.

The wind was still howling and the jet-black clouds above were spitting up huge fat raindrops that chilled the skull and made you wish for a hat. I made it to the workingmen's car out of breath and found things had gotten both better and worse. On the better side, there was water ready and more volunteers and some offered-up sheets that despite having seen better days would do the trick. On the worse side, the stench had worsened and the nursing crew was in a terrible confusion, everyone except Ella Bradna bickering and grabbing at sheets and generally showing the effects of fatigue and disorganization. When they spotted me they stopped, and something that hadn't occurred to me before became clear: nothing but nothing was going to get done without me being there.

It was basically triage, this, the sort of rough nursing that gets done after battles and bombings. Only problem was, I'd never had wartime experience, and had about as much of an idea as to how to proceed as the others. Still, it was more than plain there was only one thing *to* do; everyone else just needed to hear it from someone they figured knew what she was doing.

"LADIES," I yelled, "WE'RE ABOUT TO GET OUR HANDS DIRTY!"

We went into that groaning reeking hell and waded through bodily muck and did what we could. At first, I thought a panic was going to break out, for every ailing workingman was calling out to be helped first—thankfully, most were too weak to stand. We figured our first job was to hand out the clean water, as most of the men were now coming down with dehydration and suffering mightily because of it. We cautioned them against gulping though of course most ignored us, seeing as their thirsts were raging, so the liquid would come back up, having gained a glutinous texture from being in their stomachs. This would leave them more dehydrated than before, so we'd give them more water along with another no-gulping lecture, finding they were quicker to listen the second time around.

Was slow, patient work, getting water into them. Some of the men were so dazed they could barely lift their heads, and the ones with a little fight left in them pleaded to have the barf and shit cleaned off them before we moved on. We made a long, slow sweep of the cars, hydrating everyone we could, and when we got to the end we went back again, handing out another series of sips, Ketchum's biggest concern being that dehydration would start killing the older ones and the liver-damaged ones. When this was finally done, we tried cleaning the floor: it'd turned into a quagmire of shittiness, ankle-high and practically seething, and if something wasn't done cholera really would break out. It was a task involving a lot of mopping and helping men outside to either puke or piss blood.

Unfortunately, there were men still far too weak to get up, help or no help, and for them we handed out plastic bowls and metal bowls and porcelain bowls and pretty much any kind of bowl brought to the car. This helped, though still there were men who didn't make it to their bowls, and there were men who'd fill their bowls in seconds, the sick overflowing and covering bedclothes and sheets. In other words, there was only so much we could do, though after an hour there were stretches of floor showing between shallow puddles of sick. Around this time I noticed Ella Bradna, barely able to push her mop, her face gone slack with exhaustion. "Go home," I told her, and when she didn't respond I put my hands on her shoulders and leaned close and said, "please."

Finally, we'd got so we could concentrate on cleaning the men themselves. Was difficult, for much of the vomit had dried, their bed-clothes sticking to their bodies with a paste of their own making. Plus it was hard to get at the men writhing on the second-level bunks and near impossible to get at the men on the top bunks. In other words we mostly couldn't change them in bed, as we'd been able to do in the performer and maintenance cars; we had to rotate them and get them to jump down, the movement itself often making them retch. Once they were down and in the aisle, we'd strip them and throw the fouled clothes outside, where the healthy workingmen were helping by boiling water and running laundry. As the man stood shivery and naked, and in some cases needing support, we'd sponge him down and put him in whatever clean clothes he had, which in some cases wasn't much. Then we'd throw down a clean sheet, not even bother-ing to tuck it in, and put him back to bed and give him more sips of water. Before moving on to the next, we'd tell him it was critical he puked and shat outside, and to call for help if he didn't think he could manage.

Which is what happened. We'd be halfway through dressing a man when a man we'd just been to would call out, and one of the recruits would have to half carry him outside where it was raining. Thankfully, the healthy workingmen were starting to help in this detail, so I had the satisfaction of seeing it actually get done. It did, however, mean both men would come back in damp. Steam started coming off bedclothes, adding a haze to the confusion. Pretty soon we were all either damp or wringing wet and talking loud because it was hard to tell where anyone was.

I started to ache. I was beyond tired, my head so weighty I swore any minute it'd start playing tricks, though by the same token I hadn't felt so valuable since John Ringling killed the cat acts in 1925 so there was an exhilaration mixed in. We were about two-thirds of the way down the second workingmen's car when I decided to step outside and have some of the coffee the cookhouse staff were handing around.

I don't think I'd ever seen such rain. Those fat splattering drops had transformed into sheets so thick it was hard to pick out individual drops. I stood in the alcove of the door to the workingmen's car; for a moment I stuck my arm into the deluge and then brought it back in, stinging. The worst thing was the winds were still terrific, so the rain didn't even seem to be falling. Instead, it was everywhere, as much hitting the ground as ricocheting back up in an upside-down rain and a sideways rain and a diagonal beating rain. Waves of it battered the sides of the rail cars, no rhyme or reason to the way it moved except for every once in a while when the wind would pick up and surge for a few seconds in a specific direction and the rain would follow. Then the surge would end and the rain'd no longer be rain again but water, coming from everywhere.

A soaked workingman spotted me and brought me coffee. As I sipped, I watched lightning light up the rail yards: people were running up and down the trains, ferrying water and towels and bedpans and men needing to empty their stomachs. Then it would all go dark. About twenty feet away Ketchum was trying to co-ordinate everything happening outside; he'd found himself a slicker and a rain hat, water pouring off him and hitting the earth in sheets. He was yelling for more water and coffee and towels and—best news I'd heard all day—cups of broth for those feeling better.

When I heard this, my exhaustion made itself known. It wasn't even so much that my muscles hurt, though they all did, but more that everything hurt. The whole of me ached, and until that happens you don't really think about this thing called your body. My eyes had sunk to half mast. My brain had slowed. Maybe this was the problem. I just sipped coffee, watching the storm and feeling proud and happy and bone-weary when it happened.

I was standing there, enjoying the way the heat from the cup was passing through my hands to my arms and then to my doused body, when I got a strange feeling. It made me feel uncomfortable and tense, though I had no idea exactly why, though maybe it had something to do with all this rain meaning something. Like maybe this rain ought to *indicate* something. Was a curious thought, this, and though I figured it was just exhaustion talking, I didn't dismiss it outright. I just kept looking at the rain, splashing dirt and hitting workingmen in the face and battering the tops and sides of the Pullman in front of me. The whole time my legs tingled with an unnerved sensation, like all this rain really was trying to tell me something.

Throughout, the wind was howling, and in that howling I was sure I could hear a voice, screaming something at me, though no matter how hard I strained I couldn't quite make out what that something was. *Mabel*, I said to myself, *you're going bonkers again, tuckering yourself out like this isn't a good idea, better watch it in the future*. I even smiled at the prospect of treating myself better when this was all over. Then it hit me. I dropped my coffee and felt it heat the tops of my boots.

Oh, God, I yelled inside myself.

Rain.

So I was running. Was like one of those dreams when you're trying to get someplace but you can't because your feet have gone heavy as cement blocks or they're sticking to the ground or you've forgotten how to run. In this case, my boots kept getting stuck in the mud, and because they were boots borrowed from Art and they were too big my feet kept lifting out. Finally, I kicked them both off and ran in stocking feet, though when you're that scared, believe me, it's the intensity of your fear makes you humiliated and not the fact your feet are without shoes and caked in mud.

I made it to our stateroom. The wind and rain had whipped the note off the door. Still, what you do is hope. You pretend otherwise. You come up that hill and you see that body heaped beside a horse and you think, *Nope, uh-uh, can't be her.* So I reached out, figuring if the door was still locked then everything was fine, Art was still in the menage tending to the elephants (which he loved more than all other animals put together, though as a menage boss would never admit it). I reached out, thinking if it was still locked then Art hadn't come back to change or have a smoke or file a broken nail.

Soaking wet, I reached out.

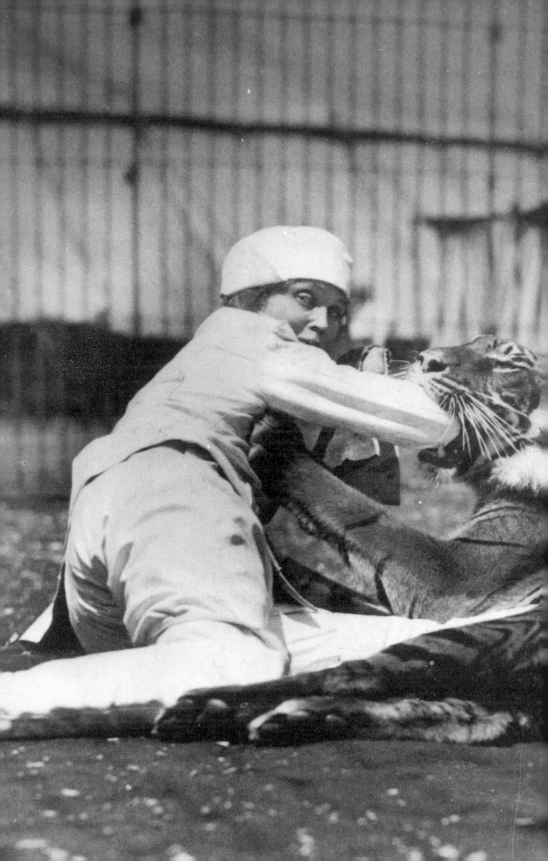

PART THREE

JOHN ROBINSON / BARNES

CHAPTER 14

LUCKY BARNES

ART ROONEY WAS BURIED THE NEXT MORNING ON A KNOLL outside of town. Was a sight, all those workingmen, heads lowered and weeping, though beyond that my memory of it's cloudy. As for Rajah, the circus was obliged by law to put him down, and all the newspapermen printed that's what happened. As usual, what the newspapermen printed and what really happened bore no resemblance. Like all big animals gone rogue, Rajah would've been sold to a Mexican circus, where he'd've fought lions or bears or small elephants for a special admission. For a while, there was a rumour saying he'd died somewhere in Nuevo Leon, torn apart by a pack of unfed prairie wolves. If it's true, at least he died to the sound of cheering.

About a week after the killing, Charles Curley visited me in my Pullman suite.

"Can we talk, Mabel?"

I stood away from the door, not particularly caring whether he came in or not. He did, and though I can't say for sure whether I offered him tea or coffee, to the best of my recollection I didn't. We sat in my living room. It was a horrible mess, papers everywhere and dirty dishes on the coffee table, and because I was known for being such a neat person it was a mess Charles Curley noticed. He looked around, uncomfortable. Then he cleared his throat.

"Mabel, I was talking to John Robinson this morning. He'd heard about your efforts during the outbreak and said you must be a real trouper."

I was noticing a stain on the wallpaper above Curley's left shoulder, not because I had any inclination to clean it but because its shape was curious.

"Mabel, he told me he's put you on John Robinson paper. He says we've wasted you here, which is true, and that it's high time someone made you a star again, and that someone's going to be him. He says he's promoting your arrival like you were the second coming. He's going to personally ensure you have a comeback."

I stared at him blankly.

"You're going to be a star again, Mabel. You hearing me?"

"Yes," I answered. "Was there anything else?"

A month or so later, I caught up with the John Robinson show somewhere in the south: Georgia, I seem to remember, or maybe across the border in Alabama. I was thirty-eight years old, and everything I owned fit in a single steamer trunk. Soon after, I started getting acquainted with the Robinson cats, who like all show animals preferred work to lollygagging. It didn't take long before one of the Bengals, a wiry specimen named Khan, was leaping through the double-flaming hoop. Along with Boston and Beauty, my Ringling twolings, I now had three cats who knew the trick; with one more I could send them all through in a continuous circle, a solid ring of black-and-orange through a tunnel of flame. Not long after that, Pasha took her first nervous steps along a single thick rope stretched taut, and I knew in no time I'd have a wire walker. The only problem was me. Here I was, the first person in the history of the world to teach these tricks, and I didn't care. For a while I thought it was the neurasthenia talking, and that one day the fog would lift and I'd be mightily impressed with myself. It didn't happen.

What did happen was I started hearing Art's voice in the back of my head—*Flash*, it said, *flash, dazzle and razzmatazz*—and it was this voice got me to thinking. One day in late February, I put my cats in the training arena and I signalled Boston through two hoops and while he soared through I figured why not? and I watched it sideways. What I saw was such a surprise I could barely catch my breath. Looking out the sides of my eyeballs, I did see beauty, but I didn't see it in Boston. What I saw there was hours and hours of rewarded behaviour. What I saw there was science. But I did see beauty in the way the other tigers were all sitting on their pedestals, with the same posture and the same proud tiger expressions, all facing in the same direction, not caring whether they got a piece of meat and not caring whether I yelled "Good kitty!" but just up there, exuding true noble tigerness. They weren't doing it to please me or an audience or anyone else. They were doing it for themselves.

That day, I dropped the hoop tricks and the wire-walking trick and started mixing the Ringling cats with the John Robinson cats. Over the next week, there were some minor flare-ups though nothing serious. Mostly I wished Art could've seen it: they were like streams of orange and black, their green eyes like stones catching light. I began to think of my display as ballet rather than a cat act, and instead of doing idiot stunts like ball rolling, I had them move around the steel arena in swirls, in patterns. As I stood in the middle of the arena, the cats would flow around me. I taught them snail patterns, figure eights, waves of movement, all of it a pure ode to Art which I figured was the least I could do. I had them sit in pyramids so unusual in shape they really weren't pyramids at all—more like shapes created by tiger. I brought down a gramophone and became the first big cat trainer to use music in a display. Sure enough, the cats learned the score and took their cues from it, so that after a while I barely needed my voice or my buggy whip to trigger the next movement. Mainly I acted as a centrepiece, my blond Eton crop a place to look when the rubes didn't know where to rest their eyes, and believe me when I say that was a startling way for a cat act to work. It got so I started thinking the ultimate act wouldn't even have the trainer in the ring (and though there were a thousand reasons why this was near impossible, it was what I was working toward). Course, word got round I'd whipped together a new kind of tiger display. One day John Robinson himself came down to the training barn and asked to see what he was taking on the road. I geared up the player. Afterwards he stood there, staring straight ahead, cigar puffing and looking fat. Also not saying a word. Later that day, I caught up to one of the managers and asked him if the boss had said anything about my act.

"He did. Said it was wondrous. And that he wished he'd seen it in someone else's circus."

I debuted the act on July 26, 1927, in Toledo, Ohio. After the peanut pitch, the matinee started with a spec called "King Solomon and the Queen of Sheba," which they billed as "A Massive and Exotic Spectacle of Ancient Days." Display number two was a polar bear act, flanked by unrideable mules getting ridden. Display number three was dog acts. Number four was ponies. Number five was tumblers doing a knock-about.

Then: the largest group of Siberian, Royal Bengal and Sumatran tigers ever assembled in a circus arena, presented by the incomparable Mabel Stark. I entered the ring, alone as always, blond hair glimmering, one hand on my hip and one hand holding a whip. This confused the rubes, for there wasn't a cat in sight. I stood under the spotlight just long enough for them to get fidgety and bored. The orchestra started up. And as it played, Old Dad, the cage boy, lifted the tunnel door and the cats filed in, and with sixteen tigers it wasn't hard to make it look like a river of tawny fur flowing into that arena. They formed a giant snail-shape pattern with me in the nexus. Was a change in the music and the tigers started moving around the arena in circles, the smallest ring and the biggest ring moving clockwise, the tigers in the middle ring moving counterclockwise. After the audience had gotten a good long eyeful of this the tigers took their seats, though instead of each one going directly to his own pedestal they filed in from two sides, leaping from seat to seat, slowly filling in the pyramid like black-and-orange liquid filling a vase. I even had two tigers share the pedestal at the summit, something that wasn't supposed to be possible seeing as tigers are so territorial. I held the pyramid through a swell of music, and then with nothing more than a tilting of chin I had the tigers forming the sides of the pyramid come down and do a simultaneous rollover, first one way and then the next, each cat so close he was in danger of rubbing the fur off the cat beside him. When they were done, they reformed the pyramid in time for my finale: with all sixteen tigers on their seats I turned my back to them and lifted my arms in the air, and *as* I lifted my arms in the air each and every one of those tigers sat up, in unison, just because they all wanted to be looked at. Believe me. Was beauty at its most honest, whether you looked at it sideways, frontward or through slits in the back of your head.

The orchestra crescendoed and I waited for the applause and it was: respectful. At most, hearty. My throat box went achy. The cats were already filing out through the tunnel. As I stepped outside the steel arena I had myself a comforting thought: maybe the small house was to blame, for if there's one thing a crowd does is breed excitement, and it occurred to me vacant seats might've caused the rubes to miss what was going on in the ring.

Display number seven was the aerial show, featuring most of the girls who'd seashelled their chests during the opening spec. Then came display number eight, performing camels in rings one and three, with the all-new John Robinson fighting act in the centre ring.

Back then, he went by the name Capt. Terrell Jacques, though later he'd poke an eye out with his own whip and change his name, becoming the famous one-eyed Terrell Jacobs. His act was a complete steal of Beatty's, the one wrinkle being he used four black-maned Nubians instead of lions and tigers mixed. Was a drum roll, and Jacques swaggered in with his animals, all of whom looked like they'd bit into something bad at lunch. What followed was an excess of snarling and charging and air swipes and pistol discharges. The lions fought so much among themselves I understood why they all had scarring on their snouts and foreheads. It took all eight minutes for Jacques to get his cats seated, though after a second and a half they came charging off the pedestals so he flung open the cage door and hurled himself to the tanbark like he was dodging shrapnel on the beaches of Normandy. Then he stood, not as drenched as Beatty would've been but close. For a few seconds, he pretended to be humbled by the near-death he'd just faced. Then he bowed and the lights came up on the rubes sitting on the risers.

Only they weren't sitting. Standing, they were. Standing and cheering and giving an ovation.

We played a few more shows before heading into Canada via Detroit and making our way northeast along the St. Lawrence. It was cold and wet the whole time and everyone got tired of shivering in the mud. You can imagine how I was feeling. In a word, distractable. Mine was the kind of act that needed constant polishing, and I confess there were days I was just too heavy feeling to squeeze in extra practise. After a couple of weeks, the tigers stopped filing into the steel arena in that beautiful snail pattern; instead, they started to look like commuters filing into a train. My concentric circles stopped moving concentrically, and when the tigers bumped into one another there were little fights I barely had the energy to break up. One day in a town called Cornwall,

Ontario, I was feeling particularly foggy. Midway through my display, I forgot where I was. To get my attention a cat named Sheik, who'd been beaten by a previous trainer and carried a meanness in his bones, came up and ran his claws down the right side of my uniform. Wasn't a bad wound, the costume taking most of it, though it looked bad and I could hear the rubes draw breath. Sheik roared, and it was clear he was fixing on finishing the job when he noticed I wasn't showing fear or concern. Not one smidgen. I was just standing there, looking at the wound as though it belonged to someone else. This chilled him, and he stepped back into the confusion of tigers circling around me, though as he did he looked back over his shoulder and glared, which was his way of saying *Next time*.

That afternoon, I got word from John Robinson he liked how I was developing my act.

The weather. Wasn't the driving rain that helped me murder Art Rooney but the chilling wet misty kind that gets in your bones and refuses to go away. It followed us all through eastern Canada, into Quebec and round the bend into New Brunswick, where the mist turned into actual rain, hitting the ground and turning into a wet haze that rose up frigid. A quiet fell on the lot, people sticking to their bunks, though when they did go out they looked hunched and miserable. Management ordered a new shipment of rubber boots, and they turned out to be just as leaky as the ones they replaced. The paraffin sealing the canvas started to soak off, the big top springing leaks. There were a lot of colds, and people feeling blue. One of the spec girls, a darty-eyed thing who suffered from real daffiness and not just everyday circus daffiness, started complaining she saw leprechauns, playing in the damp, fearsome ones with sharp teeth. The next day she was given a train ticket home.

Sometime in late May, we crossed back into the United States at a place called Houlton, Maine. As usual, we were held up for hours, the border officials combing the train for gypsies, opium takers, fugitives and distempered livestock. Finally they let us go, having arrested a cookhouse helper who turned out to have plugged his wife somewhere in Mississipi. We all hoped the change of country might stop the rains, as if rain clouds pull up at borders too.

A day later, we pulled into Bangor.

Finally we had nice weather, sunny and hot and sticky as a Danish, though with all the rain of the past few weeks the fair grounds were mud and nothing but. The guy-out elephants kept getting stuck in the earth, and the workingmen kept losing their boots. The big top steamed. By the time the tent was up and the cookhouse serving coffee, it was after six in the evening, management furious the matinee had been cancelled. Everyone else was tired and hungry, including the animals.

My cages pulled up just moments before the show began, so instead of going to the menage where the cats would've been fed and watered, they got lined up directly behind the arena tunnel. A blind man could've seen the cats were in no mood—no surprise, seeing as they'd spent a full day on wet bedding. They were growling and displaying teeth and trying to swipe each other through the cage bars. I went on anyway. Fact was, I was eager.

Once inside the steel arena, I signalled Old Dad to send in the cats. They filed in looking slinky and tough, heads low, panting and barking because mud was getting between their claws. Sensing a melee was about to break out, I didn't cue the orchestra; instead, I called, "Seat," and when this didn't work I called it again though louder. One of the dumber cats, a female named Belle, settled on the wrong seat and of course that seat belonged to my mean cat Sheik. Seeing this, Sheik blamed me, and he came up and gave me a swipe on the left leg that wasn't in any way a warning: his claws tore through bone and pretty near took the leg off above the knee. I dropped like a sack. When I got up, the left side of me felt wobbly, like it couldn't be trusted.

Old Dad started rattling the door and Sheik went for the tunnel. We were using the old swing-type door, and in his panic Old Dad swung the door into another tiger, and that tiger was none other than my oversized Bengal, Zoo, who'd nursed a grudge ever since the time I hit him for refusing to ball walk. He jumped straight into the air and came down resentful. He lit on me as I was struggling to get up, taking a big gnaw of muscle from my right leg. I hollered and he let me go and I somehow got to my feet, though as I did I could hear blood swishing in my boots. I took my whip and hit Zoo hard, sending him to the far side of the arena. At this point, I was so light-headed I started to think I could finish my act so long as I got that demon Sheik on his pedestal. So I called, "Seat," while looking Sheik straight in the eyes. When he didn't move, I buggy-whipped him on the nose. He approached his pedestal, stopped, thought about his pride and charged. On my broken leg I sidestepped him, though the sudden move sank my left boot in mud and mired my foot. Suddenly I was as stuck as sin.

Throughout, Old Dad had been hollering and waving and rattling the cage door like mad and for some reason Sheik chose that moment to respond. Problem was, he responded at the same time as a tiger named Mary, who was one of my quieter cats and had probably figured she'd seen enough. The two collided at the tunnel entrance. Mary howled and Sheik went insane. Came straight for me, not making a sound, mouth wide open, murderous. I jammed my training stick hard down his throat, though Sheik was so mad he howled and swiped at the stick while I pounded the tip again and again into the back of his throat, all of which might've saved me had Zoo not decided to attack. I didn't see him until his jaws seized my right leg and slammed me into the mud, a motion snapping the ankle that'd been mired. On my way down Sheik hit me with a roundhouse to the head and though it was a glancing blow he'd used full claws so it took off a big piece of scalp and a thicket of my precious blond hair. This angered Zoo, and he tore apart Sheik's right shoulder, Sheik backing off for fear of having the same done to the other side. With Sheik banished, and me driven halfway into the mud, and the other cats either backed up or on their pedestals, Zoo relaxed. Took his time, even. He looked down at me, licked his chops, and with forepaw nails peeled back my belly, from navel to rib cage, like he was opening a can of herring.

Then he bent over and dined.

It's hard to say why I didn't die that day. All I know is I should've, and that I wouldn't've even minded, what with Art six feet under and Rajah fighting somewhere in Mexico. Often I feel like I've got two angels following me around, one good and one bad, neither one of them gentle, and they were duking it out that day. Question is, was it the good angel decided I was going to live, or was it the bad one?

At any rate, two people also helped out that day. The first was me. Though my memory is foggy past a certain point, I'm told that after having his first mouthful or two of stomach muscle Zoo was so pleased with himself he picked me up by the hip and shook me like a ragdoll while roaring. This freed my right arm and I somehow got my pistol out of the holster and fired it point-blank into the big cat's face. He got singed bad with powder and backed off quick. The second was none other than Capt. Terrell Jacques, the future one-eyed Terrell Jacobs, who ran in the cage when no one else would and started dragging me out. Hunks of me were coming off in the mud, so after a foot or so he picked me up and being a strong, squat man carried me out like a bride.

I spent much of the next two years in hospital. Though I don't remember a lot, I do remember the drugs they gave me were full of the same analgesics I'd once taken for marital impediments, and because I had bad associations the hallucinations were frightful. Still, they were preferable to the pain, which I can't in any accurate way describe.

At times they'd think I was getting better and they'd let me out. I'd return to the circus, where they'd have me count tickets or invoice costumes, though after a few days or a few weeks something would go wrong. I'd have doubling-over pain, and the doctors would have to go in again, rooting around with needle and thread, looking for some tear they'd missed or something new that'd opened up since the last time. After a month or so, they'd release me, and something else would foul up. Infections were always setting in, the fevers horrendous. Was one period I couldn't make waste properly, causing me to swell up and turn orange and feel like I'd swallowed a watermelon whole. Back I went to hospital for more operations, and more recuperations, and more doctors huddled around my bed, stroking their chins. By the time I was shitting properly, my eyesight problems kicked in again. The partial scalping Sheik gave me—I wore hats now—had monkeyed with my vision, and there were days I couldn't see much more than quarter-sized circles of light surrounded by pitch-black. So I went in for the operation that scared me the most. Thank God, when they took off the bandages I could see what I was supposed to, though the headache caused by all that light made me wish I couldn't.

You name a problem, I had it. Arthritic pain from having my legs broke? Yep. Migraines from blod clots? Uh-huh. Nightmares? Panicky feelings? Digestive incidents? Indeed. Waking up in the morning with hardened blood on my lips and cheeks? With it cracked and dry in the folds of my neck?

Back I'd go.

Worry was another problem. Back then, circuses had a policy saying troupers paid their own medical bills. Each time I left hospital, the amount of money I owed the doctors grew, the numbers getting so big after a while they practically lost meaning. Each time I stared at one of those gargantuan bills I'd tell them the same thing: "Suppose about all I can do is try."

When I finally left the hospital for the last time, in 1930, I reckoned I owed almost $4000. An orderly wheelchaired me and my suitcase to reception. I stood, heart pitter-pattering, something that made my insides hurt. (Laughing, breathing heavily and coughing had the same effect. For hiccups I practically needed morphine.) Meanwhile, the woman at reception got my papers ready. I signed on dotted lines, not bothering to read what I was signing, figuring whatever it was was bound to be bad. Then the woman put her elbows on the desk and smiled and wished me luck.

"Aren't you forgetting something?"

"I don't believe so, Miss Stark."

"The bill. The bottom line. How much?"

This triggered a look of confusion on the woman's face, and she began looking through the papers in my file.

"No ..." she said. "It says right here you're paid in full."

I looked at her piercingly, though why I'd do that to a person who'd just given me such good news is hard to say.

"Well, that makes me want to ask a question. Who in Sam Hill paid it?"

The woman's face furrowed and she thumbed through my file again. Then she shook her head and clucked.

"It doesn't say. Do you really want to know?"

"I really want to know."

She got up and wandered into a back room. I heard conversations. After a minute or two she reappeared, holding a sheet of paper that had the crinkly look of a receipt. She came back toward the desk.

"Apparently," she said, "it was the Ringling Brothers Barnum & Bailey Circus."

By this time, John Ringling had bought out Mugivan's American Circus Corporation, the story being that Ringling and Mugivan met in a hotel in Peru, both parties knowing they couldn't survive with each other as competition. Was a coin flip, the winner having the option of buying out the loser. If nothing else, this should teach you about the quirkiness of fame: had Jerry Mugivan won a single coin toss, history probably would've made him famous and not John Ringling.

Ringling now owned every decent-sized circus in America (excepting a few renegade outfits operating out of Hugo, Oklahoma), and I suppose he thought he was being nice when he took me off the Robinson show and sent me back to the Al G. Barnes Wild Animal, which he now owned lock, stock and barrel as well. Mostly what it was was sad. Al G. hadn't had anything to do with the show since he'd sold to the Mugivan crew in 1929. Apparently most of the acts left too, feeling the Al G. Barnes Circus just wouldn't be the same without Al G. himself at the helm. Others who didn't care, workingmen and first-of-Mays, had long since moved on. Fact was, I didn't know a soul and didn't have much energy for socializing. Even winter quarters had changed; the show now bunked in a town called Lodi, a few hours south of Venice. Though the new quarters were cleaner and bigger and more efficient, something about them made me pine for old companions.

I started working up an act with eight Barnes tigers, which put me face to face with all kinds of things I wasn't exactly feeling strong enough to go face to face *with*. Ambition, for one. Memories of Art, for another. Or this: pondering why it is that chasing the exquisite should be so all-fired risky. Believe me, these were heavy questions, the kind that open up stitches if you think about them too much. No matter how hard I tried to push them away they kept coming: in dreams, in the quiet moments of morning, during the lull following a meal eaten alone.

This time I faced facts. For the first time in my life I made concessions. I didn't like doing it but I was too hurt inside to do otherwise. I taught the cats rollovers, sit-ups, hoop jumping, everything rubes liked in a picture act. Even trained up a ball roller, a trick that took me all of two afternoons. This got me written up in *Bandwagon* and *White*

Tops and the local paper, though of course a lot more ink went to the Barnes fighting act, a young good-looking guy by the name of Bert Nelson. Whereas I had the third display, he went on as close to the end as was possible without bumping the flyers. When reporters came, it was his tent they crowded. When wild animals were portrayed on Barnes paper, they were his yellow lions and not my well-trained Bengals. I was no longer marquee status, and with my head half tore off I can't say I was the least bit sorry.

I started spending a lot of time in my rented bungalow, a neat little house with a backyard in a neighbourhood filled with Barnes troupers. It was a nice place, with shrubs and a sunny kitchen and more hot water than a single person could ever use. In the backyard I put a chaise longue, and in the morning I'd sit and watch the sun come up, a wool cap and sweater keeping me warm. I did a lot of knitting, and I followed Jack Benny. At night I ate early, and went to bed around the time most people start thinking about what they're going to do with their evening.

Then, one night, the taste of supper still lingering, there was a knock on the door. I answered it, and saw a person I'd never realized meant so much to me.

I pulled him to me.

"Jesus, it's good to see you!" Though he was wearing his serious face, a second tight hug turned it into the beginnings of a smile. "Well, don't just stand there—come in."

Dan nodded and took off his hat and stepped in. In the eleven years since I'd seen him, he'd made the switch from middle-aged Negro to elderly Negro, and it looked like the switch could've gone more smoothly. There was grey in his hair, mostly at the temples, though if you looked close little individual grey hairs spotted his entire head, not unlike the odd blue fibres in a red mohair blanket. He'd lost only a little weight, but since he didn't have much to lose in the first place, the impression he gave now was one of ricketiness. Plus all that stooping from worry had crooked him over for good, so that he now carried his spindly frame in the shape of a question mark. On the positive side, he wasn't suffering from any obvious disfigurements, Dan having always been one for staying out of fights.

I couldn't stop hugging him—it was like he was some totem from better times sent expressly for my relief. After a bit he got embarrassed. Started blushing and gently easing me away, so I sat him down and got us both a can of beer and started with "So how *are* you?"

Here he gave one of those shoulder-bobbing chuckles old black people give when contemplating hardship.

"Can't rightly complain. Retired, of course."

"You living in Venice?"

"Oh my, yes. Took the train down when I heard you was back with the Barnes show. Them trouping days is over for me. I'm settled now. In one spot."

"Takes some adjustment, doesn't it?"

"It sure do, ma'am. It surely do. Had Sunday-night insomnia for near half a year."

"I tried it once myself. Remember when I married that millionaire and settled in the Cajun end of Texas? One of the main reasons I upped and left was I found being stationary a chore."

"Well, I know what you mean, Miss Stark. I know what you mean fo' sure."

"You renting a bungalow?"

"Nope. Living at the St. Charles."

"The St. Charles? *That* old place? What's it like now?"

"Different. Filled with folk less reputable than circus folk."

"Jesus, I didn't know that was possible."

"Well, it is, Miss Stark! It surely is!"

Here we both laughed, heartily, though when we stopped there were long moments of silence.

"Do you have enough money to live on, Dan?"

"I wouldn't say enough exactly. But some."

"It's a crime, what happens to circus folk, isn't it?"

"It surely is, Miss Stark. It surely is."

That silence, again.

"Dan, was money the reason Al G. sold his circus?"

"Course. He'da never sold otherwise. Not him. Got taken to the cleaners by Miss Speeks. I suppose she got herself better lawyers than Mr. Barnes's first wife had. Was a crying shame, seeing what it did to Mr. Barnes. One day I walked into his office, and his head was in his hands and he said, 'It seems, Dan, I have found myself in a deplorable situation financially.' Can't you just hear him saying that? In that way he spoke? It was the *way* he said it scared me, like the fight had gone out of him and that was something I never thought I'd see happen to Mr. Barnes. A week later Jerry Mugivan came calling with an offer."

"Was it a good one?"

"Maybe yes. Maybe no. He never told me. Suppose it don't matter, because Miss Speeks got most of it. Miss Speeks and other assorted vermin. Course, I don't think Mr. Barnes cared a tinker's ass—oops, sorry Miss Stark, here I am getting burned up just thinking about it. I don't think Mr. Barnes gave two hoots about the money. He sold off that half-built ranch in Nevada and that didn't seem to bother him either. Was losing the circus broke his heart. That's what I believe, anyway. Broke it right in two."

Here he looked down and started turning the brim of his hat in his hands.

"Dan," I said. "How is he?"

"'Fraid that's what I came all this way to tell you, ma'am. Truth is, he's poorly."

"How poorly?"

Dan's eyes glanced up for just a second. They'd gone milky with age, the brown of his irises having turned into a colour that was practically robin's egg.

"Poorly."

My taking the train back north with Dan wasn't a problem; I picked a cage boy to feed and water the cats and I knew they'd be fine. We did have to put up with some fairly nasty looks on the train, though, my being a white woman travelling with a black man; least we weren't in Alabama or Mississippi, or we might've been tossed in the slammer. When Dan got off in Venice I hugged him in front of some people who'd been giving us the dirtiest of looks, just to rile them further.

It took a day and a half more to reach Portland. As I didn't want to waste money on a berth, I slept sitting up, and by the time I reached the rainy part of the country I wished I hadn't: all that jostling had pained my stitched-together insides something fierce. After deboarding, I rested awhile and had myself a frank with sauerkraut in the station diner. Mostly it refluxed and tasted terrible, and I wished I'd stuck to cottage cheese and a banana. Afterwards, I took a taxi to the address Dan had given me. Though it wasn't in the part of town where Al G. used to go whoring, it was getting there.

The taxi pulled up in front of an old five-storey building with a fire escape running down the front. The entrance was dark. Though I didn't exactly trust the lift, I took it anyway, three flights of stairs being a little much after that long train ride. I knocked on Al G.'s apartment door and wasn't surprised when a woman answered. What did surprise me was this woman's appearance, for she couldn't have been plainer. Her dress was long and grey and uncinched at the waist, her shoes a muddy brown colour. Her red hair sprung out in frizzy shocks. Her face was too round and freckly, and her nostrils flared sideways, the upshot being her features reminded me of a pig with a clown's wig on. Basically, she was one of those woman who inspire a feeling of superiority in other women, though as soon as this feeling hit I remembered I was no one to talk, what with my droopy eye and a big hunk of scalp that wasn't ever going to grow hair again. I decided I'd be as nice to her as I possibly could, no matter who she was.

"Hello?" she said. Her voice was so kindly I immediately knew why Al G. had picked her for his last days. I held out my hand, and she took it. Her grip was as warm as a steamed bun and just about as comforting.

"My name's Mabel. Mabel Stark. Al G. and I trouped together for years and years."

"Really? How interesting. My name's Margaret Welsh. I'm Al G.'s wife. Pleased to meet you."

"Pleased to meet you."

"I'm glad you're here. Al G. would love a visitor."

I stepped in and she took my coat. When she went for my hat, I flinched, so she let it be, immediately pretending it was common for people to keep their hats on indoors.

"How long have you and Al G. been married?"

"Well, that's the thing of it. Not long. Not long at all." As she spoke, she put my coat in the closet. "Four weeks, actually. Our one-month anniversary is tomorrow. I was his nurse after the third attack."

"You're a nurse?"

The suddenness of my question made her hesitate for a second. She looked worried she'd accidentally committed some rudeness.

"Yes."

"I was, too. Long time ago."

"Really? Where?"

"St. Mary's Catholic Hospital. Louisville, Kentucky."

"What happened?"

"Suppose you could say the circus came to town."

"Really? How wonderful. How wonderful, indeed. Have a seat, Mabel. I have to explain something to you. I don't know if you've been told but Al G. isn't well. In fact, he's very, very ill. The doctors say he hasn't much time left but Lord knows they've been wrong before. You see, it's his heart. It's not circulating the blood properly so he's weak. Stress and fried foods, as far as I'm concerned. But I'm confident he'll be fine. I'm *sure* of it."

"Knowing Al G. he'll pull through. He'll probably have himself another circus before the year is out."

"Well, I wouldn't be too sure about that but your confidence is heartening. Would you like to go in now?"

I followed her to a door leading off the back wall of the living room. During those five or six steps, I was thinking how Al G. was such a slippery operator this probably *was* some sort of ruse, a hoodwink designed for him to lie low and get creditors off his back while he thought up his next operation. If his latest wife had turned around, she would've caught me with a little grin on my face.

Margaret pushed open the door and we went inside.

"Al G.?" she said softly. "Al G.?"

Though it was gloomy in the room, there was enough light peeking through the break in the curtains I could see him on his bed, mouth cratered open and blankets pulled chin-ward. Right off I knew this wasn't a ruse, and that if he was going to get better it wasn't going to be anytime soon.

We approached the bed. Al G.'s face'd gone gaunt, his cheekbones as pronounced as eggs, his eye sockets grown slightly too big for his eyes. The only other parts of him visible were his hands, which were folded over the hem of the blanket. Blueish and thin, they were, with valleys between each knuckle.

"Al G.?" Margaret said again, though this time she was gently nudging one of his shoulders. "Al G.? You have a visitor...."

Because she thought I was looking at Al G., her cheeriness vanished and was replaced by nothing but a sorrowful concern. After a second she took a sharp breath, and her smile popped back as surely as a duck in a shooting gallery.

"He just took his medicine. He needs his rest. Perhaps you'd like to keep him company?"

She motioned to a chair beside Al's bed, and I sat. Margaret left, returning a half-minute later with copies of *The Saturday Evening Post*.

"Here," she said. "You can look at these if you get bored."

I took the magazines and she left and for the longest while I didn't know what exactly it was I was supposed to do. Mostly I watched Al G. breathe, which in itself was a scary business: sometimes he'd go so long between inhalations I'd swear he'd taken his last one ever, and I'd be fighting the urge to pound his chest and scream for Margaret when it would finally come: a deep, rasping, chest-rising suck of air, which he'd hold for ages. When he'd extracted every last bit of oxygen he'd exhale slowly, making a sound like a sigh.

The only other movement was the odd flutter of his eyes behind lids grown thin as tissue. There was a bowl and cloth on Al G.'s bedside table, and with the radiators making the room so dry I'd dampen his lips every five minutes or so. Beyond that, there wasn't a lot of nursing I could do for him, my only hope being he sensed my presence and it was a presence comforting to him. After a bit of useless fretting, I moved my chair to the opposite side of the bed, where it caught whatever light was sneaking into the room. I picked up a magazine. After an hour my insides started to hurt so I got up and went into the living room.

Margaret was working in the little galley kitchen on the far side of the room. From the smells emanating I guessed she was making soup. She heard my rustling and came into the living room, wiping her hands on an apron decorated with pictures of kittens.

"Oh, hello. Did your visit go well?"

"He slept the whole time."

"Well, he needs his rest. Tell me. How long will you be in Portland?"

"I'm not sure. Four or five days, I think."

"Good!" She fished in her apron pocket and pulled out a sheet of paper. "You could pick up some things for Al G. and me and bring them when you come tomorrow morning. Could you do that?"

Without waiting for an answer, she handed me the list and went searching for her purse. Before she could pull out any money I stopped her, putting my hand on hers and saying, "Oh no. It's on me. It's the least I can do. With this damn Depression, Lord knows every penny counts."

She looked at me, lips parted.

"Thank you, Mabel."

"You're welcome, Margaret."

The next morning, I brought Margaret her groceries and her soap and went to have another session visiting with Al G. He looked exactly as he had when I'd left him, except his pyjamas were changed and his bedding smelled faintly of lemon juice. I dampened his lips and sat down to have myself a read. After about five minutes I heard sputtering, and when I looked up some saliva was bubbling on Al G.'s lips. Then there was a little groan. His eyes popped open like they'd been dynamited apart, and I was relieved to see the one thing Al G.'s illness hadn't touched was the royal blueness of his eyes.

Seeing he had a visitor, Al G. sat up sharply, his back against the headboard. Though he was still rail thin and his skin deathly pale, was no denying something vital had popped into him when he'd come awake, and the only thing I could figure was it was the same force that'd always made Al G. the whirlwind he was. Felt like turning cartwheels, I did.

"Kentucky!" he said in a strong voice. "What on earth brings you here?"

"Dan told me you were sickly."

"Dan? Well that son of a preacher. I *told* him I didn't want anyone seeing me like this."

"Like what, Al G? I can promise you you aren't the first circus owner who's had himself a heart attack or three."

"If you're saying it's an occupational hazard, then I'm afraid I would have to agree."

We both laughed.

Al G. said, "I read in *Billboard* that you had some fairly grievous health problems yourself."

"You could say that."

"What happened?"

"There was a deluge and we were late and the cats didn't get fed. I went on anyway."

"Now, Mabel, why on earth would you do that? Why would that damn John Robinson let you?"

"I guess what it boils down to is he didn't know."

"Well, I can tell you *I* would have known and there's no way *I* would have let you perform. I would've had two big workingmen carry you off. Three, if that's what it took. I know you, Kentucky." Here he seemed to be studying me, those blue eyes flickering.

"Boy, it's good to see you, Kentucky. I'm glad Dan broke his promise. I'd offer you a Calvados if Margaret let me have any. You look good. Really good."

"That's because the curtains are drawn and I'm wearing a hat and foundation."

"We all have our battle scars, Kentucky. The ones who wear them on the outside are just a little more honest about it, that's all. Believe me. You look as pretty as you did that day we first met on the old Parker show. Remember that? Beside that ratty old Siberian? It seems like yesterday, doesn't it?"

"Sure does," I said in my maudlin voice. "At the same time, it seems like lifetimes and lifetimes have passed."

"See? Now there you go, Kentucky. Getting all broody. Dwelling on the bad. You always were that way, weren't you? Listen to me,

Kentucky. Who cares about a little misfortune when you compare it to the experiences we've had? Remember that time in Oregon when a lion got free during parade? Or that time we blew down in Montana when the rubes were still in the tent? Or the time I tried hiding from John Ringling with those lunatic Doukhobors? Or that time we ..."

Here his voice trailed off, and I was thankful he didn't complete what he was going to say: *Or that time we had dinner in San Francisco.*

"Is there anything you need, Al G.?"

"Well, as a matter of fact there is, Kentucky. As a matter of fact, there is. You wouldn't happen to have ten thousand you might want to invest? I've been thinking, Kentucky. The public's growing tired of the huge five-ring extravaganzas people like John Ringling put on. I think the public's ready for smaller, more intimate circuses. One ring, with nothing but human acts. Knockabouts and contortionists and acrobats and jugglers and rolla-bolla artists and teeter-board wizards. Each one the best of its kind. It could work, don't you think? With $10,000 I could purchase a canvas and hire some Europeans. Maybe even some Chinese chair stackers. What do you say, Kentucky? Do you have any money?"

"I'm afraid I don't, Al G."

Here he looked at me and grinned. "Ah, that's all right. Not too many people do these days."

I grinned too. A short silence passed.

"Can I ask you something, Al G.? Something I've wanted to know for years?"

"Of course, Kentucky."

"Why'd you change your mind and let Rajah go? Why'd you do that?"

"Kentucky! I did *not* change my mind."

I looked at him, confused.

"What do you mean?"

"Just that. I never changed my mind. I was going to let that tiger go all along. Unless of course you'd changed your mind and asked to stay. That would have been a different story. Tell me, did I ever say, straight out, that you couldn't have Rajah? Tell me, Kentucky, have you ever heard me say no to anyone? Much less a woman with curls and a prettiness about her?"

I thought about it hard, and realized I hadn't.

"So Rajah was mine all along?"

"Of course," he said. "For Pete's sake, he would have killed anyone else who tried to wrestle him. Common sense, Kentucky."

We talked a little while longer, mostly about the old days. Then, as suddenly as he'd woken, he tired. Seemed like one minute he was gesturing with his hands and the next minute he was sinking back on his pillow and pulling the blankets to his chin and saying in a voice gone breathy, "Maybe you should go, Kentucky. I'm feeling a little punk...."

A second later he was asleep. My cheeks dampened, for he'd been so animated and Al G.-like I'd forgotten the reason I was visiting was his being on his deathbed.

I stayed in Portland a lot longer than I'd originally intended. I'd visit during the mornings and run errands for Margaret in the afternoons. Often she'd invite me to stay for dinner, but I'd always beg off, saying I had plans with other friends in the city. If I was hungry I'd go eat someplace, though mostly what I'd do was spend the night walking. Truth was, having spent the better part of two years in a noisy hospital, I liked roaming around by myself, freer than most, the city quieting itself down.

As for my visits with Al G., they were variable. Some mornings I'd do nothing but thumb through magazines, Al G. asleep the whole time. Other times he'd come awake groggy, and murmur and grunt and make strange comments before drifting back to motionlessness. Other times he'd pop awake, as alert as you or me. I'd give him a little apple brandy I'd snuck in, and we'd talk about silly things, like fashion or news. One morning he taught me to play Chinese checkers, which I found a hell of a lot more interesting than American checkers. Other times I'd read dime novels to him; he liked westerns and gangster tales.

One morning, after I'd been coming for almost ten days, I stepped in the apartment and realized something: I hadn't once, in all that time, seen Margaret go outdoors, which may've accounted for the pastiness of her complexion.

I marched straight up.

"Margaret, you're taking the morning off."

"I beg your pardon?"

"You've been cooped up in this apartment for ten whole days and how much more before that I hate to think. Take the morning off. Go get your nails done. Visit your mother. Take a long walk. I'm not asking, I'm telling."

Competing thoughts swirled through her head. Slowly, she raised a hand toward her brow. "Well," she said hesitantly, "I suppose I *could* get my hair done."

"Now you're talking."

"And I *have* cleaned him...."

"Well then, nothing's keeping you here. Don't you worry. I'm a trained nurse, so he couldn't be in better hands. Go on, now. Scram. Take a powder. And don't come back till people on the street start wishing you a good afternoon."

Slowly she turned and put on her coat. Before leaving she turned and said, "Thank you, Mabel."

After tidying a little, I went into Al G.'s bedroom and sat with him while he slept. At around ten o'clock, he sputtered and came fully awake, groaning and waving his arms and sitting up simultaneously.

"Jesus, Al G. You scare me when you do that."

"I'm sorry about that."

"Well, the next time you come out of your coma, would you do it a little more peacefully?"

He yawned and stretched and looked full of hope. "Ah, I'm getting better, Kentucky. I can just feel it."

"Glad to hear it." The truth was, he did look a little pinker that morning. "So, Al G., tell me. What're you in the mood for this morning. Some crime stories? Those Chinese checkers? How about a coddled egg? Margaret's gone out, so you're all mine."

He didn't answer, unless you counted the grin that was in the process of crossing his features.

"What is it, Al G.? What's running through that head of yours?"

He suddenly looked a little embarrassed.

"It's just that ... well ... the thing of it is ..." He took a deep breath and collected himself, an action that made him wince. "Have a seat, Kentucky. I need to explain something. You see ... it has to do with Margaret. It has to do with ... well, what I'm trying to say is she's a wonderful woman and she excels in many departments. Cleaning and making soup, for instance. And keeping her hands off my money, not that I have any money for a woman to keep her hands off nowadays, but if I did I know I wouldn't have to worry. There is, however, one area in which she's proven a little, shall we say, reluctant?"

I looked at him, less confused than I pretended to be.

"You see, Kentucky, whenever I wake up fully rested and full of vim and vigour, like right now for instance, I have a tendency to suffer from a certain, uh, shall we say, sprightliness?"

Here I suppose I should've been offended, but the fact was I was just too amused by the mischievous little boy still inside Al G. all the heart attacks in the world weren't about to curb that rascal. To make sure Al G. and I were talking about the same thing, I reached under the covers and let my hand travel southward and sure enough he was stiff as a man in traction.

"Goodness."

"Jesus, Kentucky, I hate asking but you're the only comely thing to have come within a country mile of this apartment for weeks and weeks. If there's anything you could do to relieve my misery I'd be grateful."

I thought about this for a minute, understanding what a kind and honourable thing it would be to help Al G. out. Only problem was, I'd made a solemn pledge I'd never be biblical with a man again, not after what I'd done to Art. I sat there weighing upsides and downsides. What finally tipped the meter was my realizing there was precious little I could do to harm him, considering he wasn't going to live much longer anyway. And even if he was, it wouldn't be in a fashion a man like Al G. Barnes could ever put up with. I decided to break my policy, just this once, and make Al G. Barnes the last man I ever joined in bed, clothed or otherwise.

"Think your heart can take it?"

"Frankly, Kentucky, I don't much care if it can."

"Will you be cold if I pull back the covers?"

"Probably."

I chuckled and pulled down his blankets and tried to keep my eyes off the spindliness of his body. He was poking up through the fly in his pyjamas, and it was nice to see his penile girth was the one thing hadn't been affected by heart disease. In fact, it looked like the property of a young man. I couldn't help but think of the first time I ever saw a thick-ened member: hard to believe I'd been so shocked and scared and curi-ous by something so out-and-out homely.

Was then I decided if I was going to kill Al G. Barnes, I might as well do it grand fashion. I bent over and geared up to do something I'd never done but had seen done twice: the first time in a sepia presented to me by Dimitri Aganosticus, the second time in a jail cell in Bowling Green, Kentucky. Yet beyond having a mind's-eye image of what was involved I swear I didn't have a clue how to start. For this reason, my first few licks and kisses were on the feeble side. Finally, I decided I'd treat it like an ice cream cone filled with my favourite flavour: with each swirl I imagined my tongue coating with strawberry. This must've been more than agreeable, for after a time the patient gave a little moan. A second later he came fountaining up. Course, *it* didn't taste like strawberry ice cream. Was more like an egg cream flavoured with anchovy.

After spitting his froth into a tissue, I sat back down and was glad to see he was still among the living. In fact, he was smiling.

"You can still breathe?" I asked.

"It appears so."

"No big pains in your chest?"

"None whatsoever."

"And you feel okay? No arm tingling? No bright lights? No visions of heaven?"

"I feel fine, Kentucky. More than fine, in fact."

"Good. I'm glad."

For the longest time, we didn't say a word, instead enjoying a moment that would've made us giggle had we been teenagers. "Thank you, Kentucky," he said, and a minute later he was asleep, his breathing deep and slow. Watching my old friend, I realized there was something else new I wanted to do that day, something I'd never done with a man (or leastways one who didn't make his eyes up with shadow).

Reached out, I did, and for the longest time just sat there, holding Al G.'s hand.

CHAPTER 15

JUNGLELAND

 Suicide note, found atop a folded child's sweater on the desk of Mabel Stark:

> *Well. Here it is, Roger. Like I promised. I made it big, so she'll grow into it. Buttons shaped like teddy bears.*
> *Yours truly,*
> *Mabel Stark*
>
> *P.S.: Hand wash, cold water only.*

RESEARCH NOTES

Charting the broad strokes of Mabel Stark's career was not difficult. The Robert L. Parkinson Library and Research Center, which operates under the auspices of the Circus World Museum in Baraboo, Wisconsin (birthplace of the Ringling brothers), has indexed every issue of *Bandwagon*, *White Tops* and a few lesser-known circus publications; I had only to write the name Mabel Stark on a sheet of paper and hand it to the head librarian, an endlessly helpful person named Fred Dahlinger, to be presented an hour later with a sheet of references. Mostly, these mentions were no more than a line or two tossed off in general news sections. My job was putting them in order.

This, then, is what we know for certain about Mabel Stark's professional life. She joined the Parker Carnival as a sideshow dancer in 1909, and that at the time she was using a Greek last name. (I saw different versions of that name, the one I preferred being Aganosticus.) She left to marry a rich man in Texas, only to get a job cooching a few months later with the Cosmopolitan Amusement Company. By the beginning of the following season, she was doing the free act for the all-new Al G. Barnes Circus, Barnes having been the head animal man on the Parker show. Later that year, she was performing a mixed act with two tigers and a pair of lions borrowed from Barnes's lion trainer, Louis Roth. Stark soon graduated to a tiger act, her career rising meteorically until, by the early twenties, her wrestling bit with Rajah was the best-known cat act in the American circus. Her fame dwindled when the Ringling circus ended cat acts in 1925, and by 1928 she was with the John Robinson show, where she suffered her worst mauling. She ended her circus career with the Al G. Barnes show of the thirties, before moving on to JungleLand.

As for Mabel Stark's private life, I refer to a series of letters written by Stark herself, which are also found at the Circus World Museum library. It seems that in the thirties, Mabel Stark wanted to publish an honest account of her life in and out of the circus. She contacted a ghost writer named Earl Chapin May, and the two started corresponding. These letters are a wealth of information; in them, she described Louis Roth as a drinker, and her next husband, Albert Ewing, as a cheque forger who left the Ringling circus owing $10,000. She described her next man, Art Rooney, as "the only one I ever loved enough to give up the tigers for," and also wrote, "I was told he never went with any girl, he was supposed to be a woman."

In another letter, this one devoted solely to Rajah, Stark revealed the highly intimate nature of her famous act: "When I turned and called him he would come up on his hind feet and put both feet round my neck. Pull me to the ground, grab me by the head, you know a male tiger grabs the female by the neck and holds her and growls till the critical moment is over. So in this fashion Rajah grabbed me and held me. We kept rolling over till he was through and while the audience could not see what Rajah was doing, his growling made a hit."

Though Earl Chapin May's book never materialized, a Mabel Stark autobiography titled *Hold That Tiger* was published by a circus vanity press in 1938. Like most circus autobiographies of the time, it was intended to promote the circus, and may have even been written by the Ringling press department. Suffice to say, it is highly sanitized and highly inaccurate; I found it useful only in its descriptions of her maulings and her animal-care methods.

Finally, I interviewed anyone I could find who knew Mabel Stark in the latter days of JungleLand (and who would also agree to talk to me). Clearly, it was Stark's opinion that a personality clash with the new owners was the reason for her firing. While this may or may not have been true, this book was written to express her point of view, and for me this was enough justification to use this rendition of events.

The rest is fiction. The characterizations of the more famous people—Al G. Barnes, John and Charles Ringling, Lillian Leitzel, Louis Roth—were the result of research.

A few more notes.

In my book, Mabel Stark has an early brush with the mental health system as it existed at that time. Though this is speculation, it is not speculation made lightly. We know that something fairly significant caused her to leave the respected profession of nursing to become a cooch. Those who knew her at JungleLand said she always lied about her age, the suspicion being that something happened to her early in her life that she worked hard to obscure. In the book *Wild Animal Trainers of America*, a circus writer named Joanne Joys claims that Mabel Stark's departure from the nursing profession was due to a nervous breakdown. Given the way that Stark's life ended, this seemed to account for the highest number of mysteries concerning her early years.

I massaged a couple of minor facts in service of the story, which I will mention as there are many circus aficionados out there, and it is not my wish to anger them. There were not one but two Rajahs (named, incidentally, Rajah I and Rajah II). As the first was by far the most important to her career, I eliminated the second. Second, Mabel Stark did marry one more time, for a few years in the early sixties, to another old menage boss named Eddie Trees. Finally, Al G. Barnes died in the state of California, and not in Oregon.

The Al G. Barnes Circus performed its last date on November 27, 1938, in Sarasota, Florida, on a bill shared with Sells-Floto, John Robinson and the Ringling Brothers Barnum & Bailey Circus.

On July 6, 1944, during a show in Hartford, Connecticut, the paraffin coating a Ringling big top caught fire, killing 168 patrons. For years, the show survived in a state of near-bankruptcy, owing to damages awarded against it. Today, the Ringling Circus is the biggest in the world and tours the United States and Canada in two units.

Mabel Stark committed suicide on April 21, 1968, through a combination of self-asphyxiation and barbiturate overdose. Her exact age was unknown.

ACKNOWLEDGEMENTS

While many people assisted with the research of this novel, there are five individuals without whose help this book would not have been possible. Roger Smith of Houston, upon whom the Roger Haynes character is based, helped immensely with my depiction of Mabel Stark in her later years. Fred Dahlinger, head librarian at Circus World Museum, unhesitatingly shipped me numerous old circus books, many of them fifty years out of print, with nothing more than my promise to return them unharmed. Michael Hackenberger, an animal trainer and owner of the Bowmanville Zoo in Bowmanville, Ontario, taught me many of the early training techniques presented in the book. Al Stencell, an ex-circus owner and girl show expert, told me everything I'd ever need to know about cooch dancing. Finally, Barbara Byrd, of the Carson & Barnes Circus, invited me to travel for a week with her circus through rural Texas, even though I made it clear I would not, in any way, be able to promote her show with my book; this, I submit, is what troupers mean when they describe someone as being "both with it and for it."

I'd also like to thank those who read the book and offered suggestions along the way: Susan Greer, Jackie Kaiser, Jocelyn Lawrence, Jan Whitford and Robert Young. My thanks also goes to those who've supported my writing in the past, either by giving me magazine gigs or critiquing earlier, unpublishable works of long fiction: Lynn Cunningham, Angie Gardos, Wayne Gooding, Angel Guerra, Marni Kramarich, John Macfarlane, Dianna Symonds, Linda Williams. Finally, my complete and unreserved gratitude goes to my editor, Anne Collins, who upon receiving highly abbreviated, yet-to-be-fleshed-out drafts never failed to say what a writer most wants to hear:

"It's getting there. Now give me more."